WISH YOU
WERE HERE

WISH YOU
WERE HERE

JOANNE TRACEY

First published in Australia in 2016

by Joanne Tracey

https://joannetracey.com

Copyright © Joanne Tracey 2016

Print ISBN 978-0-9943134-7-8 | Kindle ISBN 978-0-9943134-6-1 | Epub ISBN 978-0-9943134-5-4

Cover design Jacinda May – www.jacindamay.com

Cover photography – BrianAJackson and Yolfran via Deposit Photos (extended licence)

National Library of Australia Cataloguing-in-Publication entry (pbk)

Creator: Tracey, Joanne, author.

Title: Wish you were here / Joanne Tracey.

ISBN: 9780994313478 (paperback)

Subjects: Australian fiction.

Dewey Number: A823.4

For Grant and Sarah ... always ...

January in the Kitchen

It might be cold and frosty outside, but it's not all bad news for the seasonal cook. While the best of the main crop potatoes have been dug out, leeks are still at their peak; you should be able to buy sweet young brussels sprouts on the stem; and purple sprouting broccoli is widely available. Oh, and turnips. I know they're good in soups, but I have to admit they're not one of my favourite vegetables. If you know, dear reader, of anything useful and tasty to do with a turnip that doesn't involve soup, please do tell me.

This month, I thought we'd look at the humble cauliflower. Although they're available most of the year, I find they taste their best when it's cold outside. Cauliflower cheese or cauliflower mornay make a lovely side or supper on a cold winter's night; and cauliflower and stilton soup is a pub favourite.

If you made a rash declaration at the stroke of midnight on New Year's Eve regarding weight loss and carbohydrates, and you're serious about meeting your health goals without sacrificing taste, why not try roasting cauliflower with some vibrant spices? It's the sort of dish that will warm you up from *the inside without weighing you down, and makes a perfect side for roasted or grilled meats. I especially love it with fish. It can also be a nutritious vegetarian lunch or supper in its own right – and it couldn't be easier. Simply take a cauliflower and separate it into florets. Don't be too precious about this. Now grab whatever spices you have in your pantry: ground coriander seeds, cumin seeds, curry, paprika or turmeric will all work. Perhaps a shake of cinnamon as well? Use them all, or just a couple – a teaspoon each will do. Stir the spices into a couple of tablespoons of vegetable oil in a bowl, and then drop in the cauliflower florets. Toss them all about until they're coated with the spices, and spread them out on a baking tray. Scrape and drizzle whatever's left of the spiced oil over the florets, and roast in a hot oven (pre-heated to around 450F or 230C) until the cauli's a little brown around the edges and beautifully tender inside. It should take 10–15 minutes. This works well in the deep fryer too – you get a really satisfying crunch.*

If by chance you have any of this nutty, spicy cauliflower left over, you can transform it easily into a spicy soup that also happens to be good for you. Simply chop an onion, a couple of cloves of garlic and another half a cauliflower and cook them all in a little vegetable oil until soft and tender. Add in a teaspoon each of whatever spices you used when you roasted the cauliflower, pour in some vegetable or chicken stock from the freezer or the pantry. If you don't have any, water will also do the job. Let it all simmer for about 15–20 minutes. Now you just need to whoosh it about with a stick blender. If you used paprika or curry powder in your mix it should now be a lovely warm colour. And the leftover roasted cauliflower? Serve it on top for some tasty texture.

If you're not in a soupy mood, try dipping the roasted cauli into some garlicky hummus – sort of a cross between aioli and hummus. Better yet, deep fry them before dunking. Seriously yummy, but perhaps not a good idea if you're watching your calories.

Another way you can use spicy roasted cauliflower is in a salad. Salad in winter? Bear with me; this one is perfect with leftover roast lamb stirred through it. It's one of those dishes you can eat from a bowl with a fork while you watch telly in front of the fire. Whip up a simple dressing of olive oil and lemon juice. Season it with salt and pepper and a few shakes of ground coriander if you have any. Toss the cauli, lamb and dressing together with some hazelnuts or almonds and some crumbled feta cheese.

We had this salad for lunch in the shop the other day with the last of the Christmas turkey mixed through it and some of Westfarm Dairy's gorgeously creamy feta. Speaking of which – have you tried the feta yet? It's good, right? Just don't tell the boss that I took some from the shop fridge. Who am I kidding? He probably knows already!

Until next month,

Max

CHAPTER ONE

'I think we'll have champagne,' James declared. 'Do you want champagne, Maxine?' He didn't wait for my answer, just turned the single page of The Lamb's wine list over and back again, grimacing at the lack of choice. 'Then again, maybe not. I don't understand why you wanted to come to the village pub for your birthday dinner. We could have tried that new Michelin-starred place in Cheltenham. Or even that pub at Sapperton you like – at least the wine list there is a little longer.'

I reached my hand across the table to find his. 'I like it here. Besides, I don't see that there's very much to celebrate about turning twenty-nine.'

'You'd be surprised, my darling. Now,' he said, turning back to the menu, 'what shall we eat? Have you decided?'

I nodded. 'I'll have the pumpkin and feta risotto.'

He wrinkled his nose. 'Really?'

While he was deliberating, another couple walked in. It was Richie Evans, my closest friend here in Brookford and the manager at Blossoms & Buds, the garden centre I worked at, with his arm around a pretty blonde woman about my age. She looked familiar. Ah yes, Angela from the hairdresser's. I watched Richie cast his eyes around the room until they settled on me. It was a cold night in January so there weren't many people out and about.

Grinning, he dragged Angela over to our table and bent to kiss me on the cheek. 'Happy birthday, Maxi.'

'Thanks,' I said. 'Hello, Angela – it's good to see you.' My smile included both of them, but Angela didn't return it.

James looked up from the menu and held his hand out to Richie. 'Evans.'

'Henderson,' Richie said and shook James's hand.

'And who is this?' James smiled widely at Angela, causing her to preen a little too obviously.

'James, this is Angela,' I said. 'Angela, meet my husband, James. Angela works for Sharon at the hairdresser's at the top of the high street. You know the one?'

I knew James didn't – he always had his hair cut in London – but he nodded as if it meant something to him.

'We were at school together,' I added.

'It's lovely to meet you,' James said, treating Angela to the full force of his charm.

I raised my eyebrows at Richie who grinned and shrugged.

'We'll leave you two to your birthday celebrations,' he said. 'Enjoy.' He bent, kissed my cheek once more and led the giggling Angela to a booth at the back of the room.

'How long has that been going on?' James asked me.

'No idea,' I said as I watched Richie and Angela snuggle into the booth together. 'It looks quite new. She used to be married to Paul – he's a butcher and was in our year at school too. I think they have a daughter together.'

'Maybe Richie needs to watch out for carving knives. Or should that be "witch" out for them?' James enjoyed making fun of Richie's New Zealand accent.

When he noticed I wasn't laughing with him, he went to the bar to order our wine and meals.

Back at our table he held his glass up. 'Here's to my beautiful wife, to us, and to new beginnings.'

'New beginnings?'

'I haven't told you the good news yet, have I? You know that tender we've been working on in the States?'

Of course I did – he'd been commuting between London and New York for much of the last few months.

'Well,' he said, 'we won the business. And I've been asked to manage the US team. New York, here we come! Da da dadada …' He attempted a Frank Sinatra impression. 'You could say I've given you New York for your birthday!'

I swallowed a large mouthful of the wine. New York? I supposed I should be pleased for him.

'It's everything I ever planned,' he said. 'A few years over there will set me up perfectly for a senior management role when I come back to London. Managing partner at forty was always the goal and now I can almost taste it.' He finally noticed that I hadn't said anything. 'What do you think?'

'It's great, of course. Congratulations,' I managed.

'You don't seem very excited.' He sounded deflated. 'This is the biggest thing that's happened to me in years. You might be a bit more pleased for me.'

I nodded and forced a smile. 'I am. You've worked so hard and you deserve it. I just don't know what it means for us.'

He drained his glass and poured us each another. 'It means we'll be together again. There'll be no more commuting back and forth, no more linking in with India for my schedule.'

India was his very glamorous assistant. James relied on her, but I couldn't stand her.

He smiled across the table at me. 'I know these last few months have been hard on you, darling. There've been too many weekends when I've been stuck over there, or unable to drive up from London, but all that sacrifice has been worth it now we have New York.'

I was saved from answering by the arrival of our food. The risotto was perfect: the feta salty, the

pumpkin jewel-bright. I made a mental note to ask
Duncan, the landlord, for the recipe. I could feature it
in *Harvest Happenings*, the monthly newsletter I wrote
for Blossoms & Buds, and perhaps plate it on the rustic
blue pottery set I owned that James hated so much.

The newsletter had started soon after I came to
work at the garden centre. Richie's idea, it was intended
to educate customers about what was happening in
the garden that month: what they should be planting,
pruning, weeding and harvesting. The plan was that
customers would read the newsletter and realise that
now was the time to buy their tomato seedlings, or a
new pair of secateurs to prune their roses, or maybe that
lovely bird bath we had on sale. I'd got into the habit
of bringing in baked treats for Richie and whoever else
was lucky enough to be working at the time, and we'd
leave what we didn't eat on the counter for customers
to sample while they were paying for their goods. One
of our regulars suggested I could include a recipe or
two in the newsletter, so I did, featuring things like
my chocolate and sour cherry cookies, orange and
cardamon sour cream muffins, and the lemon drizzle
cake that Richie had declared was his favourite.

Richie had taken the newsletter to the next level
with his idea to feature ingredients from the garden.
'It makes sense, Hendo,' he'd said. 'We're telling them
what they should be harvesting, so let's also tell them
what they can do with that produce.'

I enjoyed every bit of the process – experimenting at home, writing up the recipe, styling and photographing the end product – Richie enjoyed eating what I made, and our customers enjoyed reading about it. *Harvest Happenings* had become so popular that we'd had to add a separate page to the website to store the recipes.

Yes, I decided, savouring my risotto, I could publish this recipe in March, and maybe do a whole feature on squash in September.

'Obviously it'll take a few months for all the paperwork to be completed,' James said as he poked and prodded at his steak to check it had been cooked the way he liked it. 'I'll continue flying in and out until then. You'll need to give notice at your job – you should probably do that as soon as possible.'

'Oh,' I said. That part of James's news hadn't occurred to me.

He laughed. 'Really, darling, the garden centre isn't exactly a career, is it?'

'Perhaps not yet,' I said, taking another mouthful of wine. 'But I might have my own cafe one day.'

'Serving other people cups of tea and bowls of soup? It's not exactly what we planned.' He emptied the last of the bottle into his glass.

'Nor was New York,' I said quietly. 'Besides, I'd hoped we might try for a baby soon.'

He put his glass down without sipping at it. 'Let's just see how this role works out.'

'You said that when we first moved back here.' I still recalled his exact words: 'A village is a much better environment to bring a child up in. We'll get something close enough to London so I can commute each day. I want my wife at home, not running about trying to juggle daycare and a career.'

He sighed heavily, as if it was a subject he was tired of talking about. 'Before we have a baby I'd like to make sure that I'm available if you need me.'

'I've got Mum and Dad and Horrie. I've got friends … I'll be fine.'

'Most of your friends in the village have families of their own,' he pointed out. 'Most of our joint friends are in London; and that other friend of yours – the large, loud and inappropriate one –'

'That would be Miranda.'

Miranda and I had been friends since art school. She had a huge personality with an appetite for everything life had to offer, and was perfectly comfortable in her size fourteen skin. To make matters worse in James's eyes, she wore colours and accessories that meant you couldn't help but notice her. Beige wasn't a word in Mirry's vocabulary, and neither was discretion. She always said that life was too short to miss out on anything, and that included saying what you thought. In her case, at the exact time she thought it. She and James barely tolerated each other.

He grimaced. 'How could I forget? Anyway she's

moved to Sydney so she'd be no help to you either.'

'I suppose,' I conceded. I missed Miranda dreadfully. 'But I don't really see the difference. You said we'd be together in New York, so I'll have you there to support me.'

He shook his head. 'No, it's not the right time.' He held his hand up to signal to Duncan behind the bar that another bottle of wine was required, which was also a signal to me that the baby subject was closed.

'I really thought you'd be happy about this.' He reached over the table and covered my hand, stroking it in a way he knew relaxed me. 'I know you're disappointed about the baby, but you'll see that I'm right. I just want what's best for our future.'

'I am happy for you – you deserve it. I just need to get my head around what's involved.'

Still looking deeply into my eyes, he turned my hand over and traced gentle circles into my palm. As he watched my breath come a little faster, he smiled slowly.

'We're both still young – we have plenty of time to be thinking about babies,' he said. 'If we have two years in the States, I'll still only be thirty-six when we get back. Besides, think of how much fun we'll have practising.' He looked towards the bar where Duncan was busy pouring pints. 'Where's that other bottle?'

His phone alerted him to a text message and he let go of my hand. 'Excuse me, darling. I need to read this.'

Although he smiled apologetically at me, his attention was already elsewhere.

'That's okay,' I said. 'I'll go and see what's happened to the wine.'

'Happy birthday, lass,' Duncan greeted me. 'How was your meal?'

'Great, thanks. Oh, while I think of it, could you ask Seb for the recipe for that risotto? I'd like to include it in *Harvest Happenings*, maybe with a photo of him?'

'I'm sure he'll be happy to give it to you.' He glanced across to where James was still busily texting. 'You'll be after another bottle?' The look in his eyes told me he'd seen James's signal and had chosen to ignore it.

'Yes, please.'

While Duncan removed the cork, my eyes were drawn to Richie and Angela.

'They look cosy, don't they?' Duncan said, reading my thoughts.

'They do. How long has it been going on?'

In a village like Brookford, if you wanted to know anything, the pub landlord was the person to ask.

'Since New Year I'd be guessing. They've been in here three times this week – although they're never in for long, if you know what I mean.'

He winked so I had absolutely no doubt what he meant. As if on cue, Richie stepped out of the booth and held out his hand to pull Angela, still giggling, towards him for a brief kiss. They stopped by the bar on their way out.

'Enjoy the rest of your night, Hendo,' Richie said.

'You too.'

'Bound to.' His grin was cheeky and Angela giggled again.

James reached for me as we walked home, pulling me into the shadows beside the sweet shop. 'It's been too long,' he said. 'I've missed you.'

With things so busy around the New York contract, James hadn't been home all January.

'I've missed you too,' I said.

He pushed me against the cold stone wall, his erection insistent against my stomach, his hand reaching for my breast. Despite an answering rush of warmth between my thighs, I moved it away.

'Not here,' I said, my head swimming. I wasn't used to drinking as much as I had tonight.

'But I can't wait,' he murmured into my throat, reaching under my skirt, smiling when he felt my desire.

I held his hand in place for a few seconds before reluctantly pushing it away, missing his warmth already. He scowled in frustration, but let me go.

Once inside our front door, he pulled me to him and kissed me, more roughly this time, forcing his tongue into my mouth and grabbing at my breast through the thin material of my dress. Impatient to feel his skin against my own, I wrestled with the buttons on his shirt, pulling it out from the waistband of his trousers, moaning into his mouth as his hand found its way inside my bra and pinched at my nipple. His hips thrust into mine until he'd forced me back against the door. He groaned as I wound one leg around his to grind myself against him, needing to feel more of his heat.

He tore his mouth from mine, panting. 'Why don't you go and change into your birthday present,' he urged. 'I've been picturing you in it since I bought it. Now I want you to put it on so I can take it off you and celebrate properly.'

He looked deep into my eyes, his finger lightly tracing the lips he'd just ravaged, his desperation of a few minutes ago back under control. I captured one of his nipples in my mouth, nipping it lightly as I ran my tongue around its hardness.

When he released me I staggered a little – a combination of alcohol and lust – and made my way up the stairs, feeling his eyes on my bottom and the sway of my hips as he followed me.

In the cold of the bathroom, I managed to get myself out of my dress and wriggled into the red lacy thong and barely-there bra. The bra was a cup-size too small and the thong bit into me in places that needed to be treated with a little more respect, but when I stepped into the bedroom where James was waiting naked in our bed, he was very appreciative.

'Now that's more like it,' he said. 'Just stand there and let me look at you.'

The path his eyes took was a promise of where his hands would follow. I felt my breasts jut forward a little more, nipples standing to attention under his gaze, my breath coming faster.

'Oh yes,' he murmured, and beckoned me towards him.

He ripped aside the thong to slide a finger into my slickness, and then another, his thumb brushing across my clit in the same rhythm as his tongue played in my mouth. Just as I was about to arch into his hand, he pulled it away to remove the thong completely.

'I can't wait any longer,' he groaned as he thrust into me.

Afterwards – too soon – he collapsed off me.

'God, I've missed you,' he said, pulling me into his chest and trailing his fingers lightly down my arm. 'I can't wait for us to be together all the time again.'

'Me too,' I murmured, but he'd already fallen sleep.

I lay in the dark for a while, listening to him snore. My head was spinning, my tummy was churning, the bra he hadn't had time to take off was cutting into my skin. Then nausea hit and I made a dash for the bathroom.

When I was done, I collapsed back on the tiled floor, resting my head against the cool of the vanity, still naked except for the tight red bra. James had always been ambitious, and a job like this would put him where he wanted to be. I was happy for him, truly I was, but as much as I yearned for us to want each other as we had tonight, there on the cold floor it seemed that what we each wanted was already miles apart. It worried me that even though we were going to be together physically, the distance between us was widening.

He'd given me New York, but right now I wanted to return it for a refund.

CHAPTER TWO

Despite our late night, I was up and walking as usual just before sunrise. Climbing to the top of the hill that ran behind the village I watched the sun come up, turning the sky lilac and then pink. There'd been a frost last night and the grass cracked beneath my feet as I walked. I sat down on the cold hillside and waited for the light to sweep ever so gradually across the fields. I loved this time of the day – the way the sun blessed every leaf on every branch of every tree as it passed, painting everything gold and reminding us that no matter what had happened yesterday, today was a new day.

From here I could see over the whole of Brookford, and watched as it came to life: wisps of smoke from wood heaters and cookers hanging in the still, cold air; the wintery landscape looking like a scene off a postcard. I wished I could keep it in the pocket of my jeans for another morning when we were far away. My morning walks wouldn't be the same in New York. I couldn't imagine replacing the green of the fields and the sound of the birds with traffic and sirens.

Almost directly below where I sat, a curving street ran all the way through the village. At one end I could see our cottage: a classic Cotswold two-storey house, set amongst a row of others almost the same, only distinguishable by their gardens, the number of windows, perhaps an extra gable. I knew that when the sun passed by each, it would warm the stone to a burnished yellow.

On the other side of the village was another row of two-storey houses built from the same local stone. I grew up in one of those houses, and my parents still lived there. My father had retired at Christmas – he'd been senior partner in one of the accounting firms in Cheltenham – and he and Mum had left last week for a long holiday in Australia with a cruise to New Zealand and stopovers in South-East Asia. They hadn't taken a proper holiday in … well, forever. I didn't think I'd ever seen my mother more excited.

My grandfather, Horrie, lived across the road from my parents. You wouldn't know it now, but in spring and summer his garden was one of the best in the village. Everything I knew about gardens I'd learnt from Horrie. If I ever needed him, I'd usually find him either working at his allotment, or checking out the form guide at a table beside the fire in The Lamb with a pint of ale in front of him and his retriever, Lucy, by his feet. He called in at Blossoms a few days a week, bringing flasks of homemade vegetable soup to share with Richie and me. My grandfather's vegetable soup was legendary.

Also legendary was his success with the ladies – although he could never remember which one he was supposed to be entertaining.

Last week Duncan had warned him: 'You need a better system to keep track of them, Horrie. You'll get yourself in trouble one of these days.'

Horrie had laughed and drained his beer. 'There's more chance of me picking the trifecta in each of the main races at Doncaster, Newbury and Carlisle than that happening. The girls keep track of my comings and goings better than I do. I wouldn't be surprised if they have their own roster for me. I might have invited Beryl, but it could be Norma's turn ... or Kathleen's. I never really know who'll turn up.' He'd turned to me as he stood and folded his paper. 'Don't look at me like that, lass. I know what your mother says: "Horrie's floozies" she calls my girls. I don't see what the problem is – we keep each other company and no one gets hurt.'

I had to agree with him. There was no competition amongst the women for Horrie's attentions, and everyone seemed happy with the arrangement. Mum pretended to be stern and disapproving, but I knew she was grateful that she and Dad could go away and be comfortable that between me and his 'girls', Horrie would be well looked after.

On a small rise at the edge of the village was the old Norman church – one of the first places to catch the golden light each morning. I remembered hearing something about how churches had been deliberately positioned for this reason, and why burials were to the south side where it was warmer – or something like that. The more important you were, the better your position in the graveyard.

James and I were married in that church. Next month it would be six years. Even though the day had been cold – as usual in February – the sky was blue, and there'd been enough snow overnight for a soft dusting to remain. James had asked me to wear something expensive and sleek, but I'd wanted vintage. I wore my mother's simple slip-style wedding dress, a faux-fur stole, and a wreath of vines in my short brown hair. Mum said I looked like a woodland nymph, and I did feel as though someone had waved a wand and cast a spell over me. The whole day was like a fairy tale – and I'd thought our marriage would be the same. Back then James and I seemed to be so well suited – almost made for each other. In London we used to lie in bed and talk about our plans for the future: the children we'd have, where we'd live. 'As soon as we can afford it, we'll move to Brookford,' James used to say. 'I've always thought the country is the best place to bring up children.' He'd grown up in London, with his father working two jobs and his mother working in a department store to send him to the best school they could afford.

Just lately, though, I wasn't so sure. I didn't think

it was just because James had been away more than he usually was. I was used to him not being here. He'd only managed the daily commute into London for one of the three years we'd lived here. After too many late nights, delayed trains and missed opportunities to entertain clients, he'd talked me into agreeing to a mortgage on a one-bedroom flat in London. 'If we factor in how many nights I've had to stay in hotels, darling,' he'd said, 'the flat will pay for itself.'

By then he was earning enough in bonuses to well and truly cover the expense. A management consultant, he worked for one of those corporate banks that sniff out investment opportunities and make deals to buy out other companies before selling them on for a lot more. The bigger the profit, the larger the bonus – and some of the bonuses James had earned over the years were obscene.

No, it wasn't that he was away more often. Until recently, the absences had made our being together all the sweeter. Because we were together so rarely, I always made an effort to make our weekends together special: I'd plan the menu meticulously and even apply makeup and change for dinner. Even if I didn't agree with James about something, I'd grit my teeth and say nothing rather than spoil our limited time with a fight over something that probably wasn't worth arguing about. His absences had made our sex life sweeter too. At times it had felt as though we were stealing time together – almost as if we were having an affair with each other. But even that had changed over the last few months, and I wasn't sure whether it was because I'd stopped making the effort or because James was too tired from all the commuting.

In London we'd seemed to need each other more; but since we'd moved here we'd built lives that only required us to come together occasionally. When James wasn't home, I spent hours in the kitchen, or working with Horrie in the allotment, or walking through the country with my camera. James hated walking and wasn't particularly keen on mud, so even if he was home he wouldn't come with me on those excursions. Instead, Richie would come, and I'd pack sandwiches and we'd walk for miles. Afterwards, I'd use the photos I took to illustrate the newsletter.

Although I would have preferred it if James was here with me, I realised that I'd built myself a life in Brookford that didn't rely on him; and he'd done the same in London, without me. I missed the way we used to be and wished we could go back there.

The sun hadn't yet reached my spot on the hill and my bottom was getting cold. I grimaced at the dirt on my hands and wiped them against the now wet bum of my jeans. James would probably have something to say about that – I giggled at the thought. Poor James; he was always so immaculately put together and I so often forgot to be.

•

An hour or so later I let myself back into the cottage and set about preparing breakfast. I'd made up a batch of potato scones before James arrived home yesterday afternoon, and planned to serve them with the smoked salmon I'd picked from the fridge at Blossoms. It was from a new supplier so I'd told Richie that I needed to test it out, just in case. I topped the scones with slices of salmon, a dollop of crème fraîche (also from the garden centre) and a sprig of dill snipped from my garden. Finally, I made tea in James's favourite pot and took it upstairs to him on a breakfast tray. James hated eating anywhere other than at the table, but made an exception for special breakfasts.

After placing the tray carefully on the bedside table, I took my wet jeans off and replaced them with some loose pyjama pants. James stirred, but didn't wake. I straddled him and moved up his body until my lips could reach his.

'Mmm,' he said softly, 'that's a lovely way to wake up.' He registered my sweater and socks. 'Have you been out already?'

'Uh-huh,' I murmured, kissing my way down his throat and across his chest. 'Just for a walk.'

'Not in those I hope.' He held me back to indicate the pyjama bottoms.

'Absolutely not.' I lowered myself down on him.

'Would you like me to get rid of them now?'

'I think that would be an excellent idea,' he said, his hands working their way under my jumper to pull it over my head.

Unlike the haste of last night, our lovemaking was slow and satisfying – the way it should be on a lazy Sunday morning. Afterwards, while I snuggled under the duvet, James went downstairs to make a fresh pot of tea. We sat up in bed and nibbled at the scones and sipped at the tea, chatting lightly about New York: the places we'd go, the sights James wanted to show me. It felt so much like we used to be that I wanted the morning to last forever. Perhaps James was right: we needed New York to bring us together again.

Too soon the mood was interrupted by a text.

James picked his phone up from the bedside table and read it with a frown. 'I'm sorry, darling, I'm going to need to leave for London a few hours earlier than I planned.'

'Was that India?' I tried to keep the irritation from my voice.

'Yes.' He sounded distracted. 'Jeremy's asked to see me before I fly out tomorrow morning.'

Jeremy was James's general manager.

'On a Sunday night?'

'We'll go to his club. You understand, don't you, darling?'

His look was pleading and I melted immediately.

'Of course I do.'

He leaned across and kissed me, but I could see his mind was already on leaving.

CHAPTER THREE

'When that kettle comes to the boil, can you move it to the window for me, please?' I asked, fiddling with the arrangement in front of me.

Outside the rain was pelting down. It was cold enough that on higher ground it was probably falling as snow.

'Won't it make the glass fog?' Richie asked.

'Uh-huh.' I checked the arrangement through the viewfinder on my camera, and moved the jam jar I'd filled with woody herbs to the opposite side of the plate. 'That's the whole idea: I want the condensation on the window in the background. It says that it's still cold outside without me having to spell it out.'

Richie nodded his understanding and obligingly moved the kettle away when the required level of fogginess had been achieved.

My subject was a plate of the peanut butter and chocolate chip cookies I'd made yesterday afternoon after James had left for London. I'd decided to shoot what was left of them before Richie demolished the lot. They were much more photogenic than the bowl of parsnip risotto I was intending to feature in the February newsletter. Even though I'd styled the soup with a drizzle of chilli oil, I was running out of creative ways to make beige food look appealing.

Richie smiled at me. 'Are you right now? Can I go back to what I was doing before you decided you needed a photographic assistant?'

'Yes, you're released from your duties. And when these little babies are released from theirs, it's your turn to make the tea.'

'You're on,' he said, returning to the papers on his desk.

The centre was empty of customers and I cursed everything about January that made work so quiet and gave me more time to think about the New York bombshell. I looked out the window. Yep, still raining. I sighed.

Richie looked up. 'That was a heavy sigh.'

'I hate January.'

'I thought you hated February more. Next you'll be telling me that you're bored.' He grinned.

'Well, I am bored and I hate them both equally: January and February.'

'Okay, I'll ask the question. Why do you hate January so much?'

'That's easy. Because I love December, and you're as far away from December as it's possible to be in

January.'

He laughed. 'You just like being able to drink mulled wine at 10 am while wearing a Christmas sweater.'

In the lead-up to Christmas I wore a different Christmas-themed sweater each day.

'What's not to like about that? And don't forget the Christmas markets – even you like those.'

'True, but January means a new year and you like new starts. Your birthday's in January – surely you like that?'

'The problem with new starts is that something else has to end – and I don't like that. Plus, my birthday is just for one day, and it's not something that anyone other than me looks forward to. Not like Christmas. That's so everywhere that the day itself is an anti-climax.' I paused to nibble the edge of a cookie. 'And the problem with February is that it's so in-between. You know that spring's coming and you have lots to do to be ready for it, but you can't do any of those tasks because the weather's terrible. It wouldn't be like that on your side of the world. I bet it's sunny and gorgeous.'

'It is down south. Up north, though, and across the ditch to Sydney, it's hot and uncomfortably humid.'

'It would still be better than this.' I sighed again. 'You stay there – I'll make the tea.'

I reboiled the kettle and popped teabags into

mugs, then rubbed at the window to look out. Yuck.

'What are you working on?' I asked as I placed Richie's tea on the coaster on his desk and looked over his shoulder at the drawings he'd been concentrating on.

He spread the sketches across the workbench. 'My garden.'

'The one you'll do for Chelsea?' Although his plan was to eventually go home to Queenstown and work in the family business designing gardens, his dream was to one day have one of his designs exhibited at the Chelsea Flower Show. 'The way you've drawn it, the garden looks almost like a lake – or a flowing river. What are you using? Flax?'

He looked impressed. 'Nice. New Zealand flax. The way it flows in the breeze sometimes looks like wind moving across water. I want the whole thing to look like Lake Wakatipu makes me feel.' He paused, embarrassed, and focused his attention on the pages in front of him.

'Don't stop. I love listening to you talk about it. It sounds wonderful.'

'It is. It's home. I'd like you to see it one day. There's an area outside of town, on the way out to Glenorchy, where the lake and the mountains seem to go forever. When you're there and seeing it, you wonder how you can ever want to be anywhere else. It's magnificent on a blue day, and intense as all hell on a grey one. It's almost as if the mountains have their own story to tell. In a way, I guess they do.' He gazed out the foggy window into the soft drizzle, but I knew that wasn't what he was seeing. 'The lake breathes, you know – in and out. The Maori say it's the beating heart of the giant who created the lake when he was killed. They say the heart of a giant can never be stopped.' He turned to look into my eyes and said softly, 'You'd love it – I know you would.'

I felt something shift in my tummy and hung my head to hide my confusion.

Then I blurted it out: 'We're moving to New York. James told me on Saturday night.'

Richie turned away and gathered his drawings, sliding them back into the pages of his sketchbook. I watched his back, waiting for a reaction.

Finally he said, 'What about you? What do you think about it?'

I shrugged. 'I don't know. It's a great opportunity for James – he's really excited. On the bright side, it means I'll see more of him. That has to be a good thing, right?' I forced a wide smile. Richie didn't smile back. 'Besides, what am I doing here? Sitting around in a potting shed playing at being a gardener, writing a silly little newsletter and taking photos of plates of food and vegetables while I wait for my husband to come home? I'm not like you – I don't have an ambition or a plan. I just have James.'

'What about your dream to have a cafe selling food

sourced from your garden? Soups, salads, muffins, all-day breakfast, mac cheese of the month … what about that? And the cookbook and recipe cards?'

I shook my head. 'That's just a fantasy.'

'It's more than that. You've planned the fit-out in almost as much detail as I've planned my Chelsea garden. Light and airy with polished concrete floors, you said. Local art on the walls, plants hanging from the ceiling, and the whole space opening up to a sun-filled pergola with wisteria providing colour and shelter in the spring and summer, and letting light through in the winter. A herb garden out the front so you can wander out and snip from it as you need to, and raised vegetable beds. Like a potting shed, but with food, and stock from local producers – like we do here. Nothing matching, you said. I've been listening.'

He certainly had been.

'I know, but it's all a bit silly when you think about it. James is a management consultant – he belongs in cities. I'm his wife, and I belong wherever he is. Anything else is unrealistic.'

He nodded slowly. 'You're right, of course.' He looked at me closely and I felt my tummy flip again. 'I'll miss you. It won't be the same without you here, Hendo.'

I felt him watching me when I turned away to look out the window.

He paused, then asked, 'When will you go?'

'Not for a few months. It'll take that long for all the visa and transfer paperwork to be done, so James will continue to commute until then. I'll need to find a tenant for the cottage. James is sorting out an apartment over there for us, and we're leaving the London flat as it is for when he needs to come back.' I didn't look at him as I spoke. 'James wants me there for summer, so I guess I'll go sometime in May or June.'

'What will you do there?'

'What does any woman do in New York?' I plastered a bright smile onto my face. 'Shop, sightsee and lunch. It's most women's dream come true – to be a lady of leisure in the best city in the world.'

'But not yours,' he said quietly. 'That's not you, Maxi. That's not who you are.'

'Maybe not,' I conceded. 'But James is my husband and I love him. My place is wherever he is.'

'Sounds like it's already decided.' There was no expression in his voice.

I turned to meet his eyes. 'I guess it is.'

'He's a lucky man, your James. I hope he knows that.'

I felt my cheeks grow warm under his gaze. He swallowed and dropped his eyes from mine.

'The rain's stopped. If you can make a start on the seedlings in the polytunnel, I'll get the furniture moved back outside. What time did you say Tom will be here to help me load the truck for the Swinbournes' delivery?'

I glanced at the clock on the wall. 'He should be here soon. I'll see you at one for lunch?'

'Thanks, but you eat when you're ready – don't wait for me today. I'll just heat some soup when I'm done.'

He pulled his boots on and went outside.

Horrie's reaction to my impending move was just as enthusiastic as Richie's had been. Monday's bad weather continued throughout the week and it was Friday before he and Lucy dropped in at Blossoms with a flask of spiced cauliflower soup. Horrie made at least one pot of soup each week from whatever vegetables were in the allotment, freezing the excess for lunches during times of the year when the garden wasn't quite so generous.

Horrie shrugged off his rain jacket and hung it with ours. As always at this time of year, he was dressed in his work pants, a checked flannel shirt under a grey chunky-knit jumper, and his well-worn black boots. He brushed a few stray raindrops from the wool before pulling a chair out from the round table where Richie and I usually ate our lunch. Lucy flopped in her usual position: on the rug near the heater.

Horrie rubbed at his left knee and grimaced when he sat down.

'Knee still playing up?' I asked.

He scratched at his thick white hair. 'It'll be right

tomorrow,' he said, grinning ruefully, his still blue eyes twinkling in his lined face.

'Hmmm.'

'Don't you be worrying about it, lass. It's just a touch of arthritis. This heater and a mug of soup will help warm it through.'

He was probably right. Although lanky, Horrie was still deceptively strong – something he put down to his daily walks, the work in the garden, good food, good women, and his daily pints. It was easy to forget he was in his late seventies.

That day we'd been offering tastings of a new cheese from Westfarm Dairy, so I dropped nuggets of it into the piping hot soup. Richie cut slices of baguette that we spread with Westfarm's wonderful butter and the three of us sat around the heater nursing our mugs.

'Bit quiet today,' remarked Horrie.

'It's been quiet all week,' said Richie. 'Aside from people coming in for supplies from the fridge, it's been dead. Half the time I think they only drop in to see what Maxi's left on the counter.' He grinned at me. 'Maybe we should post to our Instagram account on the days she brings in baking – we'd be bound to get extra traffic.'

I shrugged, an innocent look on my face.

'All I've sold today is firewood and feta,' he continued. 'I had to call Westfarm this morning to order more. Can you let me know in advance what you'll be featuring in February's newsletter so I can stock up? I think half of the Cotswolds have been making cauliflower salads this month.'

'You know I don't plan these things in advance,' I told him.

'Don't I just. I'm impressed you've already started on February's column – makes a nice change. What's going to happen next? You'll clean your desk?'

'When I'm this bored, anything is possible.'

'Young Jim home this weekend?' Horrie asked, ignoring our banter. His grin told me that he didn't need reminding how much my husband hated being called Jim.

'No.' I looked away, unable to meet Horrie's eyes. 'The thing is … well …'

'You getting a divorce, lass?' Horrie didn't appear upset about that possibility.

'No! Of course not.' I looked at Richie for support. He raised his eyebrows to indicate I was on my own in this one. 'Why would you think that?'

Horrie shrugged. 'No reason. But it's not much of a marriage when you never see each other.'

I thought about making an appropriate retort, but caught Richie's warning glance just in time. 'The thing is, James has been offered a role in New York and … well, we're moving over there. It won't be forever – just a couple of years – but it'll set James up to come back to something really senior.'

I held my breath and looked into my soup mug while I waited for Horrie's reaction. I didn't need to wait long.

'Yeah, I heard something like that. I was wondering when you were going to tell me.'

I wasn't expecting that. 'Where did you hear about it?'

I sent an accusing glance to Richie who shook his head.

'Duncan might have mentioned something.'

'But how did he … Never mind.'

If you wanted to know anything in a village, ask the publican.

'I told him the same I'll tell you – I think it's a bloody stupid idea,' Horrie said, his whiskery chin firming. 'What do you think you'll do over there?'

'It's not about me, Horrie, it's where James will be working. It's a good thing, really it is.' I didn't know who I was trying to convince: him or me. 'Isn't it, Richie?' My eyes pleaded with him to support me.

'Don't involve me in this. Anyone need more bread?'

'Did you have a say in the decision?' Horrie's gaze was sharp as he waited for my answer.

'It means we'll be together again – James won't be travelling as much.'

We both knew I'd avoided the question.

'Hmmm.' Horrie didn't sound convinced. 'You

probably won't see any more of him – you'll just be in the same country is all.'

I shrugged, unable to argue with that. James had always worked long hours, and entertaining clients and colleagues outside the office had always been part of the job.

'Have you told your mother?'

I nodded. 'I emailed her the other day. We haven't talked about it, but I'm sure she'll support the decision.'

'I wouldn't be too sure, lass. She could just be biting her tongue until she's home.'

I felt my own chin beginning to jut out. 'I'm twenty-nine years old, Horrie – there's not a lot she can do about it.'

'Here we go,' Richie muttered and he shifted in his chair.

'You haven't answered my question: what will *you* be doing over there?' Horrie's tone was even, but it felt like his eyes were piercing mine.

'Oh, you know: what every woman dreams of doing in New York. I'll shop and lunch and get my nails done.' I glanced down at my stubby unpainted fingernails. 'That's probably not a bad thing.'

He grunted. 'That'll keep you occupied for the first couple of days. You're not that kind of woman.'

'Well, maybe it's about time I grew up and became that kind of woman.' I glared back at him.

Richie stood up and collected our mugs. 'Okay,

I've seen that look on both your faces before. Anyone else for a soup top-up?'

Horrie and I ignored him and he escaped into the shop.

We glared at each other for a few more seconds. I was the first to drop my eyes.

'Perhaps you're right,' I said. 'I'm doing it though. I have to – he's my husband and my place is with him.'

Horrie relaxed as well. 'That's as maybe, lass, but you also deserve to be happy and I can't see you being satisfied with that sort of life.'

'James makes me happy,' I said quietly. 'There'll be time for me to follow my dreams when we come back. Please, Horrie – I know this wasn't my decision, but I'm going with him.' My eyes were pleading with him to understand. 'I'd prefer to do it with your blessing.'

He nodded thoughtfully. 'I wish you luck then.' He stood and whistled for Lucy, then kissed my cheek. 'Just be sure that it's Jim who makes you happy, not the thought of staying married. Remember, lass, you have choices too.'

I couldn't think of an appropriate answer before he called goodbye to Richie and left.

The shop remained annoyingly quiet for the rest of the afternoon, so in the absence of anything more meaningful to do I played around with some parsnip recipe ideas for next month's newsletter. That kept me occupied for all of about ten minutes – parsnip wasn't the world's most interesting vegetable. Try as I might, I couldn't forget Horrie's comments. Why had he jumped straight to divorce? Surely he knew I loved James? I'd always known that Horrie didn't have a lot of respect for James – at times it felt as though he was laughing at him – but I still didn't know where the divorce idea had come from.

'Why do you think Horrie jumped to that conclusion?' I asked Richie later that afternoon.

'What conclusion would that be?' I heard the patient smile in his voice as he looked up from the accounts.

'When he asked if I was divorcing James, of course.'

'Is that what you've been mulling over all afternoon?' Richie pushed his paperwork aside. 'I don't think he meant anything by it, Maxi. You know how Horrie likes to light your spark every so often. I'd say he was just a bit pissed that he found out about the move from Duncan.'

My shoulders slumped. 'I suppose so. How does Duncan know these things?'

Richie shrugged. 'It's a talent. Perhaps Horrie assumed you wouldn't want to leave Brookford and that's why you hadn't said anything to him.'

'He's right on that count – I don't want to leave Brookford. I have everything I need here.'

'Except James.' Richie said it so quietly that I wasn't sure at first that I'd heard him.

'Do you think it's a stupid idea – me going to New York?'

He groaned. 'Oh, Maxi, don't ask me that. This has nothing to do with me. Besides, you've made it clear that you are going.'

'But what do you think?' I knew the question I was asking was impossible for him to answer. 'Please, Richie, I want to know.'

'I think it's a big decision to have made without consulting you.' He paused. 'I think that's the point Horrie was trying to make too.'

I opened my mouth to argue, but he stopped me.

'Don't say it. I know my track record with long-term relationships isn't great so I have no experience of these things, but I'm pretty sure I wouldn't make a call like that without talking it through with my partner.' At the look on my face he shrugged one shoulder. 'You asked me the question, and I answered it. I'm sorry if you don't like the answer.' With that he piled up the papers he'd been working on and moved across to the filing cabinet to put them away.

I walked around to where he was and stood with my hands on my hips. 'I'll have you know that even though I didn't get a say in it, I think this could be a good thing – for both of us.'

'That's good then.'

'I could have a rooftop garden like in *Sex and the City* – you know the episode where they have a hotdog party on the roof?'

'No, I'm not familiar with it – I didn't know you were either.'

I waved his comment away. 'I'm not really, but Mirry was addicted so I had no choice. But my point is, I can have a rooftop garden, and shop at farmers' markets. In the movies they always shop at farmers' markets.'

I made a mental note to google farmers' markets when I got home.

'Yes, I'm sure they do.' His sigh was audible.

'So whatever you say, I think I can build a life for myself in New York. It won't be the same as in Brookford, but that doesn't mean I won't enjoy it.'

Richie finally turned and looked at me. 'I thought the whole point of this was so you could build a new life for both of you – together.'

Our eyes met and held for a few heartbeats.

'That's what I meant,' I said softly, my eyes dropping to the floor.

My words to Richie were braver than I felt. In truth I had no idea what I'd do with myself in New York. James had told me I wouldn't be able to work – something to do with the terms of the visa – but had added with great pride that he'd be able to look after me in a manner he hoped I'd grow accustomed to.

'There'll be plenty for you to do without having to go off to a nothing job,' he'd said.

I'd bitten my tongue before I could blurt out that my nothing job incorporated everything I loved to do: growing, cooking, styling, photographing and writing about food. It mightn't pay much or be as important as his job, but I considered myself fortunate to work with my best friend doing something I loved.

At home, I defrosted a single serve of Napoletana sauce I'd made from Horrie's tomatoes last summer, and popped some penne into a pan of boiling water. As the pasta cooked I wondered whether I could grow tomatoes in the rooftop garden I'd convinced myself we'd have. Perhaps I could continue my blog from there, experimenting with different vegetables and discovering new farmers' markets.

Balancing my plate on the arm of the couch I flicked through the channels, landing on an old episode of *Sex and the City*. After the conversation with Richie this afternoon, it seemed like a sign that this would all turn out for the best.

I reached for my phone so I could tell James so, but my call went straight to voicemail. I didn't bother leaving a message.

February in the Kitchen

February might be the shortest month of the year, but it always seems so long. Is that just me? When you're feeling like that it's difficult to find some enthusiasm in the kitchen. It doesn't help that there's nothing new coming into season, but it is the last month for the best of some of our winter standbys. Parsnips, brussels sprouts and Jerusalem artichokes are all on the way out for the year. Before the brussels disappear, you should try this fabulously simple salad. No, don't give me that look – this tastes nothing like brussels sprouts when your mother overcooked them.

Shave or slice the sprouts finely – if you have a mandolin, it's a cinch. Just don't rush it – my fingers are still covered in plasters from when I made this last week. Lightly toast some walnuts – say, a cup – in a pan, and then crush them in your hands. Don't be too precious about this – you don't want walnut crumbs, but rather walnut pieces. Grate over some pecorino or parmesan, and toss it all together. As for a dressing, whisk a few tablespoons of lemon juice into a quarter of a cup of good olive oil. To finish, some crispy fried bacon bits give a delicious crunch.

We're well and truly over spiced parsnip soup here at Blossoms. Most weeks I've made a batch, varying the spices each time to add a little difference to the sameness. I've done a version where I roasted the parsnips first in the spices, and another where I cooked the parsnip in spiced milk. The Lamb here in Brookford has been doing a lovely parsnip soup with pear and ginger; and I tasted one last week in a pub on the road to Cheltenham that included apple. For me it was just that tiny bit too sweet, but (thankfully) we all have different tastes.

You know that pumpkin makes a fabulous risotto – remember the one I posted in October's newsletter? It was made with sage and pancetta, just a touch of chilli, and finished with creamy mascarpone. I'm hoping to persuade Seb from The Lamb to part with his recipe this time, so watch this space.

Parsnip works well in risotto too. Simply peel a couple of large parsnips and chop them into small pieces, and do the same with an onion. Heat a dollop of butter in a pan large enough to hold your risotto – the unsalted butter we've been getting in from Westfarm Dairy is well worth trying – and crush a clove of garlic. Actually, crush two – no recipe ever really calls for one clove of garlic, does it? Besides, garlic helps keep winter colds away – possibly because no one comes close enough to pass on their germs.

Cook the onion gently in the butter for a couple of minutes – you don't want it to colour too much – and toss in the parsnips and garlic. Cook these down until the parsnip is tender and your kitchen smells wonderfully garlicky. The arborio rice can be added now, and a splash of wine. (Just pour some out of the glass you're drinking.) Now make your risotto as you usually would – adding ladlefuls of simmering vegetable or chicken stock, stirring until it's absorbed and then adding another. You'll know it's done when the rice is tender but not soft inside – a fine, but not insignificant detail. Finish it off with handfuls of parmesan and plenty of butter. I've added some chilli oil too – not just because it looks better in the photo, but because it gives a little extra kick. You can serve this as a side dish or a stand-alone one-bowl, one-fork meal.

Given February's the coldest month of the year, it's only fair to share a variation of the ultimate comfort food with you: a leeky cheesy mac. Yes, macaroni cheese with finely julienned and fried leeks stirred through the sauce before baking. For even more luxury, fry up some diced bacon, then toss some fresh breadcrumbs into the bacony fat, and scatter both across the top before you pop the dish into the oven. For best results on this one go for a less saucy sauce – if you know what I mean.

Also, because it's February and we all need a little decadence to cut through the gloom, why not try my peanut butter chocolate chip cookies? Perfect with a cuppa on a cold wintery afternoon. Full recipes are available, as always, on the website.

Don't worry, spring is just around the corner.

Until then,

Max

CHAPTER FOUR

George, the owner of Blossoms & Buds, made a rare visit in the middle of February. He'd moved to Spain some years ago and managed his several UK-based businesses and various ex-wives from there. Although he was in the habit of dropping in once or twice during the summer, we'd never seen him at this time of the year before. I said as much to him.

'Trust me, Max, leaving Spain at this time of year is not something I do lightly. But I had some other matters to attend to, so here I am, freezing my arse off. Reminds me why I left this country in the first place.'

Hands on hips, he surveyed the shop. Since his last visit Richie had put in a wide open-fronted fridge and a tall upright freezer for displaying and storing the perishables. Condiments were arranged on a wooden table that ran almost the entire width of the shop, with large baskets holding bread at one end, while at the other were small piles of diaries, journals and other gift items. On a ladder in one corner hung tea towels, aprons and pot holders.

'It looks good. Is it all locally produced?' George asked.

'Everything,' replied Richie. 'Even the paper products and baskets. Nothing has travelled more than fifty miles.'

George nodded thoughtfully. 'Christmas numbers were up,' he said as he walked around the shop picking up jars of this and bottles of that. 'Mostly due to what you've got on offer here rather than what's for sale out there.' He indicated towards the nursery.

'Yeah, we were kept busy in the lead-up to Christmas with people dropping in for hampers and the like. We're still trying out new suppliers, and have more phoning us asking us to try them.' Richie smiled at me. 'The biggest issue we have is keeping up with demand when Max features a product in her newsletter. I lost count of the times I had to restock the feta last month.'

I didn't hear George's response as he and Richie went into the office and closed the door. He didn't stay long, dropping into the shop on his way out to say goodbye. I was unpacking a delivery from the trout farm. He wrinkled his nose, declared he didn't like fishy shit and had to keep moving, raising a hand in the air as he walked out.

'What was that visit in aid of?' I asked Richie.

'I have absolutely no idea,' he said slowly, as if trying to make sense of the words before he spoke them. 'He wanted to talk numbers, of course – and seemed impressed by the results we've brought in this winter – but I couldn't get a handle on what he was after.'

'Maybe he really was just in the area and decided to drop in?'

'Hmmm.' He didn't sound convinced. 'That's not normally something George does. Are you just about done with that fish? It must be time for tea – and I do believe it's your turn.'

I grinned. 'Really? My turn comes around a lot. While I think of it, did you want to come by for supper tonight? I'm experimenting with sweet potato macaroni.'

'Sounds great, but I'll need to rain-check – I've got a date.'

'Angela? Still? Wow, that's lasted more than a month. You'll be changing your relationship status soon.'

'I wouldn't think so,' he said with a wicked grin. 'Way too limiting.'

Another reason I disliked February was that it always seemed to be when I caught my annual cold. This year was no different, except for the fact that no sooner was I over the cold when I managed to get really sick with a tummy bug. James had been home for the weekend and we'd been out for dinner to celebrate our anniversary and talk through the logistics of the move to New York, which I was still struggling to get my head around.

'I'm wondering whether we should sell the cottage rather than renting it,' James had said, almost to himself, as we lingered over coffee, the smell of which was making me feel sick. 'I don't think there's much more capital gain to be made here over the next two years, so we might as well realise it now.'

I'd felt a jolt somewhere in my stomach at his words. All along we'd been talking about coming back to Brookford – or rather I'd been talking about coming back. If we sold the cottage, we'd have nothing to come back to.

I opened my mouth to tell him that, but suddenly felt nauseous and had to make a quick exit to the bathroom.

As I sat down, James looked at me with concern. 'Are you okay?'

I shook my head. 'I don't think so. Something hasn't agreed with me.'

'Well, I don't know what. You haven't eaten much tonight and you've barely touched your wine.'

I shrugged. 'I don't know, but I think you'd better get me home before I make a mess in here.'

He wrinkled his nose in distaste. 'A little too much information, darling,' and indicated to the waiter that he needed the bill.

Once home, I'd gone downhill quickly, so James had left early the next morning.

'I'm sorry, darling, but if this isn't food poisoning I can't afford to get sick, not with everything we have happening at the moment. You'll be alright, won't you?'

I'd nodded miserably from where I was tucked up on the couch, trying desperately to keep down the dry toast I'd attempted to eat.

Although I wasn't well enough to cycle into Blossoms on Monday, I very quickly tired of my own company and was back at work by Tuesday. My tummy was still queasy and all I wanted to do was sleep. I'd never known tiredness like it.

On Thursday, Richie took me aside. 'I know you've not been well, but I really need to talk to you when we have a moment.'

'Why not now? There's no one in just yet, and with this drizzle I think we'll be quiet most of the day. How about I make us a cup of tea to have with these muffins I've brought in, and you can tell me what you need to tell me?'

'Are they your special chocolate ones with the gooey centre?'

'Uh-huh.'

'In that case I'll make the tea.'

I watched him as he took the first bite from his muffin, closing his eyes to savour the chocolatey goodness.

'Man, that's good,' he declared.

I broke the top off mine, but after nibbling the

crunchy bits around the edge decided I wasn't hungry. 'So … are you going to tell me?'

He ate some more, swallowed far harder than he needed to, and said, 'I may as well just spit it out – George has sold the garden centre.'

'Oh.' The news hit me like a blow. George may have been an absentee landlord, but I supposed I'd thought Blossoms & Buds would be here forever. 'Who to?'

'One of the national brands. They'll take over just after Easter and probably close in spring for rebranding.'

'That's what he was here for the other week,' I guessed. It was only ever a matter of time. George had inherited the garden centre from his father, but had never shown any real interest in it.

Richie nodded.

'What are you going to do?' I asked.

He reached for another muffin, breaking off the crumbly top to dig at the fudge inside. 'They've offered me the manager's job. I might take a holiday first though. My friend Brad – he's a landscape architect in Melbourne – emailed me the other day. He's been offered a fellowship in Denmark, so I might spend a week or so there. It sounds interesting – they're looking at permaculture and alternative planting systems. I might even go home for a visit. It's been a few years since I saw Mum and Dad.'

'Oh.' The few crumbs I'd eaten weren't sitting well in my tummy.

What could I say? I felt my eyes well and turned my head so he wouldn't see. This was ridiculous. I swallowed, but my muffin was coming back at me and I made a dash for the bathroom. When I finally emerged, Richie's face was concerned.

'It's this flu,' I explained. 'I can't seem to shake it.'

'You look tired.'

'Of course I'm tired,' I snapped. 'I'm exhausted trying to get my head around this New York business – there's so much to do. Last night I sat down to watch telly before dinner and woke up at midnight. I can't seem to stay awake. And I'm emotional over ridiculous things. This damn tummy thing has really hit me hard.'

'Hmmm.'

'What does that mean?'

'Are you sure you're not … Look, forget I said anything – it's none of my business.'

'Am I sure I'm not what?'

'Pregnant. Isn't that supposed to make you sick and tired and teary?'

'Yeah, but so does packing up your house, having the flu, and watching your husband fly off to New York. Of course I'm not pregnant. How could I be?'

He shrugged, and in my head I began calculating dates. Had I missed my last period? I realised it had been a while, and I was normally as regular as clockwork – but that could have been the stress associated with the move. Besides, I was diligent with my pill – I always had

been. But the night James had told me about New York
I'd been ill from all the alcohol – maybe I'd thrown
up my pill? Thinking about it, I had been feeling off
for a couple of weeks and my breasts were incredibly
sore, which I'd put down to my period being due. Then
there was the debilitating exhaustion and the crying at
Labrador puppies in tissue ads. A sliver of excitement
circled around the edges of my brain, but I kept my
face expressionless.

Richie shrugged and said, 'It was just an idea. It's
been dragging on for a couple of weeks though, so
maybe you should get yourself off to a doctor.'

'I will,' I promised.

'Is James home this weekend?'

'Yes. He's flying back on Friday, but has a client
thing on Friday night. He says I have too much to do
to bother travelling down for it so he'll go on his own
– although India will be there, I suppose. He'll drive
up here on Saturday. I haven't seen him for nearly a
month, you know.'

'Well, soon you'll be seeing him all the time,' Richie
said, and busied himself with some order forms.

'Yes.' My mind was full of the possibility of a
baby: surely James would be happy?

'How about you try that again with enthusiasm
this time?' Richie's smile was sardonic.

'Sorry. Of course I'm excited to see him.' Even I
wasn't convinced, but I was saved by the shop bell as

someone pushed the door open. 'I'll get it,' I said.

It was Angela, and by the look on her face she wasn't happy. I'd seen that look on Richie's other women over the last couple of years and knew exactly what it meant.

'Hi, Angela. Richie's out the back.'

She didn't return my greeting, just pushed past me to get through to the office.

'Just go on in,' I said unnecessarily, and headed out into the drizzle to leave them to it.

A baby. The tiny spark of excitement that had flared when Richie first suggested the possibility was now raging through me so warmly that even the rain couldn't dampen my mood. I wandered into the polytunnel to check on the progress of the seeds I'd sown last week, but now the idea was in my head it was all I could think about. I had no idea how I'd manage to concentrate on work until this afternoon when I could pick up a pregnancy test.

I heard the slam of a car door and the sound of wheels spinning too fast on gravel and assumed that Angela's talk with Richie hadn't resulted in a happy outcome.

'Is it safe to come back inside?' I asked when he joined me not long after to see if I was ready for some soup and sandwiches.

'Yeah, she's gone.'

He didn't expand on that, and it was only much

later when I was cycling into town after work that I remembered I hadn't asked him what had happened. I decided that if he'd wanted to talk about it, he would have found some way to bring the subject up. I pedalled harder, anxious to reach the pharmacy before it closed, and didn't give Richie's love life another thought.

CHAPTER FIVE

The test was positive. I did three – just to be sure – and bundled the little sticks together so I could show James on the weekend. I knew this was something we hadn't planned, but I hoped he'd be happy about the idea once he'd had a chance to get used to it.

I was tempted to call Mum or Mirry, but decided that James deserved to know first. I could wait another few days, and Mum would be home next week anyway. In the meantime, I googled pregnancy do's and don'ts. I didn't usually drink a lot so going without alcohol wasn't going to be a problem, but eight months without soft cheeses or anything made with raw eggs was going to be difficult. Not that I could stomach much food at the moment – I was finding it difficult keeping down anything more than a cheese sandwich. Far from morning sickness, this was all-day general queasiness.

On Friday afternoon, Richie and I were packing up for the day when James phoned me. 'Hello, darling, I just thought I'd let you know I landed okay.'

'Thanks.' I tried to keep the surprise from my voice.

Although he thought it ridiculous that I worried about him, usually he just sent me a quick text. Something like *Landed* or *Here*, or *All OK*.

'Also, something's come up here in town tomorrow night. I'm not going to be able to make it to the cottage this weekend.'

'Oh.' I couldn't hide my disappointment. 'Do you want me to come to London instead?'

'Of course I do, darling, but as much as I want to see you, you haven't been well. At least if I'm not there to bother you, you'll be able to get some rest. You're going to need it!'

'It's just that I miss you.' Out of the corner of my eye I saw Richie walk out of the office and into the shop, presumably to give me some privacy. 'And there are things to talk about.'

'It can wait until next week. I'm sure you can handle whatever it is you need my input on. In only a month or so you'll be in New York and we'll be together all the time. We've been apart for so long that it's going to be like when we were first together – new and fun.'

'I guess.'

'Darling, please don't be like this. I hate the situation as much as you do, but with everything else I've got on, I don't need you at the other end of the phone giving me grief. It's a few weeks and a bit of packing and some cleaning. I really think you can manage that, don't you?' His voice softened. 'Of course, I wish I could be there with you. I'd be there if I could.'

'I understand.' I didn't. Not really.

'Good, I'll see you next weekend.' And with that, he was gone.

Richie gave me another couple of minutes to compose myself before coming back into the office.

'He's not coming this weekend,' I told him.

'Yeah, I got that impression.'

'Something's come up.'

He nodded. 'I thought it might have.'

'He'd be here if he could.' I felt as though I should be defending James.

Richie didn't comment.

'He would, you know,' I said again.

Richie sighed. 'Of course he would. Given that you're now at a loose end do you want to drop in at the pub for a drink and an early dinner?'

I considered it for just a minute. 'Sure, why not? I'm in no mood for my own company tonight so I may as well inflict myself on you. Aren't you seeing Angela though?'

'To be honest, she's not very happy with me at present.' At my blank look, he added, 'Remember she called by the other day? We had words – or rather, she had words, an awful lot of them.'

'What's happened?' I asked, taking my jacket from the hook and pulling it on. 'I thought you two were getting on well.'

He shrugged, closing the door behind us. 'Yeah, nah ... now we're not.' He unlocked his car and opened the passenger door. 'Are you coming or not?'

'Okay,' I said a short time later, shuffling into a booth at The Lamb. 'What's the story with Angela?'

'Drinks first. What are you drinking?' Richie asked.

'Just soda and lime for me, thanks.'

He looked closely at me, but said nothing until he was back at the table with our drinks. 'Congratulations. How do you feel about it?'

I didn't pretend to misunderstand. 'Excited, scared, thrilled.' I shrugged. 'I've wanted a baby for so long.'

He reached over and patted my hand. 'I'm really pleased for you, Maxi. You'll make a great mother. What was James's reaction?'

My smile faltered. 'I haven't told him. I was supposed to tell him tomorrow.'

He nodded, but said nothing.

'Oh, who am I kidding? If he really wanted to see me, he would have tried harder.' I scowled into my glass.

'Do you think he'll be happy about the baby?'

'I have no idea. Probably not to start with – he wanted us to wait another couple of years.'

'He should have been more careful then.'

'It was my fault. That night he took me out for my birthday, when he told me about New York – I had too much to drink and I think I threw the pill up, and ... I'm getting into too-much-information territory, aren't I?'

He grinned. 'Why stop now?'

'True. I'm hoping he'll come around … Not that he has a lot of choice in the matter – the baby's coming whether it fits with his schedule or not.'

'So when will you tell him?' he asked.

I shrugged. 'He says he'll definitely get here next weekend. I suppose the conversation can wait until then. After that there's only another month or so before everything has to be packed up and I head over there.' As I said the last sentence, Richie looked away. 'Can you imagine if I don't get to tell him before I go? He'll see my boobs before he sees me! They're huge at the moment. Had you noticed?' I cupped my hands under my bra for emphasis.

He shook his head and laughed. 'Do you really want me to answer that? If I say no, you'll wonder why I hadn't noticed; and if I say yes, you'll want to know why I was checking them out.'

I acknowledged the truth of his words.

'Having said that … yep, they're fabulous.'

I grinned. 'They are rather, but so sore.'

'James is a lucky man.'

The smile fell off my face. 'If only he were here to appreciate it.'

'Why don't you go to him? I'll even drive you to the station seeing as how you've sold that rust bucket of yours. Speaking of which, I can't believe someone bought that car. I would have thought the wardrobe of clothes you kept in the back was the only thing holding it together. I'll bet James is pleased you finally got rid of it.'

'He is.' James hated my car. So much that he'd always refused to get in it. Or that could have been because he hated my driving too. I thought about Richie's offer. 'You're right. There's nothing stopping me hopping on a train. I can even go with him to whatever he has on tomorrow night. In fact, it's such an obvious answer I can't believe I had to wait for you to think of it.'

He tipped his glass in a silent toast. 'Pleased to be of service.'

The waitress, a local girl named Helen, came by with our meals – fish and chips with mushy peas. As she laid the plate in front of Richie, she said, 'I should tip this in your lap in support of Angela.'

'Yeah, well, I appreciate it that you didn't,' he replied, and she stalked off.

'What was that about?' I asked.

'I told Ange the other day that I'm thinking of going to Denmark for a few weeks in June. I think she was hoping we'd go on holiday somewhere together.'

'And you're not ready for that?'

He shook his head. 'You'd really enjoy what we're doing in Denmark. I think you'd like my mate Brad too.'

'Well, if I change my mind about New York, I'll know where to find you.' I said it with a laugh, but he didn't join in. 'Why aren't you taking Angela away somewhere?' I added. 'I thought you two were getting quite close.'

Richie delayed answering. 'You know – the usual.'

'Too much too soon?'

'Something like that. I'll have to get around to finishing it, I suppose – or make it up with her … I haven't decided. I might go and see her later.' He looked intently at me. 'Did you know immediately when you met James?'

'That he was the one?'

He nodded.

'No. At first he was just one of the managers in the company I was working for. I was too busy having a great time – you know what it's like when you're out of home and earning money for the first time.' I paused to nibble on a chip.

'I've never asked – how did you end up working there? I can't picture you fetching and carrying in an office.'

I let out a short laugh. 'I'm not really sure what I was doing there either.' I'd faffed about with food technology at college, but somehow came out with a design degree. 'The grand plan was to save up and go travelling for a bit, then come back and work in food – although I hadn't decided if I wanted to grow it, cook it, photograph it, write about it, style it … or all of the above. The admin job seemed as good a place to think about it as any other.'

'And James? Did that start immediately?'

I shook my head. 'I'd noticed him – James is one of those men you can't ignore.' I traced the condensation on my glass and smiled as I remembered. 'Of course he's handsome, but it was more than that: he had this charisma about him that made you hold onto his every word.'

Even back then James had a sleek, sophisticated and very polished veneer – the sort you only get from going to a good school and being with other people who have that sort of polish. He'd been to a good school, but not *that* good. From ordinary middle-class stock, he'd deliberately cultivated the rest – dressing in the right brands, being seen at the right restaurants and clubs, learning how to drink the right wines. By the time he graduated from Oxford with an economics degree, he already had around him the beginnings of a useful network. None of the boyfriends I'd had before – and there weren't many – had prepared me for James. Once he decided on something, argument was futile.

'Once he turned his charm on me, I didn't stand a chance. He dazzled me, swept me away. But I wouldn't call it love at first sight.' I shrugged. 'Sometimes I wonder what he saw in me. Before we started dating, I'd seen him with these gorgeous model types on his arm – women like India. I'm nothing like them. I don't care about my nails, or the latest designer bag. I don't really care about my hair … which is lucky given I'll never be able to set foot in the local hairdresser's again once you break it off.'

He laughed at that. 'Yeah, sorry 'bout that.'

'So no, I didn't know immediately. Have you ever – fallen in love at first sight?'

He smiled ruefully. 'I have – the very first time I laid eyes on her. I was just going about my business as normal and all of a sudden she was there. My head was full of her and, yeah, so was my heart. The same thing happened with my dad. He fell for Mum immediately too. Wham bam. As far as he was concerned, no one else would do. It took some time for her to catch up with him, but all these years later they still only have eyes for each other. My mate Brad said the same happened with him. Sometimes I think it's something that happens to guys more than girls – the lightning bolt thing.'

I frowned as I pondered the idea. 'Perhaps. You know, Horrie always said it was like that with Gran – it's why he didn't marry again after she died. And I remember Dad saying he decided to marry Mum after their first date – she thought he was joking. I'd think it was more of a guy thing if it wasn't for Mirry and Oliver – she decided she wanted him and the poor bugger didn't stand a chance!' I sipped at my soda. 'Yours didn't work out? The one you fell for?'

'Obviously not.'

She clearly wasn't smart enough to appreciate a

good thing when she came across it.

'Is that why your relationships don't last long? Do you compare them to her?'

'I try not to, but yeah, probably.' I waited for more, but he changed the subject. 'Are you going to finish those chips?'

'No, take what you want.'

Soon after, the tiredness hit me in the way it had been lately – not so much sneaking up on me as whacking me about the head.

Richie noticed almost immediately. 'I'd better get you home before you fall asleep on me.'

He helped me to my feet and, once outside, put an arm around me. I rested my head against his shoulder and we walked the short distance to my place like that.

At the cottage he took my keys and unlocked the front door. 'You get a decent night's sleep. I'll pick you up around one and drop you at the station.'

I smiled gratefully. 'Thanks, Richie. I really appreciate this.'

'You're welcome.' He kissed my forehead. 'Sleep well.'

The first cramps hit soon after I got home. They started as a low pain somewhere in my pelvis, dull to begin with, but enough to send my heart racing into my throat. I put a DVD in the player and tried to relax. It was nothing. Everything would be alright.

Within an hour the pain was coming in waves, starting at my side and sawing through my belly around to my back, and then starting all over again. When I couldn't avoid it any longer I went into the bathroom. As I'd feared, my pants were stained with blood. I rested my head against the tiled wall for just a minute, then cleaned myself up as best I could.

I phoned James, but the call went straight to voicemail. So I called Richie. He answered after just a couple of rings.

'Hey, Hendo, it's late. Are you okay?'

'I'm sorry to disturb you, but I think I might need a lift to the hospital.' Somehow I managed to say it without crying.

There was a few seconds of silence, then he said, 'I'll be there in five.'

I wrapped a cardigan around the waist of my denim skirt and waited outside for him. When he pulled up and raised a questioning eyebrow at me I shook my head. 'I'm sorry, I'm going to need a towel to sit on in the car.' My voice broke and my eyes began to well.

He put his arm around me and, without saying a word, led me to the car. Once I was settled, he put his hand over mine and squeezed it once, tightly.

We drove to the hospital in silence, me looking out the window at the descending dark, tears streaming down my face, willing everything to turn out alright – even though I knew in my heart it wouldn't be. It already wasn't.

Richie concentrated on the road ahead, but every so often I felt him sneaking a sideways look at me. It felt like we'd been driving for hours, but it was probably only around thirty minutes. I tried phoning James another few times, and sent a single text: *Please call me.*

When Richie pulled up at the hospital entrance, I stopped him from getting out. 'I'll be fine from here. Besides, you can't leave the car here.'

'I'll come in with you,' he offered, a worried look on his face.

'No, Richie, it's fine. You've done enough – there's nothing more you can do for me.'

I didn't tell him that I didn't need him to see me like this; I thought he knew. James was the only man who should be seeing me like this, but he was in London not answering his phone. Without him it felt lonely.

I shut the car door and went to check myself into Emergency.

CHAPTER SIX

Some hours later, a tired-looking doctor not much older than me didn't quite meet my eyes as he told me what I already knew. 'I'm sorry, Mrs Henderson, but you've lost your baby.'

I sat on the edge of the hospital bed in my hospital gown and nodded slightly. Why did they say that: you've lost your baby? As if a baby was something you could put down and forget to pick up again.

'Can I go home now?'

'Do you want to ask me anything else?'

What else could I ask? The baby had gone, before it had even had much of a chance to exist. Nothing this poor over-worked doctor could tell me would make any difference to that.

'Can I have my clothes, please?'

He looked uncomfortable. 'There's been quite a bit of bleeding so I suspect you've passed the pregnancy naturally. The bleeding could continue for another week or two, but if it becomes heavier, come back in. The nurse will give you a leaflet on what we consider abnormal or worrying symptoms. As for the pain, it should be just like regular period pain, so feel free to take some paracetamol.'

Regular period pain. Did he have any idea what that felt like?

'Can I have my clothes, please?' I asked again. I didn't want to sit here and listen to him reading me the textbook spiel.

'Your clothes are quite heavily stained. Is there someone we can call to bring you something else to wear home?'

'No. They'll have to do. I just want to go home – can I have them, please?' My voice was beginning to rise.

A nurse pushed the curtain aside to enter the cubicle. 'I'm sorry to interrupt, Doctor, but Mrs Henderson's friend has been waiting outside for hours. He's brought her some clean clothes and will see she gets home safely.'

For a split second I thought she meant James, that someone had managed to get hold of him.

Richie poked his head around the curtain. 'Is it okay if I come in now?'

I nodded and held my arms up to him, burying my head into the warmth of his chest. 'You came back,' I mumbled.

He sat down beside me, one arm pulling me into his side, the other hand reaching across to hold mine. 'Of course I came back. I couldn't just leave you here

to go through this on your own. Besides, I knew you'd
need something else to wear. I hope you didn't mind
me going through your stuff.'

I shook my head. 'The baby's gone,' I told him, my
eyes welling again.

'I know, Maxi.'

He rested his head against mine and held my hand
tighter as I sobbed for the life that James hadn't even
known about, but that I'd already loved. He didn't tell
me that it would be alright; I think he knew it couldn't
be. He just held me and let me cry.

Richie didn't ask me about James until we were on our
way home. 'Is James coming back?'

I looked blankly at him.

'You haven't told him?' he guessed.

'No.'

I didn't even know if James had tried to call me
back. I checked my phone. He hadn't, so I switched
the screen off and, tipping my head back against the
headrest, shut my eyes.

At home, Richie took the bag of soiled clothes
straight into the laundry. I heard him switch on the
washing machine as I stood in the hall unsure of what
I should be doing.

'How about you go and get into bed? I'll bring you
up some tea and toast.'

'I'm not hungry.'

'I'm sure you're not, but I am, and I need to be doing something for you.'

He smiled gently and I slowly climbed the stairs.

He sat on the edge of the bed and watched me nibble at the toast he'd prepared, waiting until I'd eaten it all.

When I'd finished, he took the plate. 'I'm not going anywhere tonight – I'll sleep on the lounge so I'll be here if you need me. Will I find a blanket and pillow in the linen cupboard?'

'Yes.' I heard him opening and closing the cupboard doors and moving about the lounge room. 'Richie?' I called.

He answered immediately. 'Do you need anything else?'

'No … just, thank you.' It didn't seem sufficient for all he'd done for me, but it was all I could manage.

He leaned forward and kissed my forehead. 'Try and get some sleep. We'll talk in the morning.'

When I surfaced the next day, Richie had already packed up the blanket and pillow and put them back in the closet. I could hear the shower running, so I made myself a cup of tea, swallowed a couple of paracetamol tablets, and popped some bread in the toaster. By the time Richie came in, I was sitting at the kitchen table and staring at the toast I'd made, wondering if I had either the strength or the inclination to eat it.

'You should have stayed in bed and let me get that for you. You're supposed to be taking it easy,' he scolded.

'It's just tea and toast.'

'Sure, it's just that the doctor said –' He saw my face and said nothing more.

We didn't talk while he reboiled the kettle and made himself some toast. He took a seat at the table and glanced out the window at the rain.

'The good weather hasn't lasted,' he said.

'It never does in spring.'

'They're forecasting some late snow on higher ground. Maybe not this far south though.'

'Hmmm.'

'Maxi ... do you want to talk about it?'

I didn't answer immediately. Instead I cut my toast into smaller pieces. 'James hasn't called me back. He didn't even know there was going to be a baby, and now there's not. I don't know how to tell him about it.'

Richie watched me for a minute, then stood and picked up the dishes. 'Why don't you go rest on the sofa? I'll put away these breakfast things, and then we're spending the day watching whatever you want.'

I felt my eyes filling again. 'Even box sets of Inspector Barnaby?'

He rolled his eyes in exaggerated relief. 'I was worried it was going to be chick flicks. *Midsomer Murders* sounds perfect.'

•

Richie defrosted some of Horrie's vegetable soup for lunch, and we ate it on the couch with toasted cheese sandwiches as we watched the body count rise in *Midsomer Murders*. We didn't talk much about anything other than subjects like:

'Remind me never to move to Badger's Drift.'

'I'm not sure whether I like the new Barnaby more or less.'

'Sykes the dog should have his own credits.'

I was curled up on one end of the couch with my knees held into my belly when I heard the key in the front door. It was early afternoon.

James took in the scene. 'Well, isn't this cosy?'

I immediately straightened at my end of the couch. Richie took his time.

'I've been trying to ring you,' I said.

'Yes, my battery needed charging. I switched it on this morning and saw all these missed calls from you. Couldn't you have just left a message?'

Richie was watching James with raised eyebrows. 'So you thought you'd come rushing back rather than phoning?'

'I thought there must be something wrong – it's not like Maxine to pester me with calls. Instead I walk in to find the two of you curled up on the sofa watching trash.' He eyed the soup plates on the coffee table. 'And lunch in front of the television? You know I don't like eating meals away from the table.'

Through my misery I felt a faint stirring of anger. Before I had a chance to explore it, James continued.

'I stopped in at the store to buy a paper and Molly was kind enough to tell me that Richie's car has been parked here all night. What's that about? Does that happen every time I'm away?'

'Okay, I'll answer this one,' Richie said, standing to face James.

I groaned inwardly. That's all I needed – for these two to strut their stuff as if they were roosters in a coop.

I shook my head, but Richie said, 'No, Maxi, he needs to know. My car was here last night because when I drove your wife home from the hospital after she miscarried your baby she wasn't in any state to be left alone – and you weren't answering your phone. If you want to have it out with me for caring about her when you're not around to do what needs to be done, fine – go for it. But right now she needs a little more consideration from you.' He turned to me. 'Call me if you need me – you know that I'll answer.' To James he said, 'You don't deserve her. I hope you know that. But if you really love her, you'll go easy on her. And as you seem so interested, I slept on the couch.'

'Awww, wasn't that a lovely speech?' James said when Richie had gone.

I forced myself to my feet and cleared the plates away. He followed me into the kitchen.

'Is it true, what he said about you having a miscarriage?'

'Yes.' I popped another couple of paracetamols into my hand and ran the tap for water.

He waited until I'd taken the tablets before speaking again. 'Why did he have to take you? Couldn't you have called for a taxi or an ambulance?'

I turned to face him and leaned against the kitchen bench for support. 'I tried calling you last night when it happened – I've sold my car, remember? There was so much blood.' I took a deep breath and looked at the ceiling. 'And then there was no baby.'

I didn't try and stop the flow of tears and he made no move to comfort me.

'When were you going to tell me? About the baby?'

'I only found out I was pregnant during the week. You know how I'd had that stomach flu? I took a test and it was positive.'

He rubbed his hand over his eyes as if trying to understand all the steps that had led to this. 'I thought you'd got over whatever it was you had the other week.'

'You never asked how I was.'

'So this is my fault?'

'I didn't say that,' I said wearily. 'I just said … It doesn't matter.' I sank into a chair at the kitchen table.

'When were you going to tell me?' he asked again.

I sighed. 'When you called yesterday to say you couldn't make it back, I decided to come to you.' A flash of something I couldn't describe passed across his face. 'I didn't want to tell you over the phone. That's why I couldn't leave a message last night – I was too upset. Besides, how do you tell someone in a text message that their baby has died?'

He pulled a chair out and sat across from me. 'What I don't understand is how this happened. I thought we'd decided that now wasn't a good time for a baby. We were going to wait.'

'No, James, *you'd* decided. My wishes didn't come into it.'

He stared at me. Then he rubbed his hands down each side of his face, the way he always did when he was trying to understand something incomprehensible. Yet this wasn't incomprehensible. It was a baby we were talking about. Our baby.

'I thought you were on the pill.'

'I was.'

He shook his head. 'Then how …?'

'It's not a hundred per cent effective, you know. And that night we went out for dinner for my birthday – I was sick. Remember how I drank too much?'

'No, I don't remember that part.'

Of course he wouldn't. He'd gone to sleep straight after.

'Are you even sure it was mine?' James spat the

words out and I felt them hit me like a slap in the face.

'How can you even ask that? Of course it was yours. Who else's would it be?'

'It could have been Richie's,' he said quietly. 'Is that why he took you to the hospital and hung around here afterwards – because he thought it could have been his?'

I stared at him. Where was this coming from?

'Richie is my friend – there is nothing more between us.'

'I've seen the way he looks at you. There's more than friendship on his mind.'

'No.' I shook my head. 'You couldn't be more wrong. I'd know if he felt anything else, and he doesn't.'

'Has he been over to our house while I've been away?'

'Sure, occasionally – for supper during the week, or a snack after we've been walking.'

'You cook for him?'

'I have done, yes. We'd otherwise each be cooking a meal for one, and it's far easier to cook for two. Besides, I like feeding people, and with you gone it gets lonely.'

'Jesus Christ, Maxine! The whole village probably knows you're having an affair. You know what this place is like – everyone minding everyone else's business. I can hear it now: "There goes James Henderson in his flashy car. He's trying to set up a dream life for his wife while she's screwing the gardener!'" By the time he'd got the last sentence out, he was yelling.

The anger built inside me. 'It isn't like that. Nobody is talking about you; and Richie and I aren't having an affair.'

'I've seen the way he looks at you,' he said again.

I let out a breath. 'Whatever it is that you think you've seen, I haven't so much as looked at anyone else in the years we've been together. The baby was yours.'

I dropped my head to the table and rested my forehead on the smooth, cool timber, squeezing my eyes shut, gritting my teeth, struggling to stay calm when all I wanted to do was scream at him until I had no voice left to scream with.

I felt his eyes on me, watching the back of my head. Finally he said, 'Okay, I accept that. And I understand that you're probably upset right now, but at least you hadn't had time to get attached to it. It wasn't real. At that early stage hardly anyone knows they're pregnant. Really, when you think about it logically, it could have just been a heavy period. This has probably worked out for the best – I don't know how we would have coped with a baby in New York.'

I didn't lift my head from the table. I couldn't bear to look at him. I couldn't bear to listen to him.

'We would have coped, James. Women have been having babies for hundreds of years in New York and somehow they cope. Let's just leave the conversation there, shall we? I can't talk to you any more about this.'

I heard his phone ping a new message.

'Who's that?' I asked as he read the text.

'Oh, just India wanting to know what the problem with you was, and to check I'll be back for the function tonight.'

And just like that my anger disappeared to be replaced by an icy nothing.

I raised my head. 'You know what, James? Go. I'll be fine now.'

He shifted in his chair. 'No, it's okay. The welfare of my wife is more important than any customer. I'll let India know I'm staying here tonight instead.'

He reached over and held my hand. It was the first sign of kindness he'd shown me this afternoon and was enough to bring the tears out again.

'I'm sorry, darling. I didn't mean what I said before. It was all too much for me to take in, so I reacted badly.'

That was so like James: to go straight onto the attack in a situation he didn't understand.

'It's just hard for me to feel anything about a baby that until an hour ago I didn't know existed. It's different for you.' He offered me his handkerchief to dry my eyes. 'How about we get you back to bed – you're looking tired.'

I smiled gratefully at him.

'Has the doctor given you time off work?'

'Yes. He told me to take it easy for a few days.'

James nodded. 'Good – and so you shall. I'll change my flight to Tuesday and stay here with you until your parents get home. You take it easy this afternoon. These dishes can wait until tomorrow, and don't worry about dinner – I'll order something in. I'm here now, so everything will be as it should be.' He helped me to my feet and wrapped his arms around me. 'I am sorry, darling,' he said again. 'For your loss and what I said to you.'

I rested my cheek against the soft wool of his jumper and allowed the tears to fall.

CHAPTER SEVEN

Mum and Dad arrived home at about midday on Monday and came straight around to see me. My eyes filled as I heard their voices in the hall.

'Oh, my darling,' Mum said, gathering me in for a hug. 'I should have been here.'

'It's okay,' I replied. 'You couldn't have done anything to help.' I stepped out of her arms and leaned back against the couch. Physically I was feeling much better, but still needed support. 'But how did you know?'

'James managed to get hold of us as we were waiting for our last connecting flight. You wouldn't have thought it was so difficult to get back here from Bali. How many flights did we have to take, Alan?'

'You will opt for the non-standard stopover,' said Dad wearily. 'It feels like we've been travelling home for days.'

Mum was about to argue with him, but James came out from the kitchen carrying a tray with mugs of soup and plates of toast. He set it down on the dining table. I didn't even know that he knew how to defrost soup, but wisely kept my mouth shut. Despite his initial reaction on Saturday, he'd been wonderfully gentle with me since – although he'd drawn the line at watching *Midsomer* episodes with me.

'I'm sorry, darling,' he'd said. 'I love you, but perhaps not *that* much.'

He'd smiled to turn the comment into a joke, and we'd spent the rest of Saturday afternoon and again yesterday with me on the couch watching Inspector Barnaby, and him at the kitchen table catching up on work but popping in periodically to check on me. I'd heard his phone pinging regularly, but it didn't really disturb me.

However, although the iciness I'd felt on Saturday at the mention of India had thawed under his attentions, I couldn't forget the words he'd said and the accusations he'd levelled at me. They'd left an ache that paracetamol couldn't ease. He'd apologised again, but I knew the thoughts had to have been festering somewhere inside him to have come out when they did.

By unspoken agreement none of us mentioned the baby over lunch. Instead James plied Mum and Dad with questions about their trip and soon had them telling us stories about Australia, their stopover in Bali, and the cruise to New Zealand they'd taken from Sydney.

'You should have seen some of the passengers, Max,' Mum said. 'Three courses piled high on a single plate – and then they'd go back for more.' Out the corner of my eye I saw James wince. 'It was an engineering marvel. It's no wonder they say the average weight gain on a ten-day cruise can be as much as fifteen or twenty pounds!'

I smiled at my trim mother. 'You two look healthy though. How did you manage?'

'Your mother had us up early to do laps around the track on the ship,' Dad said. 'It meant I could sneak in an extra pastry at breakfast.'

'And I could justify an extra martini at dinner,' Mum added.

'You two should do a cruise sometime, Jim,' said Dad. He was as bad as Horrie when it came to his attempts to annoy James. 'Get Max away for some rest and relaxation before the big move.'

James forced a smile. We all knew that a cruise would be his worst nightmare. 'It certainly sounds tempting, Alan. Unfortunately the way work is at present I can't manage more than a few days. But don't worry, I have plans to whisk your daughter away for a romantic long weekend before we leave.'

He put his arm around me and pulled me to his side, smiling down at me. 'Speaking of leaving, I'm sorry, darling, but I'm going to have to go now if I want to get organised for tomorrow morning's flight.'

Mum saw my chin begin to tremble and attempted to defuse the situation. 'She'll be absolutely fine, James. I'll see that she gets enough rest.'

James left soon after, pulling me in for a final hug – the picture of a concerned husband, even though it felt like he was off-loading the responsibility of me onto my parents just as he'd outsource any other task he didn't want to be distracted by. I pushed that disloyal thought from my head, reminded myself that he'd delayed his flight for me, and smiled when he kissed me goodbye.

My parents took me back to their house so they could, in Dad's words, 'keep an eye on you over the next couple of days'. They were tired as well and couldn't be doing with going backwards and forwards from mine when what they really needed was sleep. So that's what we all did for the next few hours – we slept.

When I woke in my childhood room, tucked up in my narrow childhood bed, I checked my phone. There was one message, from Richie: *Hi, just checking in on you. How are you doing?*

Dear Richie. Before my eyes welled again I tapped out a quick response: *On the mend. Mum and Dad are back so I'm spending a few days at theirs. James has gone back to London.*

His reply was quick: *That's a great place for you to be – you'll have no choice but to take it easy. Look after yourself and call me if you need company.*

I replied with a smiley emoticon, and snuggled down into bed. I slept for a few more hours, and when I woke didn't feel up to doing anything more than curling up on Mum and Dad's couch with yet another episode of *Midsomer Murders*.

Mum made one of my favourite comfort food dishes for supper – pumpkin and ricotta macaroni, scented with rosemary from the garden – and I even went back for seconds.

Rested and fed, the three of us sat around the kitchen table and had the talk that needed to be had.

'How far along were you?' Mum didn't look at me as she asked the question.

'Not far. James said that meant I hadn't had time to get attached to it.'

Mum reached out and hugged me. 'Oh, Maxi, I miscarried a few times before we were lucky enough to have you. I was "attached", as James so beautifully put it, right from the start. What did he say when you lost it?'

I didn't answer her immediately. 'I only found out during the week … I was waiting until he came home to tell him. He didn't know that I was pregnant until I wasn't.' I faltered on the last few words and bit the inside of my mouth in an attempt to keep the tears at bay. 'He seemed more concerned about why Richie's car had been parked outside our house overnight.' I laughed ruefully. 'He actually accused me of sleeping with Richie – said the baby must be Richie's, not his. I tried to tell him that I haven't looked at anyone else since we've been together, but he had this idea in his head and ...' I couldn't finish the sentence.

'What was Richie doing there?'

'When the cramps and the bleeding started I tried calling James ... I knew he was in London because he'd phoned me on Friday afternoon to tell me that he'd landed but wouldn't make it back this weekend because of something or other. Anyway, his phone went straight to voicemail. I'd sold my car so I couldn't drive to the hospital, so I called Richie.'

'Oh, sweetheart,' Mum managed, her eyes glistening. 'We should have been here.'

'It couldn't be helped, Mum. Besides, Richie was wonderful. He didn't ask me any questions, just bundled me into the car and got me to the hospital. Then he waited until it was over and took me home again and stayed with me. I don't know what I would have done without him. He even made sure I had some fresh clothes to wear home.'

Mum and Dad exchanged glances.

'You were lucky he was there,' said Mum.

'He's a good man,' agreed Dad. 'Pity he follows the All Blacks.'

I smiled at that. 'He was still there on Saturday afternoon when James arrived. That's why James got angry.' I took a sip of my tea as I tried to find words that would paint James in a better light. I didn't want to say anything I'd later regret. 'I don't know, I think James was just taken unawares and that's why he reacted as he did. After all, I'd known I was pregnant, but he didn't.'

'Or perhaps he was feeling guilty that someone else had taken care of you and been there for you in the way that deep down he knew he should have been,' suggested Mum.

'You could be right. James does tend to attack when he's on the defensive.'

'I don't know about you, love, but it felt to me this afternoon as if he was off-loading you onto us so he didn't have the responsibility of worrying about you – and could be sure that Richie wasn't taking care of you.'

Even though Dad's words were close to my disloyal thoughts of earlier, I felt I should defend James. I'd always known my father wasn't James's biggest fan, but this was the first time he'd actually said anything to criticise him.

'That's not fair, Dad. He's my husband – of course he cares about me. He was so kind to me afterwards. He was supposed to fly out to New York on Sunday morning but he changed it to Tuesday. I'm sure he was grateful to Richie for taking me to the hospital; it's just that he was trying to process what had happened. And if I'm that much of an inconvenience to everyone –'

Mum patted my hand. 'Settle down, dear, that's not what your father meant.'

Dad raised his eyebrows and mumbled under his breath, 'Not the bit about you being inconvenient anyway.'

'The thing I can't get out of my mind is how he said it was probably for the best because we wouldn't have been able to cope with a baby in New York, that the timing was wrong.'

'Don't people have babies in New York?' asked Dad.

Mum shook her head at him. 'Are you telling me it wasn't planned?'

I nodded. 'James wanted us to wait until we got back from this posting. To be honest, I think he was a little annoyed with me that it had happened. I tried to explain that it was an accident, but I think that's also why he said what he did. He didn't mean it; he just doesn't like things to be outside his control. I'm sure we'll be fine again once we move and he's no longer commuting. He gets so tired, you see. I don't blame him for not wanting to get in the car for another ninety minutes after he's flown across the Atlantic.'

Even to my ears it sounded as though I was scrambling for excuses.

'Well, darling, you've got a few days now to do nothing except read and watch Inspector Barnaby.'

'That sounds good to me.'

I'd just gone upstairs to bed when James phoned.

'Hi, darling,' he said. 'I just wanted to check that you're feeling better.'

'Thanks, I am. I had a nap this afternoon and I'm

taking it easy.'

'Good.' He paused for a second. 'I can't wait until you're in New York with me.' I heard the smile in his voice. 'There are so many places I want to take you. It will be just like it was when we first started dating. I know it's been tough for you with me travelling – it's not how we planned it to be. But that's nearly over, and when we're settled again the hard work and separation will have been worth it. And then in a few years when I take over from Jeremy, we'll have everything we've always dreamed of.'

I didn't know what to say to that. We'd only ever spoken about his ambitions, not my dreams. Perhaps they were meant to be the same. Perhaps he assumed they were the same.

'I mightn't say it as often as I should, but you know I love you.' His voice was confident, yet it didn't warm me as it used to.

'I love you too,' I replied softly, feeling a shameful sense of relief when he hung up soon after.

He'd said he wanted things to be like they used to be. Only a few days ago I would have said the same. Now it felt as though it was already too late to go back, but I had to believe we could.

CHAPTER EIGHT

While Mum and Dad were wonderful, and my time with them was healing, by Wednesday I'd exhausted both my box sets of *Midsomer Murders* and my available reserves of self-pity. I needed to be occupied with something other than the crime wave in Midsomer County, and what might have been. There were boxes to be packed and arrangements to be made.

I hadn't spoken to James again, although a ridiculously large flower arrangement had arrived at my parents' house on Tuesday afternoon.

'See, darling, I told you he was thinking about you,' said Mum.

'He probably got that assistant of his to send them. He should be here with her instead of sending flowers.'

'At least he remembered to ask India to order them,' Mum said with a warning look at Dad.

I hid my face in the blooms and pretended to smell their perfume. They were both right – he probably did have India send them, but at least he'd thought to ask her to. Even though I would have preferred James to be here rather than these beautiful hothouse flowers that would fill the centre of my kitchen table, I still felt numb whenever I replayed his words from Saturday afternoon. I didn't want to think about what that meant.

Richie called around after work on Wednesday afternoon and offered to drive me the short distance home. He met me with a light hug and a kiss on my cheek. 'All good?'

'All good.' I smiled weakly at him.

He greeted my parents warmly. 'It's good to see you back. Maxi probably thinks I've come to see her, but I'm really more interested in hearing what you thought of New Zealand.'

'We've got so much to tell you,' said Mum. 'Sit down and Alan will pour you a beer. Now, why didn't you tell us how beautiful your country is?'

The next hour or so was taken up with talk of the ports the ship had docked in and the places they'd seen.

'You really must convince James to take you one day, Max,' said Mum. 'You have to see it to believe it. The sheer size of Mitre Peak – that's in Milford Sound, you know – against the ship, well –'

'Sorry, Claire, but we'll need to continue this conversation another time,' interrupted Richie, who'd been watching me closely. 'This one's starting to fade so I think I should be getting her home.'

On the short drive, neither of us referred to the

events of the previous weekend until we were almost at my house.

Concentrating on the road and not looking at me, Richie said, 'James seemed pretty angry to find me here on Saturday. I hope it didn't cause any more trouble for you.'

'I think his reaction was more guilt that he hadn't been here for me. James doesn't like things to be outside of his control, and that was.'

Richie's chin firmed slightly, but other than that he showed no emotion. 'As long as he didn't give you a hard time about me being there.'

'No, he understood. I haven't thanked you properly … for what you did.' I thought I saw a pulse in his jaw. 'I mean it, Richie – you were there for me when I needed you, and I really appreciate it.'

'It's sweet, Hendo. I only did what any friend would do.' He glanced at me and smiled. 'Besides, I don't mind Detective Inspector Barnaby.'

I searched his face for something more, but he was turning into my lane. He waited with me while I unlocked the door and dropped my bag inside, then turned to leave.

'Do you need me to bring you something for dinner?' he asked.

'I'll be fine, thanks. I don't feel that hungry – I'll just defrost some soup or something. I'm sure I have some pasta sauce if you want to stay and have some with me?'

He looked at his feet as he answered me. 'No, I won't, not tonight. I'm meeting Ange down at the pub. But if you need me ...'

I felt a pang of something low in my tummy and smiled to cover it. 'Are you two back on then?'

He shrugged. 'Sort of. Are you still determined to come in tomorrow?'

I nodded. 'Absolutely. I'm pretty sick of myself, and I've got to get the March newsletter out before it's April.'

'Okay, but you're not riding to work. No,' he said as I opened my mouth to argue. 'I'm well aware that the doctor didn't specifically tell you not to cycle, but I'll be picking you up until I've decided you're well enough to climb back on that bike.'

After he left I swallowed another couple of paracetamol, but they didn't take away the pain in my middle.

Over the next few days I felt almost unnaturally calm, as though something was brewing outside of me and I was battening down the hatches to withstand it. I still wasn't strong physically or emotionally, so I was grateful to Richie for driving me to and from work. In the evenings I'd come home and go straight to bed, feeling an emptiness that went beyond my womb. I still hadn't managed to draft the March newsletter. It was too difficult to talk about the new life that came with spring when the new life I'd been growing had died. In some way it felt as though my old life had died with the baby and I didn't know what was going to take its place.

James drove up to see me the first Saturday. Where only last week I would have greeted him with joy, this time I smiled, kissed him hello and continued with my baking.

'How are you feeling?' he asked.

'Physically I'm fine.'

I rolled another spoonful of the cookie mix in my hands and placed it on the tray, flattening it slightly with the heel of my palm before pressing a fork onto its surface.

He looked around the kitchen. 'Did you get the flowers I sent?'

'Yes, thanks.'

'It's just that I don't see them anywhere.'

I sighed. 'They were lovely, thanks, James. But the arrangement takes up most of the kitchen table, so I've moved it into the sitting room.'

'Oh, right.' He watched me work a while longer. 'So you're feeling better then? You know, over it?'

I counted to ten as I slid the tray into the oven, then stared directly at him. 'Over it?'

He held my gaze for a second or two, then dropped his eyes. 'I'm sorry, darling, that was the wrong choice of words.' He walked across the kitchen to hold me. 'I have no idea what the right thing is to say in this situation.'

I let out the breath I'd been holding and relaxed into his arms. Perhaps he was right: how could he know? I stepped back in his arms and looked up into his handsome face. There were faint lines and shadows around his eyes that I hadn't noticed before, and a tightness around his mouth that I was sure wasn't there a month ago. He'd flown out to New York on Tuesday morning, had probably worked sixteen-hour days, flown back again last night, and driven straight up here this morning – to see me.

I raised one hand to stroke his smooth jaw. 'You look tired,' I said gently. 'Did you manage any sleep on the plane?'

'A little, but it's fine. I wanted to see you.'

I nodded slowly. 'How about you sit down and tell me about what's happening in New York while I make us a frittata for lunch. Then you can turn your phone off, go upstairs and sleep for as long as you need.'

He pulled me back into his chest and kissed the top of my head. 'All of that, my darling, sounds wonderful. But can you make it with extra egg white instead of yolk, and no toast on the side?' He patted his flat stomach. 'I'm off carbs at the moment – have to stay in shape.'

While James was sleeping I wandered up to the allotment. Although I still wasn't up to working in the garden, I hadn't seen Horrie in over a week. When I arrived he was over in the neighbouring plot talking to 'old' Tom about tomatoes. Horrie's tomatoes were considered to be the best in Brookford. Lucy was flopped down in her favourite spot beside the shed – she could keep an eye on everything from there.

'There you are, lass. I was hoping I'd see you today. I was just telling old Tom here that I've found a little olive oil in the soap spray helps get rid of the aphids. It helps the soap stick to the little buggers' lungs, you see.'

I smiled fondly at him. 'Do aphids even have lungs, Horrie?'

He rubbed at his whiskery chin. 'Course they do. How else are the little blighters going to breathe?'

I acknowledged the logic of his comment with a nod.

He looked me up and down, his blue eyes as sharp as ever. 'You're looking a little bit peaky there, lass. Let's go have a cuppa. My knee will be grateful for the break.'

The short walk had taken more of my energy than it should have so I was glad to drag Horrie's chairs into the sun and slump into one while he put the kettle on.

'That sprouting broccoli looks ready to pick,' I said once he'd handed me a mug of tea and gingerly sat down beside me. Lucy did her flop-dog impersonation between us.

'Aye, it's good this year. I'll give you some to take home. You can have some for supper when young Jim's gone back.'

James wasn't as much a fan of purple sprouting broccoli as I was.

We sat together in companionable silence for a few minutes, enjoying the warmth of the still-weak spring sun on our faces, the buzz of the bees as they worked their way from flower to flower, the sound of chatter and spades from the adjoining plots.

'Your mother told me about your bad luck,' he said.

I swallowed to move the lump that had made its way into my throat.

'I remember when she went through the same thing. She thought her world was ending, but she was lucky – she had Alan there to stand by her. I don't think he left her side for days afterwards.' He looked hard at me. 'And then she got lucky when you came along.'

'James delayed his flight until Mum and Dad were back.'

'And from what I heard, he couldn't wait to leave as soon as they were.'

'You've been talking to Dad.' I reached down to scratch Lucy's head. 'There was nothing more he could do. Besides, I'm fine now and he's home this weekend.'

'That's good then.' Horrie drained his tea. 'Remind me to cut you some asparagus too before you go.'

'I'd like that. Another?' I held up my mug.

'Not for me, but you help yourself, lass. It was lucky young Richie was around to take you to hospital,'

Horrie added when I came back with a fresh mug. 'I don't imagine Jim was too happy about that though?' He didn't look at me as he said it, instead gazing out across his garden.

'Have you been talking to Mum?'

His face was innocent as he turned to look at me. 'Might have been. Jim's not the only one not happy about it. Duncan was telling me that Richie's girl – that Angela from the hairdresser's – was in a state about him leaving her to go and help you. The way Duncan tells it, Richie was at Angela's house when you called him – if you know what I mean.'

I remembered the argument Richie'd had with Angela. He must have gone over to make it up with her after he'd walked me home.

'I can't see that lasting anyway,' Horrie said. 'That girl's not had a sensible thought in years, and Richie needs someone he can talk to.'

I looked away from the intensity of his stare. 'Yes, well, maybe talking isn't what's on his mind when he's with her.'

'Ah, lass, that part's easy. It's the rest that's difficult.' He got to his feet, groaning slightly and rubbing his knee. 'Anyway, can't be sitting around here all day. Come help me pick you some vegetables. My knee's not as good as it used to be – either that or the ground's further away.'

CHAPTER NINE

James was still asleep when I let myself back into the house. We weren't due at my parents' for supper until much later, so I decided to let him sleep as long as he needed.

The new owners were due to officially take over the garden centre in another month or so. They were closing it during June for rebranding and refurbishment. I hoped that didn't mean the produce section would go, but they weren't giving away their plans yet. Richie had tried to tell them to take advantage of the summer business and close in the autumn, but they hadn't taken his advice. We supposed this way the closure would coincide with him going on holiday and the notice I'd given, leaving them time to recruit a replacement for me.

George had agreed that I owned the recipes and photos I'd uploaded to the website over the months, and I'd told Richie about my idea to continue my blog from Manhattan under my own name.

'It's a great idea, Hendo. You can explore all the

markets in Manhattan and get a whole new audience, and it'll give you a social media platform for when you're ready to launch your recipe cards or whatever. You do know it's all about the platform these days, don't you?'

I'd nodded. 'Yeah, that's what I thought.'

'When you're ready, I'll help you if you like.'

I didn't know whether his enthusiasm was for the idea, the task, or simply that the work might get my head out of this empty place it'd been in since I lost the baby. I knew I needed to get myself out of it and start thinking about something else – like packing and moving.

First, though, I needed to get this March newsletter written before it was April. I made another cup of tea, opened my laptop, gritted my teeth and tried to think happy thoughts.

March in the Kitchen

I don't know about you, but as spring … well, springs, there are signs of new life all around. It's still a few weeks too early for cuckoos and bluebells, but I swear I saw some snowdrops yesterday and the first of the jonquils. Plus, the other day I went outside without a jumper. Yes, really. Even though you know there's still the possibility of late snow or a cold northerly, there's something about the promise of blossoms and fresh green that's really exciting.

Things are heating up in the garden too. Although our warmer weather favourites aren't ready yet, purple sprouting broccoli, or PSB as we like to call it, is particularly good at the moment. I love this vegetable. It's not pretty and proud like calabrese broccoli. Instead it's untidy and leafy, sort of a little clumsy – as if it hasn't grown into its legs just yet. It's the colour that gets me: so much deeper and more vibrant, with a purple cast to the florets.

Don't think PSB is limited to a side vegetable – it's so much more versatile than that. However you choose to serve it, remember that these young stems need just a few minutes' cooking, no more. They should still hold their colour and be slightly tender with a delightful crunch. Serve them with butter and lemon – or just lemon if you're feeling virtuous.

For a little more interest, fry some finely sliced garlic in a little vegetable oil – or a mix of vegetable oil and sesame oil – until it's golden. Toss in the steamed broccoli and, if you like more texture, serve with a scattering of sesame seeds. Or some fried herby breadcrumbs will add crunch.

If you're still going with your healthy-eating New Year's resolution (well done, you!) freshly steamed PSB makes a perfect carrier for dip, especially tuna dip. And it couldn't be easier to make. Simply whizz a can (including the oil) of tuna in the blender; add some crushed garlic and, if it needs it, a little more olive oil. Too easy. Sort of like a broccolini tonnato – and not a starchy carb in sight.

You could also try sweating some anchovies into a good-sized knob of butter, stirring until they almost *dissolve, and then tossing lightly boiled broccoli into it. Take it one step further and mix through some pre-cooked pasta, finishing with a good squeeze of lemon. A complete supper in as long as it takes you to boil up the pasta. Of course, if you're anti-anchovy (and I know some of you are) you can leave them out and stir through a tin of tuna instead. I'm not anti-anchovy, and have been known to chop some into creamy scrambled eggs to serve with long-stemmed PSB beauties on a Sunday night.*

Speaking of eggs, PSB is also perfect with poached eggs and hollandaise. Naturally add some salmon if you're so inclined. You don't need to buy a fancy pre-made hollandaise or be a MasterChef contestant to make one. I cheat and whisk melted butter, a little at a time, into an egg yolk, finishing with a squeeze of lemon juice and seasoning. It's far from perfect, but generally holds its form for as long as it takes me to eat it in front of the telly.

As always, the recipes are up on the website – and I'd love to know what you do with your purple sprouted beauties this month. Drop me a line, or better yet pop a photo up on Instagram. If you tag us and use the hashtag #psb you'll go into the running to win this month's prize pack.

Until next time,

Max

The newsletter done, I began the laborious task of copying all the posts from the Blossoms & Buds website. The photos and recipes I already had saved.

Who knew how long the website would stay online until it disappeared? Probably until the next domain name payment was due, I supposed. As I worked, I tried to picture myself in New York doing the things that James had told me with great enthusiasm I could look forward to doing: shopping in Manhattan; lunching with other expat wives; endless hair and nail appointments; decorating James's arm at some event or dinner; listening and nodding and speaking only when a question was directed at me. I could form the pictures in my head and see James clearly in each, but I couldn't place myself in any of them.

I shook my head to clear it. It didn't need to be like that. If I had my own website up and running it could be different. I forced myself to consider a new set of possibilities: baking in the kitchen in our new apartment; tending pots on the rooftop garden with the roar of the city far below; wandering through farmers' markets and photographing the seasonal produce; dropping in at delis for picnic foods for us to share on strolls through Central Park; tapping away on my laptop while James relaxed in front of the television. There was no reason why I couldn't begin to develop a set of recipe cards illustrated with my own photographs. It was a business I could set up and run from a New York apartment.

It wasn't just that he didn't like walking – James's idea of exercise was membership to a gym or a golf course – or picnics. No, the reason I couldn't picture him in my version of our life was because I knew deep down that he'd rarely be at home. Despite what he said about wanting us to be together again, his idea of that was to sleep in the same bed in the same city.

It wasn't that I didn't like New York; I just didn't want to live there. James had taken me there last year as an anniversary surprise – only for a long weekend, but it had been a magical few days. The snow was thick on the ground and we strolled through Central Park, stopping to watch the ice skaters, mugs of hot cider in our hands. We made love in a plush hotel high above the city, feeding each other champagne and strawberries from a room-service trolley, just like in the movies.

Nor was it that I wasn't a city girl. I'd enjoyed the years I'd lived in London. Sure, winter could get claustrophobic – leaving for work in the dark and arriving home in the dark – but there always seemed to be a green space just around the corner. I'd spent hours walking through the parks on weekends; and when I really missed the feel of dirt under my fingernails I'd hopped on a train and was in Brookford in less than two hours and working in Horrie's allotment or my parents' garden shortly after.

No, it wasn't any of those things. It was more a realisation that the life James wanted for us was different to the life I wanted – different to the life I'd envisaged us living. I knew he was more ambitious than

I was, but I'd figured that even though our career goals were different, deep down we wanted the same core things – and that included a family.

We'd talked about it early in our marriage. I recalled one conversation soon after we were married. We were tucked up in bed and full of dreams of the future.

'I'll come home on weekends and we'll do the things that families do,' he'd said. 'My father worked two jobs to send me to the school I went to and to give me the opportunities I've had. But it meant that he wasn't around, and I want to be there for our boys.'

James's dad had been determined he should have the best education they could afford, but had died of a heart attack just before James had been accepted into Oxford.

'I'll take the boys to Oxford and Gloucester to watch the rugby. And your father can take them to the football – if he absolutely feels that he should.' He'd pulled me closer. 'You can take the girls to London for shopping and shows and special teas.'

'We can go for long walks and picnics, and pantomimes at Christmas,' I'd continued.

'Let's not go to extremes, darling,' he'd laughed.

James's goal was to be managing partner in his firm by the time he was forty. I respected that – and had supported it. My goal was much different. In my version of our life, I was running a small cafe out of Blossom & Buds. The blog posts would have grown into a series of recipe cards, and the recipe cards into cookbooks, which I styled and photographed myself. None of that included New York.

Except for being with James, the little voice in my head reminded me.

Maybe James was right: perhaps it was best to wait until we were back in England before starting our family. It was just a few years, after all; I'd still only be in my early thirties. In the meantime, I could get my business up and running. Besides, I'd want my parents and Horrie to be involved with our children. And even though James didn't have a lot to do with his mother at the moment, I was certain that his attitude would change when we had children. He'd surely want her to see them, and there was no way she'd be able to afford to come to New York regularly.

James's mother had remarried soon after his father's death and James didn't approve of her choice. 'It's not that I care that Peter's a tradesman. It's just that Mum's worked so hard all her life, it would be nice for her to have some breathing space now,' he'd told me the first time he took me to meet his mother and stepfather. 'She was so quick to marry Peter that people will think they were having an affair.'

'Don't you think it's nice that she's fallen in love again? Besides, what does it matter what other people think?' I didn't like to point out that by this time his father had been gone for some years.

'Of course it matters what other people think,' he'd snapped at me. It had been the first time I'd seen James even close to losing his temper, and he was very quick to regain it. He'd taken one hand from the steering wheel and reached across to pat mine. 'I'm sorry, darling. It's just that Peter's not a patch on my father.'

I'd understood that his real problem wasn't with Peter, or even the speed of the marriage, but the fact that his father had been replaced.

James appeared, yawning in that way people do when they've slept too long and too heavily in the middle of the day. He came over to where I was working and kissed the top of my head.

'What are you up to, darling?' he asked, looking at my laptop screen.

'I'm uploading all my content from the Blossom & Buds website. George has agreed that it's my intellectual property and he's happy for me to republish it under my own name on my own website. It's something I can keep going when I'm in New York.' I looked over my shoulder at him and smiled. 'I just need to think of a name. What do you think of *Brookford to Brooklyn*?'

He laughed and ruffled my hair before moving away. 'I suppose if it gives you some connection to back here, it's a good idea. You'll soon be so busy in New York that you won't have time to be playing around with photos and recipes.' He opened the biscuit tin and looked inside before determinedly closing it again. 'What do you think is so important that your parents need us and Horrie over tonight?'

I refused to allow James's dismissal of my blog to hurt my feelings. 'Maybe they just want to show us their photos.'

James sighed. 'It sounds like my idea of the perfect Saturday night.'

I feigned innocence. 'Great. You won't be disappointed then.'

CHAPTER TEN

Mum and Dad waited until after we'd eaten to drop their bombshell, although in hindsight I should have known something was up when Mum produced her chocolate bread-and-butter pudding for dessert. The last time we had it was when they announced Dad was retiring and they were off to the other side of the world for a long holiday. The time before that was a year or so ago when she'd told me about some minor surgery Dad needed done on his shoulder. This time, I just assumed it was Mum's way of making me feel better.

Horrie looked up when Mum set the enamel baking dish on the table. 'What's this in aid of then?'

'Do I need a reason to prepare Max's favourite pudding?' she replied, spooning him out an extra big helping.

'Suppose not.' Horrie bent his head and tucked in.

'Seeing as you mention it though,' Dad began once we were all in squidgy, chocolatey heaven.

'We're moving to Cornwall,' Mum announced, looking anywhere but at me.

The spoonful of pudding lodged halfway down my throat and wouldn't move any further. I took a sip of water to help it on its way.

'What?' My question came out as a cross between a squeak and a splutter.

'We're moving to Cornwall,' Dad repeated. 'We've bought a house by the sea.'

'It's the one we stayed at on that long weekend we took last year – or was it the year before?' Mum frowned. 'It doesn't matter when, but surely you remember us telling you about it, darling?'

'I remember you talking about how fabulous it was, but I certainly don't remember you saying you'd bought it.'

As I spoke I looked across the table and saw Horrie frown at me. The smile had fallen from Mum's face and something more like worry was taking its place.

'I'm sorry,' I said, 'it's just such a surprise. Tell me about the house.'

Horrie nodded once in approval.

Dad put his arm around Mum and smiled into her eyes. 'We both fell in love with the house when we were there that time, so when we heard it was on the market we put in an offer immediately.'

'It was on the last day of our cruise and we got talking to another couple about Cornwall and retirement,' Mum said.

'As you do,' I muttered under my breath.

Mum continued. 'Somehow we started talking about that village and it turned out their daughter and her family live there. On their last call home their daughter had mentioned how the white house at the top of the hill overlooking the sea had recently gone on the market. Well, Alan and I looked at each other and both got a bit excited. As soon as we were back in Sydney and had reception, we looked it up on the real estate site and it was the house we'd stayed at.'

'Our offer was accepted the same day, but we didn't want to say anything until the contracts were exchanged – and that happened yesterday,' explained Dad. 'There's no chain or finance involved, so from here it should move quickly. We saw Marcia today and we'll be renting this place out for now.'

'It's all fallen into place so easily it feels as though it was meant to be,' Mum said.

I bit back my own words when I saw the tender look they exchanged. Instead I plastered a bright smile onto my face and got out of my chair to hug them both. 'Well, no wonder you baked the special pudding. That's fabulous news.'

James, who hadn't said anything throughout the announcement, shook my father's hand. 'That's great news, Alan. Congratulations – I'm sure you and Claire will be very happy.' He put his arm around me. 'With you going to Cornwall and us moving to New York, it's all happening!' He turned to Horrie. 'It's up to you now to fly the flag for Brookford.'

'Aye, I won't be going anywhere. Who else will tell those buggers how to manage aphids?' He reached down to ruffle Lucy's head. 'No, I'll leave the gallivanting to you youngsters. Claire, did you say something about putting the kettle on?'

'Absolutely. How about we move into the sitting room. I'll just clear these things first.'

'No, Mum – you go through. Let me deal with the dishes,' I said.

'If you're sure, darling.'

Once alone, I scraped the remnants of our pudding into the bin and put some plastic wrap over what was left. If I left it out of the fridge Mum could be tempted to send it home with me.

Rather than placing everything in the dishwasher, I decided to hand wash it all. To say my parents' announcement was a surprise would be understating it. I was pleased for them, truly I was – they'd worked so hard over the years and things were now really falling into place for them. But how could they leave me like this? With no warning? It would feel strange not having them here in the village.

I smiled ruefully into the sudsy water when I remembered that I wouldn't be here either. I wondered how they'd reacted when they received my email telling them that news. Because I'd been so upset about the miscarriage, we hadn't really spoken about my moving away. They'd just sent a short return email from the ship with their congratulations. Somehow, it seemed easier to miss them when I could picture them doing familiar things with familiar people here in Brookford. I couldn't picture Cornwall at all.

I stacked the plates carefully on the draining rack and stared out into the darkness of the garden. Had me leaving helped them make this decision, or would they have gone anyway? What if I wasn't going to New York? What if I didn't go? I quickly pushed the idea back to wherever it came from.

Mum entered the kitchen so quietly that I didn't realise she was there until she'd picked up a tea towel and was wiping plates.

'How do you really feel about this, Max?' she asked.

I forced a smile. 'I really am happy for you. It just seems as though too much is happening too quickly. I'll be fine once I get my head around it.'

'We worried about whether to tell you tonight – you've been through so much with the baby – but we couldn't leave it any longer. Anyway,' she gave me a watery smile, 'you're starting a new life too. Things wouldn't have been the same without you here, so it makes sense for your father and me to be doing this now. We have to find our new normal – one that doesn't constantly remind us of you. I know we've always talked about retiring to Cornwall, but if you'd stayed and had a family, we'd never have been able to drag ourselves away. Your email was a sign that the time was right for us to be moving on too.'

My eyes filled and I blinked to send the tears away. 'Talking like that you'll fit in well in Cornwall. How many crystal shops does this village of yours have?'

She laughed and reached across to hug me.

'Well,' I said, pushing open our front door later that night, 'I wasn't expecting that.'

'I'm just glad there were no slides involved,' joked James. 'Retirement plans I can deal with.'

'But Cornwall?'

'Why not? They love it there.' He hung his jacket in the hall closet. 'You said yourself that they've always wanted to retire down there. What did you expect — that they'd wait until they were too old to enjoy it?'

'Well, no, I suppose not.' I undressed for bed, leaving my clothes on the floor where they fell. 'I just didn't expect it to be now.' I pushed aside the images I'd conjured up this afternoon: my parents helping me with our children while I built my food empire. 'And what about Horrie? We'll be moving soon too — who's going to look after him?'

'He'll be fine. He's a fit old guy —'

'With a bad knee.'

'— who's quite capable of looking after himself.' He climbed into bed. 'Darling, even Horrie is happy for your parents. Besides, he's got his girls to look after him.'

'I guess. But fancy Dad making an offer on a house without even seeing it. That's an awfully spontaneous thing to do, and my father doesn't do spontaneous – he's an accountant.'

'Well, he's done spontaneous now. Besides, they have seen it – they stayed there once on a mini-break.' He patted the bed beside him. 'Come to bed, Maxine.'

I climbed in and lay on my back, staring at the ceiling. 'I'll miss them.'

'Darling,' he said, irritation in his tone, 'we'll be in New York. You would have missed them anyway.'

'I know that, but they were supposed to be here when we came back.' He didn't need to know the rest of the fantasy.

He sighed. 'Things change, people move. Did you really expect Brookford and everyone in it to remain exactly the same while they waited for you to come home?' He kissed me. 'Now turn the light off and go to sleep. I've got a big week ahead and want to get an early start tomorrow.'

He turned away from me, his soft snores beginning soon after. I lay awake in the dark for much longer. It felt as though all the ties I had to Brookford were beginning to sever, and as they dropped away it was as though my choices were dissolving with them. We were leaving; Mum and Dad were retiring to some cottage

on the coast they'd only seen once; and Blossoms &
Buds was closing.

I was pleased for my parents: Cornwall was what
they'd always spoken of. It was just that I'd selfishly
assumed everyone I loved would be here waiting for
me when I got back from New York. I couldn't help
thinking that it was James's promotion that had started
all of this, and now it seemed as though everything was
spiralling too fast out of my control. Even if I didn't go
with James, there was no way now of taking everything
back to the way it had been before my birthday.

CHAPTER ELEVEN

James drove back to London early Sunday morning, leaving me at a loose end on a day that was too nice to spend inside. The doctor still hadn't given me the all clear for anything other than light exercise, so a long ramble through the woods or across the fields with Richie was out of the question. Because I'd made cookies yesterday, and Horrie had sent me home from Mum and Dad's last night with a fresh batch of soup, there was nothing much I could do in the kitchen either.

I wandered down to the allotment to see if Horrie was there, only to be told by 'young' Justin (so called because he was a sprightly fifty something) that Horrie had a lunch date with Maureen … or was it Barbara? 'Your grandfather couldn't remember. He said he'd be happy to go out with whichever one turned up.' Typical Horrie.

Walking back through the village I mentally ran through everyone I could call on a sunny Sunday and concluded that there was no one else — other than Richie, of course. When had my social life shrunk to this? I wished Miranda was still in London – I might have gone back with James to see her.

When we first moved back to Brookford, I'd reconnected with the few people I'd known from school. They'd all married and had their own families, and their husbands worked long hours during the week – commuting to London, or Oxford, or other local towns – so they wanted to spend every available moment of the weekend playing happy families. I couldn't blame them – I was the same. On the weekends when James was home – or due home – I'd got into the habit of making sure I was completely free to spend time with him. I supposed people had got tired of me always declining their invitations on the off-chance that James managed to make it home. The more James travelled, the more isolated I'd allowed myself to become – when it should have been the opposite. I had plenty of things I could do to fill the time so hadn't noticed how lonely I was until now. I was twenty-nine years old and relied on my parents, my grandfather, Richie and an assortment of old gardeners to keep me amused when my husband wasn't here.

Walking past The Lamb, I checked my watch. The pub kitchen would still be open. As I was contemplating going in, Angela came out. When she saw me, she brushed the tears from her eyes and spat out, 'I hope you're happy.' Then she pushed past me and stalked off down the street.

Bloody hell. I assumed Richie was the cause of the tears.

Once inside I caught Duncan's eye. 'He's out the back, lass. Better take him a drink and another packet of crisps.'

'Anything I should know before I go out there?'

'Lucky you've got short hair – you'll be needing to find a new hairdresser.'

I laughed. 'Thanks, Duncan.'

I took our drinks out to the courtyard. Richie looked up, surprise – and, I suspected, relief – on his face. 'I'm glad it's you, Hendo.'

'Did you think I was Angela back for round two?'

'Round three more likely. Or is it four? I've lost count. How did you know?'

'You mean aside from the fact that you look beaten up? She said a few choice words, pushed past me and left in rather a hurry.' I grinned. 'And then, of course, Duncan might have said something.'

He shrugged and gave a rueful smile. 'Duncan doesn't miss much.'

I raised my glass to his. 'Cheers.'

He smiled and clinked. 'What brings you in here on a sunny Sunday afternoon? I thought James was in town.'

'Yeah, he was, but he had to leave early.' I stretched my legs out along the bench and raised my cotton skirt to my knees to get some of the early spring sun. 'I baked yesterday, and I'm not allowed to walk too far yet. Hopefully I'll be able to get out and about properly again next week, and then it'll be almost as if it never happened.'

We both knew what I was referring to.

'Anyway, as I was walking past, Angela was coming out and I put two and two together and figured you'd be in here.' I leaned back, supporting myself on my elbows so my face was tipped to the sun. 'Speaking of which, what are you going to do about that? Or has it already been done?'

He gave a half-laugh and took a mouthful of beer. 'We had fun, I guess, but it was never going to last. I couldn't talk to her. Once we got over the first sexy part, it was boring.'

I laughed. 'Delightful!'

He attempted to justify his words. 'She's pretty enough, but she's got nothing remotely intelligent to say. All she wants to do is giggle and gossip.' He screwed his nose up and shook his head. 'Boring as batshit. What else is happening?'

'Mum and Dad are moving to Cornwall.'

'Did you see that coming?' There was surprise in his voice, and something else … concern, perhaps?

I shook my head. 'Absolutely not. Horrie didn't seem so surprised though.' As I said it, I wondered why that was the case.

'There's not much that gets past Horrie,' Richie

said. 'Between him and Duncan they have all the news covered. How do you feel about it?'

I paused before answering. 'I don't know … there's not much I can say really. After all, I won't be here to miss them.'

I swung my legs back to the ground and drained my drink.

'No, you won't,' he said, his eyes meeting mine for a beat too long. 'Another?' He indicated my empty glass.

At my nod, he stood and went inside to the bar.

Duncan bustled around collecting empty glasses. 'He alright?' he asked.

'I think so.'

He looked at me closely. 'Are you alright?'

'Sure, why do you ask?'

'Well, I know you had some bad luck, and with your parents moving south …'

'How do you know that? I only found out last night.'

He tapped the side of his nose. 'It's my business to know these things.' He straightened the teetering tower of glasses he was carrying. 'Everyone's leaving us: first you, then your parents, and now the lad. Cornwall's not far, and I dare say we'll see Alan and Claire back in from time to time; but once the lad goes – well, New Zealand's a long way away.'

If Duncan hadn't been standing in front of me, I would have doubled over from the pain. It felt as though I'd been kicked and all the wind knocked from my body. Somehow I managed to stop the surprise from showing on my face.

'He's only going for a few weeks though. He'll be back.'

I held my breath as I waited for him to reassure me.

Duncan's eyes were sympathetic. 'No, lass, he won't be. Anyway, this isn't getting these cleaned up.' He added our glasses to his tower of empties and went back inside.

The ache in my belly moved through my body and settled somewhere in my chest where it sat like a lead weight, pushing down on my lungs and restricting my breath. I was still gasping for air a few minutes later when Richie sat down and placed fresh drinks on the table.

'When were you going to tell me?' I asked.

He saw the pain in my eyes and didn't pretend to misunderstand. 'Maxi —'

'My best friend is leaving the country and I had to find out from the publican.' He opened his mouth to speak, but I carried on. 'How long have you known?'

He shrugged and didn't quite meet my eyes. 'I've been thinking about it since January, but made up my mind a month or so ago. It's time I went home and got on with my life.'

'When were you going to tell me?' I asked again.

I watched him swallow and move his finger through the condensation on his glass. A fresh wave of heaviness hit my chest and I found it hard to breathe through it.

'You weren't going to tell me, were you?'

He didn't respond.

'I was going to go to New York with James, and you were going to wave me goodbye and not tell me that you were leaving too.' If I had come back, he wouldn't have been here. Then it came to me. 'You're going before I do, aren't you?'

He nodded slowly.

I wanted to shout at him – to tell him that he couldn't go away, that he was supposed to be here when I returned – but I knew none of that was fair. Instead, I watched him reaching for something to say, trying not to look at me, and then I couldn't see him any more.

I grabbed my bag and stood to go – too quickly. The blood drained from my head and I staggered, grabbing at the side of the table and toppling my glass over. He reached for my hand, but I tore it away and shook my head.

'I'll see you home,' he said. 'You're still too –'

'Too what? Too gullible? Too stupid? Too naive?'

His eyes finally met mine. 'Too fragile.'

'I'm stronger than you think.' He stood to follow me. 'No – don't. I can't talk to you about this right now.'

This time when I walked by the allotment, Horrie and Lucy were there.

'I was hoping you'd come by again, lass. Young Justin told me you'd dropped in earlier.' He winced suddenly and used the garden fork he'd been turning the ground over with to support himself.

'Knee?' I eyed him with concern. 'Don't you think it's time you went to the doctor?'

'It'll be right tomorrow, lass. Now, what's with your long face?'

'Everything's changing, Horrie, and I'm not ready for it,' I wailed, the tears I'd been holding in burning the back of my eyes.

He nodded slowly. 'I see. Is this about your parents moving south or that young man of yours going home?'

'You know about that?' Why did everyone in this village know everything before I did? 'Anyway, he's not my young man.'

Horrie shrugged. 'You've always known your parents would move south one day, and you've always known Richie would go back to New Zealand. Besides, what does it matter? You're moving away yourself – you won't be here to miss them.'

I nodded through my tears. 'You don't need to tell me that. It makes no sense for me to be this upset. I suppose I just thought that when I came back, they'd all still be here like normal.'

'Ah, lass. Don't you mean that if you change your mind about going to New York with Jim, it could be as though you'd never thought of leaving?'

I stared at him with my mouth open. Sometimes it seemed as though Horrie could read my mind.

'I have no intention of not going with James. Where did you get that idea from?'

'No need to take that attitude. Maybe I got it wrong. I just thought you wanted more from life than shopping and lunches.'

I lowered my eyes to the ground. 'What I want doesn't come into it. James is going to New York so I am too. I have no choice.'

'That's where you're wrong, lass. You always have a choice.'

'I just don't see why things can't stay the same,' I grumbled, knowing he was right and that I sounded like a spoilt brat.

'Where would we be if everything stayed the same? Nothing would grow – that's why we have seasons and weather. Things happen because they have to in order for other things to happen. That's why your parents are moving – they need to get on with the next phase of their life.'

'But aren't you angry about that? Who's going to look after you when I'm gone and they're gone?'

'Who says I need looking after? I'm not on my deathbed just yet.' He spoke to me the way he used to when I did something naughty. 'I've got plenty of people who'll look in on me, and your mother's only going to be a few hours away.' He leaned on his garden fork and stared into my eyes. 'Don't try to make this about me, lass. And don't try and make it about your parents.'

I was silent.

His tone was gentle. 'Jim's moving up in the world, and you're going with him. It's time for Richie to go home and get on with his life.' He rubbed his knee. 'When should Richie have told you he was moving? Be honest, lass – there hasn't been a right time.'

'He should have talked to me when he was considering it. What did it matter that I was leaving? He still could have told me.'

'When did he decide?'

'He said he started thinking about it about back in January, but he made up his mind a month or so ago.'

'I see.'

'What does that mean?'

'He was only ever going to stay a year, and he's been here for much longer. He only stayed because of ... because of the friends he's made and the work he was doing. You were a large part of that. With you going, he had nothing left to stay for. There was no right time for him to tell you.' He looked at me. 'You hadn't thought about it like that, had you?'

I shook my head, more miserable than when I'd arrived. Now it was misery with a side serve of shame for my selfishness.

'Call him, talk about it ... and try and be happy

for him, lass. He's going back to do what he's always wanted to do. And while you're at it, do the same for your parents – they've always been supportive of you. How do you think it was for them losing their only daughter to London when you went away to college? And when you told them about New York, did they try and stop you?'

'No, but you did.'

'Yes, because I thought it was a bloody stupid idea. I still do – but it's your choice and I'll support it. Besides,' he grinned cheekily, 'I'm old, I can say what I think.'

I giggled at that.

'There's more, isn't there?' he said.

I nodded, and then blurted it out. 'Mirry and Olly have gone to Sydney and are building a house and a business; Mum and Dad are retiring; Richie's going to be a fabulous garden designer; and James is getting the promotion he's been working towards. I'm just going along with him for the ride.' I hung my head again, embarrassed at how ungrateful I sounded. 'Even though I'm leaving too, part of me feels like I'm being left behind.'

Horrie was silent for a few seconds. When I risked a glance at his face, he wasn't watching me, but rather looking across the allotment and the lengthening shadows.

'I can see how it must feel like that, lass. You

need to decide what's really important to you and be brave enough to make it happen. Or be happy to watch everyone else move on without you.' He paused. 'Answer me this: do you want to go to New York?'

I shook my head slowly, feeling like I was betraying James for even contemplating the question.

Horrie nodded. 'Thought as much. Don't say you'll go with him if your only reason is to take things back to how they used to be. Too much between you and Jim has already changed.' His face was serious. 'There's no shame in doing it alone – if that's what you decide.'

I looked at him in surprise. Was he really suggesting what it sounded like he was suggesting?

To cover my confusion and lighten the discussion I smiled. 'That sounds like something out of one of Mum's new-age self-help books.'

He chuckled. 'No, lass, just common sense.' He looked up at the darkening sky. 'It's getting cold, so I might get these old knees back home.' He reached for my hand and patted it. 'You be off home too, and call that lad and be friends again.'

I attempted to smile past the lump in my throat. 'I'll do that,' I managed. 'Thanks, Horrie.'

'Anytime, lass.'

Back home I took the leftover chocolate pudding from the fridge and scooped a generous helping into my bowl, then poured cream liberally over its surface.

Leaning against the kitchen bench I ate a spoonful, and then another, closing my eyes briefly in appreciation.

Horrie had a point: there hadn't been a right time for Richie to tell me he was leaving. I'd been too full of myself about the changes in my life – and then I'd lost the baby. He must have known that whenever I found out I'd be upset about it.

There'd never been any doubt that he'd go home some day. For him it wasn't just the expectation of taking over the family business; it truly was what he wanted to spend his life doing and where he wanted to be doing it. I'd always known that – we'd talked about it many times. Perhaps – like with my parents' retirement – I hadn't thought the time would ever come.

James wanted me to put my dreams on hold until he was ready for me to live them; until he was finished living his. Why should Richie put his dreams on hold until I was ready for him to live them? It was unfair of me to even think it. Rather than feeling envious that he was leaving to see more of the world and take control of his life – because that's what, in all honesty, this boiled down to – I should admire him for having the courage to do that.

The truth was, I'd never taken control of my life or made a decision that I hadn't already drifted into. When I finished college, I took the first job I was offered. I might have intended for it to be short-term while I figured out where in the world I wanted to see and what I wanted to do, but once I started dating James none of that mattered. I loved him, and I wanted to build a family and a life with him. I'd thought he wanted what I did. Back then he might have done. These days, though, the gap between his goals and my dreams was very wide. I supposed the big question was whether either of us was prepared to bridge that gap. In giving up my job and following James to New York, I'd be putting my independence into his hands too. I was no longer sure I was prepared to do that.

I couldn't do anything about James right now, but I could fix the situation with Richie.

Curling up on the sofa, I texted him: *So when do you leave?* Then I waited for my phone to ring.

'Hiya, you.'

'Hiya, yourself,' he said.

Then we both said it together: 'I'm sorry.'

I laughed. 'Well, that was unplanned.'

'I'm sorry you found out the way you did. I should have talked to you about what I was thinking about doing – there were plenty of opportunities.'

'I think I understand.'

'Do you?'

'Sure. You must have thought I had enough on my plate with the move and then the baby that I wouldn't have had space in my head to listen to you properly.'

There was a pause at the other end of the phone. 'Yes, something like that.'

'And I over-reacted. After everything you've done for me, I shouldn't have gone off at you the way I did.'

'It's okay, Hendo. I get it.'

There was an awkward silence for a few seconds.

'I really do want to hear about Queenstown,' I said.

I could hear the grin in his voice when he said, 'And I really want to tell you about it.'

Richie picked me up on Monday morning to drive me to work as usual. I was probably fit enough to cycle the short distance by now, but when I mentioned it he waved the idea away. After I'd spoken to him yesterday afternoon, I'd dropped in on my parents to have a similar conversation with them, so I filled the short drive to Blossoms with talk of Mum and Dad's new house, their village and the views.

It wasn't until we were in the office grabbing a cup of tea between customers that I brought up the argument. I'd salvaged the last of the chocolate pudding for him.

'I am sorry, you know.'

'Yeah. So am I. But we're sweet now, right?'

'Sure we are.'

He took his first mouthful of pudding. 'This is amazing. Why haven't you made me this before?'

I laughed at the look of rapture on his face. 'It was always Mum's go-to pudding whenever I'd had my heart broken or before a big exam. Somehow after eating this I was able to talk about whatever was worrying me – like a chocolatey truth serum. Lately she's made it whenever she's needed to tell me something she hasn't wanted to tell me.'

'Well, it would certainly distract me from bad news. I'd have to be careful not to tell all my secrets.'

'I'll have to remember that.' I grinned. 'The knowledge could come in handy some day.'

'That it could.'

Our eyes held for a second too long. He was the first to break the mood.

'Man, am I going to miss your muffins.'

'Just my muffins?' I smiled cheekily.

'No, I'll miss all your baking – but especially your muffins.' I thumped him on the arm. 'It's true – no one feeds me as well as you do. On the upside, I might have a chance to get rid of this belly.' He patted his flat stomach, grinned and reached for the pudding bowl, dragging his spoon around the edges to get the last of the squidgy goodness. 'I should have said something to you, Maxi – about what I was thinking about doing. The truth is, I didn't tell you because I didn't know how to say it. I suppose I thought you'd always be here, and when you told me you were going to New York, it hit me like a ton of bricks.' He looked away. 'I couldn't stay here when one of the reasons I've stayed so long was moving away. I realised I had no input in the decision you'd made – and why should I?'

I'd never thought about it that way – that Richie might have felt as winded by my news as I had been when I found out about his. The same as Mum said she and Dad had been when they got my email.

'But –' I started.

'You don't need to say anything – I know you didn't have a choice. Your place is with your husband. That doesn't mean I didn't wish you weren't going with him. It was the signal to me that it was time to go home and get on with things.'

I stared at him with my mouth open. 'But you never said.'

'What could I say? Something like "Don't go and be with the man you love. Stay here instead"? No. We're friends – I could never do that to you. Then when you lost the baby, there was no way I could tell you what I was doing – I didn't want to upset you any more. But I hurt you anyway – by not sharing it with you – and I'm sorry for that.'

'I am too ... sorry for not thinking about it from your point of view.' I tilted my head to the side and smiled at him. Then I leaned forward and lightly punched his arm. 'Sweet as, right?'

He smiled back. 'Sweet as.'

April in the Kitchen

The first of the season's spring onions were picked the other day. They're still thin and straggly, but will soon be much plumper – if only I can leave them in the ground for just a little longer. We're also getting some curly lettuce and cucumber, and a few skinny spears of asparagus. In another few weeks we'll start to see fresh peas and artichokes, then broad beans, tomatoes, and then ... I could go on.

It's about this time of year that we start to shed our layers, see what's underneath and vow to make better friends with salad. Which leads me into dishes that go well with salad, or dishes that salad goes well with. There's a difference. Even in the middle month of spring there are days when we need comfort, something warm in our belly, but without the richness and heaviness we look for in winter. Take cheese, for example. Whereas in winter we might long for creamy mornays or cheddar-rich macaroni cheese, now we're after something a little lighter. Ricotta fits that brief.

Of course you can buy ricotta – we stock a particularly good one from Westfarm Dairy – but it's easy to make it yourself. All you need is a saucepan, some milk, and lemon *juice or vinegar. Heat, Curdle, Drain – One, Two, Three. It couldn't be easier.*

Step 1: Heat. Pour two litres of whole milk (don't even think about attempting this with skimmed or semi-skimmed milk) into a saucepan. If you want a creamier ricotta, add a couple of tablespoons of cream to the milk. Season as required. Heat until it's almost at the boil. You can use a thermometer if you must, but really, just bring it to this side of a boil.

Step 2: Curdle. Add four tablespoons of white vinegar or lemon juice. The purists use citric acid, but I find you get a good curdle from vinegar or lemon – and a good curdle is exactly what you want. Stir gently, then bring the mix to a simmer for a couple of minutes before removing the pan from the heat. Once the mixture's sat for about ten minutes you'll notice that the curds have floated to the top and the whey is at the bottom. We're only interested in the curds for ricotta – although there are plenty of uses for whey. I'll leave you to google those.

Step 3: Drain. Line a sieve with cheesecloth or something similar (I find clean pudding cloths are perfect) and balance it over a large bowl. Pour the mix through and allow the whey to drain away. The longer you leave it draining, the more solid your ricotta will be.

This is a fresh milk product so you'll need to store it in the fridge and use it within a few days, but as ricotta is so versatile that's not difficult.

You can crumble it into an omelette, over a salad, or

on top of your tagliatelle carbonara – remember, no cream in the carbonara, we do it the Italian way! The ricotta is also lovely on hot toast with some cinnamon shaken over the top. You can even use it whenever you'd normally use Greek yoghurt – not that you'd use Greek yoghurt on toast, but you get the idea. It goes especially beautifully with bananas, strawberries and honey. Speaking of honey, have you tried the local honey we have in the shop at the moment?

My favourite use for ricotta, however, is in little gnocchi-type dumplings. I love gnocchi, but let's face it, they can be temperamental. If the potato isn't cooked exactly right, or dried out enough, or worked too much, your perfect little gnocchi can easily taste like rubber. You won't have that problem with these ricotta dumplings. I serve them with a smoky, sweet red pepper sauce. Coincidentally, peppers are coming into season next month. I'll pop the recipe for both the dumplings and the sauce up on the website.

Until next time,

Max

CHAPTER TWELVE

Mum and Dad moved to their new house in Cornwall in the middle of April. We had a farewell party of sorts for them at The Lamb. At the last minute, James called to say he couldn't make it home to say goodbye to them. 'Tell them we'll be down for a weekend before we leave,' he'd said. Mum had smiled and said it would give her something else to look forward to. Dad muttered something about not holding his breath.

The Saturday before he left, Richie and I walked the few miles through the woods to Sapperton. It was one of those days you sometimes get in early spring when you can smell the fragrance of the new growth in the breeze and it's easy to believe that every day will be as perfect as this one. The bluebells were out and carpeted the fields as if someone had taken a giant paintbrush and a giant tube of watercolour and washed it across the landscape. It made me want to skip – so I did.

I heard Richie's laugh as he jogged to keep up with me. 'Were you skipping?'

'Yep, what of it?'

'Only little girls with pigtails skip.'

'I'll have you know, mister, that anyone can skip when it's bluebell time.'

I stopped in the centre of the path and gazed around at the beauty. Up close the flowers were such a deep blue as to be almost purple.

'I bet you don't get colours like this at home,' I said.

'No, but in Sydney you get the jacarandas. Just like there's no other colour on earth like bluebell blue, there's no other colour like jacaranda purple. When Cate, my sister, was a little girl she used to call them fairy flowers.' He thought for a second or two, a smile on his face. 'I think she still calls them that.'

'And Queenstown?'

'Lupins. So many colours, more than you could ever imagine. The best are a few hours' drive out of Queenstown, up the road at Tekapo.' He looked into my eyes. 'Something about the blue of the lake – an icy, milky turquoise – makes the colours appear even more vibrant, as if they've been photoshopped in.'

'They sound beautiful.' For some reason I couldn't move my eyes away from his.

'They are. I'd like to show you some day.' He held my gaze a few beats more, then took my hand. 'Come with me.'

He led me to a spot where the sun was shining through the trees across the dappled blue carpet. Releasing my hand, he lay down.

'You too,' he urged.

I looked around us, but we had the place to ourselves, so I lay down beside him.

'What happens now?' I asked.

'Shhh,' he said, rolling onto his side and laying a finger briefly against my lips.

I had the strangest urge to open my mouth and draw it in – maybe to nip it, maybe to kiss it, or to reach forward and kiss him. Before I could give in to the temptation he'd rolled onto his back and shut his eyes.

'Let's just lie here for a minute,' he whispered.

'James is driving up this afternoon,' I reminded him. 'I'll need to be home by then.'

I mentioned James's name to cover the confusion whirring around in my brain.

He reached his hand out and held mine. 'I know.'

I turned my head to look at him, but his eyes were shut and his jaw relaxed. I wanted to trace his jawline with my finger, to kiss his closed eyes, his mouth. I wanted a mental photograph of this moment, of this man lying in the bluebells – something I could remember in my heart when he was in New Zealand and I was thousands of miles away in New York.

I lay back, the sun warm on my face, my hand still in his. I must have dozed, because when I woke the sun had gone behind a cloud and it was suddenly chilly. Richie was still beside me, but awake and lying on his side watching me. Somehow I knew that he'd been watching me for a while. Again the urge to reach up and pull his head down to mine was overwhelming.

His smile grew wider.

'What's so funny?' I asked. 'Was I snoring?' I felt my face grow warm with embarrassment.

He laughed and reached out a finger to touch the corner of my lips. 'No, but there's a little bit of dribble just there.'

I smacked his hand away and, pushing myself into a seated position, rubbed at my mouth. 'There is not!'

'Maybe not, but it was fun to watch your face when I said it.'

His grin was so cheeky that I couldn't help but laugh with him.

He stood and held out a hand to pull me to my feet. Still holding it, he looked into my eyes and said, 'I'm going to miss this … us …' He swallowed hard. 'I'm going to miss you.'

Something clamped in my chest and the tears that hadn't been far away for the last couple of weeks rushed to my eyes.

I pulled my hand from his and, turning away, muttered, 'Yeah, me too.'

'Maxi,' he said quietly, 'look at me.'

I shook my head and walked a few steps to the closest tree, biting the inside of my mouth, digging my nails into my palms, trying to force the sobs back down where they belonged. I'd given up attempting to hold back the tears – they were running freely down my face.

'Maxi?'

I turned to face him, leaning back against the tree, trusting that it would support me.

'Oh, sweetheart,' he said, 'this is for the best.'

In that moment I knew that he'd felt the same urge as I had in the bluebells.

'I know,' I managed to say through the tears.

'It's not goodbye forever. We'll stay in touch by email, and Facebook and Instagram.'

'I know.'

'Who knows? One day you could come to New Zealand.'

I nodded.

We both knew that once he left he wouldn't be back, and there was no chance James would ever let me go anywhere he knew Richie was.

I struggled to stem the tears, but the pain forced itself into my throat, leaving me gasping. I pounded my chest in a vain attempt to relieve the pressure within. I wanted him to hold me but knew that if he touched me the sobbing would start, and once it had started I was afraid it would never stop. I was afraid that if he held me I'd want him to kiss me. I was afraid that if he kissed me I'd never want him to stop.

'I'm afraid to touch you,' he said, his eyes glistening.

I nodded. 'I know.'

He swallowed again and then somehow he was in

front of me, pulling me into him, hugging me tight as the sobs finally found their way past my throat. I thought I felt him kiss the top of my head. He held me like that until the shaking stopped and I had myself back under control, until I forced myself out of his arms and turned my back on him, afraid of what I'd see in his face, scrabbling through my pockets for a halfway clean tissue. I pushed my forehead into a tree trunk and rested it there. I felt his eyes on me, but he said nothing.

Finally I was able to face him. 'I'm sorry. I'm so happy for you … going home and everything. It's what you've always said you wanted to do, and now that it's happening I know I'm being selfish. It's just … it's just that …' I screwed my eyes tight and bit down on my bottom lip. 'I thought I was okay about this, you going and everything … but maybe I'm not.'

'You're going away too,' he said quietly. 'To New York. With James.'

I opened my eyes and stared into his. 'Yes, I am.'

I didn't tell him that going to New York with James was the real problem; that since I'd admitted to Horrie that I didn't want to go, I was no longer sure that I would be going. But staying here on my own when nearly everyone else I loved had gone? I didn't want to think about what that meant.

Perhaps all of that washed over my face because he reached for me again, and we stood there together for a few minutes, maybe more, my head resting on his chest, his cheek against my hair. When I pulled back, his face looked as sad as I felt.

'Please be happy,' he said. 'I just want you to be happy.'

I nodded. 'You too.'

I thought I saw something change in his eyes, but then he pulled back and said, 'We'd better be getting you back. At this rate, James will beat you in.'

I nodded miserably.

'You'll be okay, Maxi. Everything will be fine.'

I nodded again, but I didn't believe him. How could I tell him that wherever he was, I'd be wishing I was there too? Telling him that wouldn't have helped either of us.

James's car was in the drive when we finally arrived home.

'Great,' I muttered.

Richie heard me but didn't respond.

'Are you having farewell drinks or anything at the pub tonight?' I asked him.

'Apparently so. You coming down?'

I shrugged, not trusting myself to speak again.

He looked between the car and the front door of my cottage. 'You'd better get inside. If I don't see you for a drink tonight, see you in the office, hey?'

'You don't want to come in? I can make you

something to eat.' I could feel the grit in my eyes as I looked up at him.

'No, Maxi, not a good idea.' He bent to kiss my cheek, leaving his hand on my shoulder for a few seconds. 'See ya.'

I watched him until he turned the corner out of my lane. He didn't look back.

CHAPTER THIRTEEN

When I let myself in, James called to me from the kitchen. 'Darling,' he said, reaching out to pull me to him. 'I've missed you so much these last couple of weeks.'

He kissed me slowly in a way that only a few months ago would have left me melting for him.

'What's wrong?' he asked, putting a finger under my chin to lift my eyes to his. 'Is everything okay?'

'Yes.' I moved myself out of his arms. 'I've just been walking – miles – so I'm a little sweaty. I think I'd like a shower.'

'Walking? Alone?'

'No, Richie came with me. We took the path down to Sapperton. The bluebells are out. It would have been a shame for him to leave without seeing them.'

Damn these tears. I turned away and busied myself with unpacking the dishwasher so he wouldn't see them.

'That's right, he's going back to wherever he came from. When does that happen?'

James was leaning against the kitchen door watching me work. I could hear the smile in his voice.

'Next week.' A tear landed on a clean plate. I wiped it dry.

'Is he having farewell drinks or anything?' Before I had a chance to answer he added, 'Maybe we should go along to make sure he does go.'

When I didn't respond, he said, 'Are you sure you were walking through the bluebells? By the look of your clothes you were rolling around in them. You've got grass stains on your jeans.'

'Yes,' I said, straightening to look at him. 'I had a fall. I decided that skipping through them would be a funny thing to do, but tripped over a tree root.' I forced a laugh. 'That wasn't quite so funny. I'm heading for a shower – do you want me to make you anything to eat first?'

'No,' he said, watching me through narrowed eyes. 'We need to go through my movements for the next few weeks leading into New York, so I'll wait for you to be presentable again. Then I thought we might go to The Lamb for dinner. I'll phone and book a table, shall I?'

'I thought I might just cook something?'

'You cook every night, so how about you let someone else do the cooking?' He moved closer and cupped my chin, raising my mouth to his for another kiss. 'Then we can come back here and I'll show you just how much I've missed you.' He smiled as his finger traced the line of my jaw, down my throat and into the shadow between my breasts. 'If you're well enough to walk for miles, you're well enough for what I have in mind for us. But first, my darling, you need to change.'

He turned me around and lightly slapped my bottom to send me on my way.

By the time I'd finished my shower, James had set up his laptop on the kitchen table. He proceeded to run through the time line (which I assumed India had prepared for him) of what I needed to have done and by when. I listened mostly without comment. India seemed to have everything covered.

'You'll be flying out in the last week of May,' he said. 'India has booked the movers, so all you need to do is work out what we'll be putting into storage and what will be coming with us. The apartment we have is furnished – it has everything we need.' He stopped and smiled at me. 'All it needs to make it perfect is you.'

I managed to smile back.

'I've arranged to have the cottage placed on the market –'

'What did you say?' His words jolted me to attention. 'We haven't talked about that!'

'Of course we have, darling.' He was still smiling, but now it was the smile of someone who knew best. 'It makes perfect sense. The market is unlikely to move further and, let's face it, when we're back from New

York we'll be settling in London.'

'What about how we talked about our children growing up here?'

He reached across the table for my hands, but I pulled them away.

He raised his eyes to the ceiling in exasperation before saying, 'Things have changed, Maxine. Your parents have retired to Cornwall, all our friends are in London –'

'Don't you mean all *your* friends? They're not mine.'

He ignored my interruption. 'Our friends are in London and our children will certainly want to be in London. If we really need a country weekender, it will probably be somewhere a little more appropriate than this.'

'I love this cottage.' I pushed myself to my feet and moved around the kitchen gathering the ingredients for the lemon slice I intended to bake that afternoon. 'And I love living in Brookford.'

'This is for the best, Maxine.'

'Whose best? Yours? It's certainly not what I want.'

I smashed biscuits into crumbs for the base layer of the slice, wielding my rolling pin as if it was a dangerous weapon. I didn't want to think about whether my anger was directed at James and what he was saying, or towards myself and how I was feeling.

'And just what is it you want? To stay here in the countryside playing around with plants and baking?

That's not who we are. We're more than that. This move isn't just the right thing for us, darling, it's the best thing for you too.'

I stopped bashing the biscuits and stared directly at him. 'I'm tired of everyone telling me what's best for me. How about you start by asking me what I want, rather than telling me what you think I should want?' I waved the rolling pin for emphasis. 'You've never even listened to what my dreams are.'

James held my gaze for a few seconds, then said, 'We're moving to New York and I'm selling the cottage. The sooner you get used to that idea, the better.'

When he left the room, I let out the breath I'd been holding. The condensed milk and butter that I'd been heating slowly on the stove had caught, and as I stirred the last of the butter through, nasty black burnt bits floated to the surface. I tipped it in the bin and started again.

My second batch didn't burn, so I mixed the crushed biscuits with some shredded coconut and a variety of jewel-bright dried fruits into it, and pressed it all into a tin. I'd ice it later, once the base had firmed up in the fridge.

While it was setting, I messed about a bit in the garden: snipping a little here, weeding a little there. I could have gone down to the allotment, but guessed James would see that as a personal affront. He'd spent most of the afternoon on his phone answering texts or emails, and sighing loudly every time he caught my eye.

A picture of Richie's face swam into my mind. I touched my finger to my lips, to where he'd placed his, as if I could feel it again. I wondered how his lips would have felt against mine, whether he would have kissed me back.

I closed my eyes and brought up the picture of him lying in the bluebells, waiting for me to wake. Somehow I knew that if I had reached for him, he wouldn't have let go, and I wouldn't have wanted him to. But we both knew that could never happen, no matter how much we might have wanted it to.

James and I walked down to The Lamb for dinner that night. It was threatening to rain, so we selected a table inside. While James was negotiating his way through the wine list, complaining as usual about its limitations, I looked around the room. In a booth in the corner sat Richie with a group of other people, most of whom I recognised. Angela was there too. She was waving her hands and flicking her hair about as she talked.

Richie's eyes met mine and he tipped his glass slightly in acknowledgement.

James looked up from the menu at the same time and nodded, without smiling, in Richie's direction. 'Is he still on with the hairdresser?'

'I thought they'd broken up. I'm surprised she's here – they didn't end well.'

'It certainly looks like they're back on again. Have you decided what you want?'

As I looked across at them, Angela reached up and kissed Richie's cheek.

'Umm, I'm not really hungry. Just some grilled fish and salad.'

I watched James as he walked up to the bar. My husband. Tall and slim, he looked almost too handsome for this village pub. It wasn't just how he dressed, it was in the way he carried himself — that confidence that came from knowing he was Something, Someone. I used to feel proud when I looked at him — proud that he was mine, that out of all the women in the world he could have had, for some reason he'd chosen me. As I watched him leaning against the bar to order our meals and talking to Duncan, I closed my eyes briefly and tried to feel some of that again — so that I'd know it wasn't gone completely, maybe just hiding away for a little while.

He looked back and smiled at me. As our eyes met, a thrill ran through me. Nothing like it used to be, but an indication that perhaps the madness was temporary. That maybe when it was just us again, with no flying in and flying out, things would get back to how they used to be. Yes, I decided, when Richie was gone and we were in New York building a new life together, everything would be fine again.

Once James had ordered, he stopped at Richie's

table on the way back to me. I couldn't hear what he
was saying, but I saw Richie's face close up. Angela
played with her hair and smiled flirtatiously at him. By
the time James had covered the few steps to where I
was waiting, he looked like a man who'd had a plan
that had come together. He stood behind me and
nuzzled my neck, turning my head so he could kiss me
properly. When I opened my eyes Richie was watching
us. It felt somehow as though James had stamped me
as his property for everyone in the pub – and especially
Richie – to see.

'What did you say to Richie?' I asked once he'd sat
down and poured me a glass from the bottle of wine
he'd decided on.

'Not much. I just wished him well on his travels.'
He took a sip of wine, swilling it around his mouth.
'Not bad – perhaps a little acidic on the palate, but it'll
do. Oh, and I might have said something about how
once he's gone he's to cease all contact with you.'

'You what?'

He held his hand up in front of my face as his
phone alerted him to a new text. I saw that it was from
India. I also saw the words *babe* and *fun*, but he grabbed
the phone before I could read any more. He read it and
said, 'Sorry, darling, I have to make a quick call. I'll be
right back.'

After he'd gone outside, Richie came over to talk
to me. He wasted no time with preliminaries. 'I'm

guessing you won't be joining us for a drink?'

'No. I …' I dropped my head and almost whispered, 'I can't.'

In those two words I meant so much more: James won't like it; I can't bear to say goodbye; I don't want to celebrate you going; I don't want to see you with Angela; please don't leave me. The last was, of course, ridiculous. After all, I was leaving too.

When I looked up he was smiling. 'I enjoyed this morning.'

'Me too.'

'I'll send you a photo of the lupins.' He bent down and kissed the top of my head. 'See you Monday, Hendo.'

He met Angela in the centre of the room and grabbed the hands she was waving in my direction. I heard him say, 'Settle down, babe,' and he pulled her towards him and kissed her. Whatever else he said I couldn't hear, but she giggled and took his hand to drag him back to their group. He didn't protest.

By the time James finished his call, our dinner was already on the table and I'd started eating.

'You didn't wait for me?' he said.

'Has something come up?'

'I'll need to head back into town tomorrow morning. You understand, don't you, darling?' He poked at his meal. 'This has gone cold.'

After the way he'd behaved with Richie, and his

high-handedness about selling the cottage earlier, I wasn't in the mood to understand.

'Why do you rush back to London every time she calls, yet you're never here when I need you?'

'It's business.'

'The last few times you've actually made it here, you've had to go tearing back early. What's so important that you can't deal with it by phone or email? You're on the bloody thing enough.'

'Unlike you, darling,' he sneered the endearment, 'my job doesn't finish the minute the door closes. My responsibilities continue far past 5 pm each day, and if India needs to contact me so I can solve problems as they come up, then that's what she has to do.'

'What I don't understand is why a text telling you about a problem that only you can deal with has the words *babe* and *fun* in it.' I took a deep breath. 'Are you sure you're not running back just so you can be with her?'

His face was tinged red and he appeared to be struggling for control. 'You've been after this fight since earlier this afternoon, but I'm not going to oblige you by having it in here for the entire village to see.' He leaned forward and lowered his voice. 'I've got no idea what's wrong with you lately. I've made the effort to come back this weekend, even though things are at a crucial stage in the States. I don't expect you to understand the intricacies of what I do. What I do expect is that as my wife you respect what I do and the sacrifices I have to make in order to build the life we want. If that means I don't answer the phone the minute you ring, or don't get here to see you every single weekend, then that's what it means.' He pushed his dinner away uneaten. 'Now you've given me indigestion.'

'Where were you that Friday night I lost the baby? Why didn't you answer your phone?'

He raised his eyes to the ceiling as if searching for inspiration – or someone to rid him of this annoying woman. But when he spoke, his tone had softened. 'I know you're feeling neglected – I understand that. But in just a few weeks we'll be together again.' He stroked the back of my hand, smiling into my eyes. 'I just need you to hold it together for a little while longer.'

I pulled my hand away. 'Were you with India while I was miscarrying our baby?'

'Is that what this is about? Me not being here while you lost a baby that not only was I unaware existed but probably wasn't mine anyway?'

I let out a breath. 'Do you really believe that?' I stared at him and he dropped his gaze. As he did the fight went out of me and I stood to go. 'If whatever it is that India rang about is that important, why don't you go back now? Tonight.'

He grabbed my hand and hissed, 'You will not make a scene here. We're walking out together with a smile on our faces.'

Once outside, I shook his hand away and we covered the rest of the distance home in silence. James left for London soon after and I didn't even go outside to wave him off.

CHAPTER FOURTEEN

In the background of my sadness about Richie going was the fight with James. But from the tone of his texts in the days since, it was as if he'd pushed the whole sorry scene out of his head. I knew we needed to talk, and I'd rehearsed what I wanted to say to him, but the truth was that part of me was worried that I'd prompted the fight to block out the guilt and confusion I'd felt about Richie and what happened between us in the bluebells. I didn't even know if I was still going to New York – even though I was continuing with everything as if I were. It seemed easier to do that than to consider the alternative.

Richie tried to talk to me about it, but I snapped at him too. 'What do you care? You're out of here at the end of the week.'

Rather than biting back, he shook his head slowly and said, 'I know you're hurting, but I'm not the enemy, Maxi. I wish you'd tell me what's wrong.'

I dropped my head in shame. 'I know you're not, and I'm sorry. It's just that James is acting like nothing has changed even though it feels like everything has changed, and I feel like I'm being forced in a direction I don't want to be taking. Does that make sense?'

He nodded. 'Sort of. I have no idea what happened between you two so I'm not even going to try and understand. But he's your husband and this needs to be sorted out, so don't leave it too long, hey?'

'I won't.' I had my fingers crossed behind my back as I said it.

'Have you talked it over with your parents?'

I unpacked a box of files that I'd just finished packing. 'No. I don't know how to tell them about James and me. I don't want them to be disappointed in him. Besides, we'll probably make it up and then all the fuss would have been for nothing.'

Richie said something under his breath.

'What was that?' I asked.

'Nothing important. Do you want to repack that box? I'll see to that couple who just walked in.'

When James phoned on Thursday afternoon, I picked up. 'Hiya,' I said, turning my chair away from Richie to give myself some privacy.

'It's good to hear your voice.'

'It's good to hear yours too.'

'Maxine, darling, I'm … I'm sorry. I shouldn't have said what I did about you and Richie. You were right to get angry.'

He paused, which meant I was supposed to fill the silence.

'I'm sorry too, James. I know how busy you are. It's just that –'

'You don't need to say it, darling. I know you don't like me being away. It's different for me – I can stay busy – but you're lonely now that your parents have gone. I can understand how it's easy for you to over-react in that situation.'

I heard Richie leave the room. I leaned back in my chair and nursed the phone between my ear and my shoulder.

'Where are you? Are you in London?'

'I landed about thirty minutes ago, but wanted to call you before I went into the office. I miss you, darling. I hate it when we fight like this and I hate having to be away from you.' He lowered his voice and it curled around me almost like it used to. 'You have no idea what I want to do to you – or maybe you can guess.' He laughed softly. 'It's been too long.'

'I've missed you too,' I managed, but I wasn't sure it was the truth.

'Remember when we stayed at that gorgeous hotel in the Borders? The place with the bath large enough for both of us?'

I remembered. 'We left such a lot of water on the floor.'

I could hear the smile in his voice. 'And then we made love in that massive bed with the drapes around it.'

The memory felt dream-like and perfect.

'How about we do it again before we leave for New York? You and me, just like we used to be?' James spoke softly, almost wistfully. 'See if we can't go back in time.'

I wondered when he wanted to go back to. Before New York? Earlier? When we first met?

'It sounds good,' I said. 'But aren't we heading down to see Mum and Dad that last weekend?'

'Let's not get caught up in the details now, darling. We can talk about it this weekend.'

'So you're coming back?'

'I sure am. I should be with you by midday Saturday. How about you cook something nice for lunch, and I'll make a booking somewhere for dinner?'

'It sounds good. James, I –'

'Sorry, darling, I have to run, but I'll see you soon.'

When Richie came back into the room I was looking at my phone and smiling.

'All sorted?' he asked.

'Seems to be. I think it was just a combination of hormones and over-reaction,' I explained.

'That's good then. What exactly did you over-react about?'

I decided not to tell him about the part where James had said he didn't believe the baby was his.

'It was silly really – I virtually accused him of having an affair with India.' I laughed. 'I know, right? How clichéd would that be.'

Richie wasn't smiling. 'What made you ask him that?'

'I saw a text come through and I'm pretty sure she called him "babe", but other than that I think I was looking for reasons why he's always running back to town rather than staying with me. It was that classic thing of adding two and two together and getting something more than four. Serves me right for over-thinking it.'

'Hmmm.' Richie had turned away and was packing a pile of receipts into a box for storage. I watched him for a few seconds.

'What's that – that *hmmm*?'

'Nothing, Hendo.'

'Richie, look at me.' He turned to meet my eyes, but his slipped away too soon. 'This is the part where you tell me I was being ridiculous, that James only has eyes for me and would never look at another woman.'

He remained silent.

'You know something, don't you?'

'Please don't ask me this. I don't want to be involved.'

'If you know something I don't, you're already involved. Come on, spill.'

He hesitated. 'I'm not certain about this, but I thought I heard him call her "babe" on the phone the other night.' He stopped and waited for my reaction. Getting none, he continued. 'It was at the pub when he was outside taking a call – I'd just been over to see you. I thought I heard him say something like, "Babe, I had fun too."'

I thought about possible explanations. 'Okay, how do you know he was talking to her?'

'I don't, not for sure, but you said he –'

I waved his words away. 'And that fun could have been on a work level?'

'Of course it could have, theoretically. But there's also –'

'So really you don't actually know anything. Do you?'

'I guess I don't,' he muttered as I got up from my chair.

'You might be prepared to think the worst of my husband, but I think I'll continue to trust him.' As I said the words, I knew I was trying to convince myself as well as him. 'Plus, he said he misses me and he's coming home on Saturday. You'll see – everything will be back to normal in no time. I refuse to let you dampen my good mood.'

'Heaven forbid that might happen,' he muttered.

'I heard that,' I called on my way through to the shop.

Too soon, it was Friday and our last day at work together. After today it would be just me – cleaning everything up to hand it all to someone else. Everything that Richie and I had done together. My tears had been hovering close to the surface all week, but somehow I'd managed to stop them from over-flowing. In my more rational moments I tried to understand why I felt as though my heart was breaking. I'd had weeks to get my head around the impending separation. None of it made sense. The only thing that made sense was that moment last week in the bluebells.

Richie had said we'd catch up – just us – sometime during that last week. Nothing serious: just a meal or a drink. But as the week flew by it became clear that wasn't going to happen. He was probably worried that I'd lose control the way I did on Saturday, I thought; that I'd try to turn our friendship into something more than it could be.

Each person who came into the garden centre on Friday came for one reason – to say goodbye to Richie. It was the comments that came next that brought me undone, all a variation on the same theme:

'The lass will be lost without you.'

'Maxine won't know what to do without you.'

'Max will be lonely in here without you.'

I was okay until they inevitably turned to me and said, 'Are you alright, dear?' I wasn't. I should have been thinking about how to make things right when James was home this weekend, but I didn't know whether I wanted to make them right. I had a lifetime to be with James, but just a few hours left with Richie. Part of me wished it was reversed – and that knowledge made me feel even guiltier.

As soon as the phone rang and I saw it was James, I knew what he was going to tell me. Richie and I had closed up early and gone to the pub for a last drink together. Now Richie went inside to the bar so I could talk to James freely.

'What's happened?' I asked before he even had a chance to say hello.

'I'm sorry, darling. Jeremy's invited me to dinner at his club. It's not something I can decline, not when it's looking as though he's anointed me as his successor when he retires in a few years.'

I'd been invited to most of these dinners in the past, and quite enjoyed the company of Jeremy's wife.

'Do you want me to come?' I asked. 'You've mentioned before how it helps in these situations.'

'Would you? That would be great.' He sounded pleased. 'But wait – there's still packing to do.' He hesitated as if running through the calendar in his head. 'No, darling, the offer is very thoughtful – and I'd love to have you by my side – but I think you'd better get started on the packing. I'd prefer we have a weekend free at the end to get away together – just us, like we were talking about yesterday – rather than have you come to London this weekend for one dinner.'

By the time he rang off a few minutes later, Richie was back with fresh beers. 'What's happened?'

'Something's come up – dinner with his boss. He can't get out of it, and when I offered to go too he said he'd prefer I start on the packing. I know he's right, but I really wanted to try and bring things back to normal this weekend. All we've done lately is fight, and I'm sure it's because we've hardly seen each other. I'd even planned what to make us for lunch tomorrow.' I'd mentally gone through what was ready to be harvested in the allotment. A risotto primavera perhaps? Or pea and goat's cheese croquettes with a pea and mint puree.

Richie took a mouthful of his beer and didn't say anything.

'James usually likes me at these things. Jeremy, his boss, is quite old-fashioned – he likes to know there's a supportive wife in the background.' I leaned back to catch the late afternoon sun on my face. 'Now I've got no excuse not to start the packing,' I grumbled.

'Would you have spent the weekend packing if he was here?'

'Well, no. Not all of it. Just Saturday morning and Sunday evening. He wouldn't have wanted me to be working when he'd made the effort to drive up.'

'If that's the case, why don't you go to London tomorrow afternoon? You'll be back here on Sunday by the time he'd be leaving anyway.' He shrugged. 'As far as I can figure it, it's a win–win: you spend time with James, and you get started on the packing.'

As he spoke I was working it through in my head.

My sleeveless black jersey would be perfect for dinner, and wouldn't crush in my bag. Plus, it would take my mind off Richie being on a plane to Denmark. Yes, this could work.

'I know,' I announced, 'I'll surprise him.'

'Do you think that's a good idea?' By the tone of his voice, Richie didn't seem to think it was.

'Of course. He'll be thrilled I thought of it.'

'You don't think you should phone first to let him know?'

'And ruin the surprise?' I shook my head. 'No, it'll be better this way.'

Soon after, a group of friends joined us, all wanting to catch Richie before he went away tomorrow morning, all wanting to know how I was going to cope without him. It was almost as if James didn't exist for any of them. Perhaps he didn't. Somehow I managed to hold it together, biting back the pain and the tears, hoping no one would see behind my smile.

At about nine I decided to leave. If it were any other night, Richie would have announced that he was going too and offered to walk me home. Tonight, he stood and hugged me briefly, kissing me on the cheek as if he would be seeing me tomorrow and the next day and the day after that.

'See ya, Hendo,' he said, holding my arm, 'Be happy.'

I searched his face for something more, but he'd already turned his attention back to the others.

At the door, I turned and looked back. He was watching me with an expression that looked the way I felt.

I managed to hold the tears at bay until I was outside, and then allowed them to stream silently down my face as I walked. Once home, I let myself in, then collapsed into a sad little bundle behind the front door, sobbing for longer than I'd thought was possible.

When I opened the door the next morning to bring in the newspaper I saw them: a bundle of bluebells tied together with a piece of gardener's string. There wasn't a note … there didn't need to be. Richie had gone.

CHAPTER FIFTEEN

James was sitting at the dining table working on his laptop when I let myself into the London flat on Saturday afternoon. As I pushed open the door he looked up and smiled. I thought his smile faltered a little when he noticed my overnight bag, but if it did, he recovered quickly.

'Maxine, darling … this is a surprise!' He gathered me in for a hug, bags and all.

I grinned and prodded him in the chest. 'Good surprise?'

'Of course. I wasn't expecting to see you until next weekend.'

I moved out of his arms and set my bags down near the table.

The flat was tiny. There was one small bedroom, with barely enough room for a bed and a small built-in wardrobe, and a pokey bathroom. It was the living space – open-plan kitchen, eating and sitting room in one – with its warm wood floors that had sold it to us. Well, sold it to me. James was more interested in the

SW1 postcode; he didn't care how small it was. One weekend when James was away, I'd commandeered Mirry into helping me paint all the walls white. We'd made a mercy dash to IKEA for some bright prints for the walls and cushions for the modern grey sofa. James had complained that the colours were too gaudy and he'd been going for something more minimalist and chic, but now, with the sun pouring through the windows, the effect was welcoming.

'It's not that I'm not pleased to see you,' he said, filling the kettle with water and getting some mugs from one of the overhead cabinets. 'It's just that I know how much you have on with getting the cottage all packed up.'

'I know, but with all the packing up at work as well, I needed a break from boxes.'

James raised his eyebrows, but said nothing. The kettle switched itself off and he poured hot water over the teabags, adding milk to mine.

'The thing is,' I started, taking a sip and grimacing at the heat before putting my mug down on the bench, 'I remembered how you said that Jeremy likes his executives to have a supportive wife by their side, so I figured I'd come and be the supportive wife.'

I opened my arms in a 'here I am' pose. I felt strangely as though I was a visitor in the flat, although I supposed it had been months since I'd been to town.

'I wish you'd called,' James said, placing a coaster

under my mug. 'You see, there's been a change of plans. When Jeremy found out you couldn't make it, he cancelled. Given I'd already phoned you, I arranged to go out this evening with some of the boys from the office. It's a sort of celebration for signing the contract in New York. It would seem you've had a wasted journey.'

I tried to catch my face before it fell too far, but failed. 'Can't you call and let them know that your wife's surprised you?'

'I could, but a few of them have had to negotiate to get time away from their wives and babies.'

It was hard to ignore the look of distaste on his face.

'That could have been us,' I said quietly.

'I know, but thankfully it's not.'

'Thankfully?' I tried to keep the emotion from my voice.

'I know you were upset originally – probably the hormones – but you have to admit it's worked out for the best now. I can't imagine being chained down like that. We wouldn't be able to get away for a sexy weekend in the Borders if you were pregnant – no champagne, remember?'

He said it with a smile like it was a silver lining. He may as well have said: I'm sorry our baby died, but at least you can drink champagne.

'How could you say that? We lost our baby.'

'I didn't want it.' His tone was flat.

I met his gaze. 'I did. Very much.'

He shrugged.

There we were, the late afternoon light streaming through the windows, him leaning against the kitchen bench, me at the dining table, each of us looking at the other and knowing that whatever was said next could completely destroy what was left of us. What he'd just said had already destroyed me.

'I love you, Maxine, but I don't want children. I thought I could be ready some day – maybe after New York – but the life I want for us doesn't include nappies and noise. I want the lifestyle that goes with my job. I thought if you gave it a chance, you'd want that too. I still think that.'

'You've always known that I want babies. I've never made a secret of it. Why didn't you tell me how you really feel? Were you planning on making me wait another two years, another six months, just until after New York, or when we can afford a house by the beach? Or until I'm too old? What then? You'd pat me on the back and say "there, there"?'

He shrugged. 'I wanted you.'

'And you didn't care what I want.'

It wasn't an accusation, more of a realisation. Needing to be as far away from him as possible, I walked across the room and sat in the corner of the sofa.

In the silence, I could hear the ticking of the clock that hung on the wall next to the kitchen. Gradually I became aware of other noises too – the humming of the fridge, the rumble of the traffic in the street below, a siren in the distance, a key in the door.

India walked in, looking her usual effortlessly immaculate self in crisp white capri pants, a softly striped grey tee, cropped black leather jacket and white sneakers. Her long blonde hair hung loosely from its centre parting. She walked towards James, smiling. In her hands were a bottle of champagne and a wicker basket.

'Babe,' she scolded gently, 'you're not ready.'

As she leaned in to kiss him, he turned his head so the kiss landed on his cheek. 'India, hi … is it that time already?'

I watched James as he watched me for my reaction. I gave him none.

She looked confused, searching his face, and, following his gaze, finally noticed me. 'Oh,' she said, 'I didn't know you were dropping by this afternoon, Max.'

'So it would seem,' I managed, sounding and feeling far calmer than I should.

James pushed her to one side and came across to me. 'I'm sorry, darling, but we're meeting the others for … for a picnic. Umm, Primrose Hill. It was such a lovely day that India suggested we start there and then move onto a bar.'

'Why does she have a key?'

'She needs a key. How else is she going to arrange for groceries and everything else I need doing?'

'She's been invited to your night out with the boys?'

'Of course – she's part of the team.' He turned to India. 'Do you want to wait downstairs? I need a few minutes to sort this out and then I'll be down.'

She nodded and left the room.

He waited until she'd closed the door. 'Now, darling, let's talk about this sensibly.'

'Which part do you want to talk about sensibly? The part about you shagging your assistant, or the part about you suddenly not wanting children?'

He searched the ceiling for inspiration, or perhaps divine intervention. 'Maybe that wasn't the best choice of words –'

'What would you have said if I'd told you I was pregnant *before* I lost the baby?'

'But you didn't.' His smile was patronising. He reached out to touch my arm. 'That's a ridiculous hypothetical and you're a sensible woman.'

'I want to know, James. What would you have said? Would you have wanted me to get rid of it?' My tone was expressionless.

'That's not the exact way I would have said it, but yes, I would have said that a baby didn't fit into our plans for New York –'

'Don't you mean that a baby didn't fit into *your* plans for New York?'

'Yes, I suppose that's what I'm saying. But you were only just pregnant, so there would have been time to do something about it.'

I shook off his hand and stood. 'Don't say anything more, James. Not now. I think you've said enough.'

'What are you going to do?'

I shook my head. 'Does it matter?'

He paused for a few seconds. 'India's nothing to me – it's you I love.'

'I wouldn't let her hear you say that.'

'Come on, darling. You've said what you want to say. There's no reason for us not to proceed with New York as planned.'

He was smiling as if everything was alright, as if he hadn't said what he'd said, as if losing the baby hadn't happened, as if he hadn't been having an affair with his assistant. I had no idea who this man was standing in front of me. It certainly wasn't the man I thought I'd married.

I shook my head. 'You go to New York, James. You and India. I'm not going with you. Not after this.'

'What about the cottage? I've found a buyer, and you've already organised the movers.'

'I don't care. I'm not going anywhere with you.'

'Where will you live?'

'I'll find somewhere.'

'You'll regret this,' he warned.

'Perhaps. But I'm willing to take that risk.'

'You'll feel differently once you calm down.'

'Will I? My baby will still be dead, and my heartless prick of a husband will still be having an affair with his assistant. I can't see how any of that will change.'

'It's obvious that now isn't the best time to try and talk some sense into you.' He waited for a response, and when there was none, said, 'You never used to be this stubborn.'

'You mean, I usually came around to your way of thinking? Not this time, James.'

I picked up my bags and rushed down to the street, slowing my pace when I saw India resting her pert little bottom against the waiting taxi as she concentrated on her phone. I didn't stop until I was safely around the corner, where I leaned against a wall until I could breathe again.

My phone was ringing – I could feel it vibrating through the leather of my bag against my leg. Pulling it out, I saw five missed calls from Mum. I called her immediately.

'Oh, thank goodness I've got hold of you,' she said.

'What's wrong? Where are you?'

'We're at the hospital, Max darling. It's Horrie. He's had a fall and they need to operate. Can you come home? Please hurry. He's been taken to Gloucester.'

'I'm in London, Mum, but I'm heading to the train now. I'll be there as soon as I can.'

Mum rushed to hug me when I ran into the hospital waiting room a few hours later. 'Oh, darling, I'm glad you're here,' she cried.

'Thanks for coming back, love,' said Dad, who'd been trying to coax a cup of dreadful tea from the vending machine. He stood between us and hugged us both.

I stepped back and dried my eyes with the sleeve of my light cardigan. 'What happened?'

'He was working in the allotment, digging up some new potatoes, I think, and he had a fall. Justin Taylor found him and called for the ambulance, then called us. It's probably his knee – you know how long he's been complaining about it. He's having some scans and things now, so we should know soon.'

'Where's Lucy?' I asked.

'Justin took her back to Horrie's,' Dad said.

'Good. Now that I'm here, why don't you take a walk to the cafeteria and see if you can get us some real tea?' I suggested to him.

He nodded and smiled weakly. 'Good idea. I just didn't want to leave your mother.'

'I know, Dad.' I patted his arm and sat beside my mother to wait.

'Did Richie get away alright?' Mum asked after a

few minutes of silence.

'I suppose so.' The worry over Horrie had put Richie's departure into perspective for me and I was able to tell Mum about it without any tears. 'It was a bit of an anti-climax in the end. We didn't even really say goodbye – not properly. And then he was gone, so quickly.'

'Maybe he couldn't say goodbye,' Mum suggested quietly.

I remembered the look on Richie's face that day in the woods, the tears in his eyes. I remembered the bluebells he'd left for me this morning. Was it only this morning?

Dad joined us and handed out watery tea and plain biscuits in little plastic wrappers. I didn't think any of us were hungry, but it gave us something to do.

'Your mother said you were in London when we called?' Dad asked.

'Yeah, I'd gone up to see James. I've left him.'

Mum rubbed my arm in comfort. 'I'm sure it's not as bad as all that.'

'I know you've always said not to walk away from something just because it's hard, but there are some things you just can't stay around for. You know, deal-breakers.' I swallowed hard as I tried to keep the tears from my eyes.

Dad patted my hand. 'And I take it James broke the deal?'

I nodded and told them about how I'd gone to London to surprise him, and ended up being surprised myself. 'We've been arguing a lot lately, and he's been working so hard, so I thought I'd go to him for a change.'

'Do you think he's been having an affair with India?' Mum asked.

I nodded.

'Did he deny it?'

'He said I was over-reacting, but he didn't deny it.'

'I see.'

There was something in Mum's tone that made me turn my head to look at her. 'You knew, didn't you?'

'Let's say that I'm not surprised.'

'I thought you liked James.'

'I did … I do … but there's something about him that makes those of us around him feel … well, ordinary.'

I searched her face, but she wasn't giving anything else away.

Dad collected our empty teacups and went looking for a bin. While he was gone I told my mother the rest of it.

'He said he didn't want children and that he's never wanted children.' I lifted my head from my knees and turned to face her. 'How do you fall in love with someone, marry them, make plans for the future and forget to tell them something like that?'

'What would he have done if you hadn't lost the baby?'

I shrugged. 'I asked him that. While he didn't actually say it, he hinted that it would have been early enough to do something about the situation. He said something about how now it had happened, we could get on with our life.' I paused and sighed. 'So I won't be going to New York with him.'

It was the weirdest situation. My marriage had died and I felt ... nothing.

Mum nodded. 'I see.'

'I was standing there listening to him go on about how nappies and noise didn't fit into our life, and I remembered all the times he'd say things like, "But that's not who we are, Maxine", and it hit me that we were living James's idea of what our marriage should be – not mine. The thing is, I can't fit into his idea of what a wife should be and look like and act like. He talks about shopping and lunches and dressing up and brands, and I don't care about any of that stuff. I don't need any of it. I happen to like what I do now, even though there's not much money and I get my hands dirty. There's still part of me that wants to see more of the world, and I want to do something to combine the cooking and the gardening – but I also want to stop somewhere at some time and have babies with someone who wants to be a partner and not just a provider. James doesn't want any of that, and I don't want what he's offering. So I guess that's what you'd call a fundamental difference of opinion.

'Then there's India. Maybe that's why he was so nice to me after I lost the baby – once he'd got over the shock, of course – because he was out with her while I was miscarrying.'

At that point my father returned, bringing with him a doctor with a clipboard and a serious face.

'Mr and Mrs Donaldson,' he greeted my parents. 'And you must be Maxine, the granddaughter? I'm glad you're here too.'

'Do you have news?' Mum was clinging to Dad's arm.

'I'm afraid I do.'

Cancer.

'What can you do to treat it?' I asked.

The doctor shook his head. 'I'm sorry, it's too widespread to be operable. Any treatment now will be palliative in nature.'

Mum looked up from where she'd buried her head in Dad's chest. 'So there is treatment?'

'He's saying there isn't – aren't you?' I looked at the doctor, who nodded. 'He's saying that whatever they do now will be for pain relief.'

'That's right,' the doctor said, 'to make your grandfather more comfortable.'

I asked the question we were all thinking about. 'How long do we have?'

The doctor shook his head again. 'I'm sorry, we don't like to give definitive times, but we're probably talking weeks rather than months.'

Dad hugged Mum closer at the news. I stood there watching them, wishing I had someone to hold me up.

'I always knew Joe would get me one day, lass,' Horrie said when the doctor finally allowed us in to see him. Joe: Joe Dancer – cancer.

'So much for the bad knee, Horrie.' I attempted a watery smile.

'A lot of fuss about nothing,' he said. 'We all have to go sometime, and I've had a better innings than the average Australian opening batsman.'

Typical Horrie.

CHAPTER SIXTEEN

We stayed at the hospital until quite late, then Mum and Dad went back to Horrie's, and I went home. They were keeping him in hospital another few days to stabilise him, but had agreed he could come home after that for as long as the pain allowed.

Back home, I didn't even try to go to bed. Too much had happened, and I had this idea that I could dislodge the mass in my chest if I just kept moving. My husband, my best friend, and my grandfather. Even though Horrie was still alive and arguing with the nursing staff, it felt as though I'd lost all three of them in the space of twenty-four hours. Regardless of what had happened between James and me, there was no question of me leaving for New York now. Not now Horrie was sick. I owed it to him – and myself – to make the most of every day we had left.

Horrie had taught me everything he knew about gardening. I'd absorbed it in all the hours we'd worked together in the allotment, in his garden, in my parents' garden, in my garden. Soon after James and I moved back to Brookford, it was Horrie who'd told me about the job in the garden centre.

'It's not much, lass, but it'll keep you busy. You don't want to be cooped up in an office again.'

'I don't have any qualifications,' I'd argued.

'Maybe not, but you know your way around a veggie patch – and you know what to do with what comes out of one.' He was marking out the holes for cauliflower seedlings. 'The lad that runs it seems a good sort even though he's an incomer. He's from Australia, New Zealand, South Africa – one of those places that plays rugby. He seems to know his stuff though.' He'd smiled at me. 'You could do a lot worse.'

So I'd applied, Richie had hired me on the spot and we'd clicked immediately. Not only had the job introduced me to Richie, it had given me a creative outlet that had been missing in the years I'd worked in an office. The job grounded me, and showed me a way back into the village that I thought I'd lost when I'd moved to London. All of that was down to Horrie. I truly didn't know what I'd do without him.

Sometime close to morning I must have finally dozed off on the sofa. I was woken by the key in the door a few hours later.

'What on earth are you doing sleeping here?' asked James.

I stood up and stretched, still in yesterday's clothes.

He noticed and raised his eyebrows. 'Letting your

standards slip a little, aren't you, darling? Or didn't you come home last night?'

Two could play that game.

'How's India? Did she come for the drive? Or is she waiting for you at the flat?'

'You completely misread the situation, and then made it all more dramatic by storming out and turning your phone off. Hopefully you're over your sulk now and ready to talk about things maturely.'

'How did I misread anything? First of all, she has a key. Second of all, she waltzes in like she owns the place. Third of all, that kiss was aimed at your mouth. Fourth of all, she had champagne. Fifth of all, since when do you do picnics? Sixth of all … I've run out of fingers.'

'Yes, well, it might sound compromising,' he said. He lifted his chin and looked me straight at me. 'But there's a perfectly logical explanation. Which is more than I can say for you. Yesterday's clothes? Is that why you turned your phone off?'

I took a deep breath, suddenly tired of it all. 'My phone was off because I was at the hospital. I only turned it on to call you, but you weren't available … for a change.'

'Hospital? What was wrong? Not another miscarriage? At least this time I'd know for sure it couldn't be mine.'

His laugh had a cruel edge that I hadn't heard

before.

'No, James – it was Horrie. He had a fall, but that's not the problem.' I sat back down on the sofa. 'The thing is, he has cancer. It's everywhere and he doesn't have long.'

James sat heavily beside me, all the fight gone. 'Oh, I'm so sorry, darling.'

I didn't know what I'd expected from James, but after our argument yesterday it wasn't for him to put his arm around me and hold me. As I sobbed, I was crying for all of it: Horrie, my marriage, my baby, and Richie.

James let me cry for a couple of minutes, then listened as I told him what the doctor had said. 'You're saying there's nothing they can do? Not even radiation?'

'Apparently it's too advanced. It's why his knee has been so bad. They offered him radiation as a palliative option, but Horrie said he doesn't want his last weeks to be about tripping in and out of hospital.'

'But if it's going to give him longer?'

I shrugged. 'It's his decision and we have to respect that.'

He was silent for a few minutes and I saw him sneak a look at his watch. I wriggled out of his arms and went into the kitchen to turn the kettle on. He followed me.

'I suppose that means you'll need to delay your departure for New York until after … well, until after …'

'Until after he's gone? Really, James?'

He looked at the floor. 'Yes, I suppose that's what I meant.'

I watched him until he looked up at me. 'I told you yesterday that I'm not going with you,' I said softly. 'That hasn't changed.'

'I thought you were just angry about India and upset about the baby and maybe even Richie. I was sure you didn't mean it … You know you didn't mean it.' He stepped closer and reached for me. 'Give me a kiss, I'll say I'm sorry, and we'll start all over again.'

I pushed him away. 'There's nothing more to talk about. You said it all yesterday. It's obvious to me that you want India; and I want a family. There's a great big gap in our expectations.' I made a show of looking at my watch. 'Oh, look at the time. You'd better hit the road if you want to make it back in time for India. You can't pretend you were staying over – you have no bags. I'm guessing you'll get a text shortly that will have some reason why you need to run back to London and be on this evening's flight, which you're probably already booked on.'

He looked at his watch – as I knew he would – and then at his phone when a text came through.

'And there it is. It was India, wasn't it?'

He shook his head. 'I feel like I don't know you any more.'

I shrugged. 'That makes two of us.'

'Shall I text you when I arrive like I always do?'

'Suit yourself. I won't be waiting for it.'

He watched me a few seconds longer, then left.

I waited until I heard the front door shut before collapsing back onto the sofa and allowing the tears to flow again. These last few months had brought so many changes, yet somehow in the last twenty-four hours, my life as I knew it had imploded. In a few weeks' time, I'd be moving out of my home with no place to go and no job.

In the kitchen my phone alerted me to a new text. It was from Richie.

Hiya Hendo. I'm in Denmark. It's all sweet – hope you are too. PS you'd love it here. Change your mind about New York and come to Denmark instead? Yeah, I know – bad idea.

Before I had a chance to reply, another came through: *Miss you already ... R x*

'I miss you too,' I said to the phone.

I thought about telling him what had happened, but decided it wasn't a good idea. He was in Denmark, then he'd be heading home to New Zealand – he didn't need to be bothered about the chaos that was happening here.

Instead I kept it brief: *Change my mind? Stranger things have happened – be careful what you wish for!* I inserted a winky emoticon and pressed send.

Then I sent another: *Miss you already too ... M x*

•

I kept myself deliberately busy over the next few weeks. Blossoms & Buds closed and was handed over to the new owners. That suited me as it gave me more time to spend with Horrie – not that there was anything practical I could do for him.

Mum had moved into Horrie's cottage while he was still in hospital. Dad had made a quick dash down to Cornwall for clothes, but now he was back and staying there as well. Plus there was a constant stream of Horrie's 'girls' turning up with food and bustling about to make sure he was comfortable and had all he needed. Just as they'd done with their social outings, they seemed to have a roster for his ongoing care. Horrie never knew who would be visiting each day, but apparently they did. They also knew Horrie well enough to understand that he couldn't abide being fussed over and treated him as though nothing had changed.

The weather had been unusually and consistently fine, so Horrie managed to get out and about for a short walk most days – usually just to The Lamb with his form guide, or across to the allotment to make sure I was keeping the weeds down. I even let him order me about, but argued back often enough that he wouldn't think I was going soft on him.

In the first few weeks after the diagnosis we spoke once about arrangements.

'You'll have to take charge,' he said. 'Your mother will go to pieces, and your father will be kept busy picking up the pieces. You know she's always been one for tears.' I nodded. 'Leave the speeches for the after-party at the pub. Make sure they know it's not a wake – and don't let your father scrimp on the bar bill.'

Since then, by unspoken agreement, neither of us had brought up the subject of his illness.

The cottage had been sold, so every moment that I wasn't with Horrie or at the allotment I spent packing up my and James's things. When I was planning the New York move, I'd booked movers to take our furniture into storage. I saw no reason to change those plans. James and I hadn't discussed what was going to happen with our joint assets. It still felt weird even referring to our things as assets.

The closure of Blossoms might have left me with the time I needed to spend with Horrie, but it brought to light another issue: I had to find somewhere affordable to live and another source of income to pay for it. I had some small savings, and along with the severance and holiday pay from George, I'd have enough money for a couple of months' rent, but I'd need to get another job quickly.

I finally found a place to live a week or so before the movers were due – stumbling across it by accident just a couple of miles out of Brookford when I was walking the same path near Frampton Mansell that Richie and I had walked on that bluebell morning back in April. I would have missed the sign on the post if I hadn't almost fallen into it. Without hesitating I walked down the lane and knocked on the door of the farmhouse.

A fresh-faced woman of about my age answered, with a baby attached to her hip. A collie pushed past her and dropped a stick at my feet.

'Bella,' she scolded. 'Let the lady be. Can I help you?'

I reached down to pat the dog. 'I hope so – I'm interested in the cottage you have for rent.'

Her face brightened. 'You saw the sign then? I only put it up this morning.'

'I did. In fact, I was so busy watching the donkeys in the field, that I didn't see a hole in the road and virtually fell into the sign.'

She laughed and the baby on her hip laughed too. 'I knew the donkeys would bring the right person to us. Come with me and I'll show you the cottage. It's not much,' she warned, 'and the furnishing is very basic, but it's quiet, it's comfortable and nothing leaks.'

'Good to know.'

I bent to pick up the stick the collie had dropped and threw it as far as I could. The dog took off after it, running low, leaping the stone stiles easily.

'She'll do that all day,' the woman said. 'By the way, I'm Gracie and this here is Milo.' She indicated the baby. 'You've already met Bella.'

I smiled and held my hand out. 'Pleased to meet

you. I'm Maxine Henderson, but please call me Max.'

Gracie led the way up a short track to a single-level stone cottage. The front faced the track and had an outlook across the valley. The back shared the stone boundary fence and looked up a green hill dotted with sheep.

'They often come down to the fence,' Gracie said, seeing the direction of my gaze. 'And in just a few weeks this field will be dotted with buttercups. It's truly beautiful in the summer. The donkeys live just down the lane,' she pointed towards a small set of wooden stalls, 'but no matter how much they ask, they're only allowed one treat per day.'

I laughed. 'I'll remember that.'

The wooden gate squeaked as she pushed it open and led me to the back of the cottage.

'Welcome to Curlew Cottage,' she announced as she opened the door. 'My husband wanted to call it Badger's Drift, but that made me think of *Midsomer Murders* – and not in a good way!'

I giggled. 'I know exactly what you mean.' Stepping inside, I gasped. 'Oh, this is perfect!'

The back door led directly into a small but serviceable stone-floored kitchen and sitting area. Behind the kitchen was a bathroom with, wonder of all wonders, a separate bath and shower. As Gracie had warned, the furniture was basic: a plain timber table with six chairs in the centre of the kitchen; and a worn two-seater couch plus two single chairs and a television in the sitting area. A screened fireplace completed the space.

Off the sitting room was a narrow hall with a door leading into the overgrown enclosed garden in the middle, and a small bedroom off each side. Each bedroom contained a double bed, a wardrobe and a set of bedside tables and lamps. Nothing matched, everything was functional and I fell in love with it all at first sight. I closed my eyes briefly and imagined myself working in that kitchen, writing at the table, and even washing up with the view of the green valley just outside the window.

'Yes,' I said. 'This will do very nicely.'

Gracie watched as I took it all in. 'Do you think your husband will like it too?' she asked, her eyes dropping to my wedding ring.

'No. He absolutely won't.' At her look of concern I elaborated. 'It will be just me moving in, so what he thinks of it doesn't really matter.'

'I'm sorry.' She dropped her eyes and shifted the baby on her hip.

'Don't be,' I assured her. 'He's going to New York and I … well, I'm staying here.' I looked around the room one more time. 'How much are you asking?'

She named a monthly price that was below what I'd been expecting.

'I'll take it,' I said. 'When can I move in?'

Gracie and Milo beamed at me. 'As soon as you like. I know you walked here today,' Gracie added, 'but do you have transport?'

'Of sorts – I cycle or walk most places. It's a fairly easy ride from here into town.'

She nodded. 'I can get my Bill to help you move your things in if you like.'

'Thanks, but my parents are in Brookford at the moment so I'll ask them. I don't have very much that I need to bring with me.'

I signed the agreement that afternoon and made arrangements to call by the next day with the first month's rent.

Walking back into Brookford, I called in at The Lamb to see if Horrie was there. He was: at his usual table with the form guide and a pint in front of him, and Lucy stretched out near the empty fireplace.

'Hiya, Horrie.'

'Hiya yourself, lass. You look like you need a drink.'

Duncan was already pouring me one.

'Thanks.' I sank gratefully into a chair across from Horrie. 'I've been out walking near Frampton Mansell – and I found somewhere to live.'

'Oh aye?'

Duncan placed the pint in front of me. I thanked him and took a thirsty mouthful. 'It's a cottage on a farm just a few miles out of town. Curlew Cottage, they call it.'

'That'd be Bill and Gracie Forrest's place,' said Duncan. 'Nice couple. Originally from up north, I think. The farm was Bill's uncle's – you'd remember him, Horrie? Ken Forrest? Passed a few years back?'

Horrie nodded. 'You'll be right there, lass.'

'I think so.' I sipped thoughtfully at my beer. 'That's a place to live ticked off my list. Now I just need a new job.'

Summer in the Kitchen

They say that sunsets are a sign that endings can be beautiful. I'm trying very hard to remember that as I write my final newsletter for Blossoms & Buds. Those of you who are regulars will know that the garden centre has now closed. It will re-open in the middle of July under a new name with a whole new look and a new website. Sadly, I won't be a part of it. I'll be setting up my own blog in a new location someday soon. I'm not sure what it will look like yet, but if you want to be one of the first to know – after I do, of course – you can sign up at the linky thing at the bottom of this newsletter.

I thought I'd make this issue – our last – a bumper crop, so to speak, almost like a summer edition. So grab yourself a cold drink and settle back in the sun.

The first of the new potatoes were dug the other day – is there anything better than boiled new potatoes with lashings of fresh butter and chives scissored over the top? No, I don't think so either.

The asparagus that started to raise their heads above ground last month are now well and truly in season, and so *good – they need just the lightest of steams and really no accompaniment at all ... although I can't resist dipping them into butter or hollandaise or my goat's cheese dip.*

Speaking of which, this is one of the easiest dips you'll ever make. Just take a packet of goat's cheese – the one we get in the shop from Eastley is the perfect size at 250 grams – and mix in a few dollops of Greek yoghurt. Snip in whatever herbs you have lying around – parsley, chives or mint are all good. That's it. In the photo I've served it on a platter with baby carrots and the first of the season's red peppers, as well as some lightly steamed asparagus. Once you finish the veggies, you can spread the leftover dip on crusty bread.

If you're lucky enough to get your asparagus young and sprightly, you don't even need to cook them. Simply shave them using a vegetable peeler into a green salad. Dress the salad with a tangy lemon vinaigrette, or turn it into a one-bowl lunch by adding some smoked salmon.

There's something about all the green this month that lifts the spirits. It's the colour of new starts, new life, new cycles. The problem is, to have a beginning you need to have an ending. Another thing about beginnings is that we often don't notice them until we're in the middle of one. Take spring: it begins as a paint wash of sea-green over the trees as the new leaves begin to sprout, and continues with the first snappy peas of the year.

These baby peas, if they make it to the stove (I love to sneak them straight from the pod), need to be boiled for just a few minutes. Toss them with some garlic, shallots and fried ham or prosciutto, add a squeeze of lemon juice, and you have a simple lunch, or a side to some grilled chicken. Take things one step further and mix through some pasta or creamy risotto and hey presto: supper is on the table. Stir in some fresh asparagus and you can even give it a romantic name like primavera. Just remember the lemon juice, zest and chopped herbs for the necessary zing.

If you only do one thing with this season's baby peas, make these fritters. They're the lightest, fluffiest fritters you'll ever taste. I don't know whether it's the addition of the baking powder or my secret ingredient (which after today won't be so secret) – super-cold soda water – that makes them puff up so beautifully. When it comes to herbs, use whatever soft herbs you have. I particularly love the combination of mint with lemon zest, but you might want to try parsley, or basil, or chervil. I especially enjoy these fritters for breakfast, but you can make tiny mouthful-sized ones for a summer garden party. Spoon on some of the goat's cheese dip from above, accessorise them with a sprig of watercress and you have the perfect canapé.

The full recipe is on the website. It's worth bookmarking as you can also use it next month when courgettes begin to come into season. You'll need about a cup of grated courgette instead of the peas – just make sure you squeeze all the liquid out before you add it to the fritter mix. I'm always surprised by how much liquid one courgette contains.

Come June there'll still be asparagus, but we'll also have aubergines, broccoli (calabrese and purple sprouting) and beetroot. And that's just taken us to 'B'. It's almost easier at this time of year to talk about what's not in season. (In case you're interested, that would be cauliflower, leeks, parsnips, turnips and squash.)

Still in the 'B's: beans – broad and green – will be ripe for the picking in June and at their best in July. I like nothing better than sneaking them fresh off the vine, but if they manage to make it into the kitchen, beans are so much more versatile than you'd think.

Try freshly steamed or lightly boiled green beans with strips of cooked chicken, a dollop of tapenade and a boiled egg for a chickeny version of a niçoise salad. I tend to boil a whole chicken when I'm making stock for the freezer, and keep the stripped meat in serving sizes in the freezer. Of course, you could just poach a breast or two.

As for broad beans? I'm sure my mother is the only mother in the history of England who didn't boil her broad beans until they were army green and tough as old boots. As a result, I'm a fan of these glorious nuggets of pure summer. There's no denying they're a little more labour-intensive than most other summer vegetables: unless you can pick them while they're still just toddlers, they will need podding after being quickly boiled. This can be quite a meditative activity, and your reward is that perfect summer green that doesn't exist at any other time of year. Try tossing them with some fried parma ham, shallots and garlic. If you have baby peas, throw those in too. Drizzle over virgin olive oil, serve with crusty bread and you have lunch or a light supper. For *a more substantial meal, combine it all with cooked pasta, some grated parmesan and a shake of dried chilli flakes for a spicy kick.*

To turn supper into a canapé, smash the podded beans with the back of a fork, add a generous squeeze of lemon juice, and spread onto excellent bread. Top with some feta if you feel like it. You could even serve this beany mash as a side dish instead of potatoes. Or dollop some butter onto them just as they are and serve with roast lamb.

For something sweet, why not try this tropical no-cook lemon slice? I'm not sure whether it's the tang of the lemon in the icing, or the coconut in the base, or perhaps the jewel-bright colours of the dried fruit in both, that make this taste like summer. Perhaps all of the above. The crushed biscuits, chopped fruit and coconut in the base are bound together with condensed milk and melted butter. Just make sure you don't take your eyes off the mixture while it's melting in the pan – it will catch on the bottom if neglected for even a nanosecond. Once all the ingredients are mixed together, press them into a lined tin and pop it into the fridge to set. Then ice it later.

If you want to spice it up a little, a few shakes of cinnamon or ginger into the biscuit crumbs would do the trick. As for fruit? I use mostly dried apricots, but like to mix it up with dried pineapple, mango or pawpaw – if I can get them. I haven't tried it myself, but I wouldn't be surprised if a touch of crystallised ginger (yes, I know it's difficult to source) didn't lift this even higher. The boss used to say it reminded him of slices his mother made when he was a boy growing up in New Zealand. That's the thing about food – it can take us to a moment, a place or a person in just one bite.

If I could have chosen any time of year to leave you, it would be now – with so much wonderful produce available, you don't need me to provide inspiration. Your garden's perfectly capable of doing that for you.

Until we meet again,

Max

CHAPTER SEVENTEEN

The weekend before the sale of the cottage was due to complete, James came up for the day to pack his clothes and the things he wanted to take to New York. When he walked in on Saturday morning, I was sitting on the living room floor wrapping ornaments into newspaper.

He bent to kiss the top of my head. 'How are you doing?'

'I'm fine.'

'You're looking good … a little pale perhaps, but nothing some makeup wouldn't fix.'

'Thanks,' I said sarcastically. In the weeks since we'd last seen each other I'd had barely a minute to think about my appearance. With so many practical things to take care of, it was no wonder I was looking tired.

'How's Horrie?'

I stopped wrapping. 'Hanging in there. He's a lot weaker, and getting more so by the day, but his spirits are still good.'

'How long do you think?'

'I don't know, James. How about I ask him how

long he intends hanging around for so you can have India plan your schedule accordingly?'

He paled at my candour. 'I'm sorry … I didn't mean it to sound that way.'

I shook my head and resumed wrapping.

He looked around the room. The cabinet I was emptying was the last one, and the floor was piled high with boxes, their contents all neatly labelled in thick black marker pen. He made no move to help me. As far as James was concerned, packing fell into that grey logistical territory that one hired help for – or wives looked after.

'Are you going to ask me how I am?' he said.

'No.'

'Well, I'm not great. I was expecting to take my wife to New York next week to start our new life there. This weekend I was planning to whisk her away to a luxury retreat where we could drink champagne and feed each other strawberries in a four-poster bed. Instead, I'm watching her wrap ornaments for storage boxes.'

'Something that would have to be done if I was going with you,' I pointed out. 'How did you think things were going to get packed? Or did your intention to be away for all that mean you didn't have to think about it?'

'Something like that,' he admitted. 'I thought you could get someone in to take care of it for you.'

'Of course you did.'

He walked through to the kitchen. I could hear him moving boxes to check the labels. 'Are you finished in here?' he called.

'Yes.'

He walked back to where I was. 'So when are you starting on upstairs?'

I looked up from the china horse I was attempting to secure against limb-break. It was a Beswick thoroughbred and I remembered James buying it for me at a little antique stall at Chepstow racecourse markets one rainy day soon after we first moved in here. We'd gone to the markets, then driven into Tintern for a roast lunch at one of the hotels. It seemed like something someone else had done in another lifetime.

'I'm done up there,' I said.

'Oh, good.'

'No, James, I don't think you heard me. *I'm* done. Your stuff still needs sorting and packing. Or not. Whatever's left will be left – if you get my drift.'

He looked confused.

'What I mean is, I'm not packing your clothes or your study.'

'But I thought that's why you wanted me to come this weekend – to take my stuff back. Either that or,' he gave me the sideways glance that used to have me melting into him, 'to tell me you've changed your mind and you're coming with me.'

I screwed up my nose. 'You were right the first

time. You were just wrong to assume that I'd have packed it for you.' I smiled sweetly at him.

'You mean …?'

'Yes, James, you need to do your own packing. Would you like me to call India for you?'

He opened his mouth to answer and thought better of it.

I finished wrapping the racehorse, placed it into the box and layered newspaper around it, then secured the lid with packing tape. I reached for the black marker and wrote *Max – living room*.

He watched me stand and wipe the newsprint from my hands. 'Are you finished down here?'

'Yes.'

'Good. Can you please come and help me upstairs? Who knows – maybe I can still change your mind?'

He waggled his eyebrows at me. I thought he intended the action to be suggestive, but it came across as comical.

'Nope, I'm all packed up, so I'm off to the pub for lunch. The house is yours – whatever you leave will be thrown out.'

I went to grab my handbag from the kitchen stool. He watched me with his mouth open.

'You're really intending to go through with this?'

I deliberately misunderstood. 'What do you mean? Do I intend going to the pub for lunch and leaving you here to take care of yourself for a change? Absolutely.'

'Darling,' he moved towards me and placed his hands gently on my shoulders, looking intently into my eyes, 'are you really continuing this pretence that you're not coming with me? I've told you that the thing you thought you saw with India and me was a misunderstanding. You've made me suffer enough, so how about we stop the game, I'll concede that you've won, and we can make up properly. What do you say?'

He lowered his mouth towards mine. I turned my head away and stepped out of his grasp.

'This isn't a game, James. I know what I saw between you and India, and I know how you feel about having a family. I want one and you don't. Even if I was prepared to turn a blind eye to the India thing, I can't ignore your attitude towards children – and I can't be with someone who treats losing our baby as something to get over and move on from. It wasn't a heavy period – it was a baby. So, no, James, I'm not going with you.'

'But what will you do? The new owners move in next week.'

'I know. I've rented a small cottage on a farm not far out of the village. It's very basic, but it has a kitchen, two tiny bedrooms and is fully furnished – sort of. It's all that I need. I moved in last weekend.'

He watched me with narrowed eyes. 'I'm not paying rent for you when you have a perfectly good apartment to move into with me.' There was a sneer to his voice. 'And don't think I'm releasing any of the sale proceeds to enable you to live away from me.'

'I'm not asking you to. I can manage.'

Behind my back my fingers were crossed. Duncan had taken some baking from me, and Hawthorne Hall had booked me to cater their open days over the next two weeks, but I needed more work and quickly.

James reached for me again, frowning when I resisted. 'I know it's been hard for you lately: you lost the baby, your parents moved away, and Horrie got sick. Plus you've lost your job – such as it was.' He paused, then added, 'I suppose Richie going away probably hasn't helped – I know you used to talk to him about these things. I might not have liked it, but I understand that women need someone to confide in – although I don't know why it couldn't have been one of your girlfriends.' He smiled encouragingly at me. 'In any case, I recognise that you're not as far along the change curve as I am, so it's not fair for me to expect you to pack up and move to New York without giving you some time to absorb what it all means. Once you do, you'll understand that it's all for the best.'

'You forgot to mention that I caught my husband cheating on me with his assistant.'

'Christ Almighty, Maxine! Enough of that already!' James turned his back on me. I watched as he took a couple of deep breaths, then turned to face me again, the uncharacteristic slip from control hidden, the

charming James veneer back. 'We've been through that,
darling. She means so little to me that I'm prepared to
fire her if you'll agree to stop this nonsense.' He gave
me the lop-sided smile that always used to win me over.
'And you know how hard it is to get good help.'

I shook my head sadly. 'I don't think so, James.
You go enjoy New York, soak it up, make the most of
your promotion and the opportunity. But I'm sorry, it's
just not for me.'

We stared at each other for what seemed an age,
but was probably only a few seconds.

Then he nodded and reached for me. 'I understand
… I think. I hurt you, and I can't take that back.' I
burrowed into his chest as my tears began to flow. 'I
love you, Maxine – I think I always will.'

I nodded, but couldn't say it back. 'I know.'

'Maybe … after we've had a break, after you've
had some space …?'

'I don't think so, James.' I pushed myself away
from him and wiped my face with the back of my
hand. 'I'll leave you to it.'

The new owners of our cottage – Janey and Alastair
– had moved in last weekend. I'd taken them some
welcome-to-Brookford brownies. They seemed nice,
almost like James and I were when we first moved in.
Almost like James and I would have been if we'd had
the baby. Alastair worked in the city, commuting by

train each day, and Janey was a stay-at-home mum to a young baby.

'This cottage is like our dream come true,' she'd enthused. 'We always said we wanted something like this to bring our children up in. We'd never have been able to afford to buy in London – you should have seen the size of the flat we were squeezing into!'

Alastair had put his arm around her shoulders. 'Janey's a keen gardener and you've done so much with this one.'

'Thank you,' I said. 'It's small, but you'd be amazed what you can produce from it.'

'Come in,' Janey had offered. 'I was about to put the kettle on. We must thank you for the folder you left us too.'

I'd put together an assortment of brochures and phone numbers that I'd thought could be useful: places to eat, walks to do, reliable tradesmen, that sort of thing. I'd thanked them, made some excuse about needing to be somewhere and left them to it. I'd loved that cottage, but that part of my life was over.

My grandfather was surveying his patch from one of the chairs outside his shed when I called by the allotment a few days later. Lucy was flopped beside him enjoying the sun.

'Hiya, Horrie,' I said.

'Hiya yourself, lass.' He offered me a papery cheek to kiss.

I bent to pat Lucy's head. 'Not working today? Those PSBs look like they're about to grow legs and sprint across the fields, and there are peas that need picking.'

'Aye, lass, that's what I've got you for.' He patted my hand. 'My knees aren't the best today so I'm going to sit right here, drink tea and let you do the heavy lifting.'

We went through much the same act each day – both of us pretending that tomorrow his knees would be better and he'd be able to help me work his patch.

He gave me a fond smile. 'Sit and have some tea before you start.' He offered me his thermos and the lid as a cup, then said, 'Now, have you heard from that young man of yours?'

'No, James is in New York. I haven't heard from him in two weeks – not since the cottage completed.'

Horrie frowned at me. 'That wasn't the young man I was talking about, and you know it.'

His gaze was keen and I squirmed under its intensity. 'Richie's going well. I heard from him last week. He's in Denmark with a friend of his working on … I don't know – I guess you'd call it a fancy allotment.' I put my tea down on the ground and ducked into the shed to get my gloves and a knife for the broccoli, raising my voice slightly so he could hear me. 'It's apparently about permaculture and sustainability. Sounds interesting. A lot of it's based on traditional techniques and companion planting – much like what we do here. It's just got a technical name over there.'

Horrie waited until I was outside again before asking, 'Will he be coming back anytime soon?'

I didn't look at him as I shook my head. 'No, he's gone.'

'I see.' He rubbed his whiskery chin in the same way he did when deciding between horses in a race. 'Maybe it's about time you saw a bit of the world too, lass?'

'Some day I will – perhaps when I've got my business up and running.' I sat down on the chair beside him, and ruffled Lucy's head. 'I can't see it happening anytime soon though.'

He nodded. 'I hope that's not regret I hear. You're not having second thoughts about not going with James?'

'God, no! We need to sort things out, of course, but he's refusing to talk about it – he won't even talk to me. He emailed and said he's giving me some space and money to get "this ridiculous independence"' – I used my fingers to make air quotes – 'out of my system. I think he thinks once I've done that I'll come back to him. It's sad, but it's over. The cottage is tiny, but cute in its own way. There are sheep in the paddock outside my bedroom window, and donkeys down the lane.'

Despite his words of the other week, James had deposited some of the settlement proceeds into my account. I was determined not to touch a penny.

'And work?'

'Blossoms is closed.' I could feel his sharp blue eyes on me as I stood and picked up the basket containing my gloves and knife. 'They'll reopen in a few weeks, I suppose. Maybe a month or so.'

'Bloody stupid idea that, closing in the middle of summer. The new owners must have more money than sense.'

I smiled. 'That's what Richie told them too. He suggested they wait until October, then reopen just before Christmas.'

Horrie nodded. 'He's a smart one. Are you keeping busy?'

'I sure am. I did cakes and muffins for Hawthorne Hall last weekend for their spring garden opening. I didn't want to commit to too much until I'd finished at Blossoms & Buds, but I've also spoken to Duncan about some regular orders for the pub, and Ivy from the teashop in town is taking muffins twice a week.'

My reluctance to commit to too many regular baking deliveries right now was all about being there for Horrie – not that he needed to know that. I was a long way off making an independent income – or even deciding how I would go about making an independent income – but I was getting there, and had plenty of ideas whirring about in my head.

'That sounds grand, lass, but I think you should take some time to have a holiday away from here.'

He didn't say it, but we both knew that he meant when he was gone.

'Oh, I don't know, Horrie. I wouldn't know where to go.' Especially considering the budget I was now working within. 'Maybe I could spend some time down at the sea with Mum and Dad.'

'What about Denmark? I'm sure that young man of yours could pull some strings and get you a room and some work?' His face was innocent, but his eyes were anything but.

'Maybe. Enough talk of holidays, Horrie. You might have nothing better to do, but these vegetables aren't going to pick themselves. Are you here for a while longer, or do you want me to drop them around when I'm done?'

He smiled back at me. 'You carry on, lass. Lucy and I'll sit here for a bit and enjoy the sun.'

I busied myself with the vegetables and pulling at a few weeds, glancing across at Horrie from time to time. Although I'd worked the patch most days over the past month, the fine weather was bringing the weeds out faster than I could get rid of them. I'd planned to start working on some recipe card ideas tomorrow, but decided to spend a few hours here instead, getting it all back under control. The parsley was just days away from bolting to seed.

Out of the corner of my eye I saw Horrie lever himself slowly from his chair, and then heard rather than saw him fall heavily.

'Horrie!' Dropping the basket, I ran across to where he lay, Lucy whining and licking at his face.

'Better call for someone, lass,' he managed. 'I heard something snap.'

I checked him over quickly. His right leg was at a strange angle – I assumed that was what he'd heard. 'You stay there while I call the ambulance and Mum.'

'I wasn't planning on going anywhere real soon.' His attempt at a smile turned into a grimace of pain.

Mum and Dad arrived almost at the same time as the paramedics did. We watched as they lifted Horrie onto a stretcher and into the back of the ambulance.

'Who wants to come with us?' one of them asked.

'My mother will,' I told them, then said to Dad, 'I'll take Lucy home and get her settled. I'll see you at the hospital.' I leaned into the ambulance. 'Hold on, Horrie.'

Horrie passed away on the operating table that night. An aneurism, they said. Whatever it was, he was gone.

I knew as soon as I saw the expression on the doctor's face. 'I'm sorry,' he said. A wave of white noise filled my head, drowning out everything else and deafening me to whatever more the doctor had to say. I thanked him and waved him away. As I watched him leave us, I gradually became aware again of the sounds of the hospital – unchanged from just a few minutes ago. How could anything be the same now that Horrie was gone?

From somewhere behind me I could hear my mother sobbing, and looked around to see Dad holding her tightly. He raised his head and opened an arm to me. I rushed into it and the three of us – Mum and Dad and I – clung to each other and cried for Horrie.

CHAPTER EIGHTEEN

The next few days were full of arrangements. As Horrie had asked, I took care of most of the practicalities. Although he had pre-planned and pre-paid his funeral, there was still a lot to do and people to tell. Horrie had moved to Brookford soon after my grandmother died – when I was a toddler – so everyone knew him and wanted to bring comfort to us. Mostly that comfort consisted of casseroles and lasagnes – the fridge was overflowing. I left my parents to deal with the kindness while I got on with the arrangements.

I posted a message on Facebook advising details of the funeral, and emailed James to tell him the same. I received a quick note back sending sympathy for our loss and regret that work commitments sadly meant he'd be unable to attend. I hadn't really expected him to anyway. Not that his absence was noticed: it seemed as though most of the village had come out for the funeral, as well as publicans and bookmakers from neighbouring villages.

Dad supported Mum as we walked up the aisle to

our pew at the front of the church. Through staying busy I'd somehow managed to hold it together over the last few days, but could feel my control teetering with every step I took towards the coffin. Any slight concern for my wellbeing was likely to tip me over, and I didn't want that to happen until after I'd got through the speeches, and preferably not until I was back in the privacy of my cottage.

As Horrie had requested, the formalities were over as quickly as these things could be over. I sat dry-eyed throughout, Dad weeping quietly beside me on one side, Mum sobbing on the other.

Back at The Lamb for the after-party, I took my place at the bar and tapped an empty glass to get everyone's attention. That's when I saw him – Richie – leaning against the fireplace, a pint glass in his hand. With a sad smile he tilted the glass in my direction. I smiled weakly and the emotion I'd been swallowing back all day rose from my chest and into my throat in one solid lump. I lightly touched the base of my throat, almost as if I could feel it there. I couldn't take my eyes off him for fear that he wouldn't be there if I looked away. He shook his head slightly and raised his eyebrows in encouragement for me to continue.

I took a deep breath, cleared my throat and fought to control the quiver in my voice. 'Horrie loved this village and everyone in it. He would have been especially happy with the turnout – all of you mattered to him.'

At a table near the front of the bar, Mum wiped away a tear. Dad pulled her close to him. Lucy lay at Mum's feet, her head facing towards the door – just in case Horrie walked through it. Five elderly women sat around one table – Horrie's 'girls'. The 'boys' from the allotment were at a noisier table, and scattered throughout the room were Horrie's friends from the village, Dad's business partners, and friends of our family – all there to offer support and condolence.

I took a breath and continued. 'Horrie had today all planned. "Do what you need to do at the church," he said. "Sing whatever songs your mother thinks right, but I don't want any of them collared buggers saying anything about me – I didn't spend enough time in there to know any of them. Save the words for when people have a pint in their hands, and don't let anyone get maudlin. I don't want any of that rubbish."' By now the tears were flowing freely down my cheeks. I didn't try to stop them. 'So, there won't be any of that maudlin rubbish.' I swallowed hard. 'Duncan, can you get me a beer, please?'

'I've already got one poured for you, lass,' he replied.

I smiled my thanks and held my glass up. 'All that's left to do is raise a pint to wish Horrie on his way, and be thankful that we all had the privilege to know and love him. Life around here won't be the same without him – although I will be able to plant out my veggies without him telling me what I'm doing wrong.' There was a ripple of laughter. 'I'll miss him being right about that. To Horrie.'

'Aye, to Horrie,' the gathering repeated after me.

'That was a nice speech, lass,' Duncan said, the Scottish accent he'd never quite lost even more pronounced in this moment. 'Your grandfather would have been proud of that send-off.'

'Thanks, Duncan,' I managed. 'I'm glad it's over.'

Richie came over, put his glass down on the bar towel and swung an arm around me, squeezing me into his side.

'You came,' I said, looking up into his face through increasingly blurry eyes.

He kissed the top of my head. 'Of course I came – how could I not? But why didn't you tell me he was sick?'

I shrugged and shook my head at the same time.

'Maxi?'

'It happened the day you left – the diagnosis. I couldn't tell you.'

He didn't say anything to that, just squeezed me tighter. I didn't want the one-arm cuddle; I needed him to hold me, properly hold me, to make me believe that everything could be alright – even though I knew it wouldn't be just yet, and even though I knew he couldn't hold me like that in here.

'I can't believe that the next time I come in here he

won't be sitting over there in that corner with Lucy at his feet, sipping at a pint and reading the form guide. It's all been too quick.' My voice broke. 'Surely it's supposed to take longer? I'm not ready for him not to be here.'

'True, but you wouldn't have wanted him to hold on either. Horrie wouldn't have wanted that. He's gone the way he would've wanted to go – quickly, but still with time to order everybody about.'

'I guess. It's just that I'm …' I struggled with the words, 'I'm going to miss him.' I rubbed at my eyes. 'I wish he was still here.'

'Yeah, I know. We'll all miss him. Your grandfather was quite the character.' He gave my shoulders another reassuring squeeze. 'No James today?'

'No – he couldn't get away.'

'What could be so important that he couldn't make it to Horrie's funeral?'

'Horrie liked to think of it as his after-party,' I corrected. 'James is busy with work.'

'Isn't he always?'

The comment didn't need a response. 'How did you know to come?' I asked instead.

'Facebook. I missed your first post saying he'd died, but saw the second with the details for the funeral, so I booked a flight back. It was touch and go whether I'd make it, but I knew I had to try.' His eyes were gentle and I felt mine filling again. 'Not just to say goodbye to Horrie, but for your sake too.'

'I'm glad you're here,' I managed. Seeing him felt as though some of the burden I'd been carrying had been lifted away.

The next couple of hours passed in a whirl of greetings and remember-whens. Eventually, late in the afternoon, people began to drift away. Soon there were just my parents, Richie and me left. I slumped into a chair in the sun and kicked my shoes off, then pulled another chair over and rested my sore feet on it.

'Really, Max?' Mum said.

I shrugged one shoulder and tipped my head back, taking the opportunity to close my eyes for one brief minute.

'You're right,' she said, and did the same. 'It's been a long day.'

'It's been a long few days,' said Dad, delivering glasses of wine for Mum and me.

He and Richie sat beside us with their beers.

'Here's to Horrie,' toasted Richie. 'May he grow the best tomatoes they've ever seen in heaven.'

'To Horrie.' We raised our glasses skywards and I finally lost the control I'd been clinging to all day. It left my body in a rush of noisy, sloshy sobs.

Mum reached across the table and held my hands. Richie put his arm around me, holding me until I had no sobs left.

'God, I'm so sorry,' I managed, pulling away from Richie and grabbing at napkins to mop up my tears. 'I must look awful.'

'She had to break at some stage,' Mum told Richie. 'She's held it together so tightly over the last six or seven weeks. So much has happened since you left: first there was that business with James; then Horrie's diagnosis; selling and packing up the house – and you know what she's like with putting things away.'

Richie grinned at that. 'Don't I just. I remember the state of her desk – and her car. And I've never known a messier cook.'

'Exactly,' nodded Mum. 'Then she had to find and move into another cottage; and finish up at work. Since Horrie passed, she's been madly busy organising everything. There's been so much happening and she's just kept going.'

'She does that,' commented Dad.

'Why not just talk about me as if I'm not here?' I scowled at them through swollen eyes. 'I'll go clean myself up so feel free to talk about me to your hearts' content.'

As I stalked off in the direction of the bathroom I thought I heard Richie chuckle. By the time I got back, Mum and Dad were preparing to go.

'We'll leave you two to catch up,' said Mum. 'How long are you here for, Richie?'

'I haven't decided yet.'

'Well, I'm sure Max is glad to see you. Where are you staying?'

'I'm afraid I haven't thought of that yet either. I flew in early this morning and drove straight up.' He shrugged. 'It'll be fine. I'll grab a room for a couple of nights here at The Lamb.'

'You don't have to do that. You can stay at mine – I have a spare bedroom,' I said. I saw the look on Mum's face. 'I don't care if there's gossip. I'm sure you took the opportunity of me being in the bathroom to tell him about James and me. The whole village knows that I've rented a cottage and haven't gone to New York with James.'

The look on Mum's face was innocence, but Dad had the grace to look embarrassed. 'We didn't know you hadn't told him, love.'

'Do you need us to drive you to the solicitor's tomorrow?' Mum asked me, but she looked to Richie for a response.

'I'll make sure she gets there, Claire,' he said.

'Are you sure it's okay if I stay?' he asked once they'd left.

'Of course it is. I'll be glad of the company. Plus, I'm assuming you have a rental car, which means I'll also be glad of the transport – you can drive me home tonight and into Cheltenham tomorrow for the will business.' I added a cheeky grin in an attempt to break some of the weird tension between us since I'd extended the invitation; or was it since he'd found out about James and me? 'I'm warning you, though, the cottage is pretty basic.'

'I'm sure I can manage. But what happened with –'

I shook my head and gathered my shoes from where they'd landed when I'd kicked them off. 'I'll tell you when we get home. That story needs wine – and food.'

CHAPTER NINETEEN

Although it felt as though the day had lasted forever, it was only around six when Richie drove us down the track that led to my new home, for now. The sun was shining on the sheep grazing behind the old stone cottage.

'Very cute, Hendo,' he said as I unlocked the door. 'But if you're relying on that bike of yours to get around, I reckon you're lucky it's been dry.'

'I know. I'll need to buy a car before autumn.' I shrugged. 'I guess it depends on where I end up settling. I took this place originally because it was available – and furnished … of sorts.' I swept my arm out towards the old wooden table and chairs in the kitchen, and the rather battered sofa and mis-matched lounge chairs around the fire and television. I'd attempted to pretty them up by throwing quilts and cushions over them, but there was no disguising their age. 'The bathroom is there behind the kitchen, and the bedrooms are behind the sitting room. It's tiny and thrown together, but I fell in love with it.'

'As I said, it's cute in a boho kind of way – and actually,' Richie grinned, 'very you.'

'I'm glad you're here,' I said, emotion suddenly getting the better of me again.

He wrapped his arms around me, holding me so tightly it felt as though I was breathing through him; as if he was drawing the pain of the past weeks from me and taking some of it for himself. I snuggled closer, feeling his warmth, the strength in his broad chest, the hardness of his body steadying and supporting me. I drew back a little and looked up into his face, surprising a look of such intensity it almost made me gasp aloud. But then it was gone, I was out of his arms and wondering whether I'd imagined it.

'Yes, well, the spare bedroom is there – you'll need to put some sheets on the bed. There's beer and wine in the fridge, so make yourself at home. I need a bath to soak the day away and then I'll make us some dinner.' My words were rambling as I attempted to fill the space between us.

'There's no need for you to cook,' he said. 'I'll duck into town and get some Chinese or something.'

'Thanks, but I'd prefer to cook. I have courgettes, broad beans and salad leaves from the allotment and some herbs from the garden here. It feels right to cook them tonight to eat with you – a little celebration of Horrie.'

He watched my face for a second, then nodded

in understanding. 'You go have a bath. I'll make the bed up, get changed and maybe introduce myself to the sheep next door.'

I smiled. 'You'll find some donkeys down the lane, and some carrots in the fridge. No matter what they try and tell you, they're only allowed one each.'

Richie had a glass of white wine poured for me when I emerged from the bathroom thirty minutes later. He'd changed out of his suit into a more Richie-like pair of shorts and loose-fitting tee-shirt. I'd shed the black shift dress I'd worn for the funeral for a pair of denim shorts and a singlet. The foamy water had worked its magic and I was already feeling better. Or maybe it was having Richie here?

'What are we eating?' he asked. He was leaning against the open back door, the warm breeze filling the cottage with fresh air.

'I was thinking the broad beans smashed with some feta on that sourdough in the bread basket. And I'll grate the courgettes into some fritters to have with the salad. I know there's no meat, but I'm not sure my tummy can take it today.'

I didn't know why I was apologising.

'It's fine, Maxi. In fact, it sounds great. What can I do to help?'

I handed him the courgettes and a grater. 'You can get started on these – I'll need to rest them for a bit in a tea towel to get the moisture out. I'll get going on the beans.'

We worked together easily, Richie filling me in on what he'd been doing in Denmark.

'It's fascinating,' he said. 'I'm learning so much – not just about working with the seasons and the cycles, but also the landscape. You just don't realise how often we try to change the landscape to fit the design, but this is about making the design fit the landscape. It's also about sustainability and organics, all those things. We're not just looking at companion planting, but also planting with the phases and cycles of the Moon.' At my instruction he wrapped the grated courgettes in a clean tea towel and wrung it out tightly, the green liquid draining into the sink. 'It's funny, but at its essence, what we're doing is planting and designing the way they used to do it – before we decided to play god with the seasons.'

He paused to pour us each another glass of wine.

'And this planting by the Moon thing – it really works. You plant things that grow below the ground during a waning cycle, and things above during a waxing cycle. Of course there's more to it than that – and some stuff about astrological signs – but it all makes sense. You can take it further into the food-as-medicine thing too, but that would be more your thing. I'm trying to limit myself to the design concepts.'

'It really does sound like something I'd find interesting,' I said as I mixed the last of the feta I'd snaffled from Blossoms with the double-podded and roughly smashed broad beans, and dolloped it onto the toasted sourdough. 'Ready to eat?'

The broad beans were like spring on a plate, and the fritters puffed up beautifully. We ate them with a dollop of crème fraîche and some lightly dressed salad leaves.

'That was fabulous,' Richie said, pushing away his plate.

'They don't feed you in Denmark?' I grinned to let him know I was fishing for more compliments.

'Not like that!' He sat back in his chair and grinned at me. 'At one of the pubs in town we get these open sandwiches called smørrebrød. Mostly they're done on rye sourdough with a variety of toppings: smoked salmon, roast meats, cold cuts, perhaps some herring or eel.'

I screwed my nose up at the mention of eel.

'Okay, perhaps not eel. Then you add toppings like horseradish, lemon, dill, remoulade, onion …It's good, but man, I've missed your cooking.'

I cast my rod back in. 'Is that all you missed?'

'No, Hendo, I've missed this too – you and me: talking, eating, working together.'

'Yeah, me too.'

Our eyes met and it felt different to how it always used to. It felt like it had in the bluebells, and when I was in his arms before. To break the weirdness I packed the plates into the sink.

'Okay,' he declared, filling our glasses. 'No more putting it off – what happened between you and James?'

'I'll do the washing up first.'

He shook his head in warning. 'No, you won't. I'll do it later. Why didn't you tell me?'

I didn't pretend to misunderstand. 'The answer to that is the same as the answer to the why didn't I tell you about Horrie question – it all happened that Saturday you went away.'

'Oh, Maxi ...'

I waved his sympathy away. 'You know how I was intending on surprising him?' He nodded. 'It didn't go well.' I told him about how Jeremy had cancelled dinner, and how James had said he couldn't put the others off because some of them had arranged time away from wives and babies, and how lucky he was that he'd dodged that bullet. 'That's when he told me that not only had he not wanted that baby, but he didn't want children at all. "No noise and no nappies," was what he said.'

'And it hadn't occurred to him to tell you this before?' Richie asked.

'No. We'd talked about children, of course. In the early days we even threw around names. He wanted Miles, Preston or Sebastian for a boy and Phoebe or Pandora for a girl. I wanted Casey for either. He never talked about not wanting children at all. When I asked him about that, he said he'd thought he might change his mind. Maybe what he really meant was that he'd hoped I would.' I sighed heavily. 'And that's when India let herself into the flat, looking gorgeous and waving around a bottle of French champagne – apparently their favourite – for the picnic they'd planned that afternoon.'

Richie raised his eyebrows and leaned forward in his seat, but made no comment.

'He tried telling me that they were starting with a picnic at Primrose Hill because the weather was so good, and that of course India was invited because she was one of the team.'

'But you don't think there was ever any boys' thing,' he guessed.

'No. That picnic basket was for two – and James doesn't even like picnics. Every time I suggested one he'd complain about peasant food and ants and sitting on blankets. Maybe it's different with a basket from Harrods, French champagne and India.'

'I'd choose your bacon and egg pie any day over a Harrods hamper,' Richie said loyally.

I reached over and patted his hand. 'See, that's why we're friends. She had a key, and after she'd let herself in she kissed him. It would have been on the mouth – properly – if he hadn't moved his head. I'm sure he would have kissed her back if I hadn't been there. When she saw me, she was all, "Oh, I didn't know you were dropping by," as if I was visiting them at their house, rather than her visiting my husband at our flat.' I drained my glass. 'That's when I told him I wasn't going with him.'

I paused as Richie topped our glasses up.

'I got the call about Horrie as I left to come home.' I took a deep breath. 'So you see, that's why I couldn't tell you – it was too much. I didn't know where to start. But even though James and I are finished and I'm living here on my own, it feels like there are more doors opening than closing – if that makes sense. Wow!' I let out an embarrassed laugh and held up my glass. 'How much of this have I had? It's obviously gone straight to my head – or I must be more tired than I thought. In any case, the experience has taught me one thing.'

Richie didn't laugh at me. 'What's that?'

'I'm never going to put my life, my dreams, my goals – call them what you will – on hold for any man ever again. And if he really loves me, he won't ask me to. He'll be happy to work with me or around me, but not over the top of me.'

'But what if you want to change your goals to fit in with someone?'

I tilted my head to prompt him to continue.

'Not change so much, as adapt or vary?' he said. 'I don't know … I guess what I'm asking is, what if you choose to change your mind to be with someone you love?'

'Then it'll be my choice to make. Next time, I want someone beside me who's willing to partner with me, listen to me, support me – the same way I want to be beside them, partnering them and listening to what they want and helping them get there.'

He was silent for a few seconds as he contemplated this.

'Aren't you going to ask me?' I prompted him. 'The what-happens-next question?'

'Do you know?' he asked simply.

'No.'

'Well, there's no point asking then, is there?' He got up, walked around to where I was sitting and bent to kiss the top of my head. 'I don't know about you, but this has been a long day and I'm ready for bed – but I want to do these dishes first.'

I moved to help him, but he stopped me. 'You cooked, so let me clean this up.' He grinned as he looked at how I'd managed to fill every square inch of my tiny bench. 'At least some things don't change – you're still the messiest cook I've ever had the pleasure to know.'

I didn't think I'd be able to sleep, but listening to Richie moving about in the kitchen comforted rather than disturbed me. I slept more soundly than I had for months. When I finally emerged the next morning in the singlet and boxer-style shorts that passed for my pyjamas, he was already up and whisking eggs for omelettes.

'Sorry if I woke you,' he said.

'It's fine,' I replied, pouring a cup of tea and sitting down at the table, drawing one leg up so my chin was resting on the knee. I sipped my tea and watched him cook. It was nice to watch someone else in the kitchen. It was nice to have someone else in the house.

He must have felt my eyes on him and looked over from the stove and grinned.

'I was just thinking how sexy it is to watch a man with a pan.' Where did that come from?

'Wait till you taste this omelette.'

I laughed. 'I was also wondering how you managed to do all this without making a mess.'

'That, my dear, is about organisation. I did try to teach you, but failed dismally.' He reached for one of the plates he had ready and tipped a perfect omelette onto it. 'Ta-dah. You start on that while I cook mine. I'll put the toast on when we're done.'

'Hah! So you still can't multi-task!'

'No such thing,' he said, smiling at me.

We'd had this argument thousands of times before: I used it as an excuse for my messy desk, messy car and messy kitchen; he always said it was impossible to do more than one thing at a time and do it properly.

The omelette was good, and we chatted lightly as we ate. I'd always been one of those rare morning-type people – and so, it seemed, was Richie.

A few hours later he drove me into Cheltenham where I was meeting Mum and Dad at Horrie's solicitor's for the reading of the will.

When we finished, Richie was waiting for us outside, leaning against the white wall of the Regency building. Regardless of how he was dressed, Richie would never blend in, I thought. He was so tall, his shoulders so broad, and his eyes so blue against his tanned face and dark hair, you couldn't help but notice him. Unlike James, he wasn't classically handsome. Instead he was good-looking in a healthy I-spend-my-life-outside-and-smiling type of way. I watched as a group of girls walked past, giggling as they checked out the biceps visible under the sleeves of his tee-shirt. He smiled slowly as they passed and then noticed us. The smile grew wider as he straightened and rubbed his hands against his jeans.

'You okay?' he asked me.

I nodded. By unspoken agreement we left the updates until we'd taken seats in one of the restaurants off the high street and ordered drinks.

'How did it go?' he asked. 'Any surprises?'

'Yes and no. Horrie's financial affairs – such as they were – were up to date,' Dad answered.

'But he'd made some changes to his will in the last few weeks,' Mum jumped in. 'I always knew he was a canny old bugger, but I don't think I ever quite understood just how wise he was.'

'Horrie saw everything,' said Richie.

'I'm beginning to see that he did,' Mum agreed, her eyes locked with his.

There was an undercurrent there that I didn't understand.

'He must have driven Mr Braithwaite – he's the solicitor – mad trying to get it all written down the way he wanted it done,' I said. 'Take for instance … Where's my copy of the will?'

Richie grinned as I rummaged around in my backpack. 'Why don't you use a handbag like most women do?'

'Because,' I counted the reasons on my fingers, '(a) I'm not like most women; (b) I cycle most places and a backpack is handy; (c) I know where everything is; and (d) –'

Before the banter could turn into an argument, Dad stepped in. 'He'd always spoken of leaving the house jointly to Claire and Maxine, but he added conditions.'

'Like what?' Richie asked.

'The cottage is to remain empty as a home for Maxine, but if she chooses to make her home somewhere other than Brookford, it's to be sold and the proceeds split. It all makes perfect sense.'

Dad liked things to make sense – it appealed to his accountant's brain.

I found the paper I was searching for. 'Here we go.

I got his share in the allotment, and whatever I want from his little shed. The condition being that if I can't work the allotment, it's to go back to the cooperative for reallocation. He always said he wanted Justin Taylor to get it. The only really surprising thing was that he also left me the contents of his bank account – "the proceeds of my little flutters over the years".' I waved away the waiter who was hovering for food orders. None of us had even picked up a menu. 'There's over twenty thousand pounds in there!'

'Did you know old Horrie had that sort of money?'

I shook my head. 'Absolutely not.'

Mum reached across the table and patted my hand. 'Even from the grave he's making sure you have a home and a choice. He said the day before he died that it hurt him watching you going along with the preparations for New York even though you didn't want to go. The changes to his will were his way of ensuring you'd always have a backup plan. He wanted to leave you enough to take a trip now – to give you the time to work out for yourself what you want to do – and a place to call home to do it from once you do decide.'

I smiled and felt a prickling in my eyes.

Richie saw me swallow and reached for the menus. 'How about we put this poor waiter out of his misery and work out what we're eating?'

Once we'd ordered our meals, the conversation

moved to more general topics. I sat back and listened as Richie told my parents about the work he was doing in Denmark, and how he was thinking about using what he'd learnt in the family business when he went home. While he talked, another part of my brain was cultivating an idea that Horrie had planted there.

'My mate Brad – he's a landscape architect in Melbourne – is doing a fellowship through the university. We work and learn, and just have to pay a small amount for accommodation and meals.'

'How do you know Brad? Is he from New Zealand too?' Mum asked.

'No, he's an Aussie, but we met when we were both at uni in Sydney – same course, but he was a year ahead of me. A year or so before I came here, we did a similar summer fellowship to the one he's doing now. That one was in Europe too. Afterwards, he went home and started designing rooftop gardens for bars and doing some corporate work; and I travelled around some more, and landed in Brookford when I answered George's ad for a manager for the garden centre. I'd almost run out of money by then. The original idea was to stay for a year, replenish the bank account and then head home via Asia.'

'How long since you were last home?' Mum asked.

He thought for a minute. 'A while – it would have been Christmas two years ago, I suppose. I stopped off in Sydney and saw my sister Cate and her husband,

Harry; and then we all travelled over together to surprise Mum. Jess – she's the youngest of the three of us – was pissed off because she'd just bought her cafe and thought she was the one with the big news, and then I turned up and trumped her.' He laughed at the memory. 'Jess doesn't like being trumped – which made it all the more satisfying.'

'Cate's your older sister?'

'Yes – she and Harry live in the eastern suburbs.'

'We loved Sydney when we were there on the cruise, didn't we, Alan?'

'We certainly did –'

'Can I come?' I said to Richie, breaking into the conversation. 'To Denmark. Can I come back with you?' His face was showing surprise. 'It would just be for a couple of weeks … But it's okay if you don't want me to … I just thought –'

His mouth widened to a grin. 'Of course you can – it's a great idea. In fact, it's the best idea I've heard in ages!'

'It was Horrie's idea.' When everyone looked at me blankly, I explained. 'That last day, before he collapsed, we talked about it: about James, New York, my plans. He told me to see more of the world, and to take a holiday before I made any further decisions. He suggested I call Richie and ask if I could join him.'

Mum wiped a tear from her eyes. 'Of course it was Horrie's idea – and it's the best possible one. In fact, why don't you also –' She broke off, then said, 'No, forget it.'

The delivery of our food filled the awkward silence following Mum's half-spoken thought. I had a fairly good idea what she'd been going to say, and I suspected from the way Richie concentrated closely on his meal that he had a fairly good idea too. Dad, of course, was interested only in his lunch and hadn't picked up on anything.

Later in the car on the way home, I double-checked with Richie. 'It *is* okay, isn't it? Me coming back with you? Brad won't mind?'

He looked at me and grinned. 'It's more than okay, Hendo. You'll love it – and I think you'll really like Brad. Now, shut up about that already and tell me what you're cooking me tonight.'

CHAPTER TWENTY

Richie caught up with friends the next day, leaving me free to help Mum clean out Horrie's wardrobe. We'd decided to give it all to the charity shop – there was nothing we wanted to keep. Poor Lucy was bewildered. Everything smelled like Horrie, but Horrie wasn't coming home.

Mum had decided that the best thing for Lucy would be to take her back to Cornwall with them sooner rather than later. 'At least that way she'll have us and her things, but none of the smells that remind her of Horrie.'

I agreed. It was hard enough for us to deal with Horrie's absence, but for Lucy it must have been very confusing.

I'd given notice on my cottage and would move into Horrie's place when I got back from Denmark. There'd be plenty of time for cleaning out properly then. That meant, of course, that I also needed to pack up my cottage before I left and store everything at Horrie's. It felt as if I'd done little more than pack up all year. Richie made arrangements to stay and help me out so the two of us could fly to Denmark together.

I made one more decision that week – to hand back the allotment. If I was going to move forward, I needed to do so without hanging onto those kinds of ties. I'd have Horrie's cottage garden for when I needed to get my hands dirty, but it was time for someone else to take over his allotment patch. The cooperative had voted unanimously to follow Horrie's wishes and offer it to Justin Taylor. Justin had been hanging around helping the old boys out for years and was thrilled that now he'd have his own plot.

The day before we were due to leave, Richie announced we'd be cleaning out Horrie's shed. 'You can't put it off any longer, Hendo.'

'I know.'

The other thing I'd been putting off was emailing James.

'I'll go in early and get a start on the shed,' Richie said when I mentioned it, 'while you email James. You'll be sweet to cycle into town?'

Once he was gone, I deliberated for ages over what to say to James. In the end I just typed:

> *Dear James,*
> *Just to bring you up to date, Horrie's estate has been sorted. He left the house jointly to Mum and me, and also some cash. I'm going*

to use some of it to take a holiday – which brings me to my next point: I'm going to Denmark tomorrow for a couple of weeks. I haven't decided whether I'll come straight home after that or whether I'll spend another month or so having a look somewhere else. You know I always fancied going to Asia – this could be the best opportunity I have to do it.

I'll call you before I leave Denmark, just so you know what's happening and so we can talk about finalising everything else.

Fond regards,

Max x

I didn't wait for the reply.

As I opened the gate to the allotment, Justin was there to meet me. 'You have no idea what this means to me. The boys told me that you gave me your blessing – so, thank you.'

'You're very welcome.' I couldn't have wished for anyone better to continue working Horrie's garden.

'I asked Richie if he needed a hand, and he said everything's under control – but I'm here if he needs me.'

I forced a smile and made my way to Horrie's plot. Richie had cleaned off the potting table that stood outside the shed and placed on it pots and tools that were still okay for keeping but which Justin had said he didn't need – we'd agreed that we'd give him first refusal. Propped up against the table was a large cardboard sign that read *Free to good home*. Already a few of the 'boys' were rifling through the stuff. Richie was carrying an armful of rubbish to the bin when I arrived, and he grinned and continued on his way.

'There you are, lass,' said Tom. 'The lad said you'd be along. It's a sad day.'

'It sure is, Tom.'

The old man shook his head slowly. 'We had some good times around this shed. I was saying to Old Alan how this will always be known as Horrie's plot.' Tom screwed his eyes up as if he was looking into the future – or back in time. It was hard to tell.

'It sure will be,' I said.

'It'll do alright under Justin. He's still a bit green, but young enough to learn.'

I grinned. 'I'm sure he'd be pleased to hear it.'

Alan joined us. 'It's a sad day this one, girlie.'

'It sure is, Alan.'

'I was telling Old Tom before how this will always be Horrie's plot.'

'It sure will be.'

The two old men gathered armfuls of pots and assorted tools to take back to their own sheds. That was how it went here: one man's trash was another's treasure.

Richie was back. He ruffled my hair. 'It's done?'

'Yes.'

He nodded, leaning against the wall of the shed, his arms folded and one knee bent, his boot resting against the timber wall. His sunglasses were down so I couldn't see his eyes.

'Did you tell him you were travelling with me?' He looked off into the distance as he spoke, towards where the green hills rolled towards Stroud.

I paused for a second or two, then slowly shook my head.

'What if you decide to come to New Zealand with me?' His words sounded casual, but the set of his jaw was firm.

'Is that likely?' I deliberately kept my tone just as casual.

'That's up to you, Maxi.' He smiled and disappeared back inside the shed. 'Did you want any of these tools for your place?' he called.

The subject was closed.

'No, they can all go out on the table.'

In the next patch, the boys were patiently waiting for another delivery to the potting bench. I joined Richie in the shed. He'd nearly cleaned it all out. There were just the seed envelopes to go, and Horrie's bar fridge, now unplugged.

'I emptied it when I first got down here,' Richie said, indicating the shelf.

There were a few bottles of beer, which we put out on the table, something that used to be milk, a bottle of tomato sauce that had seen better days, and a tub of butter. The freezer compartment was still full of ice that had started defrosting, a pool of water creeping out past the towel Richie'd thought to lay down in front of it.

I looked around Horrie's shed. It had been nearly two weeks since he'd died, but now, emptying out the place where he'd spent so much time, where he and I had spent so much time together, it all seemed so final.

So much of my childhood was associated with these few square feet. When I was little, there were the countless afternoons after school and weekends that I hung about here with Horrie, learning about plants and growing cycles and seasons. I learnt how to spell the names of flowers before I knew how to read. It wasn't so much that Horrie had lectured me, more that I'd learnt simply by working beside him. Somewhere in my mid-teens I discovered that boys and friends were more interesting than a bunch of old men talking about how to get more from their beans, or when was the best time to plant snow peas. Then came the London years, when my visits were restricted to the occasional weekend drop-in.

There were times in the city – especially during winter– when I yearned for a few hours of daylight and the earth to ground me. I tried to explain it to James once: how I wanted simply to plant a seed and watch it shoot green, hopefully through soil I'd turned myself. How being close to nature helped me feel as though I was connected to something in a way that a crowded bar or a posh restaurant never could.

He'd looked at me as if I was speaking another language. 'Really, darling,' he'd laughed, 'is that a hint that I need to buy you flowers more often?'

'No, I'm simply saying that I miss having a garden to work in.'

'I couldn't think of anything worse than having to spend my weekends mowing lawns. One day we'll have a large house with someone to mow the lawns. You can have a glasshouse to potter about in if you like.'

'I don't want to play about with hothouse flowers,' I'd said. 'I want to grow my own vegetables and eat them.'

I might as well have said I wanted to run away and join a nudist colony.

'Maxine, darling, people like us don't grow our own vegetables. We go to the shops and buy them. Speaking of which, how about you put on something pretty and we'll go out for lunch.'

Since we'd moved to Brookford, I'd spent hours down here working beside Horrie, chatting about the produce, planning what I'd do with it, photographing the plants and the vegetables and the old boys. I looked around the shed at the bare benches and wiped away a tear. If Horrie were here he'd tell me to just get on with it. He'd say something like, 'Tears won't help you get the work done, lass.'

I held my fists to my eyes to force the tears back, shook my head and got on with the business of mopping up the water on the floor with the towel. It was when I opened the door to check how the defrosting was going that I saw it. In the back of the freezer compartment was a flat plastic container – the sort you might store sliced cheese or cold meat in. And wrapped in plastic inside it was a letter to me.

Hiya lass,

If you're reading this letter, it means you've cleaned out the shed. My darling Max, I know you well enough to know that if you've cleaned out the shed it means you're handing the allotment back. I know what that little plot of land means to you. It's not just about the earth and the vegetables – it's about the memories. I've taught you all I know about gardening and plants, and you've taught me so much more. That's how I know that if you're handing it back, something's happened.

Because I'm not around for you to get upset with me, I can say that I hope it's not that you've changed your mind and are moving away with James. You've always known he wouldn't have been my first choice for you, but until recently he's been good to you and I'll always be grateful that he brought you back to the village.

If you are back together, I wish you every happiness for what comes next and ask you to ignore the rest of this letter. I also ask that you keep your dreams alive, and have some independence. Maybe the little bit of money I've put aside will help you do that.

If you're reading this letter because the two of you are moving on separately, use the money to follow your dreams. Travel, see more of the world, fall in love again — with someone who respects you, wants to partner with you and doesn't expect you to live your life through their goals.

I lost your grandmother way too early, and never found anyone who could measure up to her. That doesn't need to be your story. I want for you what I had with my Shirley, and what your parents have with each other. You'll know who he is when you feel like you've come home — wherever in the world he might be. I have a feeling that you won't have to look too far or too hard for that. I hope I'm right.

I wish you all the happiness in the world, lass, and wherever I am, know that I'll be missing you.

With regret that I'm not there to see your
dreams come true,
   Your loving grandfather,
   Horrie

Richie came into the shed as I finished reading, tears streaming down my face.

'He left me a letter,' I said. 'In the freezer.'

Without saying a word he opened his arms and I burrowed into them. Eventually, I pulled back and gave him the letter to read.

When he'd finished, he folded it and handed it back to me with a weak smile. 'Your Horrie was one of the wisest men I know.' He put his arm loosely around my shoulders and pulled me into his side for a brief hug. 'Any ideas what you'll do?'

'He said to use the money to follow my dreams – so that's what I'll do. Perhaps I'll come back from Denmark and open that garden cafe I've always talked about, or start a catering business. Maybe I'll invest some in a range of recipe cards. I'm still not sure, but I'll use the time in Denmark to think about it.'

He smiled slowly. 'You've got plenty of options – and the space now to think about them. Speaking of which, we'd better get back and finish packing if we're going to be in time for your farewell dinner with your parents.'

•

The smell of Dad's roast lamb hit me as soon as Mum opened the front door.

'Is that what I think it is – one of Alan's roasts?' Richie asked as he kissed Mum on the cheek.

'It certainly is. But we'll have it with a roast pumpkin, rocket and feta salad seeing as how the weather's so nice. And I'm doing one of those lemon puddings you like so much, Richie.'

When Dad took Richie into the garden for a beer, I helped Mum prepare the salads for dinner.

'I thought we weren't doing roast veggies?' I asked, watching her slice potatoes finely.

'I couldn't resist these.' She stood the slices vertically in the pan, like a stack of dominoes, and drizzled butter over the top. 'They feel more like summer so they don't count as roast veggies, not really, and they're very more-ish. Besides, you're still looking a bit thin, and I know Richie loves his potatoes.'

'It's no wonder he was quick to agree to the invitation,' I said, smiling. 'You spoil him.'

'He's easy to spoil. Speaking of which, did you tell James that you were going to Denmark with Richie?'

'No.' I screwed up my nose. 'I told him that I was going away and that I'd call him when I got back. He would have put two and two together though. In his reply he asked me outright whether I was travelling with Richie.'

There'd been an email waiting when I got home

that afternoon.

> *Dear Maxine,*
> *Can I assume that you're travelling with Richie?*
> *Regardless of what you might choose to think, remember you are still my wife.*
> *With love,*
> *James xxx*

I hadn't replied.

'Do you think you'll come straight back?' Mum asked.

I shrugged. 'I honestly don't know.'

She nodded and put the potatoes in the oven. 'Did you bring the letter your grandfather wrote you?'

'I did, but I wasn't sure if you'd want to see it.'

I rummaged through my backpack and handed it to her. She sat down and read it, smiling sadly as she folded it and gave it back to me.

'Your grandfather saw more than we thought he did.'

Dad and Richie chose that moment to come into the kitchen so I didn't get a chance to ask her what she meant.

Over dinner Mum took the opportunity to find out more about Richie. 'Have you always lived in New Zealand? I thought you mentioned the other day that you went to university in Sydney.'

'That's right,' he said, reaching across for more potatoes. 'These spuds are amazing, Claire. Yeah, Dad was a London boy originally and wound up in Australia playing football – soccer. My older sister, Cate, and I were both born in Sydney. We moved to NZ when I was just a toddler.'

'And you mentioned you have a younger sister too?'

'Mum,' I scolded gently, 'what's with the questions?'

Her look was innocent. 'I'm just getting to know Richie better, that's all.'

Richie grinned at me. 'It's okay. Yes, Jessica – Jess – is about three years younger than me, so Max's age.'

'Do either of them have children?'

I glared at Mum and she smiled back.

'No – much to Mum's disappointment. Cate and Harry are married and living in Sydney, but so far no kids. Jess lives close to home – she runs a cafe in Queenstown. She complains that the only men she meets are just passing through. She's right into tramping as well – that's what we call walking or hiking back home. She does some guiding in the summer, and Mum runs the cafe when Jess is on track.'

'On track?' I hadn't heard that expression before.

'Yeah, a lot of the really famous walks, or tramps, in New Zealand are multi-day walks. You might have heard of some of them? The Milford Track, Routeburn Track, Hollyford Track?'

I nodded. 'I've heard of Milford.'

'Yeah, most people have. Queenstown's the centre for some of that activity, and the company Jess does some work for has accommodation on track.'

'It sounds interesting,' I said. 'Have you … tramped … any of the … tracks?'

He laughed at my awkward attempt to get the terminology right. 'I sure have, but not the posh way Jess does it with a guide, a comfy bed, a hot-water bottle and a three-course hot meal. I did them carrying everything in and out on my back, and staying in the DOC – sorry, Department of Conservation – huts. Cate and I laugh at Jess and tell her she's gotten soft over the years. You don't know you're alive until you've tramped through the rain on Routeburn for a day, shared a freeze-dried meal with strangers, curled up in wet clothes in the sleeping bag you've carried, and then pulled your wet boots on to do it all again the next day. The mob Jess works for even have drying rooms so you don't have to wear wet clothes or wet boots.'

He was talking to us, but his gaze was somewhere a long way away. 'I stir Jess up about it, but in truth it's great that the track is accessible to a wider group than super-fit twenty-something backpackers. There's something about being out there and knowing you're walking tracks that were tramped by people hundreds of years ago. The landscape changes from rainforest to alpine to plains, and often the only sounds are wind, water and birds. It's magical. You'd love it,' he said to me, his gaze intent. 'I know you would.'

Our eyes held for what seemed like ages, but must have been just seconds. The mood was broken by the oven alarm alerting us to the lemon pudding being ready. I stood and packed up the dinner plates.

Richie moved to help me and I stopped him. 'No, you stay here. Pour some more wine. I'll get these few things cleaned up.'

The day had been so beautiful that Richie and I had left the car at my cottage and walked the couple of miles into town. It gave us the opportunity to work off some of the pudding and potatoes on the way home.

'I'm sorry about Mum and the twenty questions,' I said. 'I don't know what got into her. You've had meals with my parents before and she hasn't done that.'

'Yes, but in the past I haven't been about to take her daughter away.'

'You're not taking me away – just to Denmark for two weeks.'

He smiled, but said nothing.

We stopped at the top of the hill just above my cottage to catch our breath, and rested against a stone wall, gazing across the valley and watching the sun go down. The sky changed from pale pink through to orange, lilac through to darker hues.

Neither of us spoke for a few moments, then

Richie said, 'Come with me.'

His eyes were intense. Perhaps it was the reflection from the sky, perhaps it was something else. It felt like it had that day in the bluebells.

'I am coming with you,' I said, frowning in confusion.

He looked out across the buttercup-and-daisy-tinted hills. 'I mean New Zealand. Come to New Zealand with me. I'd like you to see my town and meet my family. Come for a month, maybe longer. We'll go via Sydney and see Cate – it's a lovely city in the winter.'

'But …'

He turned from the view to face me. 'Come on, Hendo, say yes. What have you got to lose? You've got nothing left in Brookford, and you haven't decided what you want to do for work yet. At the very least it'll give you some more thinking space, and you'll get to see New Zealand as a bonus.'

I searched his face. He was unsmiling, his head tilted a little as he waited for my answer. If I didn't know him better, I would have thought he seemed nervous.

He was right: I had nothing to lose. I'd been considering spending some time in Asia anyway, so why not go to Australia and New Zealand instead? I could have a holiday with Richie and still be back home in a couple of months to start my new life.

'Why not?' My smile was wide as I looked into his eyes and nodded. 'Yes, I'll come to New Zealand with you.'

He turned back towards the disappearing sun, his face beaming. 'Sweet,' he said. 'That's sorted then.'

Rambling Rose

What do you think of the new name? I'll miss *Harvest Happenings*, but this is a new blog and a new chapter in my life.

Although I'm writing this in the kitchen of my cottage on a farm in the Cotswolds, by the time you read it I'll be in Denmark working on a project that I hope is going to teach me a lot about sustainable gardening.

I also hope to learn about Danish food, which I'm sure is about more than smørrebrød – essentially open sandwiches. Speaking of which, that's what I prepared for breakfast this morning: fine slices of radish and cucumber layered on thin slices of toasted rye with crumbled feta on top. A tearing of mint and a turn or two of pepper and I had the perfect start to a summer day. (Keep an eye on my Instagram if you want to follow what I've been eating.)

As for what's in season? Nearly everything you want to eat at this time of year!

I've been making a lot of tray-bake meals that you can slide into the oven and forget about. Things like chicken with fennel and orange, or chicken with garlic and lemon, or a combination of all of the above. You don't need much more than some steamed beans or a bowl of new potatoes on the side.

One of my favourite ways to do chicken at this time of year is with tarragon and mushrooms. The French call it poulet à l'estragon. This is a classic recipe that you can posh up a bit by serving the chicken and sauce separately, with some fresh pasta or new potatoes and a green salad. Or you can dish it into bowls with lots of fresh crusty bread to dunk into the sauce. It involves a little bit of love, care and patience as you reduce the garlic-and-wine-flavoured stock, but grab yourself a glass of white and a friend you haven't seen for a while and the time will pass in a flash. If you're time-poor, you can make a cheat's version using cream to add the richness you would otherwise get from the slow reduction. Cream can feel a little heavy at this time of year though.

For dessert, why not take advantage of the fabulous raspberries available right now? I'm lucky to have a ready supply right here on the farm. They add colour and vibrancy to a lemon drizzle cake; drama when thrown over the chocolate ganache on a mud cake; and are an absolute must with crushed meringue in an Eton mess.

I've been having them for breakfast, stirred through yoghurt with some honey and oats; but you can turn breakfast upside down, add a dram of whisky, call it cranachan and have it after supper. In its simplest form, cranachan is a Scottish trifle and couldn't be easier to put together. *Simply toast some oats in a pan – taking care not to burn them – then whip some cream until the peaks are soft and loose. Now fold through whisky, honey, and raspberries. How much whisky? Well, that's entirely up to you! I tend to go two parts whisky to one part honey, but I like my scotch. Spoon the mixture into a dessert glass and top with the oats.*

You can get a little clever and deconstruct it if you like. Leave the raspberries and honey out of the cream and layer them all instead – raspberries, cream, oats, honey – and repeat. Finish with a final drizzle of honey and a few more oats. Take it one step further and soak your oats overnight in whisky. Now, there's an idea.

I like to serve this with a wee dram on the side. Any excuse will do ...

Until next time,

Max

CHAPTER TWENTY-ONE

After a two-hour drive from the airport, Richie and I arrived at the university campus that was to be our base for the next two weeks. I'd been given the room next to Richie's. It was simply furnished with a single bed, a table and chair in front of a window that looked across fields, and a small pine wardrobe. There was a sink in the corner, and unisex bathroom facilities down the hall.

'Dump your stuff, have a wash, and we'll go down to the bar and meet Brad,' Richie suggested. 'I don't know about you, but I could do with a drink – or three.'

'Yeah, me too.'

We'd been up early to get to the airport, and even though the flight was just two hours, by the time we'd factored in travel to London, traffic, and then the drive out here, it felt like we'd been travelling all day. I supposed we had been.

'Just knock on my door when you're ready,' Richie added.

I didn't bother with unpacking, just settled on a quick face wash, some tinted moisturiser and a slick of lip-gloss. The evening was warm so I changed from my travelling clothes into a short cotton sundress and some sandals, and knocked on Richie's door. He answered wearing just a pair of shorts, with flip-flops on his feet and a towel in his hand that he was using to dry his hair.

'Sorry,' he said. 'I needed a quick shower. Have you ever noticed that no matter how long or short the flight is, you still feel dusty at the end of it?' He didn't wait for an answer. 'Just sit over there – I'll only be a few minutes.'

He'd put his backpack on the chair, so I perched myself on the end of the bed and watched as he unpacked the clothes from his trip back to England. I could see in his wardrobe that he'd neatly separated his Danish summer clothes from those he'd need for winter in New Zealand. He'd told me that the rest of his things were being shipped across.

When he zipped up his bag and stowed it neatly beside the wardrobe, I made a mental note to do the same thing. Although knowing me, I'd probably be rummaging through my suitcase the whole time we were here.

He must have felt me watching him because he turned around and grinned. 'I'm guessing you didn't unpack?'

'Nope. Couldn't be faffed.'

'Ha! It takes just five minutes, and you'll know where everything is.'

'Whatever. Just hurry up, will you? I'm thirsty.'

He smiled again and turned to hang his tee-shirts in the small wardrobe, and I watched the muscles ripple in his back. I'd seen Richie without a shirt before, but I'd never noticed how strong he looked. It felt almost as if I was seeing him for the first time.

Just above the waistband of his shorts, I could see the top of his underwear and dragged my eyes back up to the biceps that flexed as he moved. I wondered if they'd feel as smooth and hard as they looked. James was fit and worked out or ran most days, but his body was built for suits and elegance. Richie's physique was that of a man used to working outdoors for a living.

My mouth went dry and I bit my bottom lip and swallowed hard. Get a grip, Max, this is Richie. It's not been that long since you saw a naked male body.

Ahhh, said another voice, but it's been a while since you saw one in that condition.

Richie turned around and the front view was just as distracting. My eyes followed the hair on his chest down to where it disappeared beneath his shorts. I felt warmth rush to my cheeks and looked out at the fields.

'It's a great view, isn't it?' I said. Lame, Max, too, too lame.

I heard the smile in his voice. 'It sure is.' Then he said more quietly, 'I'm glad you're here, Maxi.'

I turned back, but he was pulling a tee-shirt over his head. 'Yeah, so am I.'

'Okay,' he announced. 'Let's go find that bar – and Brad. Although knowing him, if we find Brad, we'll find the bar.'

'Maaate!' Someone tall, dark and very handsome greeted Richie with a hug and an enthusiastic handshake. After watching the rugby on TV with Richie and seeing this man, I was quickly becoming convinced that the Antipodes issued their men in one size only – large – and one variety – hot.

'And you must be Max?' Brad shook my hand. 'I'm glad you could join us.'

'Thanks. It's good to be here.'

His eyes crinkled around the edges as he smiled. 'I've seen a couple of those newsletters you used to do. I tried your zucchini fritters last summer – the ones with mint, lemon and feta. Richie tells me I have to try them with fresh peas as well. Your styling in those food shots is great – I might get some photography tips off you while we're here. My website could do with some updating, but I don't have the time or energy to call in a professional photographer.'

'It's good to meet you too,' I said. 'Richie's told me a lot about the work you've done around Melbourne. I've never been to a rooftop bar – there's not a lot of call for them where I come from. It's a weather thing.'

'Richie needs to bring you to Australia some time and show you around. There aren't many better ways to spend a summer evening than lounging about on top of the city having a few beers with your mates and listening to good music. Speaking of beers, I'll grab you both one.' When Brad came back, he directed us to some tables and chairs outside. 'On nights like this, when it's this warm, we tend to gather out here.' He waved at a couple walking past. 'Enjoy the long twilight.'

'What do you do for food?' I asked.

'It's laid out inside. They do a buffet — meats, salads, veggies, pasta. It's not great, but it's filling. We're just one of the summer programs underway here, so in about half an hour this area will be full. They run a shuttle into town if you want to have a meal in a hotel, but usually we hang out here.'

'How long are you here for?' I asked him.

'I've taken a fellowship, so I'll be here until August. I'm sure Richie said something about how you'd gone to New York with your husband. How does he feel about you tripping away with Richie?'

I shrugged. 'My plans changed.'

'Sounds like there's more to that story,' Brad commented.

I nodded. 'Yeah, it's complicated.'

'Maybe you can tell me about it later?'

Was that a twinkle I saw in his eye? 'Maybe I can.'

Richie stood. 'This is getting to be a dry conversation. Same again?'

Both Brad and I nodded.

'He's talked a lot about you,' Brad said once Richie had left us.

'Really? All good, I hope.'

'Absolutely – or you wouldn't be here with him.'

'Oh, I'm not with him – like *with* him. Richie and I are just good friends. Best friends, I suppose.'

'Nothing more?'

I shook my head. 'No, nothing more.'

I'd thought that with cycling to and from work most days, and the normal amount of digging and lifting associated with a job in a garden centre, I'd be physically prepared for the work we would be doing. Boy, was I wrong. By the end of the first day on the dig as I was now calling it – much to the amusement of Richie, who reminded me that digs were something archaeologists like Indiana Jones did, not something that gardeners like us did – all I was capable of was falling weakly into a chair and pleading for someone, anyone, to get me a beer.

Richie laughed and told me to 'Harden up, princess,' but Brad grinned and said, 'You did better than most do on their first day. You stay there and let me look after you. You too, Richie, the first one's on me.'

Richie collapsed into the chair beside me with a groan.

'Ha!' I said. 'I knew it. You're as stiff and sore as I am.'

He smiled sheepishly. 'Uh-huh. You'd think I wouldn't have fallen out of condition so quickly.'

He reached behind his neck to rub at the muscles, grimacing. Without thinking, I struggled to my feet and managed to walk the few inches to behind his chair. He jumped when I put my hands on his shoulders.

'Stay still,' I said. 'You did more digging and shovelling than I did.'

As my fingers kneaded along the top of his back, he tipped his head back and shut his eyes. 'Mmm, that's nice.'

His muscles felt smooth and strong through the thin cotton of his shirt, the power in them contained – for now. I remembered how his back had looked last night without the shirt, the way the muscles had rippled under his smooth brown skin, and took a deep breath. He smelled of the sun, of gardens and work. I wanted to close my eyes and run my tongue up the back of his neck, behind his ears, and nuzzle in down the line of his throat. I swallowed hard, almost tasting the saltiness of his skin.

Brad broke the spell. 'Hey, when you're finished there, feel free to start on me.'

I laughed, but it sounded uncomfortable even to my ears. 'Nope, that's all he gets. You'd think he'd be used to a little bit of work.'

I moved back to my own chair, groaning as I sat down.

'Obviously he's gotten soft since he's been in England,' Brad teased.

Richie grinned. 'I wouldn't think so. But if you're both quite finished hanging shit on me …' He tilted his bottle in our direction.

We all clinked and took deep swallows of the beer. I met Richie's eyes. He smiled, then looked away, joining in with Brad's good-natured bantering, leaving me wondering what the hell was wrong with my breathing and why my mouth was so dry.

Richie drained his beer and stood. 'I'm off for a shower. I'll see you two later for dinner.'

Gripping the sides of my chair, I levered myself up. 'I'll join you.' When I realised what I'd said, I blushed. 'Not in the shower, of course. Rather, I need a shower too so I'll leave now as well.' They were watching me babble and smiling. 'And now I'm making no sense at all, am I?'

'Not much,' said Brad.

'Very little,' said Richie. 'But you are welcome to join me if you'd like.'

I rolled my eyes in an attempt to ignore the wave of moist heat that swept through my core, and made my way down the corridor to my room. Richie caught up with me just as I was turning the key in the door.

'Enjoy your shower,' he said, grinning. 'Knock on my door when you're done and we'll go down to dinner together if you like.'

Knocking on his door raised a very real possibility of seeing him shirtless again, and with the images now in my head of shared showers that wasn't a risk I was prepared to take – regardless of the view.

'No, it's fine. Don't wait for me.'

I delayed under the shower, hanging my head back and letting the hot water run through my hair and down my body, soothing the aches and pains. I closed my eyes and imagined a naked Richie in the cubicle with me, taking the soap from my hand and saying 'Let me'.

I snapped my eyes open and coughed as I swallowed a mouthful of soapy water. Ridiculous. I turned the cold tap on hard and gasped as the icy water chilled my skin.

When I made my way back to the common room, Brad and Richie had already filled their plates with food and were well on the way to emptying them. One of the girls, Anna from Sydney, had taken the seat next to Richie and was showing an awful lot of tanned shoulder as she leaned across the table to demonstrate a point to Brad.

I selected some salads and cold roast meat and joined them, taking the seat beside Brad. Anna smiled at me and continued with her conversation, which was, as far as I could tell, something about patriarchy, matriarchy and how a woman's value in a male-dominated society was based purely on looks.

'I spent three months in Ubud before coming

here,' she said. 'It's in Bali, you know. Indonesia.' We nodded. 'I came away with a whole new perspective on societal norms.'

As she spoke, she leaned back in her chair and lifted and bent one long brown leg, reaching around to hug her knee. I saw Brad watch the action carefully. Richie seemed to be concentrating on what was left of his dinner.

'Three months in Ubud sounds wonderful. What did you do for all that time?' I asked, keen to change the subject.

'Oh, I stayed with a group of wonderful women. It's so freeing and empowering to be away from the distractions of men, don't you think?' She didn't give me an opportunity to respond. 'We talked, we practised yoga, and I took some classes in interpretative dance, Mayan astrology and breath-work. Have you ever done breath-work?'

'No –'

'Oh, you must – it's so powerful it will change your life. There's something about working with other women that allows you to be who you're meant to be.' She lowered her leg to the floor and leaned forward again, her sleeve falling off her shoulder. 'And who you really are should have nothing to do with the way you look, should it?'

'Absolutely not,' I agreed, hiding my smile as I concentrated on my dinner.

'Yes,' she mused, 'there'll be some changes to my relationship when I get home.' She flicked her hair over her shoulder and attempted to make eye contact with Richie.

'Is there someone waiting for you?' I asked.

'My boyfriend, Hugh. We've been together since uni.'

'He didn't want to join you here?'

'No, he understands that this break is about me finding myself. Of course I miss him, but relationships can be restrictive after a while. I truly believe that marriage is a construct of patriarchal domination – and very disempowering for most women. Your goals get lost in his.' She shrugged, dislodging her top again. 'It's just how it is. We women give up what we want in order to keep the relationship going.'

'Surely it doesn't have to be like that?' said Richie. 'I'd like to think that if you love someone, you also respect and support their dreams. That's what partnership is about.'

Brad nodded. 'I agree.'

'Of course you do – you're men.' She laughed and looked to me for support.

'When do you go home?' I asked her.

'We have another week – I'm here with my friend Kelly.' She pointed out an attractive brunette on the other side of the room. 'We'll start to make our way home – via Paris and London – after that. I need to be back at work by the middle of July.'

'Where do you work?'

'*On Point*,' she said. 'It's a fashion and beauty magazine. We aim it at women like us,' she looked at me as she spoke, 'single, independent, and with a love of great clothes, great products and looking as fabulous as we can. It's not just about the brands though. Just before I came away I worked on a story on those new corsets – you must have seen them advertised? Waist-trainers?'

I shook my head. 'Sorry.'

'Oh, really? Anyway, they give you an incredible hourglass shape. You get a tiny waist and exaggerated breasts and bum. I don't use one, but it's great for women who don't have much of each.' She eyed my small frame.

'Presumably at the cost of your internal organs,' Brad muttered.

I thumped his leg lightly.

'What was the story about?' I asked Anna. 'How they're trapping women in the attitudes of the past and are symbols of female disempowerment?'

She looked at me with confusion. 'No. Just how amazing they look.'

'Oh.'

Beside me I felt Brad attempting to hold back laughter.

Anna leaned into Richie, resting a hand on his

arm. 'It's such a pity you only just arrived. Oh well, we have a week to get to know each other better.' She beamed at him.

'Drink?' asked Brad.

'Yes, please. I'll come with you,' I said.

'I'll get them,' offered Richie.

'No, mate, you stay there. We won't be long.'

As we walked the short distance to the bar, Brad said, 'Did I detect some relief there?'

'Umm, yeah. Did you hear her?'

'Sadly, yes, but she's a lovely girl. Her heart's in the right spot.'

'I'm sure it is.' I looked back and saw her leaning into Richie again.

Brad followed my gaze. 'He's not interested in her, you know. For a start, he knows she's in a relationship.'

'It doesn't matter if he is. As I told you last night, we're just friends.' But my reply sounded stiff.

I was exhausted so retired to my room relatively early. I tossed and turned in bed until I heard the key turn in Richie's door. While I could hear him moving about and getting ready for bed, there was nothing to indicate he had anyone with him. Then I heard his door shut again and a soft knock on mine.

I got out of bed and opened it enough to see it was Richie.

'Are you okay?' he asked.

'Absolutely. Why wouldn't I be?'

He searched my face. 'No reason. It's just that you left quite early and you didn't say goodnight.'

'I'm tired.'

'Okay, if you're sure that's all it is.'

'Yes. I'm tired – and standing here talking to you isn't improving that situation.'

He smiled. 'I can take a hint. Sleep well, Maxi.'

CHAPTER TWENTY-TWO

That first day set the pattern for the next five. The weather remained fine and warm, so we worked hard during the day and relaxed with a few beers at night. Members of the group came and went, as did participants in the other summer programs being conducted at the university. As he was here for the whole summer, Brad was one of the few constants. On the whole, everyone was friendly and easy to get along with; and it sometimes seemed as though every nation in the world was represented in the common room in the evenings.

We weren't scheduled to work on weekends, so on Saturday morning, after sleeping late and lingering over breakfast, the three of us borrowed bikes and cycled the short distance into town. After a wander around the small town centre, we chose a local hotel for some lunch.

'You have to try the smørrebrød,' Richie said. 'Remember the open sandwiches I told you about? How about I go and order a selection for us? Trust me, you'll wonder why you've never had one before.'

Once he was gone, Brad asked me how I was settling in on the project.

'I'm really enjoying the work,' I said. 'There's something about physical work and dirt that clears your mind, you know?'

He nodded his understanding.

'I'm not here for the design or planting ideas – not like you and Richie are. It's more about the produce for me: how I can use it, style it … work out what I want to do in my own business when I get back.'

'What is it that you want to do?' Unlike James, there was no sneer in Brad's voice – he was genuinely interested.

'I was originally thinking of baking for different outlets around town, but that would leave me dependent on their decisions for my income, and I want to be responsible for my own money now that … Well, now that I can't rely on anyone but myself, I suppose. Being here has helped me see how much I didn't allow myself to think beyond what I thought I could do.' I looked at Brad. 'That probably makes no sense at all to you.'

He smiled. 'It actually makes perfect sense.'

Richie was back with some beers. He slid into the booth beside me, the length of his thigh pressing against mine. 'What are you guys talking about?'

Brad reached across and clinked our glasses in a silent toast. 'Max's plans for the future. She was just about to tell me about the business she'll launch when she gets back to England.' His eyes were on Richie, not me, as he said it.

Richie nodded and smiled in reply.

To cover my confusion at the hidden meaning that I'd obviously missed, I focused on Richie's hands, on the finger that was tracing patterns in the condensation of the glass. For a few seconds I allowed myself to imagine that finger tracing patterns on my skin, the strong thighs that were pushing into me in the booth pinning me down. As a method of distraction it was very pleasant.

'What are you thinking about doing?' Richie asked. His eyes met mine and their blue seemed deeper, as if they could reach into my brain and pull out the thoughts I'd been indulging in.

'I'm sorry,' I said, feeling the warmth that had been filling the lower half of my body move up into my face. 'What did you say?'

He grinned as he repeated his question, the look in his eyes sending spirals of heat through my body. 'I was just asking what your plans are for when you're back in England ... or maybe you're no longer thinking of going back to England?'

I swallowed a mouthful of beer, feeling the cool liquid calming the heat of my thoughts. 'Of course I'm going back – I mean, I have a return ticket.'

I felt Richie move away slightly, enough to leave some space between us; enough for me to think more clearly, yet at the same time miss his closeness.

'Tickets can be changed,' he said with a shrug, as if he didn't really care one way or another.

'So,' encouraged Brad, 'your plans?'

'I'm thinking I might put a proposal to the new owners of Blossoms & Buds – that's the garden centre Richie and I used to work in,' I explained. 'I know they're going to go to tender for an operator for the cafe they're putting in, and I'm going to make a bid for it. I've been jotting down menu ideas and designs. Even though I have no previous experience, I know Brookford, and Brookford knows my cooking. I figure I have as good a chance as anyone. In the meantime, I'll keep the monthly blog going, but maybe increase the frequency to show places I've travelled to and ingredients I've tried. I'll use that platform to launch a range of cards with my photos and my recipes … and that's just for starters.' I looked across the table at Brad, suddenly embarrassed by my enthusiasm. 'Anyway, that's what I'm thinking right now. Of course, it could change by the time I get home in September, and I could be getting ahead of myself, but –'

'But nothing,' said Brad. 'It's good to have a dream, a goal – call it what you want. Don't let anyone tell you otherwise.'

'That's what my grandfather used to say,' I said, missing Horrie again.

I felt Richie's smile in my direction and the warmth

of his hand on mine, but couldn't look at him in case the tears came back.

'You don't need to be in Brookford to follow that dream,' Richie said quietly.

'Maybe not, but it's my home.'

'You know what they say,' said Brad. 'Home is where the heart is.'

I was saved from responding as wooden boards containing slices of rye bread and assorted toppings were placed in front of us. Richie was right – the open sandwiches were wonderful. I made a mental note to record in my journal all the toppings we'd had. It would be a great menu idea and a good use of seasonal produce.

We were back on campus by mid-afternoon. Someone had moved the beanbags and deckchairs outside so we spent the next few hours lounging about on the lawn in the sun. Anna, Kelly and some of the other girls had stripped down to skimpy bikinis and were stretched out on towels working on their tans.

I already had a pair of shorts on, but went to my room to change my tee-shirt for a bikini top, and my sneakers for a pair of flip-flops. Grabbing a book, sunscreen and a hat, and remembering to pop my sunglasses back on my head, I joined Brad and Richie on the lawn. They'd left a deckchair free between them.

Both had taken their shirts off and had sunglasses

on. Brad, having come straight from summer in Australia, was deeply tanned, and Richie, despite the break in England, had also quickly gone nut-brown. Brad was reading, and Richie had his sketchbook beside him. Both smiled at the sight of my bikini top, Richie's eyes lingering on my curves for longer than they needed to. It had been a while since a man had looked at me in that way, and I could feel my body responding.

'Do you need some help with that sunscreen?' he asked.

I blushed. 'No, I think I can manage.'

His eyes twinkled as he said, 'No problem. Let me know if you can't.' He picked up his sketchbook and settled back in his chair.

I applied my sunscreen with more awareness than usual. Although both men were lounging back in their chairs and had their glasses on, I imagined I could feel their eyes on me as I smoothed the lotion evenly into my limbs, yet when I looked across at Richie I could see that his eyes were closed behind the sunglasses.

I indulged myself and allowed my gaze to follow the dark hair across his chest, around his nipples, down his flat stomach, and below the waistband of his shorts. The thought of what was beneath those shorts made my mouth dry. Reluctantly I dragged my eyes back up to his face to see him watching me watching him. He'd pushed his sunglasses on top of his head and the look on his face was one I'd seen before – that day in my cottage after Horrie's funeral. Then the look had gone almost before I knew I'd seen it, but now its intensity lingered and fired a desire deep within me, stronger than anything I could recall feeling.

His eyes moved from my face down to my breasts and the two triangles containing them. I could feel my chest rising and falling and hoped it wasn't visible, that he couldn't see how my nipples had responded to the attention. He reached out a finger and caught a bead of sunscreeny sweat just above the shadow of my cleavage and held it there for just a second. His gaze captured mine, his eyes darkening from blue to deep navy. My breath caught in my chest and was suspended by the finger that gently rested there, releasing in a sigh when he moved his hand away. He watched the flush that spread from my breasts to my face, grinned and lay back, closing his eyes.

I sat back in my chair and glanced at Brad. The way he smiled at me told me he'd seen the exchange.

I placed my hat over my face, willing my breathing to return to normal. It was months since I'd had sex – all that was going on here was my body reminding me that it had been neglected for too long. Besides, Richie was my friend. Anything else was out of the question. It would make more sense if I was having these feelings for Brad – perhaps a quick holiday fling was what I needed. I discounted that idea quickly. The burning, yearning need I felt right now was only for

Richie. It had been waiting to come to life since that day in the bluebells and now I couldn't ignore it. How on earth was I going to keep these feelings sufficiently hidden to cope with being in such close proximity to Richie for another six weeks or so?

At some point I must have drifted off. My hat and glasses flew off my face as I jolted upright when Richie planted a cold bottle of beer on my navel. He sat on the side of his deckchair, his elbows resting on his knees, a cheeky grin on his face.

'It's warm out here,' he said, and I wondered whether he could see through my eyes into the fantasy I'd had. 'I thought you might like something cold.' He glanced down to where a drop of condensation from the bottle remained on my stomach.

After the episode earlier, I brushed it away with a flick of my fingers before he could do it for me.

Brad also sat up and put his book down. Richie leaned across me to pass a bottle to Brad, his arm brushing my breast and lingering there far longer than it needed to. The contact caused my nipple to pop up again. Really, Max?

Anna bounced over in her red bikini and took the beer from Richie's hand. 'Come on,' she said, pulling him to his feet. 'We need you for volleyball.'

'Can I at least finish my beer first?' His protest was half-hearted.

'Sure ... if you hurry.' She placed her hands on her

hips, pushing her breasts out in his direction.

'You go on ahead,' he told her. 'I'll be there soon.'

She pouted as she bounced away.

I picked up my book and relaxed back in my chair. Brad got up and walked around to where Richie had been sitting to pick up his empty beer bottle. Seeing the sketchbook on the ground, he opened it and began flipping through the pages.

'Have you seen this?' he asked me.

'Richie's drawings? Sure. He's constantly adding ideas for designs and gardens. It's like a visual diary for him.'

'Hmmm. He's good.'

I smiled. 'He is. This Chelsea garden – when he finally creates it – will be incredible.'

He looked at me again. 'Yes, it will be.'

Richie ran back across the lawn and took the sketchbook from Brad's hands. Brad raised his eyebrows in a silent question, but I couldn't see Richie's expression.

'I figured I'd better get this back inside before you two have another couple of beers and forget about it,' he said.

He was soon back and joined Anna and the others. I watched them. The bikini Anna almost had on was seriously lacking suspension, but no one seemed to mind. Kelly, on the other team, was dressed almost identically and attracting just as much attention from their audience as Anna was.

Richie leaped up to punch the ball over the net to win the point. Anna raced up to him and, cupping his face in her hands, kissed his mouth, pushing her breasts into his chest. He pulled away before she could deepen the kiss and moved to the back of the court to prepare his serve. I wondered whether his eyes had deepened to the same navy as when he'd looked at me earlier.

Anna pretended to be embarrassed, looking away from him and then back, smiling and flicking her hair. I'd seen enough and gathered my things. The sharp pain I felt in my belly absolutely wasn't jealousy.

'I'm going in for a shower,' I told Brad.

'I'll let Richie know.'

'Somehow I don't think he'll care too much.'

His smile was gentle and understanding. 'See you at dinner.'

An hour or so later, I heard Richie moving about in his room. He knocked on my door and called softly, 'Hey, Maxi, are you in there?' Then he knocked again.

I pretended I hadn't heard.

After dinner, Brad and I took our drinks to a couple of the beanbags. The night had turned too cool to be outside, and Anna had dragged a protesting Richie off to another group of people. I wondered how long he could hold out against her efforts and whether his resistance was because of my presence. Then I remembered our exchange on the lawn this afternoon. I knew I hadn't imagined either the intent in his eyes or the desire in my belly.

Brad's voice broke into my thoughts. 'I won't be sorry to see her go tomorrow.'

'Anna? Really? I thought you liked her.'

'Sure, she's nice, but she's that girl, you know? For all her talk of independence, she's the type that always has to have some guy interested in her to make her feel good about herself.'

'Did she hit on you?'

He nodded. 'She set her sights on me the first week she was here, and once she realised that I wasn't interested, moved on to Pete.' He pointed to a blond American man leaving the common room with Kelly.

'Wow, Richie didn't tell me this project was party central!'

He laughed. 'It's a bit like that. We're all here for different reasons. Some of us are here to work and get exposure to new ideas, new ways of doing things. Some are here to help with the research side of things – they're the science guys. To be honest, I have no idea why Anna and Kelly came. I suspect they didn't know they'd be getting dirty.'

I giggled. 'I think you're probably right.' I took a deep mouthful of beer. 'So Anna got nowhere with you?'

'No. I'm not sure if Richie mentioned it, but I

have someone at home – well, I hope I still do.' As he spoke he played with the label on his beer bottle.

'Are you talking about Abby? Richie told me about you two. Because you're here for as long as you are, I thought you might have broken up.'

'We're on a sort of break, I suppose, but Anna doesn't compare to Abby. No one does – or could.'

'You miss her.' It wasn't a question.

'Yeah. Every day.'

'Richie said it was love at first sight with you two.'

'He said that?' He smiled into his glass. 'Yeah, it was. We were childhood friends but lost touch for many years. Then the minute I saw her it was as if I'd been waiting to find her again for my whole life. She's never said, but I'm pretty sure it was the same with her.'

'What went wrong?'

He shrugged. 'I'm really not sure. I want us to be together – I even asked her to marry me. It wasn't the best proposal ever, more of a spur-of-the-minute thing – and she said no. I know she loves me, but there's something, some reason, why she doesn't want to commit.'

'She gave you no indication?'

He shook his head. 'There's been something up with her that I haven't been able to put my finger on. I'm hoping this time apart will help her realise just how much we're meant to be together.'

I covered his hands with mine. 'For your sake, I hope it does.'

He smiled into my eyes. 'Thanks for that.'

I looked up and saw Richie watching the closeness between Brad and me, my hands on his. He looked away as soon as our eyes met.

Anna was watching him watching me. She playfully kissed his cheek, and I turned away before I could see his reaction.

'Don't worry about her,' Brad said. 'He's not interested, but she's very persistent.'

'Oh no! We're not like that. We're friends – there's never been anything more between us.'

'But you'd like there to be?' He tilted his head to the side and smiled knowingly.

I opened my mouth to deny it, and instead nodded.

He nodded too, slowly. 'What are you going to do about it? You know it'll need to be you, right? He won't make a move on you unless you initiate it. Your friendship's too important to him.'

I smiled ruefully. 'It would never work between us. He's heading back to Queenstown to live, and I'm on holiday. Soon I'll be going back to England. We each have our lives elsewhere, so even if I wanted to go there with Richie–'

'Which you do.'

'–it's completely hopeless and couldn't go anywhere. I can't risk losing him by turning this into something it can't be.'

'It could, you know, with compromise …'

'No. I'm through with changing my life and my dreams to fit in with my partner.'

'Are you two right for a drink?' Richie's voice cut into our conversation. I searched his face to find some sign that he'd overheard us, but if he had, he was giving nothing away.

'Not for me, thanks,' I said. 'I'm off to bed – I'll see you two in the morning.'

That night when Richie went into his room, there was a knock on his door soon after. At first I thought it was him knocking on my door, and I sprang out of bed and rushed to open it, stopping just in time as I heard Anna's soft giggles.

Even though the walls weren't that thin, I didn't want to risk hearing anything so I popped in some earplugs. But they didn't stop the pictures in my head – her long brown legs wrapped around his neck as he pounded into her, her hair spread across his pillow, her eyes closed in ecstasy as she moaned and urged him on, her fingers pressing into the muscles on his back. Even with the pillow over my head, I saw the images in my dreams when I fell into a restless sleep.

CHAPTER TWENTY-THREE

I slept badly and was slower than usual to get moving the next morning. As I was heading to the bathroom with my washbag, I passed Richie coming back from his shower. He was whistling tunelessly in that way people do when they're in a happy place. It must have been a good night.

He stopped me, saying, 'Hey, you.'

I had difficulty meeting his eyes. Given the alternative was his bare chest, I forced my gaze upwards. 'Hey, yourself.'

'You're sounding tired.'

'No, I'm fine.'

He shrugged. 'Good. I'll see you at breakfast then.'

I watched him walk away, and went to attack with cold water the images that were clamouring for attention in my brain.

As I walked into the common room later, Anna pushed past me to leave. I looked across at Richie who was tucking into his breakfast. Brad raised one shoulder in response to my unasked question.

I filled a bowl with my usual fresh fruit and yoghurt, poured some hot water over a teabag, and sat down beside Brad and opposite Richie.

'What's wrong with Anna?' I asked Richie.

He grimaced. 'Fucked if I know. She's leaving today, maybe that's the problem.' He didn't look up from his bacon and eggs.

Brad met my eyes. Richie did look up then, shook his head slightly, and concentrated again on eating.

'Looks like rain,' Brad said. 'I guess the weather had to break at some stage. We've had over a week of sunshine and good temperatures.'

I shook my head at him. 'Really? We're talking about the weather?'

He grinned. 'My mother always says if you don't have anything nice to say, you should say nothing at all – or talk about the weather.'

Richie looked between the two of us and said, 'Yeah, I reckon it could rain,' before taking his plate to scrape the leftovers in the bin, and leaving the room.

'Did they …?' Brad asked.

'I think so. I heard her come to his room last night.'

'Maybe that's the problem.'

He watched my face for more, but I turned my head.

That was when Anna came back in and leaned over the table until her face was inches from mine. 'It's your fault,' she spat. 'Women like you make me sick. You act all innocent, as if butter wouldn't melt in your mouth, but in the background you like to control everything. Why can't you be happy with him,' she tossed her head to indicate Brad, 'and let Richie have some fun with someone else.' Then she was gone.

'I think you need to go find Richie,' said Brad. 'You two have some talking to do.'

I started to shake my head, but he stopped me. 'No, Max. It's time – go to him.'

Richie opened the door at my knock. He didn't say anything, just held the door open for me to enter the room. I rubbed my hands against my denim skirt. He turned to the desk where he must have been sitting before I came in and shut his sketchbook.

'I'm sorry – I've interrupted you,' I said.

Richie often went for his sketchbook when things got complicated. He said it calmed him and helped him make sense of things.

He shrugged.

'What's wrong with Anna?' I asked.

'I think she's disappointed. She had certain … expectations, and things didn't quite go the way she thought they would.'

'I heard her come here last night.' I forced myself to say the words, even though they had to fight their way past the lump in my throat. 'To you.'

'Did you hear her leave not long after?' He lifted

his head and met my eyes. There was no expression in his.

I shook my head. 'I put in earplugs. I didn't want to hear anything. You know … you … with her. I didn't want to hear it.'

The heat ran into my face, as if he could see into my brain and knew what I'd been thinking and picturing.

'I saw you with Brad,' he said. 'I don't want you to get hurt. He's not over Abby, and even if Abby wasn't a factor, he knows —'

'What are you talking about?'

'Last night – you were holding hands.'

'Holding hands? No, we weren't. I put my hands over his to comfort him. He was telling me how much he missed Abby and we'd been talking about some other things.' I considered the rest of the sentence he didn't finish. 'What does Brad know?'

'How could you think I could be with Anna when I know she has someone at home? Someone who probably trusts her the way you used to trust James. Is that what you think of me?'

His tone was even, but his eyes had darkened – with anger or some other emotion? He turned away and gripped the top of the chair he'd been sitting on before I came in.

I dropped my head. 'No,' I said miserably. 'I didn't even think of it like that. I knew she wanted you, and when I heard her come to your room …'

He was still facing away from me. 'What else were you and Brad talking about?'

'I'm sorry?'

'You said you were talking about Abby and some other things?'

It was now or never. I took a deep breath. 'He said that if I wanted you I'd need to make the first move.'

I said it so quietly that I wasn't sure he'd heard. I held my breath. He didn't turn around, but I saw the muscles in his back tense and he held onto the top of the chair more tightly.

'And do you?' he said. 'Want me?'

I nodded, even though he couldn't see the movement. 'Oh, yes. So very much.'

I waited for one heartbeat, two, three … He turned to face me, his smile wide, and somehow I was in his arms, my breasts pressed hard against his chest. He lowered his head and kissed me gently, his mouth moving softly, hesitantly, over mine. His tongue reached out to taste mine, tentatively, slowly, as if he wanted to make that first sip last.

He raised his head and looked into my eyes. 'I've wanted to do this for so long,' he murmured, his breath catching on the words.

I knew what he meant – the kiss had so much longing in it. It felt as if I'd been waiting for it to happen since the day in the bluebells, maybe even before that.

'Me too.'

This time when I reached up to pull his mouth down to mine, there was nothing gentle about the kiss, or the fire that was raging deep in my belly and the rush of heat between my thighs. I pulled his shirt up, refusing to let his mouth leave mine – not even for the brief second required to drag his shirt over his head. The muscles in his arms felt hard and smooth under my hands, his skin tasted divine under my tongue. As I licked and nipped along his chest, his mouth was nuzzling down the side of my throat, his hands busy under my top, kneading at my breasts. I could feel the length of him straining against his shorts as I struggled with the button and fastenings.

'Hey,' he said, pulling back and removing his shirt completely.

The air between us hit me and I suddenly felt shy, the blood rushing into my face. He placed one finger under my chin and tipped it up to look into my eyes. His were intense, the deepest blue, darkening as we continued to stare at each other. He smiled, and kissed me again, pushing me back onto the bed at almost the same time my legs were unable to support me any longer.

'It's been hell sleeping so close to you and wanting you so much, but knowing it was too soon and I had to wait until you were ready.'

His words hit me like a glass of cold water. What

was I doing? I'd only been separated from my husband for a couple of months. What if this was another mistake?

He felt me pull back slightly. 'You're not ready, are you?' His face showed disappointment but his voice was understanding.

I shook my head. 'I don't think so.'

'I can wait,' he said.

I stared into his eyes and my resolve began to falter. He kissed me softly and pulled back and away from me, retrieving his tee-shirt from where it had landed and pulling it over his head. I straightened my top and pulled my skirt down.

He leaned across and kissed me again. 'You just let me know when you're ready.'

I nodded. 'I'd better go.'

I was wondering already whether I'd done the right thing; missing his arms already.

He walked me to the door. 'I'll get Brad and we'll head into town for lunch, hey? With luck we'll even beat the rain.'

His words sounded so normal, as if those heated moments hadn't happened.

'That sounds good.'

Before he opened the door, he pushed me back against the wall, kissing me soundly. 'Take your time,' he said. 'I need a cold shower before I go anywhere.'

My cheeks grew warm at the reason why, and a

very insistent part of me was already regretting my decision to walk away.

On the walk into town and at lunch, neither of us mentioned what had happened – or what had nearly happened. Anna was obviously off the list of appropriate subjects, and we'd agreed not to talk any more about the weather. Instead, Brad and Richie chatted easily about rugby, arguing good-naturedly over who would win the current series between Australia and New Zealand. Richie turned to me from time to time, attempting to involve me in their banter, his arm resting lightly over my shoulders, his hand touching my arm every so often to make a point. Brad watched us, a small smile playing around his lips.

When Richie left to replenish our drinks, dropping a kiss on the top of my head as he stood up, Brad took the opportunity to talk to me.

'I take it you two sorted a few things out.' His grin was wicked. 'It's about time.'

I blushed. 'I think so … I don't know … maybe … ' My cheeks grew even warmer at the memory of Richie's kisses.

Brad raised his eyebrows and I shook my head.

I watched Richie at the bar, laughing at something the bartender said, and suddenly knew that I was ready. Everything that had come before had been leading us to this moment. There was nothing in what I knew of Richie to indicate that this would end up the way James and I had. It was all so different. So what if I was on holiday? I had another six weeks with Richie, and I didn't want to waste one minute of it. I'd already wasted more hours than I'd needed to.

When Richie returned to our table, Brad made an excuse about needing to talk to one of the program leads who was at a table on the other side of the room.

'About this morning,' Richie started. He smiled, tried to stop it, then let it happen. 'I know I should say I'm sorry, but I'm not. Kissing you is something I've been wanting to do for a very long time.' He reached out for my hands. 'And now that I've done it, I very much want to do it again.' He watched my face as his thumb stroked the tension from my hand and set free the butterflies resting in my chest. 'And again.' The heat circling through my belly moved lower. 'Besides, it felt very much to me like it was something that you want too?'

I swallowed hard and nodded.

He leaned over and kissed me, with just enough tongue to make me wish we were somewhere more private.

'I want to do so much more than kiss you.' His words hung in the breath between us. 'But only when you're ready.'

'So do I,' I admitted, mesmerised by his lips and willing them to cross the few centimetres back to mine.

Unable to wait I captured his bottom lip between mine, closing my eyes to hold the sensation, but finding I needed more.

'I think maybe we should head back,' I murmured, holding his gaze as he brought my hand to his mouth, his lips grazing the path his thumb had taken, his smile telling me that he knew exactly what he was doing to me. 'I shouldn't have stopped us this morning.' I leaned across to kiss him again. 'I've been regretting it ever since.'

'Are you sure?'

I nodded. 'Let's get out of here.'

Brad sat back down, breaking into our mood with a cheeky grin. 'Well, kids, I think we'd better drink up – it looks like it's going to pelt down out there.'

Once outside, Richie pulled me to him and kissed me briefly. Despite the difference in our heights, he held my hand tightly the whole way back, as if letting go would somehow break this new connection between us.

The rain hit us about a kilometre from home, so by the time we made it back we were wet through. We stopped in at the common room for a whisky. Brad and Richie each downed theirs in one gulp, grimacing as the alcohol hit the back of their throat. I sipped at mine, feeling the lovely warmth spread through my chest.

'Okay,' said Brad, 'I'm off for a shower and some dry clothes. Although it's very tempting to stay here and admire the view.'

My tee-shirt was almost transparent, and my nipples were clearly visible through the thin cotton. I folded my arms across my chest.

Brad laughed. 'I'll catch you guys later.'

I walked around to sit next to Richie on the lounge. He tilted his head, resting it against the back of his hand.

'Do you want another drink?' he asked.

'No.'

I unfolded my arms and his eyes moved down to my chest. My nipples hardened under his gaze, the spirals of sensation moving through my belly and heading lower.

'I need to get out of these wet clothes. Want to help me?' I said it softly, without smiling.

His gaze moved slowly from my breasts to my lips and back to my eyes. 'More than I think I've ever wanted anything.'

I got up and walked down the hall. He followed, just a few steps behind. I paused at his door.

'Mine?' he asked.

'It's probably neater than mine.'

He grinned, leaned forward to kiss me, and unlocked his door.

'Do you want a drink?' he asked, offering a bottle of scotch.

'Sure, why not?'

I watched as he poured us each a measure into

a glass tumbler. We clinked glasses and I took a sip, as did he. Then he took the glass from my hand and set it on the desk, holding my gaze the whole time. He swallowed hard, pulled off his shirt, and his wet shorts and stood before me in just his boxer shorts. My mouth was dry and I bit my lower lip at the sight of his maleness. I reached out and traced his length through the fabric, moving closer so I could feel his cock growing and pulsing under my hand.

He closed his eyes briefly and groaned, gently moving my hand away. 'It feels like I've been hard since this morning, and this is going to be over too soon if you keep touching me like that. Besides,' he peeled my wet tee-shirt from me, 'you still have way too many clothes on.'

I forced myself to stand still as he unbuttoned my skirt and dragged the wet denim down over my hips. I stepped out of it and turned so he could unclip my bra. He reached around to catch my breasts in his hands, running his tongue oh so slowly down the back of my neck, his erection insistent against the cleft of my bottom.

I felt his breath on my buttocks as he slid my pants down, holding them so I could step out of them, and then running his fingers up the insides of my legs with a touch so light that I could have imagined it if it didn't feel so incredibly sexy.

Still on his knees, without saying anything, he

prompted me to turn and replaced his fingers with his tongue, teasing my legs apart, and bringing me quickly to an orgasm so powerful and unexpected that I cried out as much in surprise as joy, and collapsed onto the floor and into his arms.

'Good?' he asked.

'Uh-huh,' I managed, leaning forward to kiss him. I could taste myself on his lips and it enflamed me even more. 'Now it's your turn,' I murmured into his mouth, pushing him back onto the floor and feasting on him through glazed eyes while I decided what part of him I wanted to savour first.

He lay there smiling, watching me, waiting for me to make my move, his chest rising and falling as his breathing grew faster. Straddling him, I leaned forward and took one pebbled nipple into my mouth, my tongue turning around and around it, my fingers teasing the other, and flicking into his mouth to wet them, before going back to his chest, rubbing myself against him as I did. It wasn't enough – I needed more of him, all of him.

Moving down his body, I drew his shorts down and off, releasing his erection. Oh my. My breath caught in my throat as I looked at him, admiring his power, imagining how he'd fill me.

'Do I pass?' he asked gruffly.

Unable to speak, I nodded. On my knees beside him, I leaned forward and licked tentatively at the tip of his cock. I felt the groan run through him, and allowed my tongue to follow the path my fingers had taken before, licking, circling, tasting, and finally taking him fully into my mouth.

'Oh, Maxi,' he moaned, pushing me away from him and rolling me onto my back. 'That feels unbelievable, but I want this to last.'

He eased himself into me, giving me time to get used to the feel of him, his eyes never leaving mine, as if he wanted the moment, our first time together, to be imprinted into my soul, and only beginning to move when I pleaded with him to.

Afterwards, we lay in each other's arms, so close we could have still been joined. The wonder that I felt was in his eyes too. It suddenly felt like too much and I burrowed my head into his chest so he couldn't see into the centre of me. I could feel his heart beating against my cheek.

'Is it always like that with you?' I asked.

I felt him laugh. 'I have no idea. Is it always like that with you?'

'No. I don't think it's ever been like that.' I meant it. Nothing I'd experienced with James had prepared me for the pleasure Richie had so generously just given me. 'I've never … not like that.'

'I'm glad,' he murmured into the hollow of my neck. 'Because it's never been like that for me with anyone either.'

I attempted to lighten the moment. 'That sounds like something a teenager would say.'

'It's how I feel,' he said simply.

I couldn't argue with that. Besides, it appeared as though he had the appetite of a teenager too, judging by the way he was looking at me.

'I don't think I'm going to be able to get enough of you,' he murmured, balancing himself on his side, his head resting on one fist and trailing the fingers of his left hand down my body. 'You feel amazing, and you taste incredible.'

Although his words made my toes curl, I ducked my head in embarrassment.

'Hey,' he tipped my chin up so our eyes met, 'what's this about?'

'It's just that … what you did … and then what you said … I've never …'

He smiled, the confusion in his eyes giving way to understanding. I dragged my gaze away. It felt weird and wrong all at the same time to be talking about my sex life with my husband while I was in bed with – okay on the floor with – Richie.

'Thank you,' he said. 'It makes me feel like you've given me something special.'

I reached up to pull his mouth back to mine. 'Thank you,' I whispered. 'Now please, make love to me again.'

He nuzzled down the line of my throat, his fingers

reaching between our bodies to stroke my slick folds and then dive into me. I arched into him.

'It would be my pleasure,' he said, watching me tilt my head back and gasp his name.

When I woke, Richie was lying on his side, tracing his finger up and down my arm. I stretched and smiled. 'Were you waiting for me to wake?'

I felt tender in places that I hadn't felt tender in for a long time. At some point we'd managed to make it from the floor to the narrow bed. When we'd finally slept, it had been in each other's arms.

'I was.' He leaned forward and kissed my lips gently. 'That's a good smile, right?'

'It's a good smile.' I pulled him in for a good-morning kiss that rapidly turned into something much more.

'We have to get up,' I said sometime later, pulling the sheet up over me.

'Do we really though?'

'Yes, Richie, we do. We have work to do, I need a shower, and the last time we ate was at lunchtime yesterday.'

'Hmmm, so it was,' he mumbled into an escaped boob.

I moaned as his tongue circled my nipple, but attempted to push him away. 'I mean it, Richie.'

'You're right, of course. I'll let you out of here on

one condition.'

'And that is?'

'That you promise me it won't burst our bubble.'

The look in his eyes as he said it caused my heart to skip around.

'It won't. I promise.'

But as I stood under the shower, a tiny voice in my head reminded me that this could only ever be a short-term thing. He was heading home, and in another six weeks or so I'd be doing the same – in the opposite direction. That's the way it had to be. It wasn't just that I'd never seen Richie with anyone long enough to call it a relationship – although Angela certainly came close. It was more that I'd promised myself I'd never again fall into the same trap I'd fallen into with James.

I pushed the thought back to where it belonged – somewhere in tomorrow. Six weeks was a long time. Anything could happen.

CHAPTER TWENTY-FOUR

Brad and Richie had already started breakfast when I walked in. Both men grinned when I came to the table with a plate loaded with eggs, bacon, mushrooms and tomatoes, and extra toast.

'Needing some extra sustenance this morning, are we?' Brad asked.

'Something like that.' I blushed and sat next to Richie, leaning in to kiss him. It felt both weird and completely normal that I could do that – kiss him.

When Richie left to refill his coffee, Brad asked, 'All good?'

I nodded. 'It feels like you described the other night – as if it was always meant to be like this.'

He smiled. 'I'm glad.'

'At the back of my mind, though, is guilt,' I added. 'What if the way I feel about Richie was always there, sitting in my heart and waiting to come out, and that's why it didn't work with James?'

'I wouldn't bother listening to guilt if I were you. Enjoy it, and see where it takes you.'

I nodded, grateful.

The rest of the week was taken up with work during the day, and lovemaking in the evenings. If I'd thought that the sex was something we needed to get out of our systems, I was happily mistaken. Every time we made love felt like a surprise and a coming home at the same time.

Although we lay in bed and talked, we never spoke about the future. We weren't looking any further forward than the long flight back to New Zealand via Sydney and Richie's sister and her husband. Neither of us knew what our relationship would look like outside of this bubble we'd created around ourselves.

When we were together, it was as if nothing and nobody else existed. Sometimes I had no idea where he ended and I began. The friendship was as it always was, but we'd slipped so easily into the next step that it hadn't even felt like a step.

I tried not to remember how in the early days James and I had done almost the same thing – although we'd lain in bed and talked of a future that was a lie. Nothing about Richie felt like a lie; it felt like exactly the opposite ... yet wasn't that how things had been with James at the start too?

James had dazzled me and taken me over. When I was with Richie I couldn't think straight, but it didn't feel at all as though I'd been conquered. Surely that was an important difference?

The closer we got to leaving, the more often the voice in my head reminded me of the plans waiting for me in England. Every time it popped up, I trampled on it. Not yet. Please, not yet.

On our last night, a Saturday, a group of us commandeered the campus shuttle and went into town for dinner at the hotel. We all had a little too much to drink. While Richie was off telling someone or other about New Zealand and Queenstown and how beautiful it was, I was chatting to Brad.

'Are you heading home soon?' I asked.

'In another month. I have no idea what I'm going home to, but my mate Todd's been keeping an eye on Abby, and he says she misses me, so I guess I have to trust that.'

'You'll invite us to the wedding?'

Even though I'd never met Abby, I had to believe that she and Brad would get back together. Otherwise what did this 'feels like destiny' thing mean?

'Abso-fucken-lutely. As long as you invite us to yours.'

'It's a deal.'

Even as I said the words, I reminded myself that I was still married. Regardless of what happened between me and Richie, I still had the remnants of that marriage to sift through and finish off. It was another thing outside the bubble that neither of us had spoken about.

I'd promised to email James and let him know my next movements, but so far I hadn't done so. Perhaps when we got to Sydney. My fear was that by contacting him I'd be inviting him into our bubble – and I wanted to keep it just between Richie and me for a little while longer.

After what seemed like a never-ending flight, or rather flights, Richie's sister Cate – apparently it was short for Catriona – met us at the airport. A tall, slim brunette, with vitality oozing from every pore, she hung onto Richie when she hugged him.

'Hey, get off,' he said without meaning it.

'I'm allowed to hug my baby brother for as long as I want to,' she said. 'Especially since I haven't seen him for years.'

When they separated, Cate was wiping her eyes, and Richie's were also suspiciously glittery. I stood off to the side, feeling awkward and, next to these two, small.

Richie reached for me and pulled me forward. 'Cate, this is Max.'

When she smiled it was like Richie's smile, wide and slow. 'I've heard so much about you, Max, it's great to finally meet you.' Without giving me a chance to respond, she continued, 'Richie, grab that trolley and we'll get you guys to the car – it costs a fortune to park here. Besides,' she directed a look of sympathy towards me, 'you two will be hanging out for a shower and a decent cup of coffee.'

'And maybe a nap,' I suggested hopefully. 'That had to be the longest flight in history.'

She laughed. 'Yes, it's a tough one. When you live on this side of the world, everywhere other than New Zealand is too far away.'

She directed us out of the terminal into the crisp blue of early morning Sydney. Within a few minutes we'd piled everything into the back of her car, and were negotiating our way out into traffic.

'It's still peak hour,' she explained, 'but we'll clear it fairly soon. Most of this is going into the city – we're heading towards the eastern suburbs.'

'That's Bondi, right?' I asked.

'Yeah. We're in Bronte, but Bondi's just up the road.' She turned to Richie. 'We've finished the extensions since you were last here. Added an extra bedroom, a study, and knocked a few walls out to open up the kitchen and lounge room. No one has separate dining rooms these days. Oh, and we've built a deck – you can see the ocean from there.'

He whistled. 'Business must be good.'

'What do you do?' I asked her.

'I'm in banking – but don't hold it against me. But it's Harry's job that pays for things like renovations. He's in management consulting. I won't even bother trying to explain it – no one ever really understands what he does. Come to think of it, no one really understands

what I do either, so I just say banking. Anyways, Harry's
in Hong Kong at the moment – some deal or another
– I gave up asking years ago. He'll be back by the end
of the week, and hopefully won't be away next week.'

Cate drove the way she talked – fast. I cringed
every time she turned to talk to me and took her eyes
off the road.

'What have you two got planned while you're
here?' she asked.

'The usual sightseeing things,' Richie answered.
'Hopefully this great winter weather will last and Maxi
can see Sydney at her best. Although, at least if the
weather turns she'll appreciate New Zealand more.' He
looked back at me and smiled. 'She also has a friend
here she wants to catch up with and –'

'Oh, really? Where does she live?'

'Umm...' I flicked through my phone for Miranda's
address. 'Clovelly. Is that anywhere near here?'

'Yeah, just down the beach a bit. What does she
do?'

'She's a designer – interiors. We were best friends at
college and did some of the same design subjects. She
fell in love with an Australian man, Oliver, at around
the time I got ... It must be six or seven years ago, and
they moved here late last year. I've really missed her.'

Richie looked back at me and I lowered my gaze.
He knew I'd been about to say 'at around the time I got
married'.

'Well,' said Cate, 'you should have a great catch-up. I've taken today off, but I'll be working the rest of the week – although I'll be home each evening, so if there's anything special you want to do ... No doubt Harry will want to take you somewhere nice when he gets home. In any case, we can try some local places over the next few nights.'

'I've got a craving for decent Thai or Vietnamese,' said Richie. 'Maxi wouldn't have tried that.' He turned back around to face me. 'Australia has some of the best Thai restaurants in the world. Sometimes I think they do Thai and Vietnamese better than the Thais or Vietnamese do it.'

'We sure do,' Cate said. 'Hey, maybe you can take Max up into South-East Asia sometime.'

She threw out the suggestion as though Richie and I were a done deal, as though I didn't have James waiting for me to finalise things, as thought I didn't have a return ticket. I wondered just what Richie had told his family about me.

'Maybe we can,' Richie said. I remained silent.

Soon we were pulling up at Cate and Harry's place. Cate drove into a small carport off the road, and helped us carry our bags inside. The entrance hallway led into a large open-plan living area and kitchen, with folding glass doors framing a view of the ocean. There was even a small in-ground pool off the deck. Richie watched me take it all in.

'It's too cold to swim, isn't it?' I asked.

'You can if you like,' replied Cate. 'We have it hooked up to a solar heater. Harry likes to swim most of the year. I don't use it as much as him – I run most days. Just down the road is the track that goes up to Bondi or down to Coogee. You should join me one morning?'

I didn't know whether she was talking to Richie or me.

'I might just do that,' said Richie. 'I feel like I need to get into it a bit more. Now I'm going home I might even start playing rugby again.'

Cate tried to grab at his non-existent love handles. 'You don't want to let yourself go,' she said. 'You're over thirty now, you know.'

'Thanks for that. I'm still in pretty good shape, aren't I?' He directed the question to me. The words were light, but the look in his eyes wasn't.

I shrugged. 'You could do with a bit of firming up. Those couple of weeks in Denmark have turned you a bit soft.'

His grin was wicked. 'Soft? Really?'

Cate laughed. 'Okay, you two … you're supposed to be jetlagged. I'll show you to your room.' She stopped. 'I'm right in putting you in together, aren't I? It's just that –'

I blushed and Richie answered for us. 'Yeah, that's fine, thanks, Cate.'

'Sorry,' she said to me. 'It's just that when Richie

first said you were coming over with him, he stressed you were travelling as friends. But when we talked last week, he mentioned that things had changed, and I assumed –'

I smiled. 'It's fine.'

The room she directed us to opened onto a balcony overlooking the water.

'You have your own bathroom here,' she opened the door, 'and feel free to come and go as you need to. I'll leave you a key. Harry and I are just across the hall. There are towels on the bed, so freshen up, and I'll put the coffee on and whip something up to eat. Toast okay? Or fruit and yoghurt? I have no idea whether you're no carb or low carb or vegetarian or gluten free. Everyone seems to be paleo these days – especially here in the eastern suburbs. I try to be, but every so often I just need a croissant, or some sourdough. You know how it is, right?'

I nodded, but I didn't know how it was, not really. In Brookford my work had been physical and, between Horrie's allotment and my own garden, most of my veggies had been fresh. I was fortunate in that I ate what I wanted to – and naturally had eaten whatever was fresh.

'I'm rambling again, aren't I?' said Cate. 'I'll leave you to it.'

Alone in the room together, I was suddenly shy with Richie.

'Cate's like that,' he said. 'She has no filter, she says whatever comes into her head. Wait until you meet Jess – she's worse.'

'You've talked to her about us?'

'Sure. She's my big sister, I tell her lots of stuff.'

I'd never had a big sister so I had no idea how that worked. 'What did you tell her?'

'What is this, Maxi? I told her originally that I was travelling with a friend. Then I told her that we got together. That's all.'

I busied myself with opening my suitcase and contemplating whether I should be unpacking. I could feel his eyes on me.

'I'm going for a shower,' I said.

'Is this a problem?'

'No, why should it be?'

'It shouldn't be, but it feels as though it is.'

I drew a deep breath. 'It's just that she seems to think we're together.'

'Aren't we?'

'Well, yes, but can we say that when I'm still married?'

'Don't you mean separated?'

'Of course, but officially I'm still married.'

I had no idea where the words were coming from; a position of no sleep maybe. Even as I was speaking I was aware that none of it was fair.

Richie squeezed his eyes shut and took a deep

breath before he spoke. 'Maxi, sweetheart, I have no idea what's started this.' He stepped towards me. 'Yes, you're still married, but we're also together. And, if I have anything to do with it, we'll stay together. So I told my sister that. Where's the harm in that?'

'How can you say that when I have a return ticket?'

He pulled me close and kissed me. I felt my anger and tiredness melt away. 'Just relax for now and enjoy what we have. There's plenty of time to work everything else out.' He kissed me again. 'We're sweet, right?'

I'd agree with anything he said as long as he didn't stop kissing me. 'We're sweet.'

Just when I thought that, despite my tiredness, it was about to get even sweeter, he pushed me away. 'Before this gets too far out of control again, you'd better go and have a shower.'

'You don't want to join me?'

He hesitated for a few seconds. 'Don't tempt me.'

'It would save on water ...'

'You have a point.'

He watched me as I pulled my tee-shirt over my head and reached behind to unclip my bra.

'I guess it also means we'll be downstairs quicker and the coffee won't get cold,' he said, unbuckling his jeans. 'And you're right – it'll save on water.'

Just before we stepped under the spray, he asked, 'Do you still think I'm soft?'

'Mmm, not this part of you.'

CHAPTER TWENTY-FIVE

After an early night and a blissfully long sleep, I was woken the next morning by Richie sitting on the bed to pull on his trainers. He was already dressed for running.

'What are you doing?' I murmured from below the covers.

'Going for a run with Cate along the coast. Although I'm a bit out of condition so she'll probably leave me for dead.'

'You seem to be in pretty good condition to me.'

He grinned and leaned over to kiss me. 'You go back to sleep, I'll be home in an hour.'

I snuggled back under the duvet and didn't wake again until a freshly showered Richie set down a cup of tea beside the bed.

He kissed an exposed shoulder. 'Hey, sleepyhead.'

'Hey, yourself.' I managed to manoeuvre myself into a seated position.

He sat on the side of the bed and watched me as I took stock of my surroundings, only reaching for the tea when I was satisfied that I knew where I was.

I sipped at it while he moved about the room folding clothes and hanging the towel I'd left on the floor behind the door. I loved how he needed some sort of order about him.

'How'd you go on the run?' I asked.

'It was tough – there are more stairs and undulations than you'd think, but it's the prettiest track you could come across. A couple of weeks of doing that and I reckon I'll be starting to get back to match fitness. Besides, I can't let my big sister beat me.'

I laughed. 'Has Cate left for work?'

'Yeah. I wanted to let you sleep as long as I could. She said hello and she'll see us for dinner.'

'What are our plans?'

'I figured we'll have some breakfast and then wander into the city for the day. What do you think?'

'Sounds good to me.'

It was Richie who inadvertently put the first teeny hole in our bubble later that afternoon. Walking back to Cate's house he said, 'I was thinking I might pop a few photos up onto Facebook from the project.' He noticed the look on my face. 'It's okay, I know you're not ready to go public with our relationship yet.'

I supposed that's what we were doing: having a relationship. It was obviously so much more than just sex, so much more than friends with benefits. It was so much more than anything I'd experienced before. By now I was sure of what I'd suspected that first night in his arms – that loving Richie as I'd always done had segued seamlessly into being in love with him. I hadn't told him, though, and he hadn't told me.

'Are you ready to go public?' I asked. Richie hadn't changed his relationship status in all the years that I'd known him.

He smiled and reached for my hand. 'I sure am. This is good, don't you think?'

'Yes, it's good.'

He kept hold of my hand as we walked. It was something he'd been doing a lot, as if he needed to be connected to me as we saw things for the first time. As if holding my hand made the already shared experience more shared. I liked it. James never liked to hold my hand. He said it was uncomfortable because I was so much shorter than him. His stride was longer, he said, which meant he needed to walk ahead. Somehow, hand-holding made what Richie and I had more like two people meeting as equals in a partnership. Maybe that was the difference: James never saw us as a partnership of equals – he was always the dominant party. He liked me to submit to him – anything else was out of the question. I liked what Richie and I had, but I couldn't forget that I still had a husband to be concerned about.

Richie watched it all play across my face. 'I haven't forgotten James. It's something we have to deal with sooner rather than later.'

Perhaps it was the hand-holding that transferred my thoughts through to him. I liked that he said '*we have to deal with it*'.

I nodded. 'I know. I suppose I'd prefer it to be later rather than sooner. I don't want to let him into this.'

He didn't say anything for a few seconds. 'No, I don't either. Has he contacted you?'

I shrugged. 'He hasn't phoned.'

'And you haven't checked your email.' It wasn't a question.

'I'll do it later.'

When we got back to the house, we unpacked our laptops. I hadn't turned mine on since I'd left Brookford. I wasn't expecting many emails – I didn't normally get too many other than fake lottery wins and requests for friendship from people I'd never heard of in places I'd never heard of, who wished to give me money for the privilege.

There were three emails from James.

The first was to the point:

> *I'm assuming you went ahead with your ridiculous idea to go to Denmark. Are you back in England yet?*

The second was a request:

When you get a chance can you check on the progress of the things we had sent over? I'm missing my blue linen jacket and think I might have put it in the pile to be sent. You should have the reference number somewhere.

The third was more complicated:

Maxine,
You haven't answered my previous two emails so I suppose that means (a) you haven't opened your laptop since you've been away digging holes with Richie, or (b) you're deliberately ignoring me.
I hope you've come to your senses and will come to New York. Let me know and I'll have India book your airfares.
Call me when you're back.
Yours,
James

I shook my head at the cheek of it and called Richie over. 'Check this out, would you? Even from New York he thinks I'm at his beck and call. Surely India can do this for him now?'

Richie read the email, smiled, and wisely chose not to get involved.

I stalked around the room as I ranted. 'How do I

answer this? He packed his shit, he can chase up where it is. This is exactly what was wrong with our marriage. He didn't listen to a word I said or consider what I wanted from life, but expected me to comply and want what he wants. He's behaving as if I haven't said the no-kids things is a deal-breaker, or I didn't catch him with his mistress.' I pointed accusingly at the laptop. 'He thinks that me not going to New York is some sort of childish tantrum and I'll fall back in line with his plans as soon as I've got whatever it was out of my system.'

'Am I something you have to get out of your system?' Richie asked quietly.

I stared at him as the implication of what I'd said hit me. 'Oh, no!' I rushed over and put my arms around his waist, resting my cheek against his chest. 'No. I don't think you're something I ever want to get out of my system.'

His arms remained by his side. 'I don't want to be some rebound against your husband.'

I looked up into his face. 'No, Richie, you're so much more than that.' I searched for the words to reassure him. 'When I'm with you it feels like I'm exactly where I need to be. It's nothing like it was with James.'

He finally put his arms around me and kissed the top of my head. 'I'm pleased to hear it.'

Then he kissed me properly and things got out of control very quickly. Later, when I was tucked in his arms, he brought the subject up again.

'You know you need to reply to him.'

'I know.' I snuggled closer into him. 'Why did I never notice how good you smell?' I nuzzled his throat. 'Or how good you taste?'

He smiled. 'And why did I never notice how insatiable you are?'

'Because I've never been like this before.'

'Don't change the subject. Did you tell him you're coming New Zealand with me?'

'No. I wasn't entirely clear about my plans. He asked if I was going to travel with you and I didn't answer him. Don't forget, we hadn't decided then.'

'Are you going to tell him about us?'

I hesitated. 'Not yet. At least not until we sort everything out.'

I felt him withdraw. 'I don't understand why. After all, he was unfaithful to you.'

'I know, but there's no reason to rub his nose in it.'

'No other reason?'

'No. None.'

There was no way I was going to tell him how James had thought Richie was the father of the baby I'd lost; how jealous of Richie he'd been. James had seen it before I did: the possibility of Richie and me. All that – just a few months ago – seemed a lifetime ago. Besides, if James knew about Richie now, he'd assume that I'd been disloyal back then too. I didn't want anything getting in the way of a smooth divorce.

'You're sure?' Richie asked.

'I'm sure. Now, shut up and kiss me again.'

I finally answered James's email after dinner:

> *Hi James,*
>
> *The correct answer to your question was option (a): I hadn't opened my laptop. I'm in Sydney and will be going to New Zealand next week. I won't be back in England until early September, so you'll need to chase up your stuff yourself.*
>
> *My decision not to come to New York hasn't changed. We need to sort out what comes next, how to finish everything up, but I'd prefer to do that face to face, so I guess that means waiting until I'm back in England – unless you'll be in Australia or New Zealand anytime soon.*
>
> *Give my regards to India. I'll email again from Queenstown.*

I checked my email before we went to bed that night.

> *Maxine,*
>
> *Am I right in assuming that you're still travelling with Richie?*

We need to talk.
James

I deleted it without responding.

The rest of our time in Sydney passed quickly. I woke early each morning and walked while Cate and Richie ran the coast track. Richie was right – it was gorgeous. All too often I'd find myself gazing out to sea as the sun came up, mesmerised by the expanse of blue. The sea at home seemed almost dull in comparison. Richie had always told me that he missed the skies of Australia and New Zealand, complaining that in England the sky sometimes seemed so close he could touch it, especially in winter. Now I knew what he meant.

The weather held and the days were mild and blue, allowing us to get out and about in the city, on the harbour, and even down to the beach for walks. As tempted as I was, I only needed to dip a toe into the ocean to remember that it was technically still winter – although I did take advantage of the solar heating in the lap pool on a few occasions. It felt good to stretch my body out in the water.

I didn't call James, nor did I reply to the email he sent asking why I hadn't called. Richie said nothing when he saw me open the email, grimace and then delete it.

We met Miranda one Wednesday for lunch at a hotel in Coogee right across the road from the beach.

'Oh, my darling girl!' She threw her arms around me and held me tight. Miranda had never been one for restraint – in anything. Her appetite for food, life and love knew no boundaries. 'I was so sad to hear about Horrie – you must really miss him.' Without waiting for a response, she pressed on. 'And James is here too … Hold on – you're not James,' she said, finally noticing Richie. 'You look nothing like James.'

She looked back at me, her eyes wide, then threw her arms around Richie almost as enthusiastically as she'd greeted me. 'Whoever you are, it's lovely to meet you. I'm Miranda.'

When it seemed she wasn't going to let go of her own accord, I stepped in to disentangle him. 'Mirry, this is Richie. He and I are … James and I are … Oh hell, Richie and I are together, and James and I aren't any more. As for the rest of it, you'll get the story over lunch.'

'In the meantime, why don't I get some drinks?' offered Richie. 'What would you like, Miranda?'

'Oh my god! Not only does he look like an All Black, he speaks like one too. No wonder you got rid of James.'

My cheeks felt warm.

Miranda laughed. 'You still blush as easily as you always did. Richie, how about you get a bucket of beers. We'll start with that and see where it heads from there.'

'A bucket?' I'd never heard the expression before.

Richie grinned. 'Oh, I've missed this part of the world.'

Miranda's eyes followed him to the bar and I brought her attention back to me. 'Eyes off the cute guy – he's mine.'

She sighed heavily and dramatically. 'I know, darling. It's a pity I'm so madly in love with my Aussie boy, otherwise I'd be tempted to try and steal him away. I have a lot to offer.' To illustrate, she shimmied her bounty, the beads she was wearing jingling with the movement.

'You sure do,' I agreed. 'Sydney obviously suits you – you look great.'

'I do, don't I? I'll never be a size eight or ten, or, let's face it, a fourteen again – and trust me, darling, anything larger than a twelve is a rarity in this part of Sydney – but I feel great. You should see how those perky little gym bunnies frown when I order bread or pastry – sometimes I think they're afraid the carbs will jump off my plate and hide in their quinoa.'

Richie was back with a metal bucket filled with ice and bottles of beer.

'No glasses?' I guessed, accepting the bottle Miranda pressed into my hand, and clinking with the two of them.

'Here's to catch-ups and surprising new men,' Miranda said.

Once I'd taken a mouthful and we'd settled back in

the winter sun, we were able to get down to some real conversation.

'How's Olly?' I asked.

He'd been offered a job here in Sydney late last year, and they'd accepted it and moved almost before I'd had a chance to process that they were going. Mirry never wasted valuable time thinking about decisions when she could be taking action. As she'd said, it was what they'd always planned. I'd remembered feeling envious when she spoke of their joint dreams, suspecting even then that was something James and I didn't have.

'He's fabulous. You know, I still want to ravish him every time I see him.' Richie choked a little as his beer went down the wrong way. Mirry smiled. 'It's true, we're as much in love now as we were back then.' She paused and looked at me. 'I was never convinced you felt like that about James.'

Beside me in the booth, Richie put his arm around my shoulders and pulled me close.

'James ... dazzled people,' she continued. 'I only met him a few times – you know how he always made excuses – but he dazzled me. There was something about him that made you think he could get whatever and whoever he wanted, and he wanted you. But I was never convinced that you were in love like Olly and I are.' Her gaze and her voice were serious for a few seconds, then she smiled widely and shook her head, the silver discs in her ears tinkling. 'Let's not talk about that right

now. What else? Well, Olly's working at his dream firm
– they specialise in high-end designs for difficult blocks
– and I've gone into business for myself. I mostly do
apartments for men of a certain age and certain salary
bracket who've recently divorced. Sadly for them, and
luckily for me, there's plenty of demand. Which is a
good thing because we paid an obscene amount for a
tiny house with a glimpse of water – if you stand in
the right spot on a box. It's what the agents like to call
"a renovator's delight", but we're having fun planning
it. It's going to be the perfect house for our children to
grow up in.'

'Oh, Mirry, I didn't know!' It had been too long
since we'd caught up.

'No, not yet – but we're working on it.' A wicked
grin spread across her face. 'We're working very hard
on it.' Once we'd stopped laughing, she changed tack
yet again. 'So, have you seen any of the old gang from
school or college? I saw Hilary briefly in March as she
was breezing through on a cruise, and she said she'd
heard that you and James were off to New York.'

'Well, he went, but as you can see, I didn't.' I
shrugged.

Richie leaned forward to drain his beer. 'Another
round?' At our nods he headed back in the direction
of the bar.

'Actually, sweetie, I'm glad you came to your senses
about James,' Mirry said. 'He was always too good to

be true. I didn't like to say anything at the time, but I'd heard he'd been seen around town with that assistant of his. What was her name? Something like a country … Peru? Cuba?'

'India,' I replied, smiling.

'Yes, her. I remember the first time you introduced me to him: he was so charming, but you were different to how you usually were when you were out with us all. More constrained, and constantly looking at him – almost as if you needed his approval. It was as if he had you on a leash.'

I recalled that night. I'd been so excited to finally introduce James to everyone. We'd tried before, but at the last minute something had always come up. We'd met in a bar near Covent Garden. Miranda was there, and some of the others from our little gang of ex-design students: Hilary, Ivy, Margie and Tom. We'd been drinking and laughing when James walked in. It was like one of those moments in a Western: everyone turned to look at him. He seemed out of place in the casual, slightly hip bar. He'd greeted me with a kiss on my lips and smiled as I introduced him to my friends. When he summoned the waiter over and ordered champagne, I felt proud that I was the one he wanted. This man who everyone looked at and looked up to, who acted as if he owned the world – or could own the world – wanted me. When he'd whispered that he couldn't stay too long, that Jeremy had asked the two of us to meet him at his club, it didn't occur to me that I was blowing my friends off.

Over the next couple of months there was always some reason why I couldn't meet the others, and eventually either they or I stopped trying. Miranda was the only one who'd persisted. When we moved to Brookford and James started travelling, I'd thought about trying to catch up, but everyone was working during the week – as was I – and weekends were for James.

Sometimes when we were in London for some event or another, I'd suggest contacting one of the old crew for a spontaneous picnic in the park, like I used to do with them. 'That sounds lovely, darling,' James would say. 'But I was looking forward to having you to myself this afternoon.' And he'd look into my eyes and I'd remember that he was flying out in the morning, and melt into him. 'Besides,' he'd say, kissing my neck, 'you know I don't like picnics.' I smiled now at the irony.

Miranda saw the smile and raised a questioning brow.

I shook my head. 'Maybe you're right. Anyway, none of it matters now. He's gone to New York, and I'm here.'

'With your All Black.'

'For now.'

'Really? You two look like you're really into each other.'

'We are. I am. It's just that …' I pondered how best to arrange the words. 'You know how you sometimes end up in places without thinking about how it happened? I didn't know what I wanted to do with my degree, and I ended up at James's office, then in his bed, then his wife. I let him take me over until there was nothing of me or what I wanted left. I know what I want to do with my life now, yet I've fallen into this completely wonderful thing with Richie. The problem is: he belongs on this side of the world – I'm just visiting. I've vowed never to put my goals aside for a man again, yet part of me is terrified that he won't ask me to do that for him.'

She patted my hand. 'I think I understand, but, sweetie, Richie isn't James. James was in love with an image of who he wanted you to be. The way Richie looks at you is completely different.'

'But what if I'm making the same mistake again?'

'I think the only mistake you can make right now is to let fear of what might happen somewhere down the track stop you from enjoying and exploring something that could be just what you need.'

'That's what Horrie would say.'

She shrugged and everything jingled. 'Great minds and all that. Oh, good … beer!'

Soon after, we ordered food, and spent the next few hours eating, drinking and discussing renovation plans and remember-whens.

At one point I relaxed back in my chair and tilted my head back, letting the warmth of the sun colour my cheeks. 'This is supposed to be winter, right?'

'Enjoy it, Hendo. Queenstown in winter is nothing like Coogee Beach – it's much colder.'

'Pity.'

Miranda made us promise to catch up again before we left for New Zealand. 'Olly would love to see you and, with the size of our mortgage, who knows how long it will be before I get back to England. Unless,' she said with a teasing glint in her eye, 'I visit you in New Zealand?'

Richie laughed and promised that we'd do something together on the weekend. 'I'll talk to Cate and Harry – maybe we can meet at a bar down on the harbour?'

'We'll look forward to it.'

CHAPTER TWENTY-SIX

Harry arrived home on Friday night, greeting Richie with a handshake and a man hug, and me with a kiss on the cheek as if he'd known me for years.

'So pleased to meet you, Maxine.'

'Call me Max, please.'

Cate he saved for last but definitely not least, gathering her into the sort of embrace that made Richie and me think that perhaps we should leave them to themselves.

'God, I've missed you,' he said when they finally separated.

'I've missed you too.' She was beaming.

'It's this bloody job,' he said to us.

'Are you away often?' I asked.

'Way too much for my liking. I'm supposed to be up there one week in every month, but lately it's been one week in every two. The travel sounds glamorous until you're doing it and it takes you away from the woman you love.' He gazed at Cate.

I turned away, feeling a bite in my heart. He had

a similar job to James, but their attitudes couldn't have been more different.

'You're never actually off-duty either,' he went on. 'There are always clients to entertain and you get sick of eating out. It's nice to come home and have something simple and home-cooked.'

I could feel Richie looking at me, so forced a smile to my face. 'I can imagine.'

'Tonight we have a treat,' said Cate. 'Max has prepared dinner – and it looks very posh.'

'It's not really,' I said, feeling a flush rise to my cheeks. 'It's just salmon and a vermouth sauce with some mash and curly kale. Richie and I went to the fish markets today. I've never seen such a range of seafood in my life!'

'Well, whatever it is, it smells wonderful in here,' Harry said. 'Have you been eating like this every night that I've been away?' he asked Cate later, pushing away his empty plate.

She smiled. 'Not every night, but Max certainly knows her way around a kitchen.'

I blushed again. 'I'm just very grateful for your hospitality, and I've been having such fun with ingredients I've never worked with before. Not these, of course,' I pointed to the now empty plates, 'but the Asian ingredients and the range of fresh vegetables.'

'And I'm very happy to be experimented on,' said Cate.

Richie grinned, reaching across to cover my hand with his. 'Maxi likes to feed people. Working with her was great – you never knew what was going to turn up for morning tea.'

'All I can say is, I haven't been able to miss my daily run since you guys arrived,' Cate added, 'and my whole paleo thing's gone out the window.'

'Has she been harping on about paleo again?' asked Harrison. 'She makes the same announcement every Sunday night. "Darling, I'm off the carbs next week … and no booze, okay? No matter what."' He mimicked his wife perfectly.

We'd finished dinner and were relaxing on the lounge in front of the television when my phone rang. I was curled into Richie, so he leaned forward to pick it up.

'It's James,' he said, handing me the phone.

'Ignore it,' I said.

'You need to talk to him, Maxi. It's time.'

I grimaced and got off the couch and took the phone through to the kitchen. 'James …'

'So, you are alive then.'

'I'm well, thank you … and you?'

There was a pause. 'I thought you said you'd call me when you got to Sydney. Are you in Sydney?'

I sighed and took the phone into our bedroom for some extra privacy. 'Yes, I'm in Sydney.'

'Where?'

'Bronte – it's near Bondi, near the beach.'

'Is Richie with you?'

'Yes, we're staying with his sister and her husband.'

'That all sounds very cosy.'

I counted to ten. 'What's your point, James?'

'My point, Maxine, is that you're married to me and you're travelling with another man and staying with his family. Are you still going to pretend there's nothing more than friendship between the two of you?'

'No. I'm not going to pretend that.'

'You admit it then? You're having an affair with Richie?'

'How can I be having an affair when it didn't start until after we were separated?'

The bedroom door opened and Richie came into the room. He sat beside me on the bed and laid a hand reassuringly on my knee.

'I thought we were just on a break,' James said. 'You told me you needed space and then you'd come to your senses.'

'No, that's what you said. I said we were over.'

'Please don't pretend that this is anything other than a rebellion shag. You were upset when you found out about India and me, so you decided to get your own back – with the gardener. It's all very lady of the manor, darling.'

My eyes filled with tears and I took another deep breath before responding. Richie's hand was gripping my knee. 'Please don't talk like that. Not about Richie.'

'You can't possibly be serious about him?'

'I am, James. I'm very serious.' I paused for a second. 'I'm in love with him.'

I heard Richie's sharp intake of breath, and felt him get up from the bed. I couldn't look at him.

'Well, hurry up and fall out of love with him. I don't imagine it will take too long. This conversation isn't over, Maxine. Your place is here, with me – and the sooner you realise that, the better.'

He hung up, and I slumped forward and rested my forehead on my knees.

From the other side of the room, Richie said softly, 'Did you mean it?'

'Which part?'

'The part about being in love with me.'

I nodded. 'Yes.'

'And you told him first? Before you told me?'

I shrugged. 'I'm sorry. It just came out. I know you probably don't –'

He moved back to the bed and raised my chin so I could look at him. He caught a tear, tracing it down my face. 'Say it to me now.'

'I'm in love with you.'

'And I'm in love with you too,' he said.

His kiss when it came was different, sweeter somehow. Or perhaps it was my imagination. Our lovemaking was sweeter too. He kept me on the edge so we came together, and when he collapsed beside me, he said it again. 'I love you, Maxi.'

'I love you too.'

As I said it, it felt almost like a sigh. Even though it was so good and so right, it also felt as if the slightest thing could come in and damage it. I held him tighter, as if that might keep the bubble around us for a little longer.

I didn't know whether it was because of the words we'd exchanged that Sunday night, but our second week in Sydney took on a dream-like quality. Even though it seemed that we didn't stop talking, neither of us brought up the subjects of James or the future.

Saying what we'd said to each other made everything all more precarious somehow, even as it brought us closer together. There was now so much more at stake. Being in love meant this could never be a holiday romance, something I could fly home from without a backward glance. Being in love meant there were decisions to be made and compromises to be reached, or hearts broken.

I wondered whether by falling in love with Richie, I'd again put myself in a position where I'd have to make a choice between him and my goals.

What Mirry had said was right though: Richie was nothing like James; and the way I felt about him was different too. Being in love with him, I had to believe that somehow, together, we'd work this out. We'd always been able to talk about everything. Surely this, and what happened after the first week of September, would be no exception?

Mum called me on our last Thursday in Sydney. It was early morning and Richie and I were sitting on Cate's deck having coffee. My eyes filled when I heard Mum's voice. Richie held my hand briefly, then kissed the top of my head before going inside to give me some privacy.

'What time is it there?' she asked.

'Just after eight in the morning. It's the middle of winter and we're sitting outside having coffee.'

'I've seen the pictures you've posted – it looks fabulous. How's Richie?'

I paused before answering. 'He's good. We're … well … I guess you'd say we're together.'

The breath I held while I waited for her response had nothing to do with how they felt about Richie – I knew they were fond of him him – but how they'd feel about me being with Richie while I was, technically, still married to James.

'Yes, I heard.'

'How?' Surely Duncan couldn't have known that piece of news?

'James phoned the other night, wanting to know if your father and I could step in to – as he so beautifully put it – help you come to your senses.'

'Oh. I'm sorry, Mum.'

'There's no need to apologise, dear, he was perfectly civil about the whole thing. In fact, he made it sound as if you were a teenager having a mini rebellion and simply needed to be taken in hand and grounded for a while.'

'Of course he did. What did you tell him?'

'That it's your life and you're a grown woman capable of making your own decisions.' She paused. 'We would never interfere in your happiness, darling. I just thought you'd like to know.'

When I didn't immediately answer, she said, 'You are happy, aren't you?'

'I'm very happy. I have no idea what will happen, or even what we're doing, but I'm happy.'

'Promise me you won't think too hard about it.'

'What do you mean by that?'

'Spending your time worrying about what might or might not happen won't do either of you any good. I've seen the way Richie looks at you. He isn't James and he won't ask you to give up anything you're not prepared to. You need to trust that.'

I forced a laugh even though my throat was choked with emotion. 'You've been visiting those crystal shops, haven't you?'

'Hold on, your father's here. He wants a quick word.'

'Hi, girl, is Richie looking after you?'

'He is, Dad.'

'Good. Don't worry about James – deal with him when you're ready.' His voice sounded gruff. 'Your mother's back. Take care.'

'Remember what I said,' Mum added. 'You don't have to have it all worked out.'

'Okay.' I couldn't manage any more.

'Love you, darling.'

'Love you too, Mum.'

Once I hung up, the tears flowed freely. I walked to the edge of the deck and stared out at the ocean. I'd miss it when we left tomorrow, but I didn't belong here.

Richie came back and, without saying anything, held me tightly until the tears stopped.

'Are you missing home?' he asked.

'No. It's just hearing their voices, you know?'

I couldn't tell him that what I was really missing was the security that went with belonging. I wasn't sure I'd belong in Richie's life in Queenstown; and I certainly didn't belong in what was left of my old life, or in James's new life.

'I know.' He tilted my head up and kissed me softly. 'Did you tell them about us?'

'I didn't need to. James called them after we spoke the other night.'

He looked into my eyes and nodded slowly. 'I see. Is that a problem?'

I shook my head and forced a smile. 'You know they like you.'

'But they're worried about the situation,' he guessed.

I shrugged in his arms. 'Perhaps.'

'Did they ask when you're coming home?' His tone sounded forced – or something.

'Why, are you tired of me already?'

I laughed and playfully tapped his chest to let him know that my words were teasing, even though the sentiment behind them wasn't. I knew that answering the question would lead to a conversation I didn't think either of us was ready to have yet.

His face was serious. 'No, sweetheart, I'm not. I can't imagine ever being tired of you.'

He rested his forehead against mine and we stood like that for a few minutes until I reached up and kissed him.

'Come on, mister, this is our last day in Sydney and I haven't been swimming in the ocean yet.'

He laughed at me. 'You're mad – it's the middle of bloody winter.'

'It's still warmer than most of the summer days back home. Are you scared of a little cold water? I'll make it worth your while later …' I waggled my eyebrows at him suggestively.

'How can I resist when you put it like that? But how about a little taster of what I've got to look forward to first – before my balls shrink to the size of raisins in that cold water?'

'Oh, you do drive a hard bargain …'

August in the Kitchen

What a difference a month makes.

Last time I was writing to you from a farm in the Cotswolds. The fields behind my cottage were dotted yellow and white with buttercups and wild daisies.

Today I'm sitting on a sun-filled deck in the eastern suburbs of Sydney, looking out at an ocean that's bluer than any ocean has the right to be. It's the middle of winter here, and the nights and mornings are cool, but the days are longer than they are in an English winter. If the sun is shining, you can be tricked into thinking the calendar has it wrong. But then a cool change sweeps through, bringing with it the same dull grey that we get in England and the jackets and umbrellas come out – for a few days at least. What's amusing is how Sydney-siders seem taken by surprise by these weather events, as if it's unusual for it to be – shock, horror – cold in winter. The newspapers are full of it.

The other day I sampled my first pho: a Vietnamese noodle soup. It's an aromatic beef broth flavoured with star anise, ginger, cinnamon, cloves and plenty of other spices, with rice noodles, thinly sliced raw beef (don't worry – it 'cooks' in the broth) and a heap of fresh herbs and chilli on the side. I had a go at making a cheat's version the other night and it turned out reasonably well – the key was getting enough depth of flavour into the supermarket-bought beef stock. To slice the beef paper-thin, I placed it in the freezer for half an hour or so first. I've popped my version's recipe onto the website, so give it a try – even if you're reading this on the other side of the world where it's still summer. It's quick enough for an express mid-week supper, and the herbs and spices will make you think you've gone somewhere exotic for your summer holiday.

Next time I post, I'll be in Queenstown, New Zealand, where I'm told I'll need my winter woollies. Don't forget, if you want to keep up with what I'm seeing and eating, you can follow me on Instagram. The link is at the bottom of this post.

Until next time,
Max

CHAPTER TWENTY-SEVEN

Richie insisted I take the window seat for the three-hour flight across to Queenstown. 'You'll see why,' he said.

I did. The views of the coastline and then the snow-topped mountains were like something out of a movie involving hobbits and journeys across made-up worlds. Richie held my hand as I watched it all.

'It's magnificent,' I told him.

His grin was proud, as if he were responsible for manufacturing the scene unfolding below us. 'Told you.'

As we came in to land I saw him brush away some moisture from his eyes. I reached across and rubbed his thigh through his jeans.

'Good to be home?'

He nodded and smiled, his eyes glistening. 'Sure is. It's been too long.'

The moment we walked into the arrivals lounge, Richie pushing the trolley with our bags, a smallish woman threw herself at him, reaching up on her toes to kiss him.

'Oh, my Ricky, I've missed you,' she said, tears rolling down her cheeks.

He held her against him, closing his eyes to savour the moment. 'I've missed you too, Mum. But I'm home now.'

A tall man with a head full of grey curly hair was waiting to the side, smiling at the reunion. As soon as his mother released him, Richie strode across and held out his hand for the half-shake, half-hug thing men did.

'It's good to have you back, Rick,' the man said. 'Back for good this time?'

'I sure am, Fletch.'

I'd been hanging off to the side to allow Richie to say his hellos. It was his mother who noticed me first. About my height, with short dark hair, and dressed in jeans with a red cable-knit jumper, she looked much younger and fitter than the fifty-eight I knew she was. There was no mystery about where Richie had inherited his smile from. Now that smile was directed at me.

'You must be Max,' she said, hugging me. 'I've been looking forward to meeting you. We're going to have such fun getting to know each other.'

'Don't listen to her, Maxi,' said Richie. 'She just wants you to help her bring the garden back to life. In case you hadn't gathered, this is my mother, Milly, and my father, Cameron – but except for Mum, we all call him Fletch.'

Fletch held out his hand for me to shake it.

Although he was smiling, it wasn't without reserve.

'Come on,' he said. 'Let's get these bags into the car and get you home. I'm warning you, though, you won't get much time to settle in. Your mother's invited Jess for dinner too.'

'I'm looking forward to seeing her,' Richie said. 'Any dramas you need to warn me about in advance?'

'Be nice about your sister,' said Milly. 'She's too busy these days with the cafe and her tramping to get herself into any trouble.' As Fletch and Richie loaded the bags into the back of the Land Rover she added, 'I know it's out of our way, but it's such a clear afternoon, so how about we take Max to that point way above the St Moritz where you get the view of the mountains and the lake?'

'Sure,' Fletch said. 'Show Rick what he's been missing.'

It was a short drive from the airport into Queenstown and then up to the vantage point. Beyond the town, as far as I could see, was a wide expanse of lake framed by a range of mountains, many of which were covered in snow.

'Magnificent,' I breathed.

'More like remarkable,' Richie said, circling my waist from behind and pulling me back into him. 'That's what they're called: the Remarkables. And that's Lake Wakatipu. The Maori say it was formed when a giant who abducted the daughter of a local chief was burnt to death in his sleep. The heat melted the glaciers around him to form the lake.'

I turned in his arms to look up at him. 'I remember you telling me about that. How the lake breathes – rising and falling with the beat of his heart. You said you wanted to show me this place. You said I'd love it.'

He kissed my lips lightly. 'So I did.'

'I think your father wants us back in the car,' I said when his eyes started to darken in that way they did. 'This can wait until later.'

Home for Richie was a long lodge-style house set on a small hill on a section – he'd already told me that blocks of land in New Zealand were called 'sections' – that ran down to the lake. The exterior was a mix of timber, corrugated iron and local stone, framed by flax of differing varieties.

'Did you have something to do with this?' I asked Richie.

'How did you guess?'

Inside, the open-plan space was warm and welcoming, with a fireplace on one side of the room, and wide windows, framed by heavy curtains to keep the warmth in, looking down the hill towards the lake. The living area ran seamlessly from sitting room to a dining space filled with a long wooden slab-like table, and into what could only be described as my dream kitchen. I couldn't help the little 'oh' that came from my mouth as I saw the double doors that opened onto a covered deck area and, beyond, what could be – with some attention – a very good vegetable and herb garden.

Milly smiled as she watched me take it all in. 'It's a fabulous kitchen, isn't it? When we built this place, Cam asked me to jot down my wish list. Somehow he managed to capture all of it. I think the garden was a little ambitious, but my intentions were good … Well, for the first few years anyway. Now that you're here, you can help me get it ready for spring.'

'I'm not sure how much help I'll be. I don't know what grows – and when – on this side of the world.'

She waved my concerns away. 'Surely it's just a matter of reversing the seasons? Between the two of us we'll be fine. Now, let me show you to your room – I think Richie and Fletch have already taken the bags – and we'll leave you to get unpacked and settled in.'

Richie had already opened his suitcase and was separating his clothes into piles: for the drawers, the laundry, and to be hung in the wardrobe.

Milly reached up to kiss his cheek. 'I can't believe you're home,' she said.

He grinned and kissed her back. 'Yeah, me neither.'

'Thanks for bringing him home,' she said to me.

'Oh, I had nothing to do with it.'

'I think you did.' Still smiling, she left us to it.

'Your parents seem great,' I said, sitting on the bed and watching him unpack.

It was something Richie did so methodically, so automatically. Where I'd toe my trainers off after a walk and leave them wherever, his would be neatly under the bed. Where I'd leave my clothes where I stepped out of them, his would be either refolded, rehung or put straight into the laundry basket.

'Yeah, they are.' He sat beside me, still holding a pile of folded tee-shirts. 'It's hard to believe I'm actually here.' He smiled at me. 'And even harder to believe that you're here with me. If someone had told me that even three months ago, I'd have thought it was the most unlikely outcome imaginable. But, man, I'm glad it happened.'

He leaned in and kissed me. 'I'd better get this done. If I know Jess, she'll be bounding in here almost as soon as that cafe of hers is closed.' He looked at my unopened suitcase. 'Aren't you unpacking? I get that you didn't for Denmark and Sydney ... but here?'

Suddenly I felt awkward. While we were travelling it had been easy to pretend that what we were doing was for real, but now, confronted with the problem of where to put my clothes, it was obvious that this was Richie's home, not mine, and that in the first week of September, I'd be the only one repacking. There was no question of him leaving here to come back to England with me.

'I left you the drawers on this side,' he said.

'But what about your stuff when it arrives from

England?'

'We'll work that out when we need to.'

We again. The smile I gave him came from my heart. We would work it all out when we needed to. Until then, I wanted to cram in as many memories with him as possible.

We'd only just slid the last of the unpacked bags under the bed when the door was thrown open and a whirlwind of a girl flung herself at Richie, knocking him back onto the bed. The women in Richie's family certainly liked to throw themselves about.

'Christ, Jess, you don't know your own strength,' he grumbled when she finally released him. 'And it's the done thing to knock first, you know – you could have interrupted us.'

'Yeah, Cate said she needed to remember to do that. She also said her water consumption wasn't as high as she'd expected with two more adults in the house,' she replied without concern. 'And you must be Max. Oh my god, Richie, she's actually blushing. I didn't know anyone blushed any more – it must be that English skin. She does have gorgeous skin. '

'Yes,' Richie interrupted. 'This is Max. She does still blush; she is beautiful; and last I heard, Australia has a water shortage. Anything to help.'

Jess had switched her attention fully to me. Instead of the instant hug I'd received from both Cate and Milly, she looked me up and down, nodded as if to proclaim I had her approval, then, smiling, stepped forward to kiss me on the cheek. 'Good to have you here.'

She thought for a second or two, then threw her arms around me. 'It's really good to have you here. Richie says you like tramping – well, you probably call it walking – so I'll show you some great tracks while you're here, and –'

'Jess! Leave the poor girl alone. In fact, get out of here and leave us both alone so we can finish unpacking. We'll be out for a drink soon.'

'You'd better be – Mum's setting out some cheese and biscuits, and she's got a roast lamb on. She reckons you wouldn't have had a decent one since you left home. I told her you probably had, but she said it wouldn't have been a New Zealand lamb. And she's done a pavlova because she didn't think Max would have had a proper pavlova before, being English and all.'

'We'll be out soon,' Richie said again, opening the door to usher her through it.

'I know when I'm not wanted,' she said. 'Just don't go taking any showers – I've heard about what you do in there.' With a cheeky grin she shut the door and was gone as quickly as she'd arrived.

'Phew.' I sat back on the bed and looked at the space where she'd been.

'Jess is like that,' said Richie. 'Always has been. Talks first, thinks later. Acts first, thinks much later.

Even as a kid she was always running off, getting into scrapes, fighting with the boys.' He smiled. 'Come to think of it, she's still doing that – running off, getting into scrapes, fighting with boys. At least these days she's too busy with work to get into too much trouble.'

He sat on the bed beside me. 'She's right though – I'd like a shower right now.' He leaned in to kiss me. 'Or something …'

'But your parents …' My protest was half-hearted as his kisses moved down my throat. I tilted my head to allow him better access.

'I'll be quick,' he promised, pushing me back.

'Not too quick, I hope.'

Dinner was a lively affair as both Milly and Jess clamoured for Richie's attention. The lamb was, as promised, divine. Milly told me the trick was – aside from making sure it was New Zealand lamb – to cook it long and slow with red wine, rosemary and garlic. The pavlova was also far more than I'd expected, the meringue lifted by the addition of dark chocolate and topped with berries and more chocolate.

'I've been experimenting a little lately,' she said. 'I found this one online. It's a Nigella recipe, and now it's Jess's favourite.'

'I can certainly see why. I've only ever had those thin crumbly versions with fruit salad and tinned passionfruit, sometimes even with canned cream,' I told her, screwing my nose up at the memory. 'It was almost enough to turn me off them for life.'

'Don't worry, dear. You'll never have a bad pav down here.'

I sat back while Milly, Jess and Richie chatted and laughed. If it were at all possible, I loved him even more as I watched him with his family, seeing the love he had for them and his pure joy at finally being home. Occasionally he'd look across at me and smile, attempting to include me in the conversation, but I shook my head and mouthed that it was alright. Tonight was his night.

Fletch didn't contribute much: a word here, a comment there. But the way he looked on indulgently as Milly fussed and Jess and Richie bantered showed me he was obviously happy to have Richie home. I just wasn't convinced that happiness extended to me.

CHAPTER TWENTY-EIGHT

'Well, well, well – Richie Evans! I'd heard you were back in town … and here you are.'

The woman standing beside our table was stunning. Although she was dressed simply in basic black, there was something about her that had most of the patrons in the busy restaurant looking at her. It could have been her height: in her high-heeled boots she would have been almost six foot tall. It could have been her hair: silvery blonde and completely straight. Perhaps it was the large-framed black sunglasses pushed up onto her head. Whatever it was, she was hard to miss, and right now Richie was the focus of her attention.

He hesitated for just a few seconds, then pushed his chair out, rose to his feet and kissed her cheek. 'Jodi Charters! Good to see you. Weren't you in Melbourne?'

'It's Spencer now,' she corrected. 'Remember, I married Byron? You were there. And yes, we were in Melbourne. He still is.'

Richie raised his eyebrows. 'Oh, it's like that?'

'Uh-huh.' She shrugged. 'It happens – you've been

away for a long time. Toby – my son – and I have come home.' She finally seemed to notice me. 'Are you going to introduce me to your friend?'

'Of course. Jodi, this is my girlfriend, Maxine. Max, Jodi and I were at school together. We also went to the same uni in Sydney – obviously not the same course though.'

She grinned and fluttered her manicured fingers. 'As if I'd ever risk breaking these nails in some dirt.'

'Pleased to meet you,' I said, offering a hand to shake. I looked around at the bustle of people in the entrance waiting for a table. 'Are you meeting someone – or would you like to join us?'

'No, I'm not meeting anyone, and I'd love to join you,' she said gratefully, wriggling out of her puffa jacket and scarf. 'I ate here with Byron and Toby in the summer when we were home to see Mum. The food was fabulous – nearly as good as in Melbourne – but I'd forgotten just how busy it gets.'

'I thought winter was the peak time here,' I said, 'for the skiing.'

'These days the summer season's almost as popular.' She summoned a waiter and ordered a glass of wine and a rice-paper roll filled with pork and salad. 'Is that an English accent? I take it you're the reason Richie stayed away so long?'

I laughed.

Richie reached across the table and put his hand

on mine. I saw her watch the movement. 'Maxi and I worked together in England, but this is fairly new.'

He smiled into my eyes and suddenly it was just us in that crowded room.

'I remember when Byron and I used to be like that,' Jodi was saying. 'All lust and hands and eyes.' She sounded wistful. 'Now I suppose he's doing all that with Meghan.'

'Really?' Richie moved his hand away to allow the waiter to place our meals on the table. 'Is that what went wrong? I always thought Byron only had eyes for you.'

She shrugged. 'Things change. Now he only has eyes for Meghan.'

Thankfully Jodi's food arrived soon after and the subject changed to one of general catch-up as we ate. Who from their old gang at school had married, divorced, had more kids, fallen off the rails, died — that sort of thing. Like last night, Richie attempted to include me in the conversation, but I shook my head slightly and smiled at him. I suspected I'd be doing a bit of that, at least until Richie had got his initial catch-ups out of the way.

'Have you caught up with Dan or any of your rugby mates yet?' Jodi asked.

'No, that's tomorrow.' He looked at me and grinned. 'I'm introducing Maxi to Kiwi club rugby. In fact, I could even be pulling a jersey back on myself this season. I haven't played for years, but Jess tells me the way we're going that won't matter too much.'

Jodi laughed. 'She's got that right. It's been a pretty dismal season so far. So does that mean you're back for good?' She lowered her eyes as she asked the question, concentrating on the half-eaten rice-paper roll in front of her.

'Yeah, it's time. It's weird – so many of us leave to see the world, yet we all find our way back. It's like we need to get out for the experience, then we come home to put it to use. What about you? Are you staying put now?'

'I'm not sure. I'm renting a place just out of Arrowtown, not far from Mum. Dad's still up in Auckland.'

'Ah, yes. I recall Mum saying he'd married again?'

'Uh-huh. Number three, I think. I've lost count.' She laughed, but it sounded forced.

'And Toby?'

'He's five now. He's settled in well at school, and is already playing rugby – much to his father's disgust. You know how staunch an AFL fan Byron is. I need to find a job though.' She shrugged. 'I haven't had a lot of luck so far.'

'What are you looking for?'

'I'm not really sure. I'd like to use my teaching degree, so maybe I'll see if I can get some casual hours at the school. But in the meantime … I have no idea. It's been a while since I worked – I didn't go back after

I had Toby. Byron was so insistent that I be a stay-at-home mum and look after Tobe and him, and look where that got me. We're finished, and I have no career.' She sounded bitter. 'Next time I'll go for a man I can rely on and who doesn't expect me to give up my life.'

Was it my imagination or did her eyes hold Richie's a few seconds too long when she said that?

He didn't seem to pick up on it. 'Let me have a word with Jess – she's often after extra hands in the cafe, especially this time of year. I can't promise anything, but it could be something to tide you over until you find something more permanent.'

'Thanks, Richie, I'd appreciate that.'

Soon after, Richie excused himself to head down the hall to the bathroom.

'It's good to see him so happy,' Jodi said. 'Especially since ...' She shook her head. 'It doesn't matter. It's just nice to see him happy.'

'You guys – you, Byron and Richie – were close?'

'We sure were. In fact, it was Richie who introduced us. It was hard for him, though, after the wedding. Then he went away. I couldn't blame him. Not really.' Her gaze seemed fixed on something long ago. I waited for her to say more. 'Anyway, enough about that. How are you finding New Zealand? Is this your first trip?'

'It is, and I'm loving it. Although we only flew in yesterday, so I haven't seen too much yet.'

She nodded. 'It's a beautiful part of the world.'

She sipped at her wine. 'And Milly and Fletch are looking after you?' She didn't wait for me to answer. 'I must get across and see them – indulge my craving for Milly's scones and home-made jam. I spent many an afternoon at that kitchen table with Milly listening to my teenage dreams, and Fletch standing in for my father. I'm sure at some stage they'd hoped ...' She shook her head. 'It all seems so long ago. There you are, Richie! We thought you'd got lost.'

He grinned at her. 'Just figured I'd settle the bill while I was down there. Saves me fighting my way through this crowd again.'

'Oh, let me give you ...' Jodi scrambled for her handbag.

'Don't worry about it – this one's on me.' He reached for my hand to pull me to my feet. 'Maxi and I have somewhere we need to be, but it was great seeing you again. I'll be sure to mention you to Jess.'

Jodi got to her feet to kiss Richie goodbye. She leaned down to give me an air-kiss. 'It was lovely to meet you, Max. I'm sure we'll be seeing a lot of each other – probably starting with the rugby club tomorrow night after the game.'

I told her I looked forward to it, but I wasn't sure I meant it.

'So where do we need to be in such a hurry?' I asked Richie.

We were heading out of town in the Land Rover – or Landy, as Richie called it – an older model than the one we'd been picked up in yesterday. Richie had explained that he'd bought this one when he first got his driver's licence, and Fletch had kept it maintained for him all these years.

Richie looked briefly away from the road and grinned at me. 'You'll see. Just be patient.'

I rested my hand lightly on his leg. 'Jodi seemed nice.'

'Yeah, she is. I was surprised to hear about her and Byron breaking up. I guess you never can tell, hey?'

'She was saying … oh!'

We'd rounded a curve in the road and were driving towards what was the most beautiful vista I'd ever seen. The clear, almost turquoise blue of Lake Wakatipu stretched wide and long in front of us, with glimpses of the road curving off to the right, and snow-covered mountains brightly white against the frosty blue of the winter sky.

'Oh my,' I said.

'It gets you like that, doesn't it.' Richie pulled into a lookout point. 'I don't think I'll ever get tired of seeing it.'

We both got out of the car and stood watching the scene in all its blue and white splendour.

'I'm not sure I've ever seen anything so beautiful.' I whispered the words, as if saying anything out loud could shatter the moment.

He took my hand and held it in his. I moved closer to him, still holding his hand, and rested my head against his arm. We stood like that for a few more minutes before he announced that he had something more to show me.

'Better than this?' I asked.

'Different to this.'

We drove through a small town at what was, Richie told me, the top of the lake. 'This is Glenorchy. That way is the Dart River – we're heading up there a bit.' He pointed towards the right.

'We're not stopping here?' I looked wistfully at some jet-boats roaring across the water.

'Don't worry – we'll be back. You're not leaving this part of the country without a jet-boat ride, or walking at least part of one of the tracks. The Routeburn Track starts not far from here.'

It was only a throwaway line, but it stung. Richie acted as though this relationship was a forever thing, but he hadn't mentioned anything about me changing my return date, and comments like that reminded me this was just a break from reality and one day I'd be going home and leaving him here.

An image of Jodi floated into my head. She'd hinted that there'd been more between her and Richie than just friendship. I looked across at him and he took his eyes briefly from the road and smiled into mine. If there had been, it didn't matter now.

Just past the Dart River bridge the road was unsealed and we jolted along through what seemed like a series of fields. Unlike the fields at home – which were small, lush and green – these were large and filled with long golden tussocks of grass. I hung onto the handle above my window to stop myself lurching around the cabin.

Richie grinned as a particularly large bump almost had me out of my seat. 'Don't worry, we're almost there.'

'I'm enjoying the ride,' I said.

We parked the Land Rover in the centre of a field, and Richie took a blanket and a basket from the back seat.

'I packed some tea and some of Mum's scones and jam,' he explained. 'I know it's cold, but I thought we could have a picnic here.'

He spread the thick blanket across the grass, while I wandered down to the edge of the water. Across the widest part of the river I could see a line of beech trees that marked a shelter of some description. A house? Or perhaps a hut, somewhere for a walker – sorry, tramper – to rest. Behind it rose a mountain covered mostly with snow. Up-river the channel narrowed; and downstream, it meandered through farmland. I could see cows grazing at the edge of the river in the neighbouring field; and in the distance I was sure I heard the bleat of a sheep. Other than that, and the wind rustling through the grasses, it was blissfully quiet. It felt as though we were the only two people alive.

Richie came to stand beside me, reaching down to pick up a pebble and skip it across the still water.

'It's beautiful. What is this place?'

'Paradise,' he said.

'No, seriously ... what's it called?'

'That's the name. Paradise.'

I giggled.

'What's so funny?'

'You've taken me to Paradise.'

'I thought I took you there last night.' His smile was cheeky and his eyes darkened as he looked into mine. 'At least twice.'

He moved closer. Oh, what this man could do to me with just a look. When he gazed at me the way he was now, I forgot everything else – who I was, where I was, the fear that this would all be over one day soon. None of it mattered. All that mattered were the waves of desire that coursed through my body and the memory of how it felt to have his lips around my nipple, his tongue in my mouth, his hands between my legs, his ...

I took a deep breath, fighting for control, anything that would stop me from doing what I so wanted to do. For god's sake, we were out in the open. Anyone could come down here. And it was cold.

I inhaled and the smell of him came in with my breath and took my balance away. I steadied my hands against his chest and leaned forward that tiny bit more so I could taste his skin at the delicious point right where his neck met his jumper. The taste of him mingled with the smell of him and the feel of his chest under my hands. The effort of absorbing it all was too much, so I closed my eyes and allowed all the senses to merge. A soft sigh escaped from my throat. I reached down between us and held the outline of his cock through his jeans, feeling him grow harder as I gently squeezed.

'Christ, Maxi,' he said, his eyes half-closing. 'Go easy.'

I relaxed my grip and took his hand instead.

'I didn't say you had to stop,' he grumbled.

'Who says I want to stop?'

I led him to where he'd laid the blanket down on the tussocked grass and took off my jacket and beanie, holding his gaze. Next came my boots and my jeans.

'Out here?' he asked as I knelt on the blanket before him, my mouth dry as I released him from the confines of his jeans.

His hands held my head as I nuzzled into his balls, licking and blowing and teasing, my fingers tracing his length, squeezing, stroking. Finally I took him into my mouth and felt his groan run all the way through him and into me. Too soon he gently moved my head away and joined me on the ground. As I would have protested, he pulled me towards him and slid his fingers into my knickers.

'It felt so good,' he said, his middle finger finding my sweet spot, 'but I want to be in you.'

I pushed him onto his back and straddled him. 'That's a coincidence,' I said, lowering myself slowly onto him.

And then he was in me, so deeply that I gasped. It felt deeper than he'd ever filled me before, deeper than I'd ever been filled before. When the orgasm came, it seemed to have come from my toes and rushed through my body to explode from my mouth in a cry. He called my name soon after, riding my wave with me before letting go on his own. I collapsed on top of him, panting. He rolled me over so we were both lying on our sides, still joined, looking into each other's eyes, holding on until we could breathe normally again.

'Wow,' he said.

I nodded and snuggled in closer.

'What are you thinking?' he asked.

How I love you more than I thought it possible to love another person. How I want nothing more than to stay here with you in this wonderful place and have your babies and grow old with you – if only you'd ask me to. How the thought of leaving you is more than I can bear. How nothing else matters but this moment with you.

I didn't say any of that. Instead, I looked up at him and said, 'I hope we didn't scare any ducks – or those horses over there.'

I felt him chuckle. 'I don't think they're easily scared.'

He was looking into my eyes rather than at the view and I thought he was about to say something else – he started to say something else – but instead he put a hand on my hip. 'You're cold, I'm cold, perhaps we should put some clothes back on and have some tea. I'd like to be back on the sealed road before the sun goes down.'

By Sunday the weather had closed in. Snow was falling in the mountains, and the forecast was for some of it to settle in town overnight. It certainly felt cold enough. Richie and I rode the Gondola up to Bob's Peak in the morning. When we set out, the sun was shining. By the time we'd looked at the view, had our coffee and were ready to head back down the mountain, the Remarkables were obscured.

That afternoon, we stood on the rugby field with Milly and Fletch as the wind whirled around us, our gloved hands shoved into pockets for added warmth. Jess spun between us and groups of her friends, while other locals drifted by to say 'Hi', 'Welcome back', and variations on 'Will we get you back on the paddock soon, son?'

I heard one old guy say to Fletch, 'It's time that boy of yours was back. He always had a safe pair of hands – we could have done with him this season.'

'We sure could have.' Fletch noticed me listening in. 'This is Max, she's a friend of his – come over for a few weeks.'

'You're not intending to coax him back over there, are you?'

The question was directed to me, but Fletch answered first. 'Not a chance. Rick's finished playing about in England now.'

Richie was so busy chatting that I didn't think he noticed that was how Fletch introduced me to everyone: as 'Richie's friend over for a few weeks'. At least twice he finished the introduction with something like, 'When are you going home?' He smiled as he said it, but it felt as if he was marking a time when I'd be gone and everything would be back to how it should be – with Richie working in the family business and in a relationship with a local girl who couldn't possible tempt him to leave again. After Jodi's hints yesterday, I was curious to know whether Fletch was reserved with her too – or whether it was for me only.

Although he said there were many new faces, Richie was greeted with back slaps as the team trudged off at full-time, and again when we moved into the clubhouse.

'How's the knee, Dave?' he asked a man who was sitting on a chair with his heavily bandaged leg resting on the seat of another.

'Munted, bro. Reckon that's me for the season,

hey?'

'Yeah, I reckon. I might just pull on your jumper next week. Didn't look like you had that much to do out there today.'

'You'll be about right in it then.'

Richie laughed and we walked across to the bar.

'Munted?' I asked.

'Umm, stuffed? Broken? Done for? Let's just say he won't be playing again this season.'

I hadn't seen Jodi at the game, but I felt her eyes on us almost as soon as we walked in, and by the time our beers were poured, she was by our side.

'I told you they needed you back,' she said to Richie after kissing his cheek.

'Not sure there's much I can do,' he replied. 'I think this season's pretty well done for.'

'I don't know,' I mused. 'I heard some old codger tell your father that you'd always had a safe pair of hands.' I reached for one of his hands and examined it, feeling his eyes burning into me. 'Looks like he was right.'

He chuckled and pulled me in for a quick kiss.

'He always had good hands. Never a dropped ball.'

Was it my imagination or had Jodi placed a deliberately long pause between those two sentences?

'Remember that last year at school?' she went on. 'You and Dan were playing in the firsts – you were the goal-kicker and potted one from the sideline right on full-time to win the premiership!'

She tossed her hair and smiled at him, obviously excluding me with her reference to their shared history. He grinned back at her, and I felt a pang somewhere in my chest, a burning in the back of my throat that left a bitter taste. It tasted like something I'd never experienced before: jealousy.

'How could I forget?' Richie said, releasing me to shake hands with another old friend. 'Yeah, good to see you too, bro.'

Jodi left soon after, citing a need to get home and rescue her mother from Toby. She had smiles and some more hair-flicking for Richie, and an air-kiss for me.

The next couple of hours passed in a blur of introductions and back-slapping. I had no idea whether I'd recognise any of these people if I saw them in the street, but they all seemed happy to welcome me into the circle. Richie was in his element: his face beaming, arguing about rugby, remembering the sporting triumphs of his youth. Every time I drifted away to give him space, he reached out a hand and hauled me back to his side. At one point he whispered to me, 'You're part of this too.'

His words warmed me, but they didn't fill the new hole in our bubble caused by Jodi.

CHAPTER TWENTY-NINE

'I know it's a lot to ask,' Jess was saying, 'but Richie says you can cook, and Cate says you can cook, and Mum's going into Wanaka for the day, and I'm desperate, so would you mind?'

'Sorry, Jess, you're not making much sense.'

I heard her take a deep breath. 'Amy, my baker, has called in sick again, and I have enough stock to get me through to lunchtime, but after that I'm stuck. I'm wondering if you can come into town and help me out? Just a slice or two, and maybe some muffins?' The silence that followed was hopeful. 'I'd pay you, of course.'

I felt the heat rush to my face. 'That's not why I was hesitating, Jess. I was running through potential recipes in my head. Do you have all the basic ingredients in stock?'

'Sure: milk, flour, sugar, eggs, condensed milk …' I giggled at that – only in New Zealand would condensed milk be a store-cupboard staple. 'And, of course, spices, chocolate, et cetera.' She paused again. 'What do you say? Are you in?'

I answered without any further thought. 'Yes, I'm in. When do you need me?' Already my head was full of possibilities.

'As soon as you can get here. Ask Richie to run you in. Mum said he's spending the day at work with Dad, so he'll be coming in this direction anyway.' She was speaking at a normal pace again, the panic gone. 'I really appreciate this, Max.'

'I wondered how long it would take Jess to ask you to help her out,' Richie said, a concerned edge to his voice. Before she called we'd been pottering about getting toast and coffee for breakfast. 'I didn't think she'd do it the first week back. You're meant to be on holiday – don't go agreeing to anything you don't want to.'

'I'm happy to help. It'll be fun to cook for someone else. Besides, if you're going into work with Fletch, there's not a whole lot for me to do around here – although I was going to ask your mother if she minded if I did some work on the veggie garden.'

'I think Mum would love that. She's always complaining that she wants to do more but doesn't have the time. And you're sure you're right with me going into work?'

I reached across the table for a slice of toast off his plate. 'Of course I am. That was always the plan – you don't need to entertain me.'

'I know, but I was hoping to have a few days to show you around before I got back into it.'

I got up and wandered around behind him, putting my arms around his neck and resting my chin on his head. He reached up to take my hand, holding it against his chest so I could feel his heart beating.

'We have the weekends,' I said. 'Besides, helping Jess out means I'll get to meet more of the locals and get a better idea of the town.'

'If you're sure.' He tilted his head back so I could kiss his lips. 'I'll miss you today.'

'Yeah, me too,' I murmured.

Since Horrie's funeral we'd barely been apart. It might be a good idea to begin the weaning process so the wrench of separation wouldn't be so bad when I left. The wrench for me, that was. He'd be kept busy with his job, but I'd be going back to nothing.

I shook my head slightly to dislodge the image before it had a chance to sit down, pour itself a cup of tea and get comfortable. I reminded myself that I'd be going back to a life I was creating for myself, which was absolutely something to look forward to. Wasn't it?

Jess's cafe was located in the street that ran parallel to the lake. The main entrance was from the shopping strip side, with a small back door that led to some outdoor seating just across the path from the lake. Given that the morning was cold and the sun hadn't yet reached this part of the lake, those tables were empty. The Monday morning breakfast rush was beginning to thin out and more people were struggling into coats and hats and gloves on their way out than were making their way in.

Jess looked up from behind the counter and greeted me with a relieved smile. She held up a finger to indicate she'd be right with me, and continued to serve the line of people waiting to settle their bills.

I took the opportunity to look around. The space was long and narrow, with tables and benches built along one wall, and a large communal table in front of the main window. People sat drinking coffee or sipping at multi-coloured juices, some working on laptops and tablets, others chatting. The main wall was completely dominated by a large aerial photo of Queenstown. It must have been taken at this time of the year as the Remarkables were covered in snow.

Where the bench seating ended, the counter began. Coffee was at one end, a blackboard behind the barista detailing the options and bean choices. A series of wooden boards should have been stacked with muffins and other sweet treats, but today the options were relatively slim – just a few paper-wrapped savoury muffins, a few that looked as though they were probably carrot cake muffins with a cream cheese icing, slices of something that looked coconutty, and a pile of afghan biscuits.

Wooden stairs led to a mezzanine level that I guessed – judging from the fit-looking wait staff clattering up and down the stairs – must be the kitchen.

Jess took money from the last person in the queue, had a few words to the barista, then came across to me. 'Phew, I'm always glad when the breakfast rush is done. On a weekend, breakfast lasts all day. During the week, though, it's done by nine-ish. After that people are either at work or making their way to the ski slopes. It'll be quieter now for a few hours – until lunch starts. People coming in now mostly want coffee and sweet treats.' She grimaced as she took in the depleted boards. 'Which is where you come in.'

I pointed to the coconut-dusted slice. 'What's that one?'

She laughed. 'This, my friend, is a Kiwi classic. It's called a lolly slice – a little retro, very sweet, but quintessentially Kiwi. You'll see it in dairies and bakeries around the country, especially in the south.'

'Where I come from a dairy's where you'd milk a cow.'

'Sorry, it's what we call a milk bar – I think you'd call it a corner shop? They sell basic groceries, sweets, newspapers, crap flowers – that sort of thing.'

I nodded my understanding. Despite speaking essentially the same language, a few years working with Richie had already exposed me to some of the differences between us: what we called flip-flops, New

Zealanders called jandals; the coffee Richie ordered for
me here had trim milk rather than semi-skimmed; and
the coolbox we'd pack for a picnic back home was a
chilly-bin here. The lolly cake, however, fascinated me.

'What's in it?' I asked.

'Condensed milk, of course, malt biscuits, butter
and Eskimo lollies. It's pressed into a log shape, rolled
in coconut and popped in the fridge to set. Simple
really – even I could make it.'

I acknowledged Jess's comment about her cooking
ability with a smile. 'Eskimo lollies?'

'Sorry, they're sweets – firm marshmallows. That's
why we use the malt biscuits – they help cut through
the sweetness. Anyway, let me show you where it all
happens.'

She led me up the stairs and to the back of the
building, behind the main kitchen activity. As we passed
she waved to someone who I assumed was the chef,
and a girl who was filling the dishwasher with plates
and glasses.

'Hey, Dan,' Jess called. 'This is Max. She's Richie's
friend – visiting from England. I told you Richie was
finally back, right?'

'You sure did. It's about time that dude made it
home. I heard that I missed him at the game and the
club yesterday.'

Dan looked nothing like a chef was supposed
to look. Tall and lanky with blond spiky hair, he was

dressed in jeans and a long-sleeved tee-shirt rolled up to the elbows rather than chef's whites, and a navy apron with the cafe's name across the front.

He held his hand out to mine. 'Nice to meet you, Max.'

'Dan and Richie were at school together. Dan went to London to train when Richie went to uni in Sydney,' Jess explained.

'The only difference is, I remembered to come home when I'd had enough of the London restaurant scene.' Dan looked at me and grinned. 'Although now I understand why Richie kept forgetting to book a ticket home.'

I blushed and looked at my trainers.

Jess laughed. 'Don't embarrass Max – she's helping us out with some baking today.'

Dan exchanged a look with Jess that I couldn't read. 'Amy's off again?'

Jess nodded. 'Uh-huh. Holly?' The girl looked up. She had a round, pretty face and short blonde hair, and I guessed her age to be around eighteen or nineteen. 'Holly's Dan's apprentice. We're hoping she doesn't follow in his footsteps and bugger off to London to some swanky restaurant.'

Holly smiled, dimples appearing in both cheeks. 'It's nice to meet you, Max.'

'We'll leave you to it,' Jess said, and turned to me. 'Amy's domain is down the back.'

Running in front of a set of windows overlooking the lake was a stainless-steel bench with two commercial mixers and neatly arranged utensils on top. Separating the space from the main kitchen was another stainless steel island bench, with a gas stove and two wide under-bench ovens encased in it.

'The store cupboard is through there,' Jess said, 'and the cool room's beside it. Under these benches we keep the mixing bowls and pans. You should find everything you need here.'

'And more,' I muttered, glancing around. 'I've never cooked in a commercial kitchen before.'

'Don't worry about it – just think of it as your kitchen at home but probably with more stainless steel. Not that I'd know what your kitchen at home looks like.'

'Nothing like this. For a start, there are no snowy mountains or a lake out the window in Brookford.' I did a quick check of the pantry, and opened a few drawers. 'You're right, everything I could possibly need is here. I'm thinking an oaty ginger slice – it's perfect with a cuppa. Maybe another one with dried fruit and a lemon icing; and something chocolatey and rich – muffins?'

'The ones Richie told me about with the gooey centres?'

'Those ones.' I grinned back at her. 'Although given I'm not friendly with this oven, I can't guarantee soft centres, but I can guarantee they'll be seriously chocolatey. If I have time I'll bake a lemon drizzle cake too. It's made with yoghurt, so you can pretend it's healthy.'

'Sounds good to me. I'll leave you to it, and get one of the girls to bring you up a coffee to help you get going.' Her face became serious for a moment. 'I really do appreciate this, Max. I know you're here on holiday, and Fletch said you probably have other things you want to do and see before you go home, so thank you.'

There it was again: the reminder. I forced a smile and told her she was welcome. Then I got on with the baking.

Five hours later, I wiped the last of the flour off the stainless-steel benches and took my apron off, throwing it straight into the laundry pile. Collapsing weakly into a chair beside the cool-room, I smiled gratefully at Holly when she offered me a cup of tea.

'I thought you might need this,' she said.

'Oh, I do.'

'I've just tried some of that ginger slice – I don't suppose you'd give me the recipe?'

'Of course I will. If you give me your email address, I'll send you the link. I used to write a blog for the garden centre back home. I featured it last year.'

Dan pulled up another chair and sat down nursing a coffee. 'What a day, hey? You did well, Max – but you're probably the messiest cook I've ever shared a kitchen with!'

I giggled. 'Yeah, I've been told that before.'

Jess came up the stairs, a plate containing sausage rolls in her hand. 'I thought you guys could use something to eat.'

'Sweet!' Dan grabbed at one before she'd even had the chance to put the plate down.

'Hey, ladies first,' she chided gently. 'Max? You must be starved.'

'Thanks.' I bit into the roll, closing my eyes briefly as I tasted the spicy filling and crumbly pastry. 'I'd forgotten I was even hungry.'

'You did well. I sold out of the oozy muffins, and the slices have gone down a treat. There's only a couple of serves of cake left, so that'll be gone too by the time we close.'

Holly appeared with another plate, a slice of lemon cake on it. 'This is the second-last piece – I figured we deserved to try some before it was all gone.'

She used a fork to cut it into three uneven portions and poured some cream over the top.

'What about me?' complained Jess.

'As if you wouldn't have already had some,' Dan said.

'Yeah, you got me there,' she admitted. 'I had to try it – just to make sure it was okay to sell.'

'Absolutely,' grinned Holly, taking a bite. 'I'll have this recipe too, please.'

I smiled, too weary to do more than eat my sausage

roll and sip at my tea.

'Is Amy in tomorrow?' Dan asked. It sounded as if there was another, deeper meaning behind his question.

'No. Apparently she's got a doctor's certificate until Thursday.'

'Hmmm. The usual reason?'

'I suspect so.'

Dan and Jess exchanged glances, then Jess looked at me.

'I hate to ask – and I know how much I'm going to owe both you and my brother – but I don't suppose you could come in again tomorrow?'

'Sure,' I agreed wearily. 'Why not?'

Her shoulders relaxed and she smiled gratefully. 'Well, that's one worry gone. The next is how I'm going to explain the situation to my brother. You're supposed to be here on holiday with him, not working for me.'

'It's fine, Jess. Richie's busy with your father, doing what he needs to do; and as exhausted as I am today, I've really enjoyed it. It was good to get the adrenaline running again.'

It had also felt good to have a purpose. Travelling and sightseeing was fun, but I'd missed having something to actually do.

'Great, that's settled. I've just messaged him to say I'll run you home – apparently Mum's doing a curry for dinner, so I may as well freeload there. Dan, Holly – get those aprons off and get your arses out of here. Sean's closing up tonight.'

'Is Sean on today? I didn't see him when I went down for the cake.' Holly's dimples came to life and her green eyes sparkled.

'Please, save me from rampant hormones,' sighed Jess, rolling her eyes. 'Sean's the Irish barista downstairs,' she told me. 'Here for the season and has kissed the blarney stone one too many times.'

Holly grinned. 'He's also seriously hot. I might see if he needs some help.' She bounded downstairs.

'The energy of the young.' Jess looked wistfully after her. 'Come on, Max. Get your bag and let's get out of here.'

Milly greeted us both with big hugs. 'Take those jackets off and warm up by the fire,' she urged. 'I wouldn't be surprised if there's snow falling up top tonight.'

Jess toed her boots off and hung her coat on the peg in the hall beside mine. 'It sure feels like it. Joel from the cafe in Cow Lane said he heard we could even get some in town.'

'Does it snow often in town?' I asked.

'Yeah, nah – a couple of times a year. It doesn't hang around for too long when it does, but it makes everything look like a winter wonderland. No matter how many times we see it, it's still exciting.'

'It's like that at home too,' I said. 'You never get

tired of waking up to see that snow's settled overnight.'

Milly poured us a cup of tea and we sat around the huge wooden table chatting. Milly told us about the friend she'd spent the day with in Wanaka. Apparently she'd just finished her final round of chemotherapy and was now anxiously awaiting the next set of test results.

'Sometimes it's nice to just do the things we did before the cancer,' she said. 'Shopping, lunch – you know, two friends catching up on each other's lives. Enough about me – how did you go in the kitchen today?'

Her question was directed at me, but Jess answered for me. 'She was a godsend, Mum. Her slices were fabulous and the lemon cake flew off the display. As for the chocolate muffins – oh my god, they were better than sex. Not that I've had any recently, but they were better than I remember it being.' She finished with a heavy sigh and placed her elbows on the table, resting her cheeks against the backs of her fists.

'That good?' Milly's eyebrows rose.

'Oh, Mum – eeeeew! Too much information! As if we need to know you're still doing it.' Jess sighed again. 'Although, apparently everyone else is – except me. Anyway, Amy's off again for the next couple of days, and Max has said she'll come in for me. I'll pay her, of course.'

Warmth rushed into my cheeks. 'Oh, you don't –'

'No arguments, Max. You're working for me –

of course I'll pay you. If you refuse, I'll have to find someone else who not only will I have to pay, but who won't be able to cook like you.'

I shrugged and looked at the table, still embarrassed.

'Oh, Mum,' Jess went on, 'I forgot to tell you who came in today – Jodi Charters, or whatever it is she calls herself now. She was asking about some casual work. I told her I'd think about it, but after the way she treated Richie she's got a damn hide.' She turned to me. 'Have you met her yet? You must have – she said she saw Richie at the club last night. She and Richie were together for a while at school until she cheated on him with that dude from Cromwell. Broke his teenage heart, she did. I was sure there was something else I heard about –'

Milly noticed my discomfort and threw her a look of warning.

'Sorry,' Jess mumbled.

'You must be exhausted,' Milly said, clearing away the mugs.

'I shouldn't be – I'm used to working in a garden. Besides, I really enjoyed myself. Once I got into a rhythm, the energy kept me going.'

'You'll get used to it again,' Milly said, 'especially if Jess continues to take advantage of you. You'll soon learn that none of us ever try to argue with Jess. She might be the youngest, but I'm sure she's the most wilfully stubborn.' As Jess opened her mouth to protest,

Milly stopped her with a smile. 'I'm only joking with you, Jessica. Now, Max, why don't you go and have a soak in the bath? Take a glass of wine and a good book. Richie and Fletch should be home soon.'

As I ran the bath I reviewed what Jess had said before Milly stopped her. So I hadn't imagined the undercurrents on Saturday and again last night – there was definitely some history there. Now it all jangled into one horrible thought: could Jodi be the woman Richie had told me about that afternoon at The Lamb, the one he'd fallen in love with at first sight?

I sank into the bath and let the scent of the bubbles, the red wine and the sheer bliss of the warm water send me into a light doze. When I woke, it was to see Richie kneeling on the floor beside the bath, trailing his fingers through the suds to tweak at the nipple that had been poking out above the water.

'Hey, you,' he said, leaning across to kiss me. 'I hear my sister wore you out?'

'Uh-huh. I have no idea where she gets her energy from.'

He watched my face as his fingers slipped further below the water. As they found their destination I bit my bottom lip and arched into them with a moan.

'Sometimes I think she manufactures it … the energy, that is,' he said.

I swallowed hard as he slid two fingers inside me,

his thumb expertly flicking at my core. What had we been talking about?

'Oh god, Richie, that feels so good.'

'What about if I do this too?'

He leaned forward and took my nipple into his mouth and all my senses exploded in one burst of light, taking my breath away for a heartbeat and bringing everything back to two things: this man, and what he could do to me. He kissed me until my moans and tremors subsided.

'Feel better now?' he asked, a wolfish grin on his face.

'I sure do. Feel like joining me?' I stretched out languorously in the cooling water.

'Somehow I think that could get messy. Let's have a shower instead.'

He stripped off and stood there naked, holding his hand out to help me from the water. As he regulated the water temperature, I rubbed my breasts against his back, pressing kisses down the length of his spine, and reaching around to grasp his hardness.

'Christ, Maxi,' he muttered, groaning low in the back of his throat. He turned around to move me against the tiled wall, pushing his erection into my belly. 'I've missed you today.'

My hips pushed back against his, wanting more, needing him to fill me. 'How about you show me how much,' I urged.

Sometime later, I sat on the edge of our bed in a loose top and knickers and watched him dress.

'How was it?' I asked.

He grinned in that way men do when they know they've satisfied their woman. 'Do you have to ask?'

'I don't mean that, you idiot. How was it working with your father?'

He pulled on a long sleeved tee-shirt, hiding that gorgeous chest of his and that flat stomach, and ... I looked away before I lost my concentration again.

'It was good,' he said. 'He listened to the direction I want to take the business in, and basically gave me the go-ahead to do more garden design and expand the shop while he continues with the landscape supplies. He's asked me to put together a business plan for him.' He smiled. 'It's good to be back. It feels like this is what I was meant to do.'

He sat on the bed beside me and took my hand. 'I really think it'll work. I've had experience overseas and now feels like the right time.' He lifted my hand and brought it to his mouth for a kiss. 'Jess was saying how well you did today.'

'I enjoyed it.'

He leaned forward and kissed my lips. 'I'm glad.'

'Jess said Jodi called in today, asking about casual work.'

'Oh, that's right. I completely forgot to talk to Jess about that.' I tingled inside as I remembered exactly what we'd done that had caused him to forget. 'What did Jess say? Did she have anything for her?'

'She told her she'd think about it, but said to your mum that Jodi had a hide asking given her history with you. What happened?'

He sighed and pulled me closer, poking a stray bit of hair behind my ear. 'I like that you've let your hair grow a little.'

'I didn't have a lot of choice, remember? My hairdresser was suddenly off-limits.'

He laughed. 'Actually I'd forgotten that. I've almost forgotten there was ever a time when we weren't together like this.' He kissed the top of my head.

I hadn't forgotten – I wished I could.

'Have you also forgotten the question I just asked you?' I said.

'I don't want to talk about Jodi – she's not important now.' He pushed me back onto the bed, his hand finding its way under my top.

I tried another line. 'Why is your surname different to Cam's?'

'Fletch isn't our father – not Cate's and mine. He is Jess's father. Ours left when I was still a baby. Fletch is the only father I've known. '

'Do you ever see him – your birth father?'

'No. It's been years. He moved across to Perth and has another life and another family, and we have Fletch.'

I twirled my finger in the soft hair on his chest. 'You said once that your father fell in love with your mother at first sight. Were you talking about Fletch?'

'That's right – I told you that, didn't I? Yes, it was Fletch – and we got lucky that he did.' His hand was idly stroking the outside of my hip.

'You told me it had happened to you too – the lightning-bolt thing.'

I looked up at him, hoping he'd take the hint and tell me something about her. His hand moved from my hip to lightly trail up my spine, sending little rivers of goose bumps across my skin.

'Speaking of sparks,' he murmured before his mouth closed over mine.

It wasn't until much later that I realised how deftly – and pleasurably – he'd avoided my questions.

CHAPTER THIRTY

I spent Tuesday and Wednesday at the cafe, baking cakes, slices, brownies, muffins and cookies. Richie dropped me off on his way through in the morning, and Milly came to collect me in the afternoon. I tried to tell her I was happy to catch a bus – the regular service between Queenstown and Wanaka ran close by – but she wouldn't hear of it.

I enjoyed the work and the camaraderie of the kitchen. The three of us – Dan, Holly and myself – worked well together, the banter enhancing rather than distracting from the cooking.

Amy was back at work on Thursday, apparently quite annoyed that I'd been allowed in her domain, and loudly critical of the cost to make the oozy muffins.

'I told her to shut up and get back to work,' Jess said. 'Those muffins sold so quickly and I've had so many requests for them – I can afford to have them on once a week and charge a little extra. Personally, I think she's a bit envious. Amy's good, but she tends to stick to the tried and true. And Dan doesn't shut up about you – I think he's a teeny bit smitten. Not that I'd say that in front of Richie.'

Which was exactly what Jess did when the three of us met up in town for drinks on Friday night.

'Max has slotted in so well in the kitchen. Dan was saying only the other day how much easier she is to work with than what Amy is. Actually,' her grin was cheeky, 'he said a lot more than that about her too – but I guess you don't want to hear that?'

'You guessed right,' Richie scowled. 'I don't want to hear it. What I do want is another beer. Same again?'

'Jodi dropped in again this afternoon. Dad wants me to give her a few shifts, but I wasn't sure how you'd feel about that,' Jess told me when Richie had gone to the bar to get our drinks.

'Why's that?' I asked, not sure I wanted to hear the answer, but knowing I needed to.

'Well, because of her and Richie. Mum gave me hell for mentioning her in front of you the other night, but as I told her, it wouldn't have been news to you – you guys talk about everything.'

I dropped my eyes and flipped a coaster around on the table.

'Oh,' she said.

I looked up at her. 'What does that mean?'

'Nothing.' She didn't meet my eyes. 'It was such a long time ago – he's probably forgotten all about it. You know what men are like.'

I nodded. 'Yes, he probably has.'

Even as I said the words I knew they weren't true. I was sure that the reason Richie hadn't told me about Jodi, about their history, was the opposite to what Jess assumed – because he *hadn't* forgotten and because it was still important. That was why I'd resolved not to ask him about her again – for fear he'd tell me the truth … and my even greater fear that he'd lie to me about her.

That didn't mean I couldn't ask Jess. 'You said they used to date?'

'For a while at the end of high school. I think they were each other's first, if you know what I mean. She left him for a fling with some guy who played rugby for Cromwell – broke his heart. And we all know you never completely forget your first. I think there might have been something when they were at university in Sydney too – but don't quote me on that. Mum's never really forgiven her for dumping him the way she did, but Dad has a soft spot for her – mainly because her father left just before it all happened.' She went to take a sip of her wine and found the glass empty. 'Where's Richie with those drinks?'

I shrugged but said nothing, keen for her to finish her story before he came back.

'After uni they lost touch for a while. She stayed in Sydney, teaching, and he went to Melbourne and trained with a landscape architect for a few years. Jodi ended up down there too, and I got the impression from her that something happened between them, but by then Richie'd introduced her to Byron and they ended up together. She must have already been pregnant with Toby when they walked down the aisle. Richie buggered off to Europe soon after that … I've often wondered if he left because she got married. He's never talked about it, but I assumed he must have been gutted when it happened. She always asks after him, but he's never said a word about it. Well, he wouldn't, would he?'

'No, I guess not.'

'Not that it matters now,' she mused. 'It's obviously ancient history. After all, he's got you now, and judging from what I've seen, he can't keep his eyes or his hands off you. What's going to happen when you go home? What are you going to do?'

I remembered Richie telling me that Jess didn't have a filter. She simply said what she thought when she thought it, without thinking.

'I'm starting my own business,' I told her. 'I'll start off with a series of recipe cards, and I'm going to submit an application to run the cafe they're planning for the nursery Richie and I used to work at. If that doesn't come off, I'll find somewhere else to run it from.'

'Cooking the way you do, it will absolutely do alright. When do you go back?'

'I leave in the first week of September.'

'That doesn't give him long,' she said, a thoughtful look on her face. 'But he obviously thinks it's long enough to work his magic … cocky bastard.'

'His magic?'

'To convince you to stay, have his babies, and work for me three days a week.'

Her face was serious, but I laughed as if it was all a big joke. I didn't tell her that he'd already convinced me – that this was the life I wanted too. But Richie hadn't asked me about my plans at all; and I didn't know what I'd say if he did. He knew that I'd vowed never to compromise again the way I had with James, but where did that leave us?

'I mean it,' Jess said. 'You're perfect for him, and perfect for me. The tramping season starts in October and Mum normally helps me out, but I think Dad would really like to take her away for a bit. If you're still here then, it would be perfect all round.'

'And it's always all about you, isn't it?' Richie was back with our drinks. 'What have you two been talking about?'

'You, my gorgeous hunk of a big brother. Max was telling me about her exciting plans for when she goes home, and I was telling her how she needs to stay here to run my business when I'm on track – and make me the occasional batch of comfort cake. Did I tell you that her oozy muffins are better than an orgasm?'

'They're good, but if you think that, you're either not doing it right or you haven't found the right man yet. Isn't that right, Maxi?' He grinned and raised his eyebrows suggestively at me, seamlessly changing the subject away from my return ticket.

My belly tightened under his gaze and heat rushed to my core.

'Oh, man, you two are going to do it again, aren't you?' Jess said.

'What's that?' Richie asked.

'Make your excuses so you can rush home and have mad toe-curling, eye-rolling sex, of course.'

'We'll let you finish your drink first,' he said, his hand on my thigh.

'Oh, just leave, the pair of you.' She was smiling as she kissed us both goodbye. 'Hey, what are you doing tomorrow?'

Richie looked at me. 'We haven't made any plans yet.'

'Good, don't. If the weather holds we'll tramp part of the Routeburn – just up to Forge Flats. We can have a picnic there and still be back before the sun sets. We can't go much further than that at this time of year. Wear layers and decent hiking boots if you have them. I'll get Mum to pack us some lunch.' She paused. 'As for Sunday – has Richie taken you to Paradise yet?'

He laughed. 'Every night, little sister, sometimes twice.'

'Get out of here.' She pulled a face and waved us away.

In the Landy on the way home, I thought Richie

might bring up what Jess and I had been talking about. I was sure I'd seen his jaw tighten just a little when she talked about my going home.

'You're right,' I told him.

'I'm right about a lot of things, but what specifically am I right about this time?'

'Jess – she has absolutely no filter. If she wants to know the answer to something, she just asks.'

'Yep, that's Jess alright.'

I couldn't see his expression in the dark. I waited for him to say something else, something that would lead us into the conversation we needed to have.

'Do you want to go tramping tomorrow?' he asked.

'Sure,' I said. 'Why?'

'It's just you've been quiet for most of the drive home. Is everything okay?'

That should have been my cue to tell him that it wasn't, that I didn't want to go back to England any more, that my exciting new plans felt as though they were diminished, that what I really wanted was exactly what Jess had suggested – to stay with him and have his babies.

'Yes,' I told him. 'Everything is absolutely fine.'

He took his hand from the wheel for a moment and rubbed my thigh. 'I'm pleased to hear it.'

I remembered back to Sydney and how I'd convinced myself that we could talk this through and sort it all out, the same way we'd always been able to

talk about everything. Everything, that was, except
my return ticket and what Jodi used to mean to him. I
hoped the two subjects weren't connected.

After walking through beech forest for a couple of
kilometres, the sound of rushing water rose to meet us.

'You'll see,' said Richie, before I had a chance to
ask the question.

Around the bend, the track took us across a swing
bridge. The water roared in frothy white torrents far
below.

'They do canyoning from here,' said Jess. 'They
slide down the rocks and into the water into the gorge.
I think there's abseiling involved too.' She shrugged.
'Each to their own, I guess.'

I shuddered. 'I can't think of anything worse.'

'I don't blame you. I'm not really into all that either
– the whole jumping off things or out of planes. Give
me a well-benched track and landscape like this and
I'm a happy girl.'

Richie grinned. 'There goes my surprise bungy
jump.'

'That was never going to happen.' I smiled back
at him.

He reached for my hand and held it as we walked
on.

The track sidled the gorge, winding and climbing
steadily but easily to Forge Flats – a grassy area that

Jess told us was once a blacksmith's camp.

'Up ahead is Routeburn Flats, and beyond that, Routeburn Falls – about another five kays, so around two hours' tramping. The last part up to the lodge is pretty steep and messy, but we're not going that far today. We're heading down there to have our lunch.' She pointed to a bend in the river and a wide sun-filled pebbly bank.

'It looks beautiful,' I said.

Richie skimmed stones across the river's surface as Jess unpacked sandwiches and a flask of tea from her daypack.

'Remember how we used to come down here in the summer?' he said. He reached in to feel the temperature of the water. 'Man, it's cold! I can't believe we ever swam in this. Did Maxi tell you she made me go swimming at Bondi when we were there? She might as well have worn a sign advertising herself as a mad pommy tourist.'

Jess laughed. 'I still swim here – every summer. We tramp Routeburn from the Te Anau end, and stop here for lunch on the final day. If the weather's good, I'll take a dip. I dive in from that rock over there – the way you taught me to.' She pointed to where a large rock jutted out from the bank over a deeper pool of crystal clear, almost jade-coloured water.

Richie laughed, his gaze on a moment in time long ago. I saw them too – gangly-legged kids on a hot summer's day jumping off the rock into water. I felt a sudden longing for the same upbringing for my children.

'Yeah, one day I'll bring my kids here too,' Richie was saying as he climbed to the top of the diving rock.

I took my sandwich to a fallen tree, and watched as Richie and Jess clowned around on the riverbank. Richie belonged here, in this place, in this country, with his family. It was where he'd marry, and where he'd bring up his children. I closed my eyes and sent a silent prayer to anyone who might be paying attention that we'd do those things together, with *our* children. It could still happen – all I needed was for Jodi to stay in the past, and James to finally accept that our marriage was over.

Over the last week I'd received another few emails from James, reminding me that I was technically still married to him, and telling me he wasn't going to release the rest of the funds from the sale of our Brookford cottage until I came to my senses. I'd deleted each of them without replying.

'Hey, Hendo!' I opened my eyes and Richie was standing there below me, his smile wide. 'Come with me.'

He held his arms out and I jumped down from the tree into them. He led me to the waters-edge and stood behind me, wrapping his arms around my middle and resting his chin on the top of my head.

'This country is what I needed you to see,' he said.

'I couldn't describe it, but it's part of my history.' I felt him drop a kiss on my head. 'One day, maybe, we'll do the whole track, but I really wanted you to see this.'

I turned in his arms. When he said things like that, our happy ending suddenly felt possible again – despite the threat of Jodi, of James, and the things we weren't talking about.

'I love you,' I said, raising my lips to his.

'And I love you.'

CHAPTER THIRTY-ONE

Fletch's attitude concerned me. It wasn't that he was actually rude to me, but he definitely wasn't as warm as the rest of the family. There wasn't a meal that passed without him making at least one reference to my holiday or how much time I had remaining. He constantly drew parallels between the work Richie had come home to do and what I would be doing when I returned home. I didn't think Richie had noticed, and I tried not to let my hurt show, but I noticed the concerned look Milly gave me after one of Fletch's comments.

Saturday night, over dinner, was the most direct he'd got so far. Although we'd made tentative plans to meet up later with Dan and a few others in town, by the time we got back from our tramp, the rain was sheeting down. Hunkered down in the warm house, with the fire blazing, Richie rapidly lost enthusiasm for the idea of going out again.

'It's a rotten night,' he said. 'Maybe we shouldn't bother?'

'Surely after a few years in England you'd be used

to a little rain,' Fletch said. 'It'll be autumn when you head back, won't it, Max? You'll be going from winter here to winter there. You didn't plan that very well.'

'I know. Somehow, other than those couple of weeks in Denmark, I've managed to miss summer completely this year.'

'There's no better place to be than Queenstown during the summer months. It's a shame you won't be here for it.' Fletch reached across and poured more wine into our glasses. 'There, Rick, I've made your decision for you – you won't be driving anywhere now.'

Richie grinned and raised his glass.

'Will you be going back to your grandfather's house in the Cotswolds?' Fletch asked me. 'Jess said you're planning to put in a tender for a cafe at the nursery where you used to work.'

'Yes. And if that doesn't pan out I'll probably head down to Mum and Dad's – they're on the coast in Cornwall – and use my share of the proceeds from the sale of the cottage to open something there. Who knows though – my options are still quite open.' I wasn't brave enough to look at Richie as I spoke.

Fletch's elbow was resting on the table, his chin on the back of his fist as he directed his questions to me. 'The beginning of September will be here before you know it. What does your husband say about it all?'

I heard Milly's sharp intake of breath. 'Cam!'

Beside me, Richie was very still.

'I haven't spoken to him for a few weeks,' I said softly.

'Are you planning to?'

'When I'm ready.' My stare was as direct as his.

'It's not good to let these things drag on,' he said. 'It's certainly one way of keeping your options open.'

'I'm not sure what you mean by that, Fletch.' I knew exactly what he'd meant.

He shrugged. 'I suppose I'm just wondering why you're not in more of a hurry to finish it off – your marriage, that is.'

'Richie was telling us about your grandfather, Max. He sounds like such a character.' Milly's voice cut across the silence.

Fletch dropped his eyes from mine and settled back into his chair.

'He was,' I said. 'He had half the widows in Brookford on a roster system. They all got along though – there was no competition or jealousy.'

'It's true,' said Richie. 'There was an entire table of them at the funeral. They all comforted each other. It's funny, for a small village there was no gossip about it; it was just accepted.'

'If your grandfather's gone and your parents have moved on, is there any reason why you have to settle back in Brookford?' Milly asked me. 'Surely, if you want to open a cafe and publish some recipes, you can do that anywhere that takes your fancy? You could even do it here.'

'Or in New York.' Fletch said it so quietly I wasn't sure if anyone else had heard him.

'That's true,' I answered Milly. 'As I said, my options are open.'

I tried to catch Richie's eye, but he busied himself with collecting the dinner plates.

'Is that what you think too?' I asked him as we were getting ready for bed. 'What Fletch was saying. Is that what you think?'

He folded his shirt and laid it on a chair before answering. 'Maxi, your marriage is your business.'

'Surely it's yours too now?'

He shook his head. 'No. *You're* my business – your marriage isn't.'

'Does it worry you that I haven't sorted everything out with James yet?'

'Of course it does, but it's not up to me, is it? You've made it clear that anything that happens from now has to be your choice. How did you say it – that evening in Brookford after Horrie's funeral? Something about never repeating your mistakes and giving up on what you want because somebody asks you to? And how if they really loved you they wouldn't ask?' He seemed to be waiting for me to say something, but when I didn't he went on. 'So, to answer your first question about me agreeing with what Fletch was saying. Yeah, I guess I probably do – but, as I said, that's your business. You'll probably tell me what you want when you're ready, and I don't want to argue about it any more.' He climbed into bed. 'What I do want is to kiss you goodnight – I'm exhausted after that tramp today.'

I lay in the dark for a long time afterwards listening to him breathing. I didn't think he was asleep either.

It should have been so easy to agree with Milly and say something like, 'Yes, that's what I'd like to do.' I could even have told Richie that I'd been considering the Queenstown option – give him an opening to ask me to stay.

But my own words had trapped me.

There was no rugby on Sunday, so Richie and Fletch spent the afternoon in the study going through numbers and business plans. When Richie made a half-hearted protest that he didn't want to leave me with nothing to do, Fletch raised his eyebrows. I was quick to assure Richie that I didn't need him to occupy me, and spent most of the afternoon curled up by the fire with Milly's cookbooks and, wonder of all wonders, some old episodes of *Midsomer Murders* on the telly. It seemed that Inspector Barnaby had a fan in Milly as well. Although neither of us could decide whether we preferred the old or the new Barnaby, we were agreed on Sergeant Jones and Sykes.

Midway through the afternoon, Richie took a call from Jodi. She was dreadfully sorry to drag him away on a Sunday afternoon, but she'd bought a bookshelf for Toby's room in a flatpack that she just couldn't make head nor tail of – her words not mine. Would he mind helping her? Would I mind loaning him out for a couple of hours?

'Do you mind?' Richie asked me.

I could feel Fletch's eyes on me as I hesitated over my answer. What could I say? If I said, yes, I did mind, it would make me look petty and jealous. After all, Jodi was a friend in need, and I should have sufficient trust in my man and our relationship to wave him goodbye with a smile.

'Of course I don't,' I assured him. 'I'll be fine here – I've got Barnaby to keep me company. You go and wrestle with flatpack furniture. Every kid needs a bookshelf.'

He smiled gratefully and kissed me goodbye. 'I'll see you soon,' he said.

After he'd left, Milly wandered into the study where Fletch and Richie had been going through the figures. Although she kept her voice low, I heard her grumble something about how Jodi had managed just fine before Richie came back.

'She doesn't mean any harm,' Fletch said.

'I wouldn't bet on that.' Milly sounded sceptical. 'You know she's always been trouble where Richie's concerned.'

Then Fletch said, 'At least she doesn't have a return

ticket out of here.'

I pretended I hadn't heard, that I was concentrating on Barnaby, but soon after I declared that I needed a nap and excused myself to our bedroom.

Richie woke me when he came in a few hours later. 'Are you okay?' he asked.

'Absolutely.' I smiled and brought his lips down to meet mine. 'I just felt sleepy. Did you get the bookshelf sorted? It took a little longer than I thought it might.' I cursed myself for the last comment.

He didn't seem to notice. 'Yeah, all done. She'd put some pieces on back to front so I had to undo it all before I could put it together again. Toby helped me – he seems like a good kid. It's a pity Jodi and Byron split, he could do with a father figure. Byron's a good guy and I'm having a tough time understanding why he wants nothing to do with Jodi and Toby.'

He looked down at me curled up on the bed. 'Not that it's something I'm particularly concerned about right now.' He lay down beside me and pulled me close. 'Thanks for understanding.'

I smiled and pretended that I did.

The next couple of weeks passed in much the same way. Weekends were spent at the rugby, or out and about with Jess, Dan, or other friends. Jodi always seemed to be at the rugby club when we were there, and was always eager to play remember-when with Richie. Now that I knew their story, I could see the game she was playing. Aside from the smiles and the hair-flicking, there'd been a few apologetic calls: asking if he'd mind picking her son up from rugby training; unblock her sink; and one Saturday morning, hang a shelf. Although I watched Richie carefully, I hadn't seen any indication from him that anything had happened between them, or that he was interested in her other than as a friend. Not yet anyway.

I was trying hard not to say anything that would prompt a fight that could drive him back into her arms and her bed, but after the third request to pick up Toby, I couldn't help myself. 'Doesn't the woman have any other friends?' I muttered. Even as I said the words I was ashamed of them.

'Really, Hendo? Remember what happened when you moved back to Brookford and James was travelling so much and your friends had all moved away? What would you have done if I'd said no any of the times you needed me?'

'That was different.'

'How?'

I nearly told him then – about how I was jealous and afraid that Jodi wanted him back. It wasn't the same thing at all. When Richie and I were friends and he'd helped me out from time to time, my reasons were innocent – I was married and had no interest in him as anything more than a friend. Jodi's motivation was less pure.

I helped out in the cafe on the days when Amy was off. I hadn't quite got to the bottom of that story, but it seemed to have something to do with an abusive on-again, off-again partner and their almost weekly break-ups and reconciliations.

'If it wasn't for the fact that she needs the stability of this job, I would have sacked her weeks ago,' Jess told me. 'Plus, she went to school with Dan, Richie and Jodi, so I feel as though I can't just kick her out. She's a competent if conservative baker, but her unreliability does my head in. The best outcome would be if I had someone who could work for me a few days a week or be on call.' She looked at me with one brow raised. 'Are you still determined to go home? My brother needs to make sure you stay – even if just for my sake. It's all about me, you know.'

I smiled and avoided answering her question.

The truth was, since the argument the other night – it had certainly felt like an argument – Richie and I still hadn't spoken about my return ticket. I thought he might when a reminder text message came through from the airline. I saw him glance at my phone, look away and continue with the conversation we were having. I wanted him to say something, *I* wanted to say something, but by the time I figured out what, the moment had gone.

How do you ask someone if you can stay when they haven't asked you to first? How does someone ask you to stay when you've already told them not to ask? It was a problem of my own making that I hadn't worked out a solution to.

On other days I helped Milly in the garden, mucked about in the kitchen, and took long walks with my camera. I'd experimented with some new recipes and styled them for my new blog. Milly was only too pleased to help. We spent hours swapping recipes, and photographing the results on different crockery and in different lights. She had a good eye for design and was a willing assistant, plus her kitchen was a dream to work in.

'Are you really determined to go home?' she asked one afternoon.

We'd prepared a batch of my fudge-topped ginger slice, and were trying out different plates to make the result look less beige and boring.

I thought for a second about avoiding the question, or giving an evasive answer, but her look had too much concern in it and I'd grown too fond of her to try and make light of it.

'No. I don't want to. I know I need to in order to sort things out, but I feel as though home is wherever Richie is.'

She seemed relieved by my answer. 'I thought that could be the case, but neither of you seem to talk about it.'

I grimaced. 'That's because we haven't.'

'Ah,' she said, 'Rick's never been good at asking for what he really wants. I should have taught him to use his words more when he was little.'

I shook my head. 'It's partly my fault – actually, it's mostly my fault. There've been times I could have said something and didn't; and he won't because of something I said when I first left James.'

'What was that?'

'Something about how I was never going to make the mistake of letting a man take me over and hold me back again, and how if he really loved me he wouldn't ask me to change my plans.'

She grimaced. 'Oh dear. Sometimes a good memory can be inconvenient.'

'So, we haven't talked about it, and the longer I leave it, the harder it is.'

Milly busied herself making tea and cutting a piece of fudge slice in half. 'I'm sure we can allow ourselves a small piece. What does your mother say about it?'

'We haven't spoken in over a week – the time zones are too difficult – but in her last email she reminded me of something she told me when we spoke in Sydney.'

'Which was?'

'That Richie isn't James and would never force me into anything I didn't want. I'm wishing I'd remembered that before now.'

'He's scared too, you know.' I looked up at that. 'He's afraid you'll leave him – and that fear is growing every day this situation is unresolved. He mightn't show it, but he's definitely putting up some protective boundaries. What else did your mother say?'

'That I can trust him.'

She nodded. 'I look forward to meeting your parents. Maybe they can visit for Christmas?'

I smiled weakly. 'I love your optimism.'

'Promise me you'll talk to him over the next week? Really talk to him. It's going to need to come from you.'

'I know.'

The following day, the Thursday of my third week in Queenstown, I received an email from James:

> *Maxine,*
>
> *It's time we talked properly. I'll be in Sydney for a series of meetings from next Tuesday. I suggest you make the appropriate arrangements to be there too. India's booked your tickets and hotel – the details are attached. You're on the Tuesday morning flight out of Queenstown. I'll call for you at the hotel at 7.30 for dinner. Wear something nice – and maybe that red number underneath. I've missed you.*
>
> *Your husband,*
> *James x*

I didn't know whether it was because of his

arrogant assumption that I'd jump as soon as he clicked
his fingers, or the fact that he was essentially ordering
me to Sydney as if I were a recalcitrant teenager, but
I closed the email without opening the attachments
and without replying. James represented a reality that I
didn't want to deal with – at least not until after Richie
and I had talked about the future. And I was now
determined that we would have one.

Things came to a head, of sorts, on Sunday night
after the rugby. We were at the club, and because the
team had had a big win, spirits were high. I wasn't
feeling great – something I'd eaten on Saturday night
hadn't agreed with me and I was still queasy. Somehow
or other I found myself clutching a glass of water and
standing in a corner at a raised table with Jodi. The
conversation started simply enough, but soon moved
to Richie.

'He seems really happy,' she commented, watching
him demonstrating a move from the afternoon's game
to a circle of mates. 'I hope you're not thinking of
dragging him back to the other side of the world when
you go home. We'd all miss him.'

I forced a smile, but there was no answer to that
question.

'When do you go?' she asked.

'My ticket's for the first week in September.'

She nodded, her eyes still on Richie. 'I suppose
you can't make too many plans just yet. Richie was

saying you're waiting for your divorce to go through. When does that happen?'

'I really don't know,' I said.

My tummy was doing flip-flops and I was feeling overly warm. Richie had spoken to this woman about me and James?

'Divorce is no fun. We've just started trying to negotiate the settlement. Byron's being difficult when really all I'm doing is trying to protect Toby's future, you know? None of what I'm asking for is for me – it's all for my child.' She shook her head. 'Sometimes I wonder how things would have been if I hadn't had my head turned by Byron, and Richie and I had ended up … He was devastated, you know, when Byron and I got engaged. But he hid it well. That's the thing about Richie – he always does what he thinks is right, even when his heart is telling him to go in a different direction.' She looked hard at me as she said it. 'But you'd know that, right? About his sense of responsibility?'

I nodded. 'He's the best man I know.' The words might have sounded simple, but they were true.

'Yes. He's the best man I know too. He would never have let Byron see how he felt on our wedding day, but he had the sense to know that he had to leave town for my marriage to stand a chance. It's why he ran off to Europe, you know. Of course, I was pregnant by then.'

She paused and sipped at her wine. I clutched my glass of water as if it were a lifeline. I was feeling weird in the head now as well as the tummy.

'Richie's fabulous with Toby. I don't know what I'd do without him helping me out. Yes, it's right that we came back here. Toby's place is with his family – if you know what I mean.'

I tried to stop the gasp that felt as if it came from my heart. Was she hinting what I thought she was hinting?

'Oh, you don't need to worry – nothing's happened between us. It won't while you're still here. Richie has too much integrity for that. He's a patient man. He's waited this long for me – he can wait another couple of weeks.'

As her words cut right through me, her gaze was firmly focused on the man I loved, a little smile on her mouth.

'Excuse me,' I muttered, and rushed to the bathroom and heaved into the toilet bowl.

It was only as I was rinsing my mouth and running cold water over my wrists to try and quell the heat within me that I realised I'd left my bag and phone with Jodi. Bugger. That meant I needed to go back.

Plastering a smile on my face and taking a deep breath, I made my way back to the corner. Richie had joined her and greeted me with a worried smile.

'Are you okay? Is your tummy still playing up?' He turned to Jodi. 'She hasn't been well since yesterday – something we ate mustn't have agreed with her.'

'I thought it might have been something I said.' Jodi's smile had a satisfied edge that I was sure was intended for me.

'Absolutely not,' I said. 'Actually, Richie, do you mind if we leave now? I feel like I could sleep for a year.'

He pulled me close and kissed the top of my head. 'Of course. You should have said so earlier and I wouldn't have kept you out.'

The concern in his eyes was real. It should have been enough to convince me that there was nothing to what Jodi had said, but it wasn't.

'If I don't see you, enjoy the rest of your stay,' said Jodi.

I thought what she meant was: 'Enjoy the rest of your time with Richie, because once you've gone, I'm moving in.'

Richie seemed oblivious to the exchange and keen only to get me home. It wasn't until we were in the Landy that I noticed the text that must have come through while I was in the bathroom. It was from James, and from where I'd left the phone, Jodi would have seen it.

I haven't received a response to my email last week, but look forward to seeing you on Tuesday. Jxx

I suspected that explained her self-satisfied smirk.

'Everything okay?' Richie asked, resting his hand briefly on my thigh.

'Uh-huh. I'm just a little queasy still. I'm sure I'll

be fine tomorrow.'

I had no intention of replying to James – not yet anyway. I'd leave it until tomorrow night when it would be too late for him to pester me to change my mind. There was no way I was wasting what little time I had left with Richie in Sydney trying to convince my husband that I was serious about divorcing him. And if I didn't intend going to Sydney, I didn't need to tell Richie about the email and how James had ordered me to fly to meet him.

I looked across at Richie's profile: the firm set of his jaw, that super-sensitive spot just behind his ear that sent goose bumps racing across his skin when I nuzzled into it. No, telling him about James's summons would only complicate the conversation we needed to have. Tomorrow, I promised myself. I'll talk to him tomorrow and we can decide together when I meet with James.

Later, in bed, Richie wrapped his arms around me to spoon me into him.

'I'm sorry,' I said. 'I –'

'It's okay,' he whispered, his hand moving from my breast to sit just below it. 'You're not well. Let me just hold you.'

After the conversation with Jodi, I didn't think I'd be able to sleep, but once I closed my eyes, the fatigue swept over me. When I woke, Richie was still holding me tight.

I told myself it was because he loved me not Jodi; that what we had now was enough to erase the memories he had with her. Although if, as she'd hinted, Toby was his son, I had no hope at all of competing with her. Richie's sense of responsibility would always win out – even over his heart. I wondered why she was waiting to play that card with Richie. Maybe her plan was to wait until I was gone so he wouldn't be torn between his responsibility to me and to her and her son.

CHAPTER THIRTY-TWO

Unusually for a Monday, Amy didn't call in sick, so I wasn't required at the cafe. It was probably just as well. Although I'd slept heavily, I didn't feel rested. My stomach was still on the tender side, so I stuck to tea and toast for breakfast.

It was raining steadily, so working in the garden was out of the question. Milly was spending the day in Wanaka visiting her friend. She'd asked if I wanted to go in for the drive, but I was working on some blog posts.

Once I'd popped a fragrant butter chicken into the slow cooker, I was happy to spend the day drafting content. I wasn't sure whether I should be writing about spring in the southern hemisphere or autumn in the north. No doubt the conversation I'd planned for tonight would decide that.

Later in the afternoon I thought about calling Mum, but it was only about 5 am there, so I wasted some time looking at cafes for lease in Cornwall – on the off-chance that the conversation didn't go the way I hoped it would.

Richie was home later than usual, arriving just in time for dinner. As he walked in, he kissed my cheek but didn't quite meet my eyes.

'You're late, Rick,' commented Milly.

'Yeah, sorry, Mum. Jodi called and asked if I could pick up Toby from football training. She had car trouble.'

Milly tried to catch my eye, but I lowered my head and made a show of setting the table.

'Well,' I said brightly, 'I hope you're hungry. There's enough food to feed a small army.' My laugh sounded false even to me.

During dinner Fletch and Milly chatted about the cruise one of their friends was taking in the spring.

'Now you're back, Rick, there's no reason why I can't leave you in charge for a couple of weeks so I can whisk your mother away,' Fletch said.

Richie smiled and nodded. 'You guys need a break.'

Other than that he was unusually quiet. Not only had he barely spoken to me all night, it felt as though he was avoiding looking at me. Maybe something had happened between him and Jodi. Surely football training for a five year old would have finished hours ago — which meant he'd been at her house for the remainder of the time. With her.

I took my barely touched plate to the sink, and cleared the table before the others could notice that I'd eaten very little. But not much got past Milly.

'Are you feeling alright, Max?' she asked, concern in her voice. 'You didn't seem to have much of an appetite tonight.'

I smiled at her. 'I'm fine, thanks. But I'm still feeling a little off-colour, so if you'll excuse me I'll take a shower.'

When I stepped out of the bathroom, Richie was sitting on the bed with my laptop open on his lap.

'What are you doing?' I asked.

'I should be asking that question of you.' He pushed the laptop over so I could read the email he'd opened. It was the one James had sent last week.

Richie crossed to the window, looking out to where the lake should have been visible if it wasn't for the rain. 'When were you going to tell me? On your way to the airport tomorrow morning?'

'I didn't tell you about it because I'm not going.'

'It has to be done,' he said.

'But –'

'But what?' he spat out, swivelling around to face me. 'You're still not ready? It's still not time? I'm beginning to think you don't want to get it sorted. You tell me you love me, you certainly act like you love me when I'm inside you,' I flinched, 'but you won't do anything about finishing what's left with your husband.'

'It *is* finished,' I said. 'I'm here with you and not there with him. Isn't that demonstration enough for you?'

'Actually, Maxi, no, it's not.'

'But I don't understand why.'

'Why? Why?' He almost snarled the words. 'Because you're still fucking married to him! That's why.'

I'd never heard Richie raise his voice before. My tummy turned over on itself and I swallowed back the bile that was rising into my mouth, leaving a bitter taste.

'I'm beginning to wonder,' he said after a short silence, 'whether there's another reason why you've avoided contact with him.' His voice was now expressionless, but his eyes had darkened and were burning into me. 'Are you afraid that if you see him again, he'll dazzle you back into his arms? "Dazzle" was the word you used, wasn't it – for the influence he had over you?'

'No,' I managed.

'No? Then what?'

'This. Because of this. Because every time he calls or emails or we talk about him, it feels like a little bit more of the bubble deflates. He makes it different just by contacting me.'

'What bubble?' He looked confused.

'The one that's been around us since the first day we made love. That one.' My stomach rose again. This time I couldn't stop it. 'Sorry,' I muttered, covering my mouth with my hand and staggering to the en suite.

When I came back out he was still in the same

position by the window. 'Are you okay?'

I nodded. 'I think the butter chicken was too rich for me. Or perhaps I had too much to drink.'

'Really? You barely touched either your food or your wine.' He watched me for a few seconds, then turned to face outside again. 'This bubble you talk about – that's not real life, Maxi. You can't live in a bubble forever. It was fine for us to be in it when we were getting used to loving each other, but you can't pretend that James doesn't exist, that you're not still married to him.' He leaned his forehead against the glass. 'The longer you avoid this, the more I can't help thinking you're keeping that option open.'

'What option?'

'Going back to him. Or going back to England. Tonight when I came in you had Cornwall leases on the screen. Jodi said you mentioned something about going home when you were talking to her at the club.' He shrugged. 'What am I meant to think?'

'What did she say?' This time the flip in my tummy wasn't from rich sauce; it was the metallic taste of Jodi.

'She said she asked you when your divorce was coming through. Then she asked how long you were staying and you told her your return ticket's in two weeks.'

'You know that. You were with me when I booked it – that day at Mum and Dad's.'

'I thought you might have changed it by now.'

I stared at him with my mouth open. 'Why would I? We haven't made any plans. I just figured that, well … you know …'

'No, I don't know. You say you love me, but this – how we live, what we do – it seems to be like a holiday romance for you. Is that what this is about, what we're about – sex? A fling until you decide what's next? You said you don't ever want to compromise again. Would being here with me be a compromise?'

He finally faced me, his eyes intense, his face otherwise expressionless. 'You can't be seriously thinking about going back to him? He didn't fuck you like I do. He didn't make you moan and plead like I do – you know he can't.'

The harshness of his words hit me like a hammer in my chest.

'You know it's more than sex,' I managed.

'Do I? If it is, why haven't you finished with him and cancelled your ticket home? Maybe you're keeping your options open because, god knows, he can give you a more comfortable life than I can. I'll never be able to offer you what he can.'

I opened my mouth to speak, to tell him that he'd never asked me to stay, but he held up a hand to stop me.

'Go to Sydney, Maxi. Go and talk to James. Finish it for good, or go back to him. This in-between isn't fair to either of us.'

I sat on the edge of the bed facing away from him, my elbows on my knees, my head in my hands. 'Is this about Jodi?'

'What?' He almost spat the word. 'She has nothing to do with this. At least she told me what was going on with you. She saw the text that came through for you —the one asking if you'd read his email and saying how much he was looking forward to seeing you tomorrow.'

'Of course she did,' I muttered. 'She's such a good friend.'

I could feel him staring at me. 'What's that supposed to mean?'

And then the floodgates opened. I stood and moved around to face him, hands on my hips. 'She couldn't wait to tell you. Just like she couldn't wait to tell me how you two used to date and how much in love with her you were. And how she's *so* glad you've finally found happiness, and how she hopes I won't mind how you feel so responsible for her and her child. How it's right you feel like that, and right that Toby's back here with family.' Once I'd started, I couldn't seem to stop. '*Is* Toby yours?'

He paled at my words.

'Oh, and then there was the comment about how her husband always knew that you'd never got over her, and she'd never got over you, and how you had to go away so her marriage would stand a chance. She told me how patient you are, how long you've waited for her, and she knows you can wait just another few weeks until I'm gone. So no, I'm sure she couldn't wait to tell you that James had ordered me to Sydney. Because that's what this is.' I picked up the laptop and waved it around. 'It's an order. He's decreed it so I must obey. He didn't ask – he just sent me the tickets. Sorry, his *girlfriend* sent me the tickets. Do you know just how humiliating that is? *That's* why I'm not going – not because I'm not keen to finish it, or because I'm afraid that I'll look at him and fall straight back into his arms, or because I want to keep my options open. I want it to be *my* decision, and I didn't want to waste the time I have left with you over in Sydney seeing him. I wanted to talk to you first and we'd decide together when I'd see him.'

I raised my eyes to the ceiling and drew breath. 'As for you being a holiday fling? I love you more than I ever thought it was possible to love anyone, Richie. And no, I didn't tell Jodi that – because it's none of her business. I love it here and I want to stay forever with you, but you haven't asked me to – stay, that is. Not once. Every time your father talks about me going home – with the emphasis on home, as if that's where I belong, not here – you say nothing. And that's none of her business either. So when she asked when I was going home, I didn't know how to reply because I already feel like I'm home, but she was reminding me in her oh-so-subtle way that I don't belong here and she does.'

I pulled out a backpack and started to force clothes into it, uncaring how crushed they were. 'I'll go to Sydney and I'll talk to James – but not because he ordered me to. Because you're right – this needs to be finished.'

He made a move towards me. 'You've got it wrong – about Jodi. And Toby.'

I held up a hand to stop him. 'No, Richie. Too much has been said tonight – by both of us. Let me finish packing.'

He watched me for a moment, then strode from the room, shutting the door quietly behind him.

Once he'd gone, I collapsed onto the bed and gave in to my tears, sobbing into a pillow so the noise wouldn't carry outside. Our bubble had well and truly burst.

Richie didn't come to bed until late. He climbed in and lay facing away from me. I lay facing the other way, wide-eyed, listening to him breathe. Finally he rolled over and gathered me to him, his arms warm around my belly, his breath soft in my ear.

'I love you,' he said. 'Please come home to me.'

I nodded, feeling tears track their way down my face. I covered his hands with mine and brought one of them to my chest, holding it to my breast.

'Maxi?'

'I promise,' I whispered, turning to face him, hoping that he was asking me to come home to him to stay, not just back to him before I left again. Hoping that he'd still be here to come home to, that Jodi wouldn't win while I was away.

Our lovemaking that night was slower and more intense than it had ever been before. Even in the dark I could feel his eyes locked onto mine, not letting go, not even for a second, not even when I would have closed them. It felt like we were each trying to imprint on the soul of the other. In case it was the last time.

I thought, despite my words, that part of him was still worried James would win me back. A very large part of me was worried that Jodi wouldn't rest until she'd won him back. He might have loved her years ago, but I was hoping that what we had now was worth more to him. As I moved against him, urging him into me, I was doing all I could to push any thought of her from his mind – to remember only this moment and me. I refused to think about the Toby factor. I could fight her, but not her child.

When Richie kissed me goodbye at the airport, his mouth crushed against mine, I willed myself to remember every second of it – how his lips felt, the hardness of his chest against my hands, the intensity in his eyes as they looked into mine.

'I love you,' I whispered when he pulled away, his face unsmiling, his jaw firm.

'I love you too,' he said, and he kissed me again, harder this time, branding me with his mouth. He pushed himself away and jammed his fists into the pockets of his jeans. 'You'd better go through.'

I stood there for a heartbeat, two, three, my eyes holding his, willing him to say something more, to ask me to stay – not just for two more weeks, but forever.

His eyes dropped. 'Go,' he mumbled.

I swallowed the ball of emotion that had moved from my chest to my throat and threatened to spill out. I turned to leave and then, unable to stop myself, spun around and grabbed handfuls of his jumper to help me reach his lips one last time.

'I'll see you in a few days,' I told him, then I walked off towards customs.

I looked back once – he hadn't moved. His hands were still in his pockets, his shoulders hunched, his face drawn. I held a hand up in a wave. He nodded, unsmiling, but I felt his eyes watching me as I disappeared through the doors.

CHAPTER THIRTY-THREE

James was waiting in the hotel lobby when I stepped out of the lift. I'd had a nap as soon as I arrived, falling into a sleep far deeper and longer than the three-hour flight had warranted. As a result, I was running late and had to make do with a rushed hair and makeup job. James had told me to dress up, so I was wearing the only good dress and heels I had with me. It was chilly outside, and I threw a long fringed scarf around my shoulders. That would have to do.

Despite my last-minute dash, I was right on time – although James was looking at his watch as if I wasn't. He looked up and his expression changed immediately when he saw me: from frowning impatience to pleased smile.

I'd seen the James charm offensive in action before, but hadn't had it turned on me since our early days together. It had worked back then, but tonight I was immune. I'd been married to this man, slept beside him, made love with him – yet looking at him now it felt as though I'd never known him. When he held my hand to pull me towards him, it felt like a stranger's hand; and when he kissed my cheek, it felt like a stranger's kiss.

'You're looking good,' he said, looking me up and down. 'More tanned, and your hair is longer. It makes you look, I don't know … softer?'

'Thanks. You look good too.'

He did, just like he always looked – smart, fashionable, slim. Richie and James were a similar height, yet beside James, Richie had always seemed huge, more powerful. Now I knew it wasn't just a muscular thing. Richie had so much more … substance about him. James looked the part; Richie was the real thing.

'Are you here on your own?' he asked.

'Of course. Why wouldn't I be?'

He shrugged. 'No reason.'

'Are you here alone?' I countered.

'I'm here for business, Maxine. Of course India is in Sydney with me.'

Of course she was.

'Anyway,' he said, taking my elbow, 'let's not argue about that now. We have plenty of other things to talk about.' He guided me out of the hotel into the street, and down towards the Opera House.

'Where are we eating?' I asked.

'I wasn't sure where you'd eaten when you were here with Richie, but I'd like to bet it wasn't at the

Opera House,' he said smugly. 'This is a little more than his pay grade.'

'No, we didn't eat there. But we went to the bar underneath the Opera House – it really goes off on a weekend afternoon. Great food, a great vibe and casual. It's absolutely perfect on a sunny winter's day.'

I remembered how we'd met up with Mirry and Oliver, Cate and Harry, and spent the afternoon listening to jazz and drinking white wine, Richie's arm around me, holding me close.

James, suspecting the reason behind my smile involved Richie, scowled. 'I think you'll find where we're going very special.'

I smiled politely and allowed him to lead me into the restaurant beneath the Opera House sails.

Once we were seated and had menus, James said, 'Let me order for you. I've always known what you've wanted.'

He'd always assumed that I wanted what he thought I wanted, which wasn't the same thing. But I chose not to point this out. It was, as it always had been, easier to allow him to take over.

He spent fifteen minutes or so pondering the menu, and then negotiating the wine list. I sat back and watched. For once I wasn't annoyed, more mildly amused. Finally he summoned the waiter – who'd been doing a fine job of waiting patiently – placed our orders, and sat back and mopped at his brow as if he'd run a marathon.

'Right,' he said. 'Let me tell you about New York.'

So he did: describing the city, the apartment, his friends, the places he went, the restaurants he ate at, the bars he drank at, the shops he shopped at. If I was supposed to be impressed, I wasn't. It all seemed so pretentious and unreal. Still, I managed to make the right noises at the appropriate times. In-between his monologue, our food and wine arrived, was eaten and drunk, and replaced with something equally as exquisite. Over a dessert that I didn't want, he finally got to the point he'd been trying to make all night.

'So, now you've heard how wonderful life is in New York, when are you going to join me? Imagine meals like this, restaurants like this, all the time. You wouldn't need to work again – I'll look after you in the way I should be looking after you. You'll have nothing to worry about other than shoes and lunch.'

My head swam, and not from the alcohol. I'd only sipped a little from each glass.

'I'm sorry, James. My answer is the same as it was months ago back in England. I'm not coming to New York with you. We're over.'

He summoned the waiter and ordered coffees.

'Not for me,' I said.

'Why not? You normally enjoy an after-dinner coffee.'

'I know. I just don't feel like one.'

Even the thought of the smell of coffee was making my tummy turn. The last time I'd felt like this – unable to stomach coffee, not wanting to drink alcohol, feeling fatigued – was back in February when I was pregnant. I remembered my sleep this afternoon – more of a pass-out than a nap. And the queasiness over the weekend.

When was my last period? Could I be …?

I hadn't gone back on the pill since I'd lost the baby, and Richie and I hadn't been nearly as careful as we should have been. There'd been a couple of occasions when things had got out of control too quickly. There was that first time on the floor in Denmark, that time in the shower at Cate's … I added the dates in my head. Yes, I was definitely late.

The joy started in my belly and worked its way up through my body to my mouth, emerging in a wide smile.

'Maxine! Is this a joke to you?'

'I'm sorry – what did you say?'

'I was asking why you think we're over when I clearly don't agree. What do you want me to do? Admit I've made a mistake and beg you to come back? If that's what you need me to do, I'll do it – even though I don't think I've done anything wrong.'

'You don't think the affair with India was wrong?'

He looked perplexed. 'You keep going on about that. India has nothing to do with this. We were discreet

– that's how it's done. If you want me to fire her and never see her again, I will – although you know how hard it is to get a decent assistant. But I'd do that for you. You're my wife and you belong with me.'

'What about love? You haven't mentioned that at all.'

'Is that what you want me to say? That I love you?'

I shook my head sadly. 'It's not what I want you to say – especially if it's not what you feel. In any case, it doesn't matter. You see, I don't love you any more. I'm in love with Richie.'

'Don't be ridiculous. The man has nothing to offer you. In comparison, I'm handing you a life that millions of women would snap up in a shot.' He lowered his voice. 'I understand if you've slept with him – I can even forgive you. No one needs to know. Although there'll be no question of you staying in touch with him once we're back together.'

'Have you heard anything I've said? You and I are over. Richie can give me absolutely everything that I need.'

'Be careful saying things like that, Maxine, darling. You've become accustomed to a style of living that he'll never be able to provide.'

James leaned back in his chair and smiled at me, confident that he'd win in the end.

'That's not why I love him. We share the same values; we want the same things. I don't need a life of lunches and shopping and brand names and posh restaurants. It's nice, but it's not me.'

He laughed. 'You say that now. We – you and I – used to want the same things.'

'We didn't, you know. I just went along with what you wanted. It took losing the baby to make me realise that you've never asked what I want. Like tonight – you've always assumed that you know best. But you don't. You have no idea what I want to do with my life.'

James's practised smile was beginning to slip. 'I know what's best for you – and it's more than digging holes, and writing ridiculous little newsletters or blogs, or playing with recipes and baking for other people.'

'So what if that's all I want? Your idea of having enough is different to mine, that's all. When we were together, I never saw you – you were never home. It wouldn't be any different in New York, except you'd be in the same country with me never seeing you. How can a marriage survive under those circumstances?'

'Plenty of marriages thrive like that. Jeremy and Helen have been married forever. She's the perfect director's wife. You could be too.'

'He's been having affairs for years though.'

He shrugged. 'So what? Helen knows the score. Besides, Jeremy likes you and he's already started making noises about how a divorce at this stage could damage my career.' He paused to consider what he was going to say next. 'If you want to try for another baby, I suppose I'm okay with that. Anything you want, darling.' He looked encouragingly into my eyes. 'We can even try tonight if you like. Did you pack the red lingerie?'

'It's a little late for that.'

'It's never too late.'

'No, James, it really is too late. I think I'm already pregnant. And this time it really is Richie's baby.'

After that the conversation deteriorated quickly.

'How could you be so stupid? The first time might have been a mistake, but a second time is just plain careless. If you've been having unprotected sex with that man, you could expose me to anything!'

'Except you wouldn't be exposed – because we're not having sex!'

'If you're expecting me to take on another man's baby, you've got another think coming.'

'That's the last thing I'd expect.'

'What about Richie? What does he say about this?'

'He doesn't know yet. I haven't told him.' I shrugged. 'Knowing Richie, I expect he'll be –'

I stopped. I had no idea what he'd say – not any more. Not since I'd told him that Toby could be his. I knew that he wanted children, and I also knew that he'd want to do what he thought was the right thing. There was no doubt that he'd want to stand by me, but the presence of Jodi and Toby complicated that. As desperately as I wanted to spend the rest of my life with Richie, I wanted all of him. And, knowing him as I did, nothing more than everything would keep him happy too.

'It's one thing to have a discreet fling. It's another thing entirely to be carrying another man's baby,' James said. 'That's unforgivable.'

That's when I cried. They were silent tears, but I couldn't seem to stop them running out of my eyes. I mopped at them with my napkin, and brushed them away with my hand, but still they kept coming.

James looked around to ensure no one else had noticed. 'Stop it,' he said. 'You're making a spectacle of yourself.'

'I can't,' I spluttered. 'I can't stop them.'

'I hope you're not expecting me to feel sympathy for you. This is all your own doing.'

'I don't need sympathy, James. I just need to end this so I can move forward – me and the baby. With or without Richie.'

He watched me for a few seconds, taking in the streams of tears that continued to flow, and seemed to give up the fight – or the pretence of the fight. I wasn't really sure he even knew what he was fighting for now. I didn't think he loved me; maybe he felt as though he still owned me. But in those few seconds, he must have decided to give me up.

'You're sure about this?' he said.

'I am, James. Please, let me go. You know you

don't love me any more, and I don't love you. This way you can be with India.'

'I'm not sure I want that,' he said. 'She's great as a mistress, but I suspect that biological clock of hers could be ticking quite loudly. At least while I was married to you there was no question of a more permanent arrangement.'

I shook my head at his cheek – or was it candour?

'Please, James,' I said again, 'let's finish this like two mature adults. No more pretending, no more recriminations.'

He nodded slowly. 'You're right … like two mature adults. We can save the money we'd otherwise have wasted on solicitors. But don't think you're getting half of our assets, and don't expect me to continue to support you.'

I didn't remind him that I hadn't touched a penny of his money since the day I'd told him we were done.

'I don't expect half,' I said softly. 'I just want this to be over.'

The next morning I went out and bought a pregnancy test. Just like last time, I got three. All were positive. I was carrying Richie's baby. The thought filled me with a glow that radiated all the way through my body.

As well as I knew Richie, I still wasn't sure how he'd react about the baby. It would come as a surprise, but I figured that, given time to absorb the news, he'd be happy about it. My main concern wasn't how he'd feel about the baby, but rather how he'd feel about me. I knew from the look on his face the other night that he'd had no idea that Toby could be his. If he was, that was bound to complicate our situation.

As for how he felt about Jodi? In my heart I knew he loved me. Any doubts I'd had were the product of jealousy. I should never have allowed Jodi to get under my skin in the way she did. If she wanted a fight, she was going to get one.

Horrie had told me to follow my dreams; and he'd also told me that I'd know I'd found my place when I felt like I'd come home. What I'd forgotten was that being with a person could feel like home; and the first time Richie and I made love it felt like we'd come home. How had I managed to forget that?

The day of Horrie's funeral I'd told Richie that I'd never change my plans because a man asked me to. Now I understood that he'd been waiting for me to take the initiative. He would never have asked me to stay; rather, he'd hoped I'd ask him. Dear, dear Richie. He'd listened to me, but I hadn't listened to him.

I sat back on the hotel bed and allowed myself to indulge in a happy family fantasy: me, Richie, and our baby. Somehow I figured he'd be a boy – not that it mattered, but in this particular fantasy he was a boy. We had a place of our own with a view of the lake. I had a garden with stone-fruit trees and enough space to grow everything I needed. We'd expanded the landscaping business to include a garden shop like the one at Blossoms, but with my harvest cafe attached. I was selling cards and recipe postcards using my own photos, and Richie was designing the large gardens he'd always wanted to design. I took the dream one step further and saw him and Brad collaborating on taking his garden to Chelsea, while I was writing a cookbook. It might be a dream, but it was also a happy combination of what each of us wanted.

James and I met again that evening and worked out an agreement of sorts. Somehow I managed to stop myself from asking whether he needed India there to take notes. When all was said and done, the ending was simple. I didn't want his money, and I certainly didn't feel entitled to it, but he insisted I accept a reasonable settlement for my share of the London flat plus the rest of my share of the Brookford proceeds. I wanted nothing to do with his pension funds.

'I know you have Horrie's cottage, but at least if Richie sends you packing once you tell him about the baby, you'll have something to live on while you get yourself sorted,' he said. 'I don't want anyone saying that I haven't treated you fairly.'

I couldn't help but smile. Now that James had accustomed himself to the separation, he was treating it as a business negotiation.

'I'll send the instructions through to the solicitors today and get the papers drawn up for the financial settlement. It will still take months for the decree to come through, but I guess that's that.' The resignation and sadness in his face was also in his voice.

'I'm sorry, James.'

'So am I. I'm sorry that you found out about India. If it wasn't for that we could have been happy.'

Inwardly I laughed. He wasn't sorry he'd had the affair, rather that he'd been caught out. Typical James.

'What will you do now?' he asked.

'Go back to Queenstown, tell Richie about the baby, and make any further decisions based on his reaction. My ticket's still booked for Heathrow in just over a week, but I'll only use it if I have to.'

Richie and I hadn't spoken since I'd left, and while he knew when I was arriving back in Queenstown, I had no idea whether he'd be at the airport to meet me. Although we'd made love on Monday night, there were things to talk about, and I was determined to get it all out in the open before I told him about our baby. If he didn't ask me to stay, I'd simply tell him that I was.

Despite what I'd told James, I had no intention of using that return ticket.

CHAPTER THIRTY-FOUR

When I walked through arrivals the following afternoon, it was Milly's face that I saw. Her smile was quick but fleeting and, after she'd hugged me, she wouldn't meet my eyes.

'What's wrong?' I asked.

'It's probably nothing to worry about. I'll tell you in the car.' She handed me the jacket I'd left behind when I flew to Sydney. 'You'll be needing this. There's been another dump of snow in the mountains overnight. This wind is coming straight from it.'

She wasn't wrong – the cold hit me as soon as we left the shelter of the airport terminal. I put the jacket on for the short walk to the car and snuggled into it.

We travelled the first few kilometres in silence, Milly concentrating hard on the road ahead.

'Did you get things sorted with James?' she asked eventually.

'Yes, it's done. Now I just need to sort things with Richie.'

'Don't you worry about him. He's hurting because

he's afraid he's lost you. Once you talk he'll be fine.' Although she hadn't taken her gaze from the road, there was an edge to her voice.

'Milly, what's wrong? Where's Richie?'

She hesitated before answering. 'We don't know. I'm sure he's alright though.'

My heart plummeted into my stomach. 'What do you mean you don't know?'

'He went tramping on Wednesday morning. Just packed his things and took off. He's done it before – when he's needed time and space to sort things through.'

'Yet you're worried?'

She nodded slowly. 'He was pretty upset when he left. After he dropped you at the airport on Tuesday he went to see Jodi and came back in a right temper. Over dinner he had some loud words with his father, and when Jess tried to make a joke of it all he flew at her too. Then on Wednesday morning he was gone. He left a note to say he'd be back to meet you.'

'But he's not yet.' I was trying to breathe normally, but every instinct was screaming at me that things were not right. My hand moved to my belly as if to protect our baby from the news.

'No.'

'And you say it snowed last night?'

'Yes. We're hoping that means he's taken shelter in a hut somewhere to wait it out. Rick might have been angry, but he's sensible and he'd never leave without the right gear, especially not at this time of year.' Her voice was hopeful rather than confident.

We drove the rest of the way in silence. I felt her eyes on me from time to time, but I couldn't meet them. I didn't want her to see the panic raging inside me. Instead I watched the landscape flying by.

At the house Fletch came out to meet us. He kissed me briefly and picked my bag up. Milly's eyes pleaded with him to have good news. He shook his head.

'Fletch can put your bag in yours and Rick's room,' she told me, 'and I'll make you a cup of tea. You look like you need it.'

I watched Fletch as he walked down the hall, the slight stoop to his shoulders the only sign that he was worried too.

'It's good to have you back,' Milly said as she placed the tea in front of me a few minutes later. 'It's only been a few days, but we've missed you – we've all missed you.'

'Even Fletch?'

She looked confused.

'It's okay, Milly. I know that Fletch hasn't warmed to me.'

She leaned across the table and patted my hand. 'It's not that he doesn't like you, love. He's worried about Rick. The situation, you see – you still being married.'

'But –'

'Don't get me wrong – he knows nothing happened between you two until you were separated. It's just that the situation reminds him so much of when he and I fell in love.' She took a sip of her tea, cradling the mug in her hands. 'Cam fell in love with me when I was still married to Cate and Ricky's dad.'

It was my turn to look confused. 'But I thought ...' I didn't know what I thought.

'It's not something we talk about. It's not that we don't talk about it either – it's just part of who we are now. Things weren't great between Gary and me. He fancied himself a bit of a ladies' man – and with his fancy London accent and his snappy clothes and fast car, he probably was. He certainly dazzled me from the start. I had no idea why he'd chosen me when he could have had his pick of anyone. Then one night at the pub he introduced me to his friend – a quiet chap. It was Cam. When Gary was off flirting, Cam kept me company. He became a good friend to me.' She sipped her tea as she spoke, her eyes focused on something over thirty years ago. 'I discovered that Gary was cheating on me the same day I found out I was pregnant with Rick. He promised me that it wouldn't happen again and I believed him. I think I had to believe him – what else do you do when you have an eleven-month-old baby and are pregnant with another? He had this way about him, you see. He finally left for good when Rick was about two months old.'

She put her mug on the coaster and smiled. 'I don't know what I would have done if it wasn't for Cam. There I was, with two kids under two – don't believe anyone who tells you that breastfeeding is an adequate contraceptive – and no husband. Cam was patient and waited until I was ready. I already loved him; it just took some more time for me to fall in love with him. When he wanted to move back here – he'd grown up here – there was no question.'

'That's a beautiful story,' I said, my eyes filling with inconvenient tears. 'But you two were okay in the end.'

'We were. Eventually. And we've certainly been very happy together. But it could very well have gone the other way. Ricky told us when he met you that you were the one for him. He also told us that he knew you could never be together – that you were married and he'd never do anything to ruin that. He said he was happy being your friend. When you announced you were moving away, he called and said he was coming home. When you fell pregnant, he said he knew that he'd lost you.

'It brought it all back for Cam. Seeing you together, knowing that you were still tied to James – well, it reminded him of how much the waiting hurt. He was worried that you weren't as serious about Ricky as he was about you; that you'd go back to England and break his heart. That's all. Besides, your place is here now.' She paused. 'Especially now.'

I looked up from my tea.

'Have you told him?' she asked.

'How did you –'

'I'm a mother. We know these things.'

'But how?'

'I always think it's in the softening of the jawline. And it's already showing in your breasts. I'm rarely wrong – and I'm not this time either, am I?'

I shook my head.

'You haven't told him?'

I shook my head again. 'I've only just found out.'

'He'll be over the moon.' She said it with so much confidence that I almost believed her.

I sipped at my tea and listened to the silence in the room. The clock ticking, a dog barking somewhere outside, the wind rattling at the windows. Richie was out in this, and it would be dark in another hour or so.

'Where did he go?' I asked.

'Probably Routeburn. But we think only to Routeburn Falls – there's a hut there and he wouldn't be stupid enough to try to tramp the Saddle in this weather.'

Fletch came into the room. 'I'm glad you're back,' he said to me. 'We were worried you mightn't come back.'

I thought he meant to say that Richie was worried I wouldn't.

'Here feels like home,' I said. 'I'm not going anywhere.'

He smiled and nodded slowly. 'I'm glad.' He was stopped by the ringing of his phone. 'It's Jess,' he told us before answering it.

'She's gone out to the Routeburn car park to see if Rick parked the Landy there,' Milly explained. 'At least that way we'll know which direction he went and can maybe reach the shelter hut by satellite phone.'

We waited while Fletch finished the call with Jess. 'She called from Glenorchy Hotel – the reception's shit out there, and non-existent on track,' he said. 'She said he's not there. He's not on the Routeburn.' He raised his eyes to the ceiling and rubbed his forehead. 'We have no idea where to start looking now.'

My gasp broke the silence. It left me doubled over and struggling for breath, as if all the wind had been knocked out of me. I thought I'd experienced pain this year, but nothing compared to this – raw fear that the man I loved more than anything was out there in the cold and unable to contact us.

Milly held my hand as I rocked backward and forward in the chair. Not Richie, please not Richie. The mantra played over and over in my head.

Unable to bear seeing the same helpless fear on Milly's and Fletch's faces, and unable to swallow back the bile rising to my throat, I raced to our bedroom and made it to the en suite just in time, heaving into the toilet bowl, holding my belly, holding our baby tight.

Long minutes later, I sat on the bed. As always, it was perfectly made. Where I had a habit of straightening the bed before I hopped back into it at night, Richie made it as soon as he got out. It was one of my habits that had irritated James, but which Richie laughed about.

I picked up his pillow and buried my head in it, smelling his aftershave. Sitting back on the bed, still cuddling his pillow, I saw his sketchbook and flipped it open. There they were, his Chelsea sketches. I turned page after page. He'd drawn detailed studies of certain types of flax, mass-planted so that when the wind hit them it appeared as though the grasses were flowing like water.

Towards the middle of the book, there were no more plants or designs. Each sketch was of me. There I was looking over the accounts at Blossoms; styling a recipe before I photographed it, biting my lower lip in concentration; curled up in the plane seat asleep; freewheeling down the road on my bike with my legs out to the side; asleep in a field of bluebells; lying back on the deckchair on that sunny Saturday afternoon in Denmark. Me. All of them. He must have drawn them from memory. The tears that rose to my eyes came from my heart.

I remembered that Saturday afternoon in Denmark, the day before we got together. Brad had picked up the sketchbook and looked at it, then looked at me. Then Richie had run back to retrieve it. That was why – because the drawings were of me. He didn't want me to see, but Brad had seen. It was why he'd pushed us together.

Towards the back of the book was a drawing of me lying on a picnic blanket half naked. My hair was messed about, my eyes dreamy. I looked like I'd been made love to very satisfactorily. It was Paradise. He'd sketched from memory that moment when I'd known that nothing else mattered – no goal, no ambition, nothing – unless I was with him.

I rubbed my hand across the top of my belly where our baby was growing. A warmth and a certainty ran through me.

I picked up the sketchbook and walked back to where Fletch was pacing and Milly was sitting with her head in her hands.

'Is there a track that starts or finishes near Paradise?' I asked.

Milly looked up and Fletch stopped pacing.

'Yes,' he said. 'The Rees-Dart Track. There's a four-wheel-drive track to Chinamans Flat – that's just a few kays from Paradise. Why?'

'I have no idea how I know, it's just that this picture …' I blushed and closed the sketchbook. 'Actually you don't need to see the drawing, but it's a special place for us and,' I lowered my head and my voice, 'I think that might be where he went.'

Fletch stared at me for half a second. 'That's good enough for me.'

Milly and I waited while he dialled Jess.

'Thank Christ you're still in phone range,' he said. 'Don't ask why, but Max thinks there could be a chance that he did part of the Rees-Dart.' He listened as Jess obviously had something to say. 'I know the conditions, and I'm not suggesting he went too far – he's not that stupid – but do me a favour and make your way out to Paradise. Check the main car park at Dans Paddock, and if the Landy isn't there, it could be at Chinamans Flat. At least there's a shelter there. And, Jess? Drive carefully, sweetie.'

And so we waited. And waited.

Finally, just after dark, the call came from Jess. She'd had to wait until she was back in a reception area.

'He was there!' She was yelling and we all heard her.

Fletch gathered Milly and me into his arms and held us tight.

CHAPTER THIRTY-FIVE

An hour or so later Jess and a sheepish-looking Richie let themselves into the house. I hung back to let him greet Fletch and Milly first, but he saved his warmest hug for me, squeezing the available air from me before kissing me soundly.

'How did you know?' he asked when he finally lifted his lips from mine.

'I saw your sketchbook and I remembered that day.'

'I'm glad you did, otherwise I would have had a very cold and hungry night.' He smiled down at me.

'That moment you drew, it was the moment I knew I'd give anything to stay with you, wherever you want to be.'

'For me, it was the moment I knew that I'd do anything to hold you here,' he said, before claiming my lips again.

Before things got too far out of control, Jess interrupted us to offer some whisky, while Milly busied herself getting dinner happening.

'Just to warm us through,' she justified.

'I thought I had it covered,' Richie said, once we were all sitting at the table. 'A couple of nights at Daleys Flat, with a side trip out on Thursday, and back to Chinamans by midday so I could meet Maxi's flight.' He smiled fondly at me. 'But when I got back to the Landy, it wouldn't start – and I had no phone reception. I figured someone would come by sooner rather than later. If not, I was ready to spend the night at the shelter and tramp out to Dans Paddock tomorrow. Thankfully, Jess came.'

'Only because Max saw some drawing you did of her there and put two and two together. Are we going to get to see this drawing?' Jess asked.

Richie looked at me and grinned. 'Probably not.'

'Well, that makes me want to see it all the more,' she laughed.

'It's enough that it led you to find Richie,' said Milly. 'And now, I think these two have some talking to do, so we might leave them to it, hey?'

'Thanks, Mum.' Richie held his hand out to me and we went down the hall to our room. Once inside, he pulled me close again. 'I've missed you,' he said, his lips meeting mine.

Somehow I managed to pull myself back. 'Do you want to know what happened with James?'

He sat on the bed and pulled me down beside him. 'Let me guess. He told you that he made a mistake, that he wants you back.'

'Something like that, but –'

'Then he said he thought he might want a family one day after all, and that he and India are finished. Did he say that?'

'Something like that,' I managed.

Richie swallowed hard, and remained silent.

'I told him I didn't want to be with him,' I said. 'I told him we were finished. Once he realised I was serious, we finally talked about the logistics. It's happening, Richie: we're finally, completely and properly over.'

'Did you tell him you're with me?' His jaw was firm as he gazed straight ahead, out towards where the lake would be if it weren't so dark.

'Yes. I said that being with you feels like coming home.'

'Oh, Maxi.' He reached his hand out, but I moved mine away.

'No – not yet. The thing is, the sight of you with Jodi made me feel sick, and the thought of what you two could be doing twisted a hole in my belly. Then when she hinted that Toby could be yours –'

'Surely you know that I love you?'

'I do know that, and whatever you had with her is in the past. But I also know that if Toby is yours, you wouldn't walk away from that responsibility. And you haven't asked me to stay.'

He shook his head, his eyes wide. 'Maxi, we dated

when we were kids. Yeah, she hurt me when she cheated on me, but we were both so young it would never have worked. Regardless of what she told you, there's never been anything between us since. I've never wanted there to be. When I introduced her to Byron, anything we'd had was long finished.'

'I think I know that now, but when she said what she said …'

'Oh, sweetheart, you couldn't be further off the mark. It's always been you. You came into the garden centre all sparky and vital with none of the qualifications I was after, but so confident that you could do the job anyway. You looked up and smiled at me and I was gone. Just like that.'

This time when he reached for my hand I let him take it.

'I wasn't expecting to fall in love,' he said. 'I'd managed to avoid it up until then, but there you were.'

'You never said anything.'

'How could I? You were married to James. I couldn't give you what he could. I couldn't compete with him. So I told myself that I was happy to be your friend.' He shook his head and looked deeply into my eyes. 'When you said you were moving to New York with him, I knew I was about to lose you. In fact, I'd decided to give it one shot and tell you how I felt about you. Put myself out there and let you decide. I figured I had nothing to lose – if you left, I'd have lost you anyway. We might have emailed for a few months, but you'd be gone.' His eyes clouded and he used his free hand to rub at his chin. 'Then you fell pregnant. That day you were going to go to London to tell James about the baby, it was the same day I'd decided to tell you what I suspected about James and India. You had to know – it was unfair for you to make the decision to go away with him and bring up a family not knowing the whole story. I had it all worked out in my head: I'd tell you, you'd hate me for a bit, but eventually you'd need me as a friend. Then, when the time was right, you'd learn to love me the way I loved you.'

'And the baby?'

He shrugged. 'It didn't matter to me that it was his. I love you, how could I not love your child too?'

'Oh, Richie.' My eyes filled and one tear rolled down my cheek.

'When you lost that baby, I didn't think any further forward than knowing I had to be there for you. I couldn't let you deal with it alone – even if that meant you might still go with him.' He looked at me and his eyes were glistening. 'But then I had to go. I couldn't stay and watch you put aside everything you wanted for someone who didn't appreciate you.'

'But you came back when Horrie died?'

'I wanted to be there in case you needed me. I didn't know you'd split with James, but I knew I had to offer whatever support I could. Staying with you in that little cottage, though, nearly brought me undone.' He smiled. 'It was torture to be sleeping so close to you, but not to have you in bed beside me. When you said you'd come to Denmark with me, I tried not to let myself hope. When you agreed to come here as well, I figured I'd been given a chance to make you love me too.'

'Work your magic,' I said.

'What?'

'Just something Jess said one night.' I thought back to those days after Horrie's funeral. 'Did Mum and Dad know?'

He nodded. 'Your mother's always known how I feel about you.'

I thought some more. 'Horrie knew too, didn't he?'

He grinned. 'Before I left, he asked me not to give up on you. I told him he should be saying that to James, and he said, "No, lad, you're the one for Max. She just doesn't know it yet."'

'James knew too – before I did. When I was pregnant, he thought it was yours.'

'I wished it was.'

He pushed me back onto the bed, lying on his side beside me, looking down at me, into my eyes, making my brain go all fuzzy and my tummy all melty.

'I'm sorry about Jodi,' he said. 'I didn't know she'd been undermining us the whole time. The things she'd been saying to you – well, she'd been saying much the same to me, just a hint here and there about James, about you staying or going. I didn't know she felt that way about me. I certainly don't feel that way about her.' He ran a finger down my cheek and across my lips. 'After you left, I confronted her and asked her to leave us alone.'

'I only left because I had to finish it,' I said. 'With James, that is. I needed to hear what he had to say – I owed him that.'

'I know. But I also knew he had some weird hold on you.'

I shook my head. 'It wasn't that so much as James likes to win. When he sets his mind on something, it's often easier to simply give in to him.'

'I was afraid that's what you'd do. I'd done all I could to show you how I feel. I had to trust that you'd come home like you promised you would.'

I reached up to stroke the side of his face. 'I came back because I love you. I was going to fight her for you.'

'You did that before you left, when you told me what had been happening.' He ran his finger across my collarbone and down to where my shirt was buttoned, leaving a trail of fiery goose bumps. 'You were magnificent in your anger – and very sexy.'

'You didn't ask me to stay,' I managed.

'How could I? You'd told me that you'd never again change your plans because a man asked you to. I had to hope that you'd change your mind on your own.'

He bent his head and nuzzled his way down my throat.

'So what happens now?' I arched my neck to give him better access.

His grin was cheeky as his fingers deftly undid the buttons on my top. 'I'm sure that by now you have a fair idea, but I'm happy to talk you through it.'

His hand reached inside and cupped one overly full breast. I moaned as his thumb flicked at my nipple, so much more sensitive than it used to be.

'Other than that,' I gasped.

'Does it matter?' His mouth took over the job his thumb had been doing.

'No. Ohhhh … Richie.'

'Are you cold?' he mumbled, his free hand already busy at the zip of my jeans.

I shook my head. His hand had slipped inside my pants and his fingers were working their magic on me, bringing me to life as only he could.

'No,' I didn't care about anything except having him inside me.

He raised his head. 'Good, because I could do with a little help getting these jeans off you.'

And then, finally, he kissed me.

Lying in his arms later, I remembered what it was that I had to tell him.

'Richie?'

'Hmmm.'

'There's something I need to tell you.'

He rolled onto his side and looked down at me. 'That sounds ominous.'

'It is, I guess.' I took a deep breath. 'I'm pregnant.'

I watched his face as he processed the news, and then as his smile grew wider. He gathered me into his arms and hugged me. When he pulled back, the grin was still there and his eyes were wet.

'But how?' he finally asked.

'Do you need me to draw you a picture?'

He laughed. 'Now *that* could be interesting.'

I lightly tapped his nose. 'Seriously, though, after I miscarried earlier in the year I never went back on the pill. And there were a few times when we weren't exactly careful – or prepared.'

'No, we weren't, were we? Just now … would we have hurt it?'

'No, it's all fine. I saw a doctor when I was in Sydney, and he said there's no reason to expect that what happened before would happen again.' I blushed. 'I also asked about sex and he said it's perfectly okay.'

'It was, wasn't it? Perfectly okay?'

'Oh, ha ha. So, you're good with this?'

'Sweetheart, I didn't think I could fall more in love with you than I already am, but somehow I have.' He pulled back to look into my eyes. 'That night when we argued, you said you never wanted to leave here. Did you mean it?'

I nodded. 'This feels like home. Where you are feels like home. Can I stay here with you?'

He kissed me again. 'I thought you'd never ask.'

Christmas in the Kitchen

Thanks to all of you who are following me on the other side of the world. It feels strange to be writing about the same ingredients that I was writing about back in June. I guess that's what happens when you turn the seasons upside down.

What has struck me about this side of the world is the variety of fruit and vegetables available. Take avocadoes for instance. I used to buy them from the supermarket in plastic wrap, after they'd been flown in from somewhere else. It seemed positively wasteful to smash up an avocado and pile it high on a slice of sourdough toast. Yet that's what I have for breakfast at least a couple of times a week. It's even more decadent with the addition of a perfectly poached egg – free-range, thanks to the girls who cluck happily around the garden.

I don't just have avo on my breakfast toast; I also blend it into a smooth guacamole to serve with crunchy corn chips or spicy fajitas, and use it in salads. The photo below is a salad I've made a couple of times over recent weeks. Essentially it's avocado, roasted sweet potato – or kumara, as it's called here – and rocket, all tied together with a spicy

Thai-style dressing. If you struggle to make friends with salad, this is a lovely one to start with, and it works well with any grilled meat.

As I write, we're preparing for my first upside-down Christmas. It feels strange. I miss the wintery Christmas markets with mulled wine – not that I can drink wine these days; I have quite the baby bump now – and the wonderful spices that seem to sit on the air. I've been experimenting with some Christmas-scented muffins that have been going down a treat in the cafe. If I close my eyes, they taste a little like mulled wine would taste if it was a muffin.

My parents are coming over for Christmas, as are Richie's sister and her husband. Friends from Melbourne will also be joining us, so Christmas will be a feast for a full house. I can't wait.

As for food? We'll be doing the traditional roast turkey, roast pork, roast vegetables, but lightening it up a touch with salads as well. We'll serve it all on platters on a long table in the garden. My father won't think it's Christmas without plum pudding, so we'll make sure he has one, but I've been having some fun with pavlovas of late. I made a batch of tangy lemon curd that I'll tip onto a lemon-scented meringue base – thanks, Nigella.

Richie's mother makes a chocolate pavlova with summer berries that's so good you absolutely must taste it. Given it's Christmas, I've managed to convince Milly to part with her recipe. The link is here. Just don't tell anyone about her secret ingredient – balsamic vinegar. Trust me, it works.

However you plan on spending the day, may it be full of joy.

Until next time,

Max

ACKNOWLEDGEMENTS

This story has been, for many reasons, a difficult one to write, and I couldn't have told it without the help of my editor, Nicola O'Shea. Thanks also to Keith Stevenson at ebookedit for file conversions; and to Jacinda Anderson for another great cover.

Gratitude also goes to Mel Kettle for helping me with marketing strategy, and to my birthday twin, Jordy, for Jess's name. To my beta readers – you know who you are – thank you. I owe you wine ... or Pepsi Max and beer.

The character of Horrie owes his name to my paternal grandfather and his occupation to my maternal grandfather. Poppa taught me about trout and how they come up for air in the creek that flows through Tumbarumba (don't believe it!), and Pa taught me anything I know about gardening. Everything I don't know is because we lost him too many years ago.

A special shout-out to Grant and Sarah for suffering through my recipe testing. I'm aware of just how difficult it must have been for you guys to have to force yourselves to sample all those cookies and slices. The chocolate bread-and-butter pudding was particularly tough.

If you enjoyed *Wish You Were Here* I'd love it if you left a review on Amazon or Goodreads. If you'd like to stay up to date with my next happy ending, you can sign up to my newsletter on my website.

You can also drop by and see me – virtually speaking, of course – at any of these places:

My website: https://joannetracey.com

Facebook: https://facebook.com/joannetraceywriter

Twitter: @jotracey_

Instagram: https://www.instagram.com/jotracey/

ABOUT THE AUTHOR

Joanne Tracey would like to say that she's a thirty-something, perky-pony-tailed marathon runner. Sadly, it wouldn't be true. What is true is that she's sometimes a corporate warrior, sometimes a domestic diva, sometimes a star-gazer, and absolutely always a believer in happy endings. Oh, and she says you can call her Jo.

www.ingramcontent.com/pod-product-compliance
Lightning Source LLC
Chambersburg PA
CBHW020241120726
47904CB00001B/52